BILLIONAIRES' INDULGENCE

Complete (Part 1-5)

Scarlett Avery

Praise for *Billionaires' Indulgence* by Scarlett Avery

I was hooked from the very first chapter. I absolutely loved this series. Jake, Hunter and Allison were amazing together and the ending was truly PERFECT. This series should be read by everyone!

— Wendy Crossley

My sweet, domineering, smoking hot, dirty talking Jake melts my panties. And the burn-the-house-down hot sex does not disappoint.

— Kimme

All five books have had me enthralled to the point of never wanting the story of Jake, Allison and Hunter to end. Such passion, love and longing between them has been unbelievable, and at times, I really felt like I was in the story. Best series ever!

— Alice C Guertin

One of the best series of steamy romance books around.... couldn't wait for each book. Highly recommended.

— Margaret J Perez

BRAVO!!! Loved it. You are truly a wonderful writer, and I enjoy your books to my core.

— Margari

Scarlett's hot, steamy and sexy series! With each book, I wanted to jump in the shower to cool off.

— Mary E.

Five+ stars! Ok, I bought and read it freaking IMMEDIATELY!!! Super steamy and definitely hot!

— *Treamer*

Well-written, interesting read!

— *Mary A. Boyce*

I read the whole series of five books. I loved the end of it. Ladies, it's always a hot, sizzling read... can't put it down. Enjoy!

— *Sylvia R. Gomez*

This was the perfect ending to the perfect series. I absolutely loved this series more than any I have read so far. Thank you, Scarlett, it was awesome.

— *Judith Shaw*

Loved all books 1-5! I couldn't have imagined the ending the series has. Muy caliente ❤! MUST READ ALL BOOKS!

— *Guadalupe Frias*

Scarlett did it again. She makes me smile the way she writes because when I read, I feel the love and passion.

— *T. Barnes*

Absolutely amazing.

— *Carly m. Milam*

Foreword

I can't thank you enough for purchasing this sizzling read.

I'm absolutely passionate about what I do. Once I start writing, I just can't stop.

It's taking me a whole lifetime to get to the point where I'm able to live out my dream every single day.

The captivating stories and the enigmatic characters live with me throughout the writing process. I think you'll quickly notice how much care and attention I put into each one of my romance novels.

Another thing you'll discover about me is how much I love my readers!

To thank you for buying this romance novel, I'd love for you to lose yourself in even more sultriness, sexiness and seduction!

When you sign-up today, I'll send you an exclusive *Secret Chapter* for this romance.

Sign-up TODAY!
www.RomanceBooksRock.com

PART 1—BILLIONAIRES' INDULGENCE

Irresistible Attraction

Chapter One

How is it possible to adore your family, but at the same time feel the urgent need to get as far away from them as possible?

As much as I love seeing my parents, they can be a bit much to handle. I know my mom wants me to be happy, but if she asks me one more time if my boyfriend Clark and I are making any plans to take things further in our relationship, I swear I'll scream. I'm sure she means well, but Mom is constantly reminding me that my three older brothers are married and I'm not. As if I couldn't figure that out on my own.

I made a special trip back home to Chicago to spend time with my brother Josh's firstborn. I had planned on spending four days doting on the sweet child like a good aunt, but since she was so sick my sister-in-law, Stefani, decided it would be best if little Kimberly didn't have too many visitors.

I could have stayed longer at my parents' house, but I saw my niece's cold as my cue to return to New York. I was supposed to catch the last flight of the day back to the Big Apple, but instead I grabbed a four-thirty flight. Since the trip is only a few short hours, I was able to land an hour ago and I should be home soon. I'm already relishing the thought of kicking back with a mouth-watering pizza in one hand and my remote in the other. If traffic isn't too horrendous, I should be sitting in front of my television by eight.

As I'm zooming down the busy streets of Manhattan at the back of the cab, I can't help but wonder if Clark will ever pop the question.

Do I even want to marry him?

I know it's an odd question considering we've been living together for a year now, but lately, it's felt like we're more roommates than boyfriend and girlfriend. I often wonder if he's seeing someone else behind my back, but Clark is always quick to brush away my concerns. Every time I broach the subject of his distant attitude, he blames his workload. It's not as if I was a skinny supermodel when he met me, but I might have put on some weight lately. In the last few months I've often caught him ogling slim and sexy women, but what can I do? As long as he's just looking, we're good, right? Where would he find the time anyway? Since his recent promotion to junior trader, he's been chained to his computer working the most insane hours. When he's not crunching numbers or analyzing graphs in the hopes of advancing his career, he's drumming up business for Venture App, the investment company he started a year ago with his colleague Jasper Reid. I know I'm being insecure for no good reason.

Maybe I should have called or texted him after all to let him know I'm coming home early.

I thought of letting Clark know I would arrive home at eight this evening instead of midnight, but I figured since he had plans to catch a Yankees game with his friends, he wouldn't be home until midnight anyways. Every time he goes to see his favorite team play, it turns into a rowdy evening with his best friends—Tim and Anthony. Since it's Tuesday, it's half-price chicken wings and beer at Atomic Bar & Grill and I'm pretty sure he'll stop there before coming home.

I could use the time alone to unpack and relax.

You'd think four days back home visiting my parents would be a vacation, but it never is. It's so hectic and now that two of my brothers have young kids, it means my time in Chicago is always crazy. There's never a dull moment in the Randall clan.

When the cab turns off the main street, I pull out my phone to check the time.

Seven thirty-five. Great. I'll have the house all to myself for at least four hours.

My eyes are still glued to my phone when the cab driver slows down in front of the house we're renting.

"We're here, ma'am. Your fare comes to seventy-three dollars. Cash or credit card?"

I can't believe how expensive it is to drive in from the airport. "Cash, please."

After parting with my hard-earned money, I climb the few stairs separating me from an evening of lounging in my little abode.

When I open the door I stumble on a pair of ridiculously high-heeled shoes. *Huh? Those aren't mine.* I drop my luggage and squat down to pick up the pair of strappy hot-pink sandals. I hold them up and twirl them in my hands with such fascination, you'd think I'm looking at a work of art. *Nope, those are definitely not mine.*

As I rack my brain trying to understand what's going on, noise comes from the upper floor. I panic at first, afraid we might be being burglarized, but then I realize I'm listening to two people moaning. *Is Clark watching porn again while jerking off?* I slowly climb the stairs and more items of clothing are scattered on each step—a woman's black lacy bra, a tiny black skirt and a matching jacket, a hot-pink bustier and a skimpy G-string.

Even though I step over Clark's favorite grey suit when I reach the top of the stairs and the grunting sounds are becoming too loud to ignore, I'm still trying to understand what I'm about to witness. It's as if I'm watching a movie of myself in slow motion walking through my home with my mouth gaping. I step towards my bedroom and I push open the door that's already ajar to find Clark balls-deep in a woman's pussy.

My eyes widen. I'm unable to believe the raunchy scene in front of me. Of course, hearing the woman Clark is hammering scream out obscenities only adds to the surreal moment.

"Yes, yes, yes, Superman, fuck me harder."

Superman?

When the woman yells out, I immediately recognize her voice—it's Paula Bullock. The woman's eyes are shut tight as my boyfriend rams into her with way more passion than he has with me in a long time, but her voice is so distinctive, it's impossible for me to not know that those skinny legs wrapped around Clark's waist belong to one of his colleagues from his trading firm. Her voice has always irritated the heck out of me since the first day I met her. I usually join Clark every Friday night after work with a few of his colleagues for happy hour at Barboncino for cheap drinks and tasty pizza—I'm very familiar with that voice.

"Shmoopie, you're so wet for me." *That's his pet name for the bitch?* "I love how I slide in and out of you so easily. It's so mind-blowing to fuck a woman with such a hot body. I almost forgot how good it feels." *Hot body?* "It's so amazing to be with a babe who appreciates sex."

"Superman, your cock is so big. Ride me like a dirty stallion."

"Your pussy feels like it's made of kryptonite. It's as if it's robbing me of my strength to resist you. Baby, you fuck me so well, I swear your sweet pussy has superhuman powers."

Seriously?

"I'm going to ride you, baby, don't you worry about it. I want to make you cry out with pure bliss when you come all over my huge cock."

Huge? As if.

"Oh, yeah, Clark, give it to me."

"I was tired of boring vanilla sex, but you're blowing my mind."

Fuck you, asshole. It's not as if you were Channing Tatum in bed.

"I can't get enough of your juicy dick. I was dying because you hadn't been inside me in over a week. I hate having to travel to our Boston office. I don't want to be away from you."

"Paula, I'm going to come, I'm going to come, I'm going to come."

"Fill me with a big shot. I'm close, Clark. Pinch my clit."

"Arghhh."

Clark and his bitch yell so loudly, I'm sure the neighbors at the end of the street hear them. I'm so shocked by the scene I'm witnessing, I'm still frozen at the doorway like an ice sculpture with my jaw dropped, watching my boyfriend fuck his colleague's brains out. Suddenly, Paula opens her eyes and we're staring at each other—the adulteress and the scorned woman.

The blood drains from her face and she panics. She tries to call to Clark, but she's so surprised by my presence she's unable to utter the words strangling her right now. She can only tug at his shoulders, desperate to catch his attention.

"What, baby? You want some more? Already?"

Obviously, Clark hasn't clued in yet and he's still flirting with Paula looking for his second fuck of the night. *God, he disgusts me.*

"Clark." Paula nearly chokes on his name as she points to the door where I'm standing.

When my boyfriend meets my icy stare, he jumps out of bed as if it's on fire.

"Allison, what the hell are you doing here?" Clark stares at me with wide eyes, cupping his family jewels like a wimp.

"What am I doing here? Are you seriously asking me that question, you jackass?" I respond with contempt, bouncing my gaze from my boyfriend to the trashy brunette sprawled across my bed with her legs spread open—on my fucking Calvin Klein sheets. I blink incredulously when my eyes zoom in between her thighs.

Of course he'd go for a skank with piercings on her clitoral hood. And of course he'd fuck her without a condom.

That's way more than I need to know about the bitch, but for some reason, I'm not surprised she's the kind of woman to adorn her private parts with jewelry. I move my unimpressed gaze to the wannabe Superman and I take in his pathetic naked body from head to toe and my skin starts to prickle into goose-bumps. A lava ball forms at the pit of my stomach.

I've always been the understanding one, the supportive one, the attentive one, the compassionate one. I've stood by Clark throughout his outrageously expensive studies to move his career forward, his long hours at the office, his business venture that sucks up any of his free time, and his recent distant demeanor. *This is how he repays me.*

I don't know if I've ever gotten mad at Clark over the six months we dated and the twelve months we've been living together. I've been pretty good at eating my emotions to avoid rocking the boat… especially since he got his big promotion at work.

He's been cold with me. He even makes sure to linger in front of the television until I've fallen asleep before coming upstairs. I've noticed, I just chose not to say anything. I honestly hoped it was something I had done or that he was overwhelmed by his new responsibilities. Being faced with the reality of his treachery is a bitter pill to swallow. I've always bitten my tongue when it comes to Clark, but in this moment, I snap.

I'm not joking. I go apeshit on him. I grab the first thing I can from the dresser to my left and throw it across the room, praying I hit him smack between the eyes. He ducks just in time and the oversize wax candle smashes against the wall behind him.

"Ali, honey, calm down."

He did not just call me honey.

"How can you possibly explain this, Clark?" I spit. "You can't worm your way out of this one."

I'm so enraged, I'm unable to speak. The humiliation of his words while his cock was buried deep inside Paula is devastating. I guess I'm not his ideal woman since I don't have a "hot body" and our sex life has been "boring vanilla" since I don't "appreciate sex". His voice is still ringing so loudly inside my head, it's robbed me of my power to tell him how I feel about him. I grab another candle and fling it at him and he jumps back in bed, trying to take cover under Paula's body. *Coward.*

Both Paula and Clark are hovering under the sheets I saved for months to afford and I'm toying with so many ways of unleashing my fury on both them. I take a step forward and both of them gasp in fear. Instead of attacking them, I head to my closet and I grab an old duffle bag my big brother Dave gave me so many years ago when I moved to New York to go to college. I unzip it and I throw in an armful of clothing. I'm in such a rush, I don't bother removing the hangers. I turn around to the other corner of the closet to grab piles of folded jeans and sweaters. I dump everything in my bag. I slam shut the closet door and I storm past the two idiots watching my every move speechless like a Trappist monk and nun who have taken a vow of silence. I get to my dresser and I pull every drawer out like a wild beast and I shove in as much as my bag can take. I don't need to have eyes at the back of my head to know that Paula and Clark are shaking and praying I don't slash their throats for their betrayal.

Once my bag is overflowing, I straighten up and turn on my heel to face the two people I hate the most in the world right now. I'm sure the expression on my face must be telling because Clark's eyes are as big as satellite dishes. *Are those beads of sweat on his balding forehead? Yeah, asshole, you should be scared.* I take a deep breath to steady my voice before speaking.

"I'll be back later this week to pick up the rest of my stuff and I'll mail the keys to you." My comment is directed at Clark, but my eyes are glued on Paula. *She's always wanted him. She's never been clever enough to hide it. Well, now she can have him.*

I walk out of my former bedroom with my head held high and my shoulders pulled back. *I won't allow him to see how much he's hurt me.* I go down the stairs and grab the small suitcase I left near Paula's hot-pink strappy sandals and I step outside in the middle of the night. I drop my bags on the top step and I reach out for the handle to shut the door.

The minute my fingers interlace around the metal handle, I lose it and a torrent of tears start pouring down my face. *I've been such an idiot.* I exhale and I slam the door shut so hard behind me I'm surprised I don't shatter the glass into a million pieces.

Chapter Two

Ten weeks later

The last few weeks have been a turning point for me both personally and professionally. I'm still having nightmares of Paula and Clark fucking. I know they say time helps you forget, and I wish I could erase that bad memory faster. As if walking in on my boyfriend's betrayal weren't enough, I lost my job as a junior graphic designer at Big Digital Communications. I had been with this agency for nine months and although I can't say I loved my job—heck, I can't even say I liked it—it was a steady paycheck. The hours were daunting and the competitive nature of the business did eat at me, so in some ways I'm not all that crushed about not having to show up there and pretend I was as gung-ho as so many of my other colleagues.

That said, it's been a sobering past few months. Within ten days I found myself without a boyfriend, a home or a job. Luckily, my best friend Gwyn insisted I move in with her and her gorgeous fiancé Gaven. They've been together for a few years now and they are so in love, it's sickening. They made the decision to start a life together and they bought a modest three-story home to accommodate a family when the time comes. I'm fortunate enough to be able to occupy the basement and live with them until I get back on my feet.

I was lucky to get a retail job at Celestial Beddings to tie me over for a bit. I'm grateful for the money, but a full day of running around in a store fetching ridiculously expensive sheets for wealthy New Yorkers leaves me drained. I'm so looking for-ward to having dinner, kicking back and allowing the blood to circulate back into my legs, but the commute home is a nightmare because of a signal problem on one of the trains preceding mine. This mess delays my journey by a whole hour. Unfortunately for me, there are no free seats when I get on the subway and I have to stand on my aching legs during this ordeal.

By the time I get off of the subway and walk the two blocks to Gwyn's house, I'm exhausted. Luckily, when I open the door, my perky best friend greets me with a warm smile. "Hey, Ali."

"Hey, I didn't expect you to be home."

"Something came up and I decided to change my plans for the evening. How was your day? Anoth-er rough one?"

"Gwyn, I can't feel my feet," I reply, collaps-ing on the barstool at the kitchen island and dropping my handbag on the hardwood floor. "When I used to be a graphic designer I'd be sitting all day, but now I count my blessings if I get to rest for thirty minutes."

My first reaction after I got canned was to jump right back in and find another job as a graphic designer, but Gwyn talked me out of it. She felt with everything that had transpired in my life, I needed time to figure out what made my heart sing and I needed time to wash Clark out of my hair.

I never planned on working in a store, but one afternoon I was in Celestial Beddings for my monthly fix. I have a thing for high-end sheets and I can never resist this chic boutique. I've been here so many times the manager recognized me and after an animated chat, she suggested I apply for a clerk's position. This new shift in my career has allowed me to take my mind off of things and I don't feel like a burden to my best friend.

"You'll get used to it. A lot of new people we hire at our Modern Crates stores have to adjust, but eventually your body will adapt and you won't be in such pain."

"If you say so," I respond before resting my chin in the palm of my hand, inhaling the tantalizing aroma surrounding me. "Are you cooking up a storm again?"

"I'm not making anything fancy. It's only the two of us tonight since Gaven is hanging out with his buddies and I thought you'd enjoy some spinach and ricotta stuffed shells. I've made enough so we can take the leftovers to work tomorrow."

"That sounds delicious and for the record, it does sound fancy," I say, licking my lips in anticipation. "So how was your day?"

"It's been so busy. Believe it or not, I'm already buying for Christmas and since business has been booming, that means I have to search high and wide for the most original gift ideas for our elite clientele."

"It still sounds like so much fun."

"Oh, don't get me wrong, I love what I do, but there's always pressure to do better than last year."

Gwyn Davidson and I have been best friends since we both moved to New York to study at the Fashion Institute four years ago. She's one year older than me at twenty-four years old and has enough ambition to fill a stadium. When it comes to dream careers, she lucked out. She's been a buyer at Modern Crates since she graduated. She works at one of New York's most stylish lifestyle décor emporiums and she always manages to surprise me with the most original gifts. We share so much in common—we're both from Chicago, we both have three older brothers, we both have long hair to our waist, we're both home décor junkies and we both love to cook. I've had many friends throughout high school, but I've never been as close to another girl as I am with Gwyn. She's model-thin and her straight long mane usually leaves me in awe. She has nearly jet-black hair, which contrasts dramatically with her light blue eyes. The second her fiancé, Gaven Henson, met her sparkling aquamarine gaze, he fell head over heels in love.

"You're so good at what you do, Gwyn. I admire you finding your passion right out of school and you're insanely well paid to do what you love every single day."

"You'll get there, Ali." She drops the knife she's holding and focuses her attention on me.

"Yeah, I hope so." I know I'm feeling sorry for myself, but how can I not be a little self-conscious that my best friend has the perfect life while mine is marred with bad ex-boyfriends, uncertainty and change?

"Do you have a cooking class tonight?"

"No, thank God. I'm way too tired. My teacher had to attend a wedding in Milwaukee and he won't be back until Saturday. I'll have class next week."

"Are you enjoying the lessons?" Gwyn places the pasta in the oven and walks to the sink to wash her hands.

"Are you kidding me? It's the best gift you and Gaven could have given me."

My best friend and her boyfriend were afraid I was going to end up moping around their home at the end of my day, so they enrolled me in a cooking class at Bonne Bouche Culinary Institute's recreational cooking school. The institute is a Godsend because it allows people who love cooking, like myself, to take our skills to the next level even though our end goal isn't to become the next bigshot chef. Since I've been talking of making money with my passion, Gwyn suggested I combine my love of food and photography to try to find a new path in life. I jumped at the opportunity. I used to prepare elaborate meals for Clark, but I'm self-taught. It's incredible what an indecent number of hours watching Food TV and months reading food blogs can do. I've considered taking classes, but money was always short since Clark's trading courses cost an arm and a leg. Since his prospects for an extraordinarily high-paying job were better than mine, we decided to focus on his education. Bad move on my part.

"The stuffed shells are going to take about forty minutes to cook. Do you want some appetizers?" She's already rummaging inside her fridge before I'm able to answer.

"You prepared appetizers? I thought you said we were having a simple meal."

"I didn't need to fuss much. It's only a plate of Italian cured meats and some Italian cheese and olives I bought earlier. I got us fresh Calabrese bread and it should hold us off until the meal is cooked."

"Sign me up," I say, looking forward to this impromptu midweek feast.

"We can't have appetizers without wine." Gwyn smiles, pulling her head from the fridge. She places the plate of meats on the counter in front of me before walking back to the cupboard to pull out two glasses. She tucks a bottle of wine under her armpit and comes to sit on the stool next me. "Since we're having Italian, I think we should keep it all Italian. That's why I selected a bold Chianti for tonight," she says, pouring wine in our glasses.

She's such a wine fanatic.

"I love the way you think."

We lift our glasses and nod. "Cheers," we both chime in at the same time before dipping into the nectar of the gods.

Gwyn puts her glass down on the granite counter and narrows her blue eyes. "When is your last cooking class?"

"I finish in two weeks. I've already been looking at the midsummer semester. I've been saving some money and I think I'll continue learning. I'm enjoying myself and it's done wonders for my self-confidence."

"I'm happy to hear that, Ali, but I think you might have to put your plans on hold."

"What do you mean?"

"You might not be in New York during the next semester."

"Huh? What are you talking about? Of course I'll be in New York. Where else would I be?"

She's not making sense right now. It can't possibly be because of the wine, since we just started drinking.

She scoots her little butt to the edge of her seat before grabbing my hands in hers. "Do you remember the contest you entered three months ago?"

"Contest?" I ask, trying to jolt my memory. "Honestly, Gwyn, there's so much that's happened in my life... I'm sorry, I don't remember."

"Let me help." Gwyn looks very serious and my heart sinks. I truly can't take another blow. "Do you remember how you spent the weekend here when Clark was away at a conference and you had so much fun you considered—although briefly—dumping Clark's sorry ass and moving in with us?"

"Sort of," I answer, vaguely remembering.

"You were sitting right here as I was preparing dinner and you were going on and on about this contest your favorite food blogger was having."

"Yes! I do remember now. Riley Carrington's assistant, Cynthia Tilley, is going on this missionary trip to Africa to help build wells to pump clean water in Uganda. Riley needed to find a replacement for her and decided to call on her readers to fill the position," I let out enthusiastically before squeezing Gwyn's hands.

"Exactly. Did you hear back from Riley?"

There goes that moment. I grimace. "Nah. I had two Skype video calls with her a few months ago and I was certain I had nailed both interviews, but I didn't hear back from her. In an attempt to keep in touch, I sent her a few emails to congratulate her on getting her own show on Food TV and I also emailed her about my new culinary journey. I even sent a few of my photos from my New York at night collection, but she hasn't shown any signs of life. It was a fun idea, Gwyn, but with my luck, there's no way I was going to be the one selected."

"Oh, why's that?"

"Puh-lease." I roll my eyes. "I never get what I want out of life. I'm used to settling. I mean, think about it—me becoming Riley Carrington's assistant and working side by side with the celebrity blogger in her state-of-the-art Colorado studio? Like that's ever going to happen." I click my tongue against the roof of my mouth. "Really, Gwyn?" I slip my hands from hers to grab my wine.

"You haven't been reading Riley's blog lately?"

"No. Not for the past three weeks. I knew she was going to announce the winner anytime now so I've been ignoring her latest posts and emails. I don't need to deal with another disappointment. In any case, when I get home, I'd prefer to watch TV than read," I lie. "It was a nice dream, but I'm sure another lucky winner must be having the time of her life."

"So I guess the hunormous basket that's sitting pretty on the credenza near the dining room table with a handwritten envelope with your name on it straight from Colorado is a mistake?"

Huh?

My glass of wine freezes in mid-air.

At first I think Gwyn is playing a trick on me, but I follow her amused gaze and stretch my body to catch a glimpse of this fictitious basket she's talking about. I blink a few times before my eyes land on the biggest gift basket I've seen in my entire life.

"Ahhh," I gasp, bringing my free hand to my mouth. "When did this come?"

"It came this morning. I left late today because I was working from home before a meeting with a new vendor at their offices. It arrived an hour after you left for work, but I didn't tell you because I wanted it to be a celebration. I wanted to see your elated reaction to the big news. I sent Gaven away for the evening so we can have the place to ourselves."

"But wait, we don't know if I've been select-ed," I interrupt. *No point in getting my hopes up yet.*

"You're right. I'm sure Riley sent this kind of arrangement to all the runner-ups. Seriously, Ali? What are you waiting for? Go open the basket and that big envelope over there," she says, whooshing me away with her manicured finger.

I'm so charged with adrenaline, my feet don't hurt anymore. I leap to my legs and sprint to Gwyn's credenza. I rip off the smaller envelope stuck to the basket and I read the note aloud.

Dearest Allison,

I know you've been a fan and a reader for a long time. Your latest culinary photos rock and you obviously know how to use a camera. Your photo-graphic skills impressed the heck out of me. Don't even get me started on your New York at night photos. Fierce. If you're still interested, I'd love for you to become my summer assistant while Cynthia travels to the other side of the world to lend a helping hand to those who are less fortunate.

Please accept this little basket as a token of appreciation for your loyalty. In the larger envelope you'll find all the details, a ticket and some paper-work for you to sign. I can't wait to meet you in person.

Riley

"Are you kidding me? Riley Carrington selected me?"

"I told you." Gwyn comes running and we both hug each other and jump up and down in the middle of her house like schoolgirls.

After a few minutes of laughter, I burst into tears.

"Ali, what's wrong? Why are you crying?" My best friend cradles me inside her arms and I unleash the ball of sadness that's been eating at me over the past few weeks. So far, I've been able to keep it together, but this monumental news breaks me.

"Gwyn, the last six months living with Clark were soul-crushing. He barely looked at me. He'd rather spend the evening in our home office watching porn. He thought I was deaf, but I could hear the moaning from the computer speakers and I could hear him take pleasure without me. When I walked in on him and Paula…" I stop, unable to speak the words, and take a breath to settle my nerves before continuing. "Then I lost my job a few days later—it's like adding insult to injury. I felt like the biggest loser in America. I had nothing left. Although I can never thank you enough for coming to my rescue, these past ten weeks have been so hard because I felt I had lost my compass. This insane opportunity is a renewal for me."

"It is, sweetie. Come on, let's go back to the kitchen for more wine," she says, dragging me away from the dining room table. "You didn't even want to send in your application because you were too afraid of leaving Clark behind while you pursued your dream."

"I know. I didn't want to admit it, but I didn't want to leave and give him a reason to have an affair. He's proved me wrong—he can have a flaming affair right under my nose."

"Did you really love him, Ali?"

"What kind of question is that? We were together for eighteen months."

"You didn't answer my question," she says, tilting her head to the side and pressing her lips together.

Gwyn's question doesn't entirely surprise me. She's asked me the same question over and over and I've never been able to give her a straight answer. I know what I had with Clark has nothing to do with what she shares with Gaven, but I was happy not to be alone.

"I'm not sure I'd know what it feels like to love someone and to be loved in return."

"You settled big time with Clark."

"But—"

"Ali, I already know what you're going to say," she interrupts, crossing her arms over her chest. "Yes, this is New York, and yes, a lot of guys only date models and wafer-thin socialites, but there are plenty of good and honest men who love women with Salma Hayek curves like yours. Clark has been lying to you for the last six months of your relationship—if not longer."

"You can't understand," I let out, irritated. "You're super-thin and you're tall. You don't have to contend with enormous 32DD breasts that seem to have a life of their own half the time, hips and a tummy on a tiny five-two frame like mine." I yank myself up on the stool, sulking.

"Honey, I'm sorry, but just in case you still haven't received the memo, your curves are all at the right places. Even my boyfriend agrees. As far as I'm concerned, you're ignoring the real issue here and we both know it has nothing to do with you gaining a few pounds over the past few months or you having boobs." She casts me a stern look and her dark gaze immediately quiets any rebuttal.

One week after I stormed out on Clark, Gaven drove me back to my former home to pick up the remainder of my belongings. Contrary to our agreement, my ex-boyfriend was there waiting for me. I couldn't even bring myself to look at his sorry ass. Before leaving the home we had shared for one year, I asked him two questions. I wanted to know how long he'd been having this affair with Paula. He admitted he had been sleeping with her since right after he got his big promotion. I mustered up the courage to ask my second question. I was dying to know if there had been others. He only lowered his gaze and whispered, "A few." I had to bite my tongue to avoid crying in front of him.

"I guess you're right," I concede.

"I think this opportunity with Riley Carrington is far more than just a job. I honestly believe being away from the city will help you reconnect with yourself. I'm certain you'll come back from this journey transformed."

CHAPTER THREE

ALLISON

I'm expecting economy class, so I'm thrilled when Riley buys me a business-class ticket for my trip to Fort Collins, Colorado. The trip is a breeze and I spend most of my time going back in Riley's blog archive to know as much as I can about my new boss.

When I retrieve my luggage and pass through the main doors leading outside of Denver airport, I immediately spot a chauffeur holding a big sign with my name in black marker. Riley is giving me the royal treatment.

At that moment, it all feels so real. Nerves start to dance inside my stomach, but I inhale deeply to suppress them. *There's no going back.* Although I'm here, I still can't believe Riley Carrington selected me as her assistant for the summer.

After quick salutations, the chauffeur grabs my luggage and I follow him to the black limo. The hour trip north to Riley's place is more beautiful than I ever suspected. Let's face it, I'm a city girl. I grew up in the Windy City and I've been living in the Big Apple for the past four years. I've never ventured into the countryside and this rural experience is quite new to me. I'm a fish out of water, but I'm so looking forward to this opportunity of a lifetime.

I spend most of the ride surfing on my iPad, obsessed with learning as much as I can to make a good first impression. I'm so immersed in my research, I'm surprised when the stretched car slows down. I lift my head to find out what's causing the change of speed. A large sign reads, *Grand Valley Colorado Grass-Fed Angus Beef & Natural Meat Ranch.*

Angus Beef Ranch?

I don't think I'm at the right location. Riley is a food blogger, not a cattle rancher. She lives in a beautiful home on spectacular land overlooking a magnificent organic garden. None of the photos on her blog post ever suggested she lived on a ranch. Confused, I lean in to ask if the chauffeur has made a mistake.

"I'm sorry, but are you sure we're at the right address?" I ask as I show him my iPhone with the last message Riley sent me.

"Yes, ma'am. Miss Riley lives here with her brother. He's owned this land for a few years now."

"Oh. I see."

Riley talks about her kids and she also talks about her nanny-slash-housekeeper Isadora Bennett, but she never mentioned her brother.

Maybe it slipped her mind. I'm a bit taken aback, but I'll roll with it. After all, it's only for a few months.

"Thank you so much." I fish through my bag to pull out a few bills to pay for my ride.

The chauffeur looks at the money and back at me. "Thank you, ma'am, but the ride's been taken care of. You don't have to worry about a thing."

"Of course," I mutter uncomfortably. "Will you at least accept a tip?"

"I've already been well tipped. This isn't the big city, ma'am. We do things different around here."

"Apparently so. Thanks again for the ride." I open the door and I circle the limo to meet the chauffeur to retrieve my bags from the trunk.

"I'm sure you'll enjoy your stay here. The Carringtons are real good people."

"I have a feeling I'm going to enjoy myself here. Thank you," I respond, smiling.

I watch the black car drive off and I close my eyes as I inhale deeply.

My God, this is it.

When I open my eyes again, I'm struck by the contrast of scenery compared to the skyscrapers I'm used to seeing everyday in Manhattan. It's so green and so wide. The sky seems so blue, lined with puffy white clouds, and the majestic mountains make it so picturesque. *I'm so ready for a fresh start.*

After a short communion with nature, I grab my luggage and I roll them towards an impressive-looking house, grinning like a kid going on a field trip. *I guess this is home away from home now.* I'm just about to climb the first step when a deep choco-latey voice speaks to my right.

"You must be Allison."

I turn around and my jaw drops when I face a tall, rugged and extremely handsome man.

He's hot.

Correction. He's smoldering.

Good Lord, does he work with my new boss? I don't think I can handle having to see him every single day.

"Welcome to our ranch. I'm Jake, Riley's brother. I was keeping an eye out for you, but I got caught up with a phone call in my office and I just noticed the car driving away."

Holy Jesus. My insides flip when he flashes me a heart-arresting smile. I didn't know Riley shared her home with a freaking *GQ* model. When the chauffeur talked about her having a brother, I surely didn't expect him to look, well, delicious.

"Oh, thank you," I respond, mesmerized by the hotter-than-hell stud standing in front of me.

"It's a pleasure to finally meet you." Jake extends his hand and I'm in such a daze I simply stare at it and forget all my good manners.

It takes me a few seconds to realize I'm acting like an idiot and I drop my luggage in a hurry to shake his hand. Since he caught me by surprise, the suitcases I was holding crash to the ground and Jake lunges forward to grab them.

"Why don't I help you with these?"

When he steps forward I catch a glimpse of his piercing blue eyes and my heart slams into my chest. *Wow.*

"Oh, thank you," I manage. I'm too much in shock to add much more.

I follow him up the stairs and I take advantage of the opportunity to check him out from behind—tight-fitting jeans, firm butt, plaid shirt rolled up to the elbow revealing muscular forearms, a black cowboy hat and, of course, a pair of sexy distressed cowboy boots.

He looks incredibly strong.

We step into the house. I nearly bump into him when he stops to drop my luggage at the door because I'm so riveted by his ass, I'm not looking in front of me. He turns around and flashes another disarming smile and I swallow hard. I know I'm quite short, but his imposing physique is such a turn-on.

Keep it together, girl.

"Riley's in town getting a few things with the nanny and then she'll swing by the day camp to pick up her kids. She should be back in a few hours and she's asked me to keep you company." He removes his hat and I take in his thick, dark brown hair.

"That's so nice of you, but I don't want to be a bother."

"Nonsense. I'm happy to hang out with you and get to know you better. After all, you'll be part of this family for the next few months."

"Good point." I smile nervously. My cheeks burn up so badly I have to fan myself to cool down, even though it's clear this magnificent home is fully air conditioned.

"Riley lives in one of the houses on the ranch. So does my business partner, Hunter Evans. We've set up one of the unoccupied houses for you, that way you'll have your own space. I'll walk you there a little later."

"I didn't expect this much attention," I mumble.

He has a business partner? Please God, don't let him be as arresting.

"Trust me, you'll be glad to retreat to your quiet space at the end of the day. I love my niece and nephews to death, but they're kids."

"I can't wait to meet them."

We lock eyes and there's an awkward silence between us, almost as if he's waiting for me to say something. My stomach clenches and my pulse quickens. Unable to withstand his gaze any longer, I lower mine and dance from one foot to the other to try to conceal my uneasiness. I've rarely had the pleasure of being in the same room as a man so dangerously hot, he could have jumped out of the pages of a men's fitness magazine.

"I'm sure the trip must have been tiring. Why don't you go upstairs to the main bathroom to freshen up? I have some towels set on the counter for you and I'll get you something to eat. You must be hungry."

The minute Jake mentions food, I remember I haven't eaten since I left Gwyn's early this morning. I'd definitely welcome a warm meal.

"Now that you mention it, I'm starved."

"Good." He smiles. "I'm no Riley in the kitchen, but I can find my way around. I'll reheat some food she cooked this morning for a new recipe for a blog post she's writing and we can sit down at the kitchen island to get to know each other better."

"That sounds good."

His presence is so intoxicating, I welcome the opportunity to take a breather to regain my composure. I climb the stairs and furtively look behind me when I reach the fifth step. Jake is already opening cupboards and pulling out plates.

Keep focused, girl. You're here as Riley's assistant. Dangerously rugged men aren't part of the agenda.

When I reach the last step I swerve in a three-hundred-sixty-degree circle to take in the upper floor. The décor is masculine and surprisingly modern for a home set on a ranch. Everything is streamlined, elegant and polished, but a few touches of wood add warmth to the home. Although he hasn't said anything, I have a feeling this is Jake's home.

When I push open the door to the bathroom, the décor is bright and fresh like the top floor. The two wooden-framed mirrors—one large one sitting on the floor near the door and another hanging above the sink—and the antique-looking chair in the corner of the room are the only country accents. The majestic claw bathtub set under the window fits perfectly against the white tile floor. I love how the smaller diamond black tiles add so much dimension and interest.

When I approach the sink, I gasp. *I look so tired.*

It's been a long trip. I had to get up very early to catch my flight. I didn't bother making any effort because I didn't expect Jake would be the first person greeting me. I take stock of my down-to-earth look and frown at myself. I'm wearing a pair of jeans and a dark green shirt on top of a white camisole with little laces at the front. It was so hot when I arrived at the airport, I undid a few buttons to cool down and when I lean closer towards the mirror, I can see the pearls of sweat against my chest.

My only saving grace is that I twisted my long hair in a tight bun to keep it neat and tidy. The last thing I wanted was to arrive in Fort Collins looking like a hot mess.

One of the advantages of working on my feet and running around all day is the fact I've been able to lose the twenty-five pounds I put on during the last months of my relationship with Clark. I'm no supermodel and I wouldn't mind dropping an extra ten pounds to feel better about myself, but at least I can fit in the clothing I already had. With all of these recent woes, I can't afford a new wardrobe. If I hadn't dropped a few pounds, I would have been in big trouble because I wouldn't have had anything to wear. But after meeting Riley's sexy brother, I wish I had been able to buy new stylish and flirty clothing because what I brought with me is kind of unexciting.

I wish I had Gwyn's exotic and seductive good looks.

I've always felt like the ugly duckling compared to my best friend—she's taller, sexier and thinner than I'll ever be.

I should get back. Jake is going to think I fell asleep in the bathtub.

I splash my face and my chest with cold water before sleeking back a few strands of hair gone loose. There's not much I can do to stand out more. The only things I have going for me are my hazel eyes, my waist-length straight blonde hair and my huge boobs. Without makeup, no one would give me a second glance.

Once I make peace with the fact I haven't been blessed by the gods, I step out of the bathroom to go back down to join Jake, but for some reason I linger at the top of the stairs.

I wonder if one of these doors is his bedroom.

My cheeks burn. What a silly thought for a woman who broke things off with her cheating boyfriend a few months ago. I shake off the preposterous idea and I go back downstairs looking forward to a good meal.

CHAPTER FOUR

JAKE

That's Allison?

I know I shouldn't stare, but how can I not?

When my baby sister announced she had hired a new assistant to replace Cynthia, I was thrilled for her. Riley's business has been bursting at the seams and there's no way she can run one of the top food blogs on the Internet and raise four kids under the age of nine.

My excitement quickly faded when she announced the winner was from New York. Both Hunter and I rolled our eyes. It's true we only lived in the Big Apple for six months after selling our tech company, but it was sufficient time to sample our fair share of skinny New Yorkers. I expected Allison to be one of those hard-edged women who lives off of beet juice and kale salad, but she's not. She's a warm and sensual woman.

The color of the shirt she's wearing makes her eyes pop. I didn't want to seem too rude so I wasn't able to tell if her eyes are green or hazel, but those eyelashes go on for miles.

I know I should have been busying myself in the kitchen since I'm sure Allison would appreciate a hearty meal, but it was way more interesting watching her climb the stairs all the way to my bathroom. Those hips wiggled with every step she took and it was impossible for me to peel my eyes off of her delicious body. I did notice from the corner of my eyes when she turned around to look in my direction, but I didn't want to scare her off by making eye contact. As charming as Riley's previous assistant Cynthia was, her boyish frame did nothing for me, but Allison's Scarlett Johansson-like physique is going to be the end of me. I mean she has curves in all the right places and her big tits make it impossible to focus on anything else.

Riley should have told me her new assistant was a bombshell.

I love how unpretentious Allison seems. I'm glad she's not one of those stuck-up women who can't even go to the grocery store without full makeup. There's something fresh and unassuming about her that's a real turn-on.

Damn, Hunter is going to lose his mind when he lays eyes on Allison. We both tend to prefer women with heavy tits and hourglass bodies. There's nothing quite like grabbing a girl from behind and slamming my dick deep inside her aching pussy while pulling her hair back and forcing her to submit to my desires. Nothing.

Sadly, life in the middle of nowhere doesn't bode well for relationships. Even casual dating can be tricky in a small rural town. Not to mention, the pace of our day-to-day life is very demanding—in fact it's almost as grueling as when Hunter and I were at the helm of our former tech company in Cali. The big difference is that instead of writing codes, we tend to our award-winning cattle, producing the best Angus beef in the state, if not the country. We start our day at six-thirty in the morning and we don't stop until four or five o'clock in the afternoon. Even with a full staff of cowboys, it's still go-go-go. When we're done taking care of our booming business, I like to spend some quality time with my niece and nephews. That usually leaves little to no time for dating.

You better keep your head in the game or else Riley will come down on you like thunder.

I shake off my improper thoughts about our new guest as I pull out the wraps from the oven. When I turn around, Allison is staring at me from the stairs. I meet her eyes and smile. She hesitates, but gives in and returns my smile. *Christ, am I hard?*

"Riley texted me to let me know she's coming back early."

"Great. I can't wait to meet her in person."

"My business partner Hunter will be here within the hour. He's also eager to meet you."

"Wow. What a welcome party. I can't wait to meet everyone," she says, coming down the stairs. I take in every undulation of her hips as she makes her way towards me. *Focus on her eyes, buddy.*

"I hope you found everything you needed upstairs. I was starting to worry you might have slipped out the bathroom window and returned to New York," I tease.

"No. I wouldn't dream of going back to Manhattan. I like what I see here," she says, raising her eyebrow suggestively.

"Do you?" I hold her gaze. The double entendre is so obvious. I know I shouldn't, but I can't resist.

"I was admiring the décor upstairs. It's not as rustic as I would have imagined."

"Well, both Riley and I grew up in LA and I spent years working in Silicon Valley. I love the sleekness of modern décor, but living out here has given us the privilege of incorporating some incredible wooden pieces. I hired the same designer who decorated my townhouse in San Francisco and I gave her carte blanche to restyle this entire home. She also decorated Hunter's, Riley's and the three other guest houses we have on the property."

"I love your bathroom. Those are such gorgeous rustic frames," she says, joining me in the kitchen.

"That's as country as I was willing to go. You won't find too many ranches around here with air-conditioning and a full wine cellar modeled after one of San Francisco's finest restaurants like I have here." I grin. *Money has its privileges.*

We both lock eyes and I try to read what I see flickering in her gaze.

"Come on and sit down to eat. I hope you like Tex-Mex?"

"I do," she says enthusiastically, pulling out a stool and sitting down.

As she settles her body on the chair, her white tank top lowers enough to reveal the crescents of her full breasts. *Wow. Those would fit very nicely in my hands.*

"Good. Riley makes an incredible chilled tomato soup and her warm chicken and avocado wraps are pretty amazing as well," I say, serving her food before sitting across from her. My hand brushes against hers by accident and the charge that travels through my body catches me off guard. I lift my eyes and I know she feels it too.

"This looks delicious, Jake." She's speaking to me, but her eyes are glued on her food.

"Riley asked me to keep it light because she's prepared her killer lasagna for tonight. I usually can't stop at one portion." I chuckle. "I'm warning you now, her garlic bread is out of this world. I'm not big on vegetables, but her Caesar salad is pretty delicious as well. It's going to be quite the feast."

"I love lasagna. I never take time to prepare it, but I order it at my favorite Italian restaurant."

"Riley has perfected this recipe. It's one we all enjoy. I'm not sure I'll have room for dessert, but I'll try since my baby sister prepared something very special for your arrival."

"She did?"

"Uh-huh. Can you keep a secret?" I ask, leaning in against the granite top. I'm so close to her, I could reach out and stroke her cheek with the back of my hand.

"I can," she answers, leaning in closer, narrowing her eyes as if I'm about to reveal matters of national security. She's so eager. If she leans anymore, she'll fall forward.

"Riley prepared her…" I let the words hang.

"Her what?" Allison frowns.

"Are you ready for this?" I tease.

"You're torturing me here. I know she's an insane baker. Please don't make me beg for it."

Her words have my head spinning. A salacious vision hits me and I moan silently. I'm dominating her and pushing her down to her knees. She's looking up at me submissively, begging for my cock. *Damn.* I blink a few times, snapping out of it. "She's whipped up her famous vanilla and raspberry cake."

"Oh my God. No." Allison leans back against her seat with her hand over her mouth. "The recipe from her blog that went viral?"

"Yup."

"The one filled with layers of mascarpone cream and raspberry compôte and then covered with white chocolate buttercream?" She lights up like a kid about to blow out the candles of a birthday cake.

"The one and only," I mock. *Thank God, a woman who enjoys food.*

"I don't know if I can survive this experience," Allison declares dramatically. "I tried to make it at home, but it looked nothing like Riley's. Her version is regal while mine was just sad."

"Yeah, she's really talented in the kitchen, but when it comes to technology, she's lost. That's why you're here."

"I don't understand." Allison furrows her brows and wiggles her button nose, surprised by my revelation. I don't know if she could be any more adorable.

"She can type and she's learned some of the basics of blogging, but I've shot most of the photos on her blog and more recently, Cynthia has been helping. Cynthia has also been the one doing all her videos for her YouTube channel. Luckily, Cynthia has a good eye or else Food TV would never have called."

"I'm surprised. Those photos are so amazing I assumed they were hers. You took most of them?"

"Yeah. I've always loved to take photos. Riley tells me you're talented behind the camera," I say, curious to know more about her. "Forgive me, I'm being so rude. I'm asking you all these questions and I'm preventing you from eating your food." She's trying to take a bite of her wrap.

"No, it's okay."

"You look young. When did you have time to develop such skills? You're clearly gifted." I know it's a bit of a personal question, but I'm hoping she'll open up more.

"I'm not that young. I'm twenty-three," she answers, raising her chin defiantly.

"I was twenty-three once," I retort, rolling my eyes.

Allison bursts into a genuine laugh that catches me off guard. Her light-heartedness is contagious and I join her. "I also love photography—always have. My dad taught me how to use a camera before I could walk."

"Are you a photographer in New York?"

"I'm not. I'm a graphic designer, or should I say I used to be."

"Oh? What happened?"

She pauses for a second before answering. "There have been a lot of changes in my life in the past few months and I've opened myself up to new opportunities."

"Is that your way of saying you lost your job?" I ask, amused.

"Gosh, I didn't realize I was so transparent." She blushes.

"I used to own a large tech company. I recognize the corporate lingo."

"You caught me."

"So you haven't always been a cowboy?"

"Oh, God. If I were to call myself a cowboy, I'd be insulting a lot of good men who come from a long line of cattle herders. Hunter and I own this ranch and this magnificent land, we've learned how to ride horses and we take care of a few daily chores, but we hire people who know what they're doing—they're the real cowboys. We're just two geeks who needed a change of pace and ended up out here playing the roles of tough guys in the Wild, Wild West."

"You're pulling my leg." She squints and pinches her pouty lips. "You were wearing the mandatory cowboy boots," she says, pointing to the entrance of the house.

"Have you ever heard the expression, 'Dress to impress?'"

"Of course."

"In New York you impress people with an expensive tailor-made suit. Preferably made with imported Italian wool. Out here, you need to dress the part to be taken seriously. That explains the boots, jeans and hat." I wink.

"Well, you could've fooled me." She crosses her arm beneath her boobs and fixes me with a smile.

I shake my head vehemently. "Look around you," I say, waving my hands above my head. "You can take a man out of California, but you can't take Cali out of the man." I grin.

Over the next hour Allison tells me about her life in New York and her childhood in Chicago. She's so animated, I find myself more fascinated by her tales than by the food in front of me. She asks me tons of questions about my tech company and I fill her in on my former life. She also seems dead set on learning as much as she can about the ranch. We're both laughing at a story about one of her clients at her retail job and this guy's incurable obsession with pricey white sheets when the front door swings open and my best friend enters the house.

"Hey, Hunter."

"Hey. Traffic wasn't nearly as bad I thought coming out of Denver."

"Glad you're back. Come over here and meet Allison, Riley's new assistant."

The blonde jumps to her feet to meet my best friend. The difference in height is shocking.

Hunter glances at me before stepping forward and I can't read the expression on his face. "Welcome to our ranch," he says, removing his cowboy hat with one hand while reaching out to greet Allison.

"It's a pleasure to meet you as well," she says, tilting her head back to take in Hunter's tall frame. I'm six-three, but Hunter towers over me by a solid two inches.

"Hunter, there are more wraps warming up in the oven. Are you hungry?"

My friend turns in my direction and the way he arches his eyebrows suggests he's as pleasantly surprised as I am to meet Allison. I nod knowingly. *She's freaking hot.*

"No, buddy. I'm good. I had a big lunch in the city." Hunter walks towards me and pats me on the shoulder. "I'll just have a cold one."

"Good idea. Grab me a beer at the same time, will you?"

"Allison, would you also like a beer?" Hunter is gripping the refrigerator door and grinning as he plays host to the newcomer.

"No, thank you, Hunter. I'm afraid I'm not much of a beer person. I prefer wine and girlie cocktails." She laughs.

"Jake's sister and Isadora are the same. We have a nice selection of wine in our cellar. I'm happy to go and grab you a bottle."

Look who's being so accommodating.

"I'm fine for now. I still haven't finished the ginger ale Jake grabbed for me a few minutes ago."

"Let me know if you change your mind."

"Thank you. I will."

"So is this your first time out here?" Hunter closes the fridge, hands me my beer without even looking at me and makes his way to sit right next to Allison. I follow him back to my seat.

"It is. I'm guilty of not travelling much."

"How are you enjoying it so far?"

"I was telling Jake how different the skyline is from New York or Chicago where I grew up."

"Yeah, not only the skyline, but the air and the open space. You'll sleep like a queen tonight."

"I'm a light sleeper and I usually need white noise to fall asleep, but it's so quiet here…"

"Trust me, you're not going to need any white noise out here."

Did he just lick his lips?

When Allison blushes at Hunter's comment, I realize I'm not the only one who heard a double entendre.

"So I hope your boyfriend isn't going to find your time away from New York too difficult to handle?"

Could he be more obvious?

"Hunter, buddy, Allison's private life is her own." I glance in Allison's direction and she's beet red.

"Uh. Gosh, you don't beat around the bush, do you?"

"It's a simple question. I was curious if you'll have any weekend visitors. We're all adults here."

"Hunter," I growl. "Enough. You're going to make her uncomfortable."

"Jake, it's okay. I don't mind answering the question," she says, curling up her lips. "I broke things off with my boyfriend a few months ago, so you don't have to worry about anyone coming around to visit me," she says, lowering her eyes to her drink.

"What an idiot for allowing you to get away."

Jesus Christ. Is he already flirting with her?

Hunter can be so forward sometimes. I tend to be more reserved at first, but once the doors are closed and I have my dick deep inside a woman's sweet pussy, I turn feral. Hunter might be an alpha male, but I'm the top dog. I just don't operate like he does.

"So, Allison—"

My best friend is about to ask a question when the front door swings open again and we hear kids screaming and yelling.

"Riley's back with the kids," I say, dropping my beer on the counter and standing up to greet my niece and nephews.

"Uncle Jake, Uncle Hunter, we're back." My four-year-old niece is always so eager to get home at the end of the day to tell us all about school.

"I can see that, sweetie. Come over here and give me a big hug." As I pick up my niece, my sister's oldest son runs into the house.

"Mom says she'll need a hand with all the stuff she bought in town."

"Zach, tell your mom we'll be out in a second." I drop adorable Erika to the floor and turn in Allison's direction. "We're going to help Riley. She usually buys up a storm when she goes into town and then she can't find the energy to carry the stuff back into the house." I chuckle.

"I can help." Before I can even protest, Allison is already on her feet.

"Nah, Riley will kill me if I put our guest to work so early on."

Right on cue, Isadora walks through the doors.

"Stay here and get to know the best nanny and housekeeper in the entire state, if not country. We'll be right back," I say, hugging the woman who's been taking care of my sister's kids for the past four years.

"Jake, what have you been telling this poor child?" Isadora playfully hits my stomach. She's so tiny, she's even shorter than Allison, who can't possibly be taller than five two.

"Nothing. I swear. I fed our guest and I kept her company, just like you told me." I kiss Isadora on both cheeks before calling on Hunter so we can bring all the food my sister bought into the house and then go drop off what she needs for her blog at her studio. "Allison, since I'll need to drive up the truck in front of Riley's house and her studio, I'll swing by where you'll be staying and I'll drop off your luggage. I'll walk you out with you later so you can get changed before dinner," I say, turning to the blonde sitting like a star pupil on her stool.

"It must be far if you have to drive." She looks alarmed.

"Not at all. It will be faster to drive by and drop all the food Riley bought than to make several trips by foot. All the homes built on this land are within walking distance of one another. You'll see what I mean."

* * *

When we get back to the house, Isadora and Allison are talking and laughing while the housekeeper tidies up my kitchen. I can't help but notice how relaxed our guest has become since arriving earlier this afternoon. I open my mouth to say something, but my sister enters the house and it's her show now.

"Allison, you're here." Riley walks right past us to hug her new assistant. When Allison gets to her feet, the difference in height is staggering. It's almost as if Allison is half her height. My sister is already a boisterous woman, and since she's five feet eleven, she stands out.

"How was the trip?"

"It was great. Everything has been like a dream since I arrived. I was able to spend time getting to know your brother and Hunter arrived not long ago," Allison says, smiling at me.

"Did my big brother feed you, honey? I hope you didn't have to eat that dreadful airplane food."

"No. It was a short flight. And yes, Jake served your amazing soup and the wrap hit the spot."

"Good. Jake, is it okay if I hang out here at your house with Allison for a bit? The kids are too noisy at my place."

"Sure. Hunter and I will go take care of some paperwork."

Before I finish my sentence, she's already turned her attention back to her new assistant, leaving my best friend and I standing by the kitchen. "Thanks. You're a sweetheart."

I'm about to step back when something my sister says makes me reconsider.

"Allison, did Jake explain the living arrangements here?"

"Uh, yes, I think."

"When I moved in with him and Hunter, we all lived in this house right here. You can imagine how crowded it was with four kids running around all day long. Jake and Hunter own so much land, they decided to build smaller homes to accommodate my little brood and they also built one for Hunter. This makes it easier for us to have some privacy... just in case these boys want to come home with a nice girl one day," my sister shouts in our direction.

"Really, Riley?" I ask.

"What? A sister can hope one day you'll find the one. And the same goes for you, Hunter. You're like a brother to me by now and I want to see you with a girl. You two are like freaking monks. At least I have four good reasons not to be dating, but two handsome, single guys like you..."

"Whatever," I answer, catching Allison's eye.

At least she looks amused by my sister's banter.

"As I was saying, we all have our living quarters and Jake also built a few extra houses on the property for guests. Isadora, my angel, doesn't stay here. She lives about thirty minutes away and she's usually here by five-thirty in the morning."

Thank God Allison lives in New York and she's used to a fast-paced life. Riley is talking so fast and downloading so much information in one shot it's overwhelming even to me.

"Oh. Did Jake tell you about the men?"

"Men?"

"You don't know yet?" Riley lifts her right eyebrow so suggestively Allison blushes.

"Well, if you're talking about the workers…"

"Honey, they're not mere workers. They're all young, drop-dead-gorgeous cowboys. My brother and Hunter employ twelve strapping hunks who come to the ranch each day at six-thirty to start their day. On hot days, by the time lunch is over, it's a girl's wet dream come true." *I can't believe she said that.* "When the sun is beating hard, the guys shamelessly strip out of their shirts and it's like walking through the gates of heaven." My sister delivers the news while fanning herself and Hunter and I roll our eyes at each other.

"I see." Allison looks slightly freaked out and I can't help but chuckle.

"Trust me, honey. The eye candy is pretty tempting… but I can't touch. I already have too much on my plate to deal with a man, but if you're single, please help yourself."

"She is."

Hunter chimes in on the conversation and I look at him, shaking my head.

"You are? Girl, I might have to live vicariously through you because God knows Cynthia was so strait-laced." My sister winks at Allison and the poor girl turns bright red again.

"I'll keep that in mind," Allison responds nervously.

"Enough about buff, handsome and semi-naked men. I should let you know that since my cooking was taking over my small kitchen, Jake built me a luxurious studio inside one of the barns, fully equipped with lighting tracks, ceiling microphones and all the outlets I need for my video segments."

"I know. You mentioned it in one of your past blog posts."

"Right. Look at you. You've done your homework."

"It wasn't much work since I've been following your blog forever."

"Good girl. I knew there was a reason why I liked you so much. Anyways, back to the studio. There's an area I use as my office and there's a desk calling your name. It's a dream space and I can't wait to share it with you tomorrow."

"I'm so looking forward to all of this."

"Not nearly as much as I am, honey. I so need your talent. I'm useless with a camera—digital or video." My sister's rollicking laugh fills the room and

Hunter and I look at each other. My best friend hasn't been able to wipe that silly grin off his face since he met Allison.

"Okay, you boys need to leave us alone now. It's high time for me to get to know my new assistant better. Don't forget, dinner is in a couple of hours right after I get the kids settled and leave them with Isadora."

"All right then. We'll all meet back right here for dinner," I say, grabbing my cowboy hat where I left it several hours ago. "Allison, we'll catch you later."

"Absolutely. I'll see you soon and thank you for everything, Jake."

"Nonsense. The pleasure was all mine."

She has no idea how much I enjoyed getting to know her.

CHAPTER FIVE

HUNTER

Jake and I walk in silence to the office we built a few miles away from the main house. Although neither of us says a word, I know he's thinking what I'm thinking because I've known him forever.

We've been best buddies since I sat next to him in the cafeteria on my first day at his high school when we were both teenagers. I'm originally from Arizona, but when my parents got divorced, my dad moved with his new wife to LA. When I turned sixteen I became so rebellious my mother couldn't handle me. After I tried her patience one too many times, she sent me to live with my father and my stepmother. Since I'm an only child, Jake is the closest I'll ever have to a brother and we've been inseparable since we first met.

Luckily the walk from Jake's home to the office is short. If it were longer, I don't think I could've contained myself. When we enter the spacious area where we usually start and end each day, Jake closes the door behind him and leans against it. Without turning around to look at him, I speak.

"Why don't I make some coffee?"

"Yeah. Why don't you?"

I focus on preparing coffee like a master barista to avoid the obvious—both Jake and I are taken aback by Allison's beauty and charm. When I return to the main room, my buddy has his feet on the desk and he's leaning back in his chair with his cowboy hat over his face.

"Here you go," I say, setting his coffee on his desk.

"Thanks." He removes his hat and grabs his cup.

I know Jake is more reserved than I am and it sometimes takes him longer to articulate things, so I decide to give him a nudge.

"Man, your sister should have warned us. I thought Allison was going to end up being a high-maintenance princess who expects to eat sushi and edamame three times a day while living on the ranch. I didn't expect this friendly and warm person. And I surely didn't expect her to look like she does."

"Neither did I, buddy." Jake jumps to his feet and paces the room, rubbing his hand through his hair. "She caught me totally off guard with her charm, her wits... and her body. Those curves..." Jake presses his lips together and shakes his head.

"I know. I couldn't stop staring at her huge tits. I can only imagine what they must look like if you rip that bra off of her. When she's on all fours, they must hang low, heavy and inviting as hell. Fuck."

"Hunter. You can't talk like that. Allison is here as Riley's assistant. She's not your plaything."

"Be honest. Tell me you didn't think the first time you laid eyes on her of fucking her from behind so you could cup her tits while you drive your cock deeper into her wet pussy." The imagery makes me instantly hard and I grab my crotch to tame the temptation. Jake can lie to himself, but he can't fool me. I've seen that hungry look in his eyes too many times in the past when he's interested in a woman.

"Thinking about something and acting on it are two different things, buddy."

"You know better than anyone what life is around here for single men. We might own a successful and lucrative ranch, but it gets lonely at the top. It's not like when we were living in Silicon Valley or New York."

"Hunter, relationships are a lot of work, and energy, and time," he says, taking a sip of his coffee. "We haven't had a lot of spare time because we've both invested our time in getting the ranch off the ground and learning everything we had to learn. You know as well as I do it's hard to find a good fit in a small town when you've lived your whole life in cities with millions of single women." He puts his cup on his desk. "Casual relationships are tricky here. And it's been a challenge finding a woman who... you know..."

"Who would be willing to give in to our kinks?" I finish his sentence.

"Yes."

"Maybe we don't have to look much further. Maybe Allison is the one. It surely would make things easier since she'll be living with us."

"We thought the same about Cynthia, remember?"

"All right, so Cynthia turned out to be a conservative good-girl who was saving herself for marriage—no wonder she's off on a missionary trip to Africa. I didn't get the vibe that Allison is a goody two-shoes. There was something about the way she looked at me from under her lashes."

"I hear you. I felt the same. The way she looked at me when she first arrived... and throughout the time we spent getting to know each other before you got back. Cynthia has always been oblivious to us and to the twelve men who come to work on the ranch every single day. Even in the midst of summer, when most of our guys are walking around shirtless, she never risked a peek, but I saw something flash in Allison's eyes that suggests she's not as innocent as my sister's former assistant."

"This might turn out to be a problem," I say, rubbing my late-afternoon stubble with the tips of my fingers.

"How so?"

"I mean, it sounds like we both find her attractive. How do we approach this?"

"We shouldn't even be having this conversation."

"But we are."

"You got me there." Jake looks so torn. It's as if he's resisting the natural urge to lose himself between a woman's thighs. In my world, there's nothing more sublime.

"Mind you…" I allow my sentence to hang to torture him a bit more into admitting he wants Allison as much as I do. "We've shared a number of irresistible women in the past when we were both attracted to the same beauty. We've even had a few wild weekends when we've been back to San Fran on vacation and left Dirk Edwards, our manager, in charge of the operations for a few days, but we've kept it to one-on-one sex for the past few years…"

"Hunter, it's a small community and people talk."

"You're right, which makes Allison so much more attractive."

During the heyday of our tech company, Jake and I used to date a lot of women. The opportunities abounded and the women were throwing themselves at us. I still remember when we sold our company and became instant billionaires, we threw the party to end all parties. We celebrated the epic event for four days straight.

Small companies being bought out by giants is hardly news in Silicon Valley. It happens every day of the week. Things were different for us because we made history. We set a milestone in the world of buyouts when Tyrion Tech was willing to pay three point eight billion dollars for the technology my best friend and I spent years perfecting. Who can blame them? We'd built an app Facebook users couldn't live without. It doesn't take a genius to figure that with Facebook's billion-plus users, Tyrion Tech was guaranteed to get back their investment in a blink of an eye.

We were wealthy before the buyout, but we become obscenely rich after it. When the news broke in the business world, we shut down our offices and flew the entire staff to Sin City. We rented four floors at the Wynn Hotel in Vegas and we partied hard. Even our newest employees made major bank from the sale of our company since we were offering stocks as bonuses. I don't remember much from those four days, but I do remember how Jake and I fought over this gorgeous busty redhead with giant tits, a tiny waist and a dreamy ass. After a few too many drinks, the vixen suggested we stop fighting and both fuck her. I couldn't walk for days after that wild weekend, but goddamn, was it ever worth it.

"I don't know, Hunter. Allison is here to help my sister. Riley will have our heads on spikes if we attempt to distract her..."

"What?" I press when he stops in mid-sentence.

"I haven't been able to shake off the visual of watching you fuck her pussy while I fuck her mouth since you started flirting with her earlier."

"This is a perfect opportunity for us. You're being overly cautious."

"Am I?" he says, flashing me a somber stare.

Both Jake and I have dated women since moving to Fort Collins—it's not as if there aren't any gorgeous women to date where we live—but after a few months, things fizzle and we usually find ourselves single again. Jake blames his wishy-washiness with women on his responsibilities to his sister, who has been raising her kids as a single mom since her deadbeat ex-husband walked out on her when little Erika was two months old, but it covers up the fact he hasn't been in the mood to make much effort in a long time. In my case, I blame my workload at the ranch, but it's just a practical excuse.

"Can you think of anything that would be more amazing than fucking her ass while I pump her pussy? I can't. I know how you have a penchant for anal sex and her ass would be oh, so sweet." The thought had flashed in front of my eyes when Allison jumped to her feet and offered to help unload Riley's car. I took one glance at her hips and I could think of nothing else.

"Listen, we don't know if she's even interested in either of us. Even if she were, it doesn't mean she'd consider having both of us at the same time." I can tell Jake is struggling with his emotions, but I'm not. "Hunter, I don't want to take any chances. This could get out of hand. I think we should give Allison some space. She's here to work and we need to respect that. So keep it in your pants."

Fuck.

CHAPTER SIX

ALLISON

Zach, Riley's eldest son, texts his mom and suddenly my new boss has to dash home. It seems her six-year-old twins, Brady and Perry, were playing and ripped the clothesline, sending a full day's clean laundry into the dirt. Riley is more amused than annoyed and she rallies Isadora to help. She also takes me back to my house so I can shower and change before dinner.

I'd love to say the walk from Jake's house is lovely and relaxing, but I can barely keep up with Riley's long strides. Obviously, Isadora, who's even shorter than I am, has had a lot of practice because she easily keeps up with the tall redhead.

After handing me the keys and kissing me on both cheeks, Riley leaves me to my own devices to discover my new abode while she rushes back to discipline her boys.

When I step inside, I take in my new surroundings. The décor is a reflection of the sleek, chic style in Jake's house. The only difference is there are many more wooden accents and it's a little quainter than the main house. There are three small, but comfortable rooms and I even have my own fully-equipped kitchen. Riley was right, this setting is a perfect way to ensure I maintain some privacy.

I waltz to the main bedroom and hoist my big suitcase onto the chair in the corner of the room to unpack and hang my clothing. As I pull out every piece I brought with me, I can't help but think how underwhelming everything looks. I was under the impression I was going to spend the summer with Riley, her four kids and her nanny and I didn't feel the pressure to look interesting, but after meeting Jake and Hunter, I regret not having anything better to wear.

What's wrong with you, girl? You've only known them for a New York minute. Calm down.

I shrug off the thought that either of these two rugged and dangerously handsome men would give me the time of the day.

I'm still taking in my summer home when my phone rings. I run back to the living room where I left it at the bottom of my handbag and I answer immediately when Gwyn's name appears on my screen.

"Hey, darling, how's life in the wild?"

"I wouldn't say Colorado is exactly wilderness."

"Honey, you're out in the middle of nowhere with no hope in hell of getting a mani-pedi during your lunch break. In my world, that's wilderness." She chuckles.

"I've definitely missed your wacky humor since leaving your place." I laugh.

"Have you settled in yet?"

"Yes, I just walked into my new house."

"House?"

"Yes, I thought I was going to end up in a small room, but I have a large house all to myself. I didn't know my new boss lived on a huge ranch. I was caught off guard. In any case, it's stunning and Riley's brother built a number of homes on his property so everyone can have their own little private hideaway."

"Wait a minute. Slow down that car, step on the brakes and now put it in reverse. Did you just say Riley's brother?"

I roll my eyes in the phone. My best friend doesn't miss a beat. "I did."

"You never mentioned a brother before."

"I didn't know. I found out when I got here and I also found out the brother, who happens to be the sexiest man I've ever laid eyes on, has an equally sexy business partner who also lives on the land."

"Girl, two hot cowboys?"

"I don't think they call themselves that," I say, shaking my head. "Jake and Hunter own this massive ranch and all this sprawling land, but they hire real, bona fide cowboys to manage the day-to-day. It's like owning a restaurant, but hiring a top-notch chef to take care of the cooking."

"I get it. How old are they?"

"Hmmm," I say, lifting my eyes to the ceiling. "I'm not one hundred percent sure, but I'd guess Gaven's age."

"So late twenties. Nice."

"Yeah. They're quite young considering their level of success. From what Jake explained, they became billionaires overnight in their mid-twenties when their dotcom company was sold."

"Holy Jesus. Are you serious?"

"I know. It's very impressive, but they're so down-to-earth and normal, you'd never know."

"Oh, honey, you're so lucky. Which one do you prefer?"

"Whoa! You're moving too fast, Gwyn. I've barely arrived. It's not as if I've had time to make that kind of decision."

"You're so bullshitting me right now. Which one is it?" she pressures me, knowing full well I've had plenty of time to check them out.

"It's all in my head. These two are both delicious and in my wildest dreams I'd love to have both, but I also know it's a dream and it will never become reality."

"Why not?"

I bite the inside of my mouth, unwilling to say the words.

"Allison, what are you thinking?"

I skirt the issue and hope I can distract her. "Riley explained there are twelve male workers who come to the ranch every single day. Perhaps I might get lucky with one of them." There's no way in hell a girl like me has a chance with either Jake or Hunter.

"You're forgetting the most important part of this equation."

"What do you mean?"

"What if you aren't interested in any of these twelve workers because you're totally into one of those ranch owners you seem to be fond of?"

"To be fair, I haven't yet met these workers. Sparks could fly."

"Allison, don't settle again. Please."

"Gwyn, I hate to admit it, but I desperately crave a man's touch. It's been over nine months since Clark last touched me and although he was an average lover, at least when we were intimate, I was able to feel his hands all over my body. These last few months have been horribly lonely and I've never felt so unattractive, undesired and unloved as I did at the tail end of my relationship. I'm sure he lost interest because I put on a few pounds."

"Any woman in your situation would feel the same way, even if she were wafer-thin. It's still no reasons to lower your expectations. You're already convinced neither of these two studs would be interested in you because you're not as thin as Keira Knightley, but you don't know that for sure, do you?"

"I guess not," I say, curling my lips down.

"Honey, I've told you before you left, Colorado is a fresh new start for you."

"Thanks for lifting my spirits. You're right. It's all behind me now. No point in getting all depressed in the face of the recent fiascos in my life."

"Exactly. You didn't accept Riley's offer just to relive every moment of your disastrous relationship with that asshole. Not when there are so many dangerously sexy men looming close by. Holy shit, imagine if it gets so hot, the men have to walk around with their shirts off… all. Day. Long. Imagine the eye candy."

"You sound like my new boss."

We both laugh.

"What are your plans for tonight? Is there anything to do out there other than to listen to crickets sing or are you going to curl up with a book in your new bed?"

"Riley is cooking a special dinner for my arrival at Jake's house."

"Jake? Her brother? What are you going to wear?"

"You're such a fashion whore. There's not much room for fashion out here and since I brought basic clothing, there's not much I can do."

"For the love of God, instead of putting yourself down, answer my question." I hear the impatience in her voice. Gwyn hates it when I'm down on myself, but sometimes I can't help it. Old habits die hard.

"I'm sorry," I say, immediately regretting my last comment. "I was thinking of wearing a pair of dark navy boot-cut jeans I got at the Gap and a button-down turquoise shirt I bought a few weeks ago on clearance at Macy's."

"Turquoise looks amazing on you."

"Yeah, I guess." I'm unsure.

"There you go again."

"Listen, Gwyn, I'm very self-conscious of the ten pounds I still want to lose."

"Sweetie, just because you have a bit of a tummy doesn't mean you're not yummy."

"You keep reminding me of that, but I'm not buying it. I don't look like you—never will. Walking in on my ex and Paula kind of confirms what I've always known down deep inside—there's nothing attractive about me. Clark professed to liking every part of me, but his words and actions suggest it was all a lie."

"Ali, you're being blind here. You can't crucify all mankind because you've dated a few idiots. Men aren't looking for perfection. They want a woman who's confident about herself—just the way she is... not the way she wishes she were. I mean, you must remember my colleague Kaileigh O'Connell from the barbecue we had at my house for Memorial Day?"

"Yeah, I do," I acquiesce grudgingly. "It's hard to forget her."

"Exactly. She has quite arresting large teeth and she has a big gap right in the middle of her pearly whites. On top of that, she has bee-stung rosebud lips, large eyes and serious dimples. But here's the thing, she's fun, joyful and bubbly. Her personality is a real magnet... and her boyfriend is smoking hot. I mean, fan-me-and-pour-a-bucket-of-ice-water-all-over-my-fiery-body hot."

"You're the least expressive person I know," I mock.

We both laugh.

"Okay, you have a point. Kaileigh bagged a hunk who adores her."

"And so can you and you don't have to look like a freaking supermodel."

"I wish I had as much confidence as you or Kaileigh, but I don't. You've always been fearless and I've always been riddled with insecurities."

My best friend has been pushing me out of my comfort zone since the day we met. She was the one who took me kicking and screaming to my first frat party and got me passing-out drunk. Her then boyfriend, Darrell Cooks, invited her to be his date at this big bash one of his friends was holding at his parents' house while they were away in Hawaii and she agreed on one condition—she had to be able to drag me along with her. I never clued in on why she insisted on bringing me because I ended up spending the earlier part of the night hugging the walls because I felt so out of place. Everyone was tall, skinny and sexy and I was not.

Gwyn wouldn't understand my angst. She's always been gorgeous and the life of any party. When she walks in a room every man stops and pays attention—I'm the invisible one following in her footsteps.

"Indulge me a little bit. What are these two Adonises you met earlier today like?" she asks.

"Honestly, it was impossible for me to ignore how strong and manly they both are when we all sat in Jake's kitchen right after my arrival. I mean, I was dizzy from all that alpha-male testosterone flying in the air."

"Damn, girl. Now I'm totally jealous. Don't get me wrong, Gaven is a nice piece of eye candy, but you get to drool over these panty-drenchers all summer long," she laughs. "Give me more details. Don't hold back."

Gwyn can turn the shittiest day into something that seems to have jumped off of the screen of a Disney movie.

"Well, Hunter, Jake's business partner, is outspoken, impulsive, rugged and very tall. His jet-black hair only emphasizes his striking dark brown eyes and makes him that much more delicious. I'm sure life on the ranch is demanding, which would explain his impressive muscle mass, but his strong lean body had such an effect on me."

"Oh, God, girl, my tongue is hanging out from that description. What about Riley's brother?"

"Jake on the other hand is more subdued. He's not quite as tall as Hunter, but I'm certain he stands at least six-three. The man is illegally hot. He's totally my type since you know I've always been a sucker for men with blue eyes. He immediately caught my attention."

"See, another reason to say amen and hallelujah your ex was a philanderer."

"You kill me. Let me continue telling you about Jake," I respond, more excited than I've been in a long time.

"Honey, don't let me stop you."

"My boss' older sibling has such a commanding presence it's disarming."

"Ohhh."

"I'm telling you, when he speaks, his deep voice reverberates through my entire body and during the time we spent together I couldn't stop looking at his hands. His very large hands."

"Hmmm, that big?"

"Uh-huh."

"Gosh, it's like you've landed in heaven."

"I think I've landed in hunk heaven for sure because when those two smile, I drool."

Suddenly I look at the clock on the wall in the kitchen and I realize I have to start getting ready for dinner.

"Listen, I love you, but I'm going to have to call you tomorrow. I still have to get ready for dinner."

"All right. I love you right back. Chin up and go get them. Both of them."

"You're crazy."

"No. You deserve it."

Once I hang up with Gwyn, I'm bursting with newfound confidence. *Thank God for her.* She's always able to help me see myself in a new light.

I quickly put my clothing away in a wardrobe and place a few folded pieces in the gorgeous antique-looking drawers. I peel off the clothes I'm wearing and hit the shower. The cool water running down my body is a welcome treat considering it's surprisingly hot in Colorado. I grab my bottle of pink grapefruit-scented shower gel and my shower pouf to lather my body. I catch sight of my stomach and wonder how much my gaining weight played into Clark's decision to sleep with other women.

Oh, well. It doesn't matter anymore. I brush off the thought and continue rinsing off my body. As I turn off the water and step out of the tub, I realize in some ways I should be grateful I walked in on my ex while he was cheating on me because what we shared had false depth and lacked any spark—I can see it clearly now. It still hurts and it's still humiliating, but at least I don't have to grovel every night for his attention anymore.

I walk into the bedroom to get dressed and to blow-dry my hair. I allowed myself two indulgences for this trip. I had no choice but to bring my hairdryer because my long mane cascades all the way down to my waist and it's so full, it takes forever to dry. I have to thank Clark for the second indulgence. People do incredible things for love, particularly for unrequited love, and I'm no exception. In a desperate attempt to save my relationship, I got rid of all my older underwear one Saturday morning and I spent hours on Rosie's Secret Lingerie's website shopping for new lingerie to ignite the fire we had lost, but not even expensive, delicate underwear and in some cases downright naughty showstoppers would convince Clark to take a second look at me—not since he had started his affairs with Paula and the other women he'd been fucking. I might not have brought fashion-worthy country-style clothing, but I have some pretty incredible lingerie no one will ever get to see.

As I shimmy into a soft pink bra and matching panties, a startling thought crosses my mind.

"Did Gwyn really suggest I go after both guys?" I say aloud.

As if that's ever going to happen. I laugh to myself. I'm too much of a chicken to be forward with one man, let alone two.

I'm still lost in my thoughts when the alarm I set on my iPhone rings, reminding me it's nearly time for dinner. Since it makes no sense to wear makeup, I get ready in a flash and after a quick inspection in the tall mirror in my bedroom I'm ready to dash off. I grab my crossbody bag and head back to Jake's house to enjoy a delicious meal. I'm so looking forward to getting to know my new hosts.

CHAPTER SEVEN

JAKE

I decide to enjoy my beer on the front porch. I love my sister, but when she gets into her frenetic mood before receiving a guest, she's like a windstorm. As I take the last gulp of my beer, I notice my best friend approaching the house. He's clean-shaven and dressed to kill. Hunter has swapped his usual work clothes for a fitted black tee shirt, a pair of sand-colored chinos and brand new boots he bought a few weeks ago.

As much as I'd like to make fun of him, I can't. After a cold shower, I traded my own dirty jeans for bone-colored chinos and a light denim shirt. I took extra time when shaving and I even spent time on my hair, which I never bother with.

Hunter lifts his eyes and meets mine before rewarding me with a grin. I can't help but smile back because it's clear both of us realize the lengths to which we are willing to go to impress the newcomer.

"Buddy, I haven't seen you so clean-shaven since we left New York to move out here," he comments as he steps up onto the porch.

"You're exaggerating," I say, rolling my eyes. "Look who's talking. You're sporting brand-new boots."

"It's important to make a good first impression."

"Too late. You nearly jumped Allison's bones in the kitchen earlier."

"You're jealous because I'm more forward than you are. How long were you sitting in your kitchen making idle conversation before I arrived? I bet you had plenty of time to make a move on her, but controlled, stoic, well-mannered Jake was prim and proper as always."

I hate him right now for being so accurate. "Am I that obvious to you?"

"I know how you work when it comes to women you're interested in. Let's just say our approaches vary greatly," he says, laughing.

"Yeah, you're right there."

"You've retreated to the porch because Riley has gone manic in your kitchen again."

"There's only so much I can take." I smile.

One of the reasons why I built my sister a separate house on my land is so I can have some peace and quiet. If she wants to cook up a meal fit for the Queen of England, I don't have to be part of it every single night. I recognize tonight is special since Allison arrived a few hours ago and Riley has been looking forward to this day for weeks now, but still, it's best for me to step out of my own home and give her the space she needs.

"It's always been go big or go home with your sister. Not to mention you know well enough how important Allison is to Riley's business."

"I know, I know," I respond grudgingly.

"Let me grab a cold one and I'll come out and join you." Before I can even agree, Hunter pulls open the front door and steps into my home. It takes Hunter no time at all to grab a couple of beers and come sit next to me. He hands me a bottle and twists the cap off of his before chugging down a big gulp.

"There's nothing quite like a cold beer at the end of a long work day."

"Amen to that, buddy."

"Well, that or you know…"

"No. I don't."

He flashes me a telling smile and I can't help but burst out laughing.

Man, Hunter doesn't waste any time.

I shake my head, reliving how shamelessly my best friend flirted with Allison when he got back from the city. She seemed a bit shy, but the twinkle in her eyes suggested she loved his forwardness. It's going to be a long summer because as much as I try to talk myself out of seeing Allison as anything more than hired help for Riley, I can't keep lying to myself—the blonde is the type of woman I gravitate towards like a bee to honey. I have to man up and I have to take the same advice I dished out to Hunter earlier in our office.

Fuck, this is going to be hard.

"You're a dirty hound-dog,"

"I'm a man. Sue me." Hunter leans into his chair and swings his long legs on a chair sitting across from him. "I wonder how things will play out tonight."

"What do you mean?"

"Now that it's out in the open we both like her, things might get weird tonight."

"Nothing has to be weird if you follow my advice," I hiss.

"I hear you loud and clear. You want me to keep it in my pants and I will. I don't know how you do it."

"Do what?"

My friend gives me a long stare before speaking again. "When was the last time you got laid?" Hunter whispers his words, aware that although Miranda Lambert's *Little Red Wagon* is blaring from my house and I can hear my sister singing along, Riley is still within earshot. "It's been a month since you broke things off with Lindsay."

Thank God that's over. I met Lindsay Corbin at a charity event in Silicon Valley. Hunter and I still keep a close circle of friends out there and we never miss the opportunity to hop on a plane and go party. The minute I saw Lindsay, I was instantly drawn to her. After a few months of back-and-forth, the relationship became taxing because as much as I enjoyed sex with her, I couldn't see things going any further. Even though she came to Denver a few times to party and to see me, she'd made it clear she could never leave San Francisco to move out here and I knew I wasn't going back there—I didn't need to. Not to mention Lindsay is a bit high-maintenance and too much of a drama queen for my liking. Since the breakup I've been a bit of a recluse, satisfying my sexual needs with predictable porn clips and jerking off any chance I get.

"I haven't seen you bring anyone around either," I reply defensively.

"You know perfectly well we have a rule not to bring women to the ranch and to keep it to hotels or their homes. At least I get some. I go to Denver any chance I have for some fun with no strings attached, but I know you get bored easily with one-night stands. A friend has a right to be concerned."

"Listen, breaking things off with Lindsay was a royal pain in the ass. Although she doesn't see herself living out here, she wanted us to keep what we had going. She keeps calling and texting in the hopes I'll reconsider. I keep turning her down, but she's unwilling to let it go. After all this, I need a break from women."

"She's still calling? She won't give up."

"I'm sure she'll find the right one, but it's not me. I haven't heard from her in a week now, so I'm hoping she's found a replacement boyfriend to latch onto. I should have never started this long-distance relationship. In the end Lindsay became needy and I had no desire to take things further, but I was dragging my feet about letting her go."

"Well, let's hope she's moved on and you won't hear from her again. I think it's high time for you to get back in the saddle."

"Don't worry about me. I'm doing fine. As for me hopping from one pussy to another… I'm not like you. I need a break between women."

We both laugh.

"As much as I love our life out here, I miss the big-city life."

Before moving to Colorado, we lived for six months in New York trying to escape our overnight fame after we got bought out. Living in Silicon Valley felt claustrophobic because of the journalists and paparazzi chasing us. They were relentless. After a couple of months, we couldn't continue being stalked by them and still hope to live a normal life. So we left.

"Damn right. We lived in the land of plenty. The Big Apple offers a tempting range of sultry women capable of fulfilling our wildest fantasies."

"Yup. In all fairness, Silicon Valley or San Fran offered a lot of amazing options as well."

"Yeah. We've had our share of unforgettable nights and insane weekends of debauchery, but out here… it's harder."

"I won't lie, Hunter. There are plenty of attractive perks in living on a ranch like this one, but it's shit for our sex life."

"Maybe our luck turned around today." My best friend raises his eyebrows and tilts his head to the right. I've seen this predatory look too many times and I know exactly what he's thinking.

"Hunter, we've already talked about this earlier."

"I get it, but when I was in the shower, I closed my eyes and..." He trails off, forcing me to lean in closer to catch the rest of his train of thought.

"And what?"

"I could only see her hips and her huge tits in my hands. I saw myself pounding her pussy until she screamed out for mercy and I also saw you looking at both of us while I took her from behind. You love watching when we both take a woman. It's been so long, Jake. My daydream felt so real. I jerked off so hard my legs were shaking after I came. Goddammit, I had to hold on to the wall to avoid collapsing. It was that intense."

I should be upset at Hunter's admission, but I'm not. I'm as guilty as he is.

"I did the same." I inhale through my nose and I run my tongue over my lip when the flashback hits me.

"What? The way you've been lecturing me about keeping my distance made you sound like a monk."

"I don't have any monastic aspirations. I also jerked off thinking of both of us taking her. Listen, I want her as much as you do."

"Doesn't sound like it," he challenges.

Hunter keeps pushing this, but I know if I'm not the voice of reason, this may get dirty real fast and we might end up compromising things for my sister.

"You won't let go?"

"No, I won't."

"Fuck, she's hot. Even after jerking off, just thinking about her gives me a hard-on."

"Good, so what are we going to do about it?"

I didn't expect to be so taken by her hourglass figure. In any case, it doesn't matter. Allison is here to support Riley's growth, not to become our playmate. But goddammit, my mind goes straight into the gutter every time she walks by me swaying those tempting hips.

"Let's see if sparks fly tonight."

"Yes!" I've barely finished my sentence before Hunter is already pumping his fist in victory.

"But there are some ground rules."

"Do we really need them?" He rolls his eyes at me.

"If we don't have them, you'll scare her. We can't put any pressure on her—you're not allowed to flirt hard like you usually do. If she shows interest in either of us, then it's worth exploring things further. If not… we back off."

"Now you're talking."

CHAPTER EIGHT

ALLISON

I'm lounging luxuriously like Khaleesi would in *Game of Thrones* and both stunning men are sitting on chairs across from me nursing beers. This evening is way up there on my list of unforgettable moments. I'll admit it was fun to be a little bit more unrestricted than I usually am. My new boss impressed the heck out of me with her ability to hold down her booze, but there was no way I was ever going to be able to compete. After a few too many drinks, I had to take a break because I'm feeling so lightheaded.

After a scrumptious dessert and piping-hot mugs of coffee with a shot of brandy, Riley retreated to her home a few minutes ago, but I'm feeling so buzzed from an exciting evening, I can't convince myself to move. The three of us are still hanging out in Jake's living room relaxing to the sultry sounds of jazz music. All in all, this evening has been so enchanting, I don't want it to end.

My eyes are half closed from the copious dinner when Jake's voice brings me back to life.

"I hope you enjoyed dinner."

I prop myself on my elbows and swerve my body to look at him. "Dinner was even more spectacular than you predicted. I had to exert some serious willpower when Riley offered me a third piece of lasagna because hers is the best I've ever had."

"I always have three servings. I can't resist. There's a reason why Riley's recipes are so popular on the Internet and she's sold hundreds of thousands of copies of her cookbooks."

"I really shouldn't be surprised since I've been following her for such a long time, but I must say this celestial meal caught me off guard."

"I'm proud of my little sis. She made history when Food TV approached her and offered her an eye-popping salary to host her own show. It's amazing considering she's a stay-at-home mom who is self-taught in the kitchen."

"I can't thank my lucky stars enough. I still can't believe she selected me amongst all of the candidates who applied for this position."

I was worried about Riley's fame before arriving here. In New York, it doesn't take much for someone to become unbearable the minute they taste a little success, but my new boss is very friendly and so down-to-earth.

"Seems like the two of you are getting along."

"I have to agree. My only challenge is your sister's frankness." I quickly bring my hand to my face, worried I've said too much. *Damn booze.* "Not quite what I wanted to say," I babble, hoping to redeem myself. "I mean, I'll have to get used to the fact she doesn't mince her words and she speaks her mind freely."

Both men laugh at my obvious discomfort.

"I've known his little sister since we were kids and Riley still shocks me sometimes."

"Yeah, I have to agree with Hunter. Motherhood has done nothing to slow her down." Jake chuckles before continuing. "She might be single, but she has the dirtiest mind."

"His sister said so many things that made you blush during dinner, I lost count. It was amusing to watch you change color."

"I noticed you guys didn't do a thing to come to my rescue." I shift my body on the couch.

"Sorry, we were in stitches."

"Yeah, buddy, I'm sorry, but the funniest was that last story your sister shared right before she served dessert. It's not the first time I've heard it and I was there when it happened, but it's still hilarious."

"Oh my God, Hunter. I nearly lost it when she shared the story of how little four-year old Erika found her vibrator by mistake and dragged it to Jake's house during a Sunday afternoon lunch."

"I didn't think I was ever going to be able to stop laughing that day."

"So it really did happen? Riley wasn't trying to be colorful?" I say.

Jake shakes his head, fighting off a smile. "Oh, it happened all right. As things were winding down, Erika declared it was time for karaoke and my little niece pulled Riley's vibrator from her Hello Kitty backpack and started singing like a diva. I squinted to take a better look at what she was holding in her tiny hands and it hit me. Riley's face was so horrified I had to bite my tongue to avoid laughing aloud. I mean, you don't want to traumatize a child for trying. Hunter was kicking my leg under the table, incredulous about what he was witnessing. Their reaction nearly sent me over the edge."

"Riley is so expressive. I could see the scene as vividly as if her daughter was standing in front of me pretending to audition for *The Voice* or *American Idol* using her mom's vibrator as a mic."

"You have no idea."

"So you knew it was a vibrator?"

Did I actually ask that question or was that my inner voice? Both Jake and Hunter are as surprised as I am by my question. *Yup, it came out of my mouth.*

"Uh-huh." Jake pinches his lips and nods.

"We've bought our fair share of vibrators. It was pretty unmistakable since I know that model really, really well."

"Hunter." Jake hits his best friend's arm and I instantly turn beet red.

"What? She asked a question and I answered." Although Hunter is speaking to Jake, his eyes are riveted on me and suddenly I'm burning up.

Holy hell. He has to stop looking at me as if he wants to devour me.

Without thinking I sweep my hand from my neck all the way down to my chest in the hopes of containing the fire that's ignited between my legs. When I realize how suggestive my actions might seem, I attempt to remove the hand resting at the swell of my boobs, but my finger gets caught and a few of the buttons pop open.

Shit.

I quickly sit up, trying to pull myself together, hoping they don't think I'm flashing them, but my fingers tremble as I try to cover up. To make matters worse, my hair falls into my face, making it impossible to see. I brush my long mane back and when I look up, I nearly gasp.

"This is so embarrassing," I manage, but neither of them say a word. They simply stare at me like they've been doing pretty much all night long.

I swear both men have been checking me out all evening. When I arrived, Hunter's expression turned shocked when he saw me and he tapped Jake on the shoulder to catch his attention as Riley hugged me. Both men were beaming like boys who had been granted permission to stay up late to play video games. It was only when my new boss made a fuss of my hair that I clued in.

Throughout the evening, I could feel Hunter's gaze on me. Every time I glanced in his direction, he'd hold my gaze for a few seconds, searing me with his brown eyes—just like he's doing right now. I found myself holding my breath every time that happened. Jake, on the other hand, had this almost boyish grin on his face every time he answered one of my questions. I became so paranoid, I excused myself to run to the powder room for a quick inspection, worried I had salad stuck to my teeth, but the only things staring at me were rosy cheeks and an air of blissfulness I hadn't seen in a long time.

"You guys don't have to look so freaked out. It's not as if you could see anything." I'm desperately trying to redeem myself, but Jake and Hunter simply bounce their gazes from my flushed face to each other.

There's a long, heavy silence, as if neither of us is able to find something clever to say. Hunter brings a fist to his mouth before clearing his throat and the next thing I know he's on his feet.

"All right, I'm off to bed. I have a long day tomorrow, but it was a pleasure spending time with you tonight, Allison. I'm looking forward to your stay here."

I try to get up from my seat to wish him goodnight, but I freeze when he leans down towards me. He drops a kiss on each of my cheeks and shockingly, the contact of his lips instantly hardens my nipples. *Oh, boy.*

"I'm sure you're going to sleep like a queen tonight, Allison. If you don't, let me know tomorrow and I'll see what I can do."

Is he coming on to me?

Either I've had one too many drinks or Hunter's comment is laced with double entendres. I take a breath in to slow down my racing heart before answering him.

"I'll keep your offer in mind, but I suspect I'll crash like a log." I try to remain as cool as I possibly can and I turn my head to avoid Hunter's burning gaze. When I swerve to the left, I meet Jake's stare and I read the same intensity I saw in Hunter's gaze a second ago. *God.*

"One last thing before I go."

"Uh…"

"Your hair," Hunter says, bringing his hand to my mane. "It's so magnificent. Why in the world would you ever put it up? You nearly gave me a heart attack when you walked in for dinner with your hair flowing all the way down to your waist. Promise me you'll wear it down more often," he says before dropping a soft kiss on my forehead.

"Hunter, stop it, you're going to scare her off. Go to bed. I'll take Allison back to her place in a few minutes." Jake's tone is stern, but the playful glee in his eyes suggests he's finding this quite amusing.

"All right. I'll be off to bed, but Allison has to promise first."

I smile, uncertain if Hunter is really flirting with me or if I'm making this all up in my head, but I feel so utterly sexy right now, I don't care. "I promise to wear my hair down more often. Cross my heart," I answer, giggling.

"Good. Now I can go sleep soundly. Good night."

"Good night, Hunter."

"Bright and early tomorrow, buddy," he says, turning to Jake.

"As always."

I'm purposefully focusing on Hunter leaving the room and I pretend to be fascinated by the front door, because I'm afraid if I turn around, Jake will see how turned on I am from this playful evening with these two hunks. I know I'm kidding myself because I feel his gaze on the back of my head and when I pivot to meet his eyes, I nearly melt. *Damn.*

* * *

I thought Jake was going to get to his feet right after Hunter retreated to bed, but instead he's been keeping me laughing with hilarious stories of his sister and her kids. I've not been this light-hearted in so long, I forgot how it felt. I could spend the rest of the night here with him, but I have a meeting at nine tomorrow with Riley so she can brief me on my new responsibilities as her assistant and I want to be fresh for my first day of work.

"I don't know how late it is, but maybe it's time for me to get some sleep. I'm sure you must be exhausted," I say, stretching out of my comfy position.

"It's not too late, but I'm sure the trip must be catching up with you. Let me put on my boots and I'll walk you to your house." He gets up and walks towards me where I've been struggling to get up. "This couch is so comfortable, when you sink into it, it's practically impossible to extract your body from it. Let me give you a hand." He reaches out for me. I extend my hand and he pulls me so hard off the couch I land on my feet before stumbling forward. Jake is quick and catches me before I embarrass myself any further. "Are you okay?"

"Yes. Thank you," I whisper. I'm suddenly aware he's cradling me against him. The heat emanating from his muscular body is making me woozy and his closeness causes my pussy to throb. To hide my nervousness and arousal, I lower my eyes, but I think he sees right through me. Jake places his index finger under my chin and forces me to meet his gaze. He pulls me closer to him and I find myself pressed against an impressive erection.

"Hunter is right."

"Umm, about what?" I ask with a shaky voice.

"Your magnificent hair. I did a double-take when I saw you walk in before dinner. Don't get me wrong, you look beautiful with your hair off your face, but when you let it flow like this…" He bites his lower lip as he strokes my mane.

I lose myself in his sultry blue eyes, even though a part of me screams to extract myself from his warm embrace.

"Both you and Hunter are full of compliments tonight." I blush.

Jake doesn't answer. He simply stares intensely into my eyes, making it hard for me to breathe.

The silence in the room is deceiving and doesn't mirror the turmoil shaking my core. There's no way this is happening, I tell myself silently, yet here I am glued against a panty-wetting guy with his cock pressed so hard against me it's as if he's trying to penetrate me without me ever removing my clothing. We're both standing there for a few lustful minutes and Jake has been gently stroking my hair until something in his gaze changes.

"Allison, I'm going to kiss you now and if you feel I'm out of line, I'll stop," he says with eyes half closed.

"Ohhh," I exhale. Instead of protesting, I get on my toes and I offer my mouth to him.

He lowers his head towards me and when our lips meet it's as if I've never been kissed before. How can this be? I met this stud a few hours ago and now I'm making out with him in his living room. For the love of God, his sister, my new boss, can walk in here at any moment and find us locking lips. This is too good. It's as if I'm living out someone else's fantasy because stuff so amazing like this never happens to me.

He's an insane kisser.

Clark was cold and distant throughout the last six months of our relationship and since I moved out two and a half months ago, it's been a really long time since a man has touched my lips—nine months, to be precise. I lose myself in Jake's tender kiss and I close my eyes, trying to drown out the cautious voice chattering inside my head. After a few minutes of this passionate embrace, I reluctantly pull myself away from him, snapping back to reality.

Oh my God, get a grip, Ali. He's your boss' brother.

"I'm sure it's the booze talking, Jake. I mean look at me." The minute the words leave my lips, I regret putting myself down like this.

"I am, gorgeous. I haven't been able to peel my eyes away from you since I turned the corner of my house and saw you struggling with your luggage after the limo driver had dropped you off. Every time you move, I'm mesmerized by your beautiful, sensual hips."

There's no way a guy like Jake can genuinely be attracted to me. "I'm sure you're just saying that." His charm is already weakening my will to refuse him.

"I never bother saying things I don't mean. I'm extremely attracted to your gorgeous body, Allison."

"You don't have to lie."

He doesn't even have to answer my question. The depth of his expression reveals that he's very serious. "Lie?" He opens his mouth to speak again, but instead, he slams my body closer to his and once more I'm pressed against his undeniable arousal. "Do you feel that?" No sooner has he pressed his body against mine does he take a small step back without taking his eyes off of me.

Hell, yeah, I feel it. I'm so turned on I can only nod, my eyes glued to his hand where he's cupping his crotch in such a raunchy and explicit way, I'm nearly salivating.

"My cock doesn't lie." The fire burning in his eyes leaves me speechless. I've never been with a man who looks at me like this.

"Jesus."

"Everything about you turns me on—your sexy hourglass figure, your huge breasts and your arousing hips. I've had many kinky thoughts since your arrival about those hips," he says, caressing my body. "This may surprise you, but not all men want a wafer-thin woman who's shaped more like a young boy than a real woman."

"In my experience men prefer skinny, model-perfect bodies."

"Fools. In my world, your body is divine perfection," he says, crushing my lips again. "I know this sounds crazy because you only arrived a few hours ago and I really can't explain this, but I do know I want more of you."

I'm torn. I've landed the job of my dreams in a scenic town, but there's this very tall, extremely sexy and oh, so turned on man-candy standing in front of me. *What is a girl to do?* Since I haven't had sex in such a long time, I'm desperate for some warmth and attention.

"You're right, Jake. This is crazy."

"It doesn't mean it can't be good, Allison. We can be discreet. No one needs to know but us," he says, pushing his thumb inside my mouth. *Christ.* "You can't deny me. I know I'm not the only one feeling this way."

I have no desire to argue with a handsome stud begging to fuck me. I offer my mouth to him again and he grabs the back of my head with both hands and kisses me so passionately I fear my heart will stop.

The next thing I know, Jake lifts me in his arms and I instantly panic. *Oh, no.*

"What?" He senses my hesitation.

"You don't have to carry me," I mumble nervously.

"I know you can walk. It's been impossible for me to ignore the sultry sway of your hips, but I want to carry you." He silences any protest with a soft kiss and I close my eyes as I wrap my arms around his neck.

He climbs the stairs as if I weigh nothing and makes his way to the end of the hallway. He kicks open the door and drops me on my feet with such care it's as if he's afraid I'll break. He closes the door behind him and walks to his nightstand to turn on the light.

"This is better mood lighting than the ceiling light." He smiles. *I'd feel more comfortable with no lighting at all, to be honest.*

I furtively scan the room, still trying to find my bearings in this new situation. *I'm standing in this hot guy's bedroom. Me.* Jake's room is spacious. Although it's very large and modern, there's still the same warm vibe that carries throughout the house. There's a sleek grey slate fireplace on the main wall flanked by an oversize brown leather chair. Right across from the cozy fireplace is a massive, California king bed covered with a dark grey duvet cover and a few accent pillows. At the foot of the bed lie stylish sheepskin and cowhide rugs. The wall right behind me is made up of floor-to-ceiling windows overlooking the ranch and the majestic silhouette of the Rocky Mountains beyond. To my surprise, a door leads to a massive wooden deck outside. His room is a reflection of him—it has a distinctive presence, but there's an unmistakably serene vibe to it as well.

I'm still looking around me when it becomes clear Jake is observing me as I take in these new surroundings.

"I like watching you."

"You do?"

"Very much so."

"You're going to make me blush again."

"Good. So where were we before we came up here?" He strides towards me with a delightfully sinful gleam before kissing my lips.

What a contrast from a few minutes ago.

I get on my toes and I wrap my arms around his neck, pulling him closer. "I'm happy one of us is keeping track." In that moment, I allow all my doubts to dissipate and I savor every single millisecond with this man.

I return his kiss with all the excitement and anticipation that's been boiling inside me since I caught him looking at me while Hunter was kissing me goodnight. Jake's kiss is deep, pressing and ravenous. *God.* These long celibate months have transformed me and to my own surprise, I press my chest against his and slip a tentative hand between us, cupping the erection I'm dying to touch. He's bigger than I imagined.

I'm even more turned on when Jake moans low in his throat as I rub him through his pants. If I needed a confirmation he was honest about his attraction towards me, I just got it.

"Allison, I didn't expect you to be such a naughty girl, but I want to enjoy your body first." Jake doesn't allow me to continue my dirty game. He takes my hands and pulls them up over my head. With his strong hands, he's able to hold both my wrists in one hand.

I look up, startled, but when I meet his lustful gaze, I quickly calm down. Slowly, like a sensual torture, he slides his other hand down, grazing my eager breasts through my shirt, moving lower, across my belly.

Oh, God, not my soft stomach. Instinctively I try to back away from him, forgetting he has me prisoner.

"Where are you going, gorgeous?"

Since I'm still swaying between burning passion and the fear this man might see all my naked flaws, I stumble all over my words. "Well... It's... You're..."

"Don't tell me you're trying to hide from me," he says, lowering his head to meet my eyes.

Since I'm still unable to find the right words, I simply nod.

"Why is it so impossible for you to believe I could be attracted to every part of you?"

God, how long do we have for me to delve into my relationship with my body image? "Because no one has ever talked about my body like you do."

"I'm very sorry you've slept with idiots in the past. If you'll allow me to fuck you until you forget their names, I'll be more than happy to make up for their stupidity, Ali." His cocky grin is irresistible. "Is it okay if I call you Ali?"

"Uh-huh." Frankly, he can call me anything he wants if he makes good on his promise.

"Well, Ali, I can't wait to devour your sinful body." Jake kisses me again as he pushes me to the edge of the bed before putting a knee on the mattress and forcing me to lie back. Without freeing my hands, he continues to explore my body with his impatient hand sliding over my shirt. He undoes each button one by one while our tongues dance together and he expertly unhooks the back of my bra. His chest is so close, I can feel the heat emanating off him. *This is too much.*

"Soft pink lace? Wow. You know how to fulfill a guy's fantasy."

"I have a thing for expensive lingerie." I giggle.

"I'm so very grateful you do. Especially considering how incredible this bra looks on you."

"Thank you," I whisper. He's boosting my confidence like no other man I've been with.

"I'm reluctantly obliged to let go of your wrists if I want to play with your nipples." He smiles.

"O-okay," I let out nervously.

"Take it off, Ali," he commands, lowering his eyes toward my chest.

Without protesting, I shimmy out of my bra and I fling it behind his head. Instinctively, I bring both hands to my naked breasts to shield them from his eyes.

"Why are you hiding these from me?" he asks, pushing my hands aside.

"I'm a little shy right now," I reply, biting my lower lip and turning my head to the side.

"Don't be. Once I'm done with you, there won't be an ounce of innocence left." He grins devilishly as he brings back my hands above my head and shackles them again. *Oh, boy.* "Not to mention your breasts are magnificent. If it were legal, I'd petition for you to walk around naked all the time."

His comment surprises me and we both laugh.

"Seriously, Ali, your breasts are huge, plump and heavy. I love your large areolas as well." Jake's voice is smooth, dark and hypnotizing. He lifts each of my boobs, evidently savoring the weight in his hand, running his fingers along the underside. I purr with pleasure as I lock eyes with him. "You're so fucking hot." He moves his fingers in a circular motion around my breasts until my nipples contract into hard buds. My body desperately craves his touch and I'm certain if I were to squeeze my legs together, I'd come. I arch, trying to get closer, and he chuckles. "You like that, don't you??"

"Yes," I hiss, lost in pleasure.

"If I weren't so eager to dip my hard dick inside your warm pussy, I'd stroke your big juicy tits and I'd pinch those perky nipples until you come. I'm sure it would be so outrageously dirty to see you dissolve this way, I'd shoot my load just watching you climax, unable to contain my own release."

"Lord," I pant. "Your mouth."

"Something wrong with my mouth, baby?" The way he asks his question so provocatively, he knows full well what his dirty talking is doing to me.

"You're so forward."

"Why skirt around the issue? What can I say? Your tits are what my wet dreams are made of. And don't tell me you're not desperate for me to take them in my mouth and suck and suck and suck."

"Arghhh, Jake." His words are so potent. My breasts are swollen, my nipples pucker at the mere thought.

"Oh, yeah, you'll be screaming out my name soon. I can guarantee it." His fingers close on my left breast, running over my areola, then tighten to the point where they nearly hurt.

Damn, this is insane.

When he draws my nipple into his mouth, his hot, wet tongue draws shudders from me as it circles the erected peak.

"Christ," I scream out, unable to contain my cry.

The minute his lips leave my boobs I'm already in withdrawal.

"Don't fight it, baby. Enjoy."

His teeth close and nip. I gasp. The pain is so pleasurable, it's a hedonistic jolt running down my spine, an electric line all the way to my core. I bring down my hands to his head and stroke his thick silky hair.

At that moment, I realize Jake isn't going to ask for my permission on anything. He's going to take anything he wants from me and I'll gladly let him.

My breath hitches even as my excitement rises to levels I never knew existed. He moves to my right breast while his fingers keep playing with my left one, never missing a beat. He takes me into his mouth, sucking hard until my nipple stands erect.

"Ali, I could suck on these all night long," he groans. "They're fucking perfect." He slides down my trembling body. "Are you okay, baby? You're shaking."

"No one has ever touched me like this before."

He stops dead in his tracks and casts upon me a heavy glance. "You can't be serious. The guys you've been with in the past have never taken the time to worship your magnificent tits?"

I shake my head in lieu of an answer. I didn't even know it was possible to feel this way until now.

"They're fools. It's their loss. Tonight I want to worship you like an empress and I want to fuck you like a queen. I hope that's okay with you." He smiles.

"I hope I can handle it."

"I'm sure you can."

Jake's mouth presses against my stomach, nibbling and kissing until I squirm under his burning touch.

"Ahhh," I let out, my heart pounding faster with every inch.

Staring at him with eyes half closed, I shiver as my mind goes blank. Nothing else matters other than indulging in every kiss, every stroke and every caress.

Just when I think I'm about to go over the edge, Jake releases my hands and sits on his knees besides me.

"As sexy as these jeans are on you, they're in the way." He reaches out and slowly unzips my jeans before tugging them down my legs. Feeling the fabric slide down my legs as he holds my gaze only heightens the moment and leaves me breathless. "Much better. I'm very tempted to rip these off you, but I'll cut you some slack for tonight. Take them off," he says, waving his finger over my pussy. I lift my hips and pull down my panties. The coolness of my sticky juices sliding down with my underwear catches me off guard. Good Lord, I'm so turned on. "Now spread open your legs for me."

I obey and part my legs even wider, accepting the pleasure he's willing to give me. I'm open, naked, displayed to him, totally powerless. Jake stares at me, his gaze burning across my skin, my breasts, my stomach, down to between my trembling thighs.

"Ah, a landing strip?"

I nod, unable to speak.

"Fucking gorgeous," he whispers as I offer myself to him.

I bite off a smile, feeling a twinge of power. I've never seen a man look at me with such hunger in his eyes before and I'm relishing every second.

He lowers his hips and starts a slow and mind-blowing tease. He's grinding against me slowly and decisively and I groan.

"You're torturing me," I plead.

"That's the point, gorgeous. I want your dripping little pussy begging for my cock. Would you believe me if I told you I've been thinking a lot about your pussy since I saw you climbing the stairs to go the bathroom earlier today?"

"Oh." I'm taken aback by his confession.

"Yeah."

His strong hands run up and down my legs, massaging the undersides of my thighs. The man is a miracle. He's touching parts of me that have remained untouched my entire life.

Just when I'm certain this can't get any better, Jake takes me to new heights when he starts rubbing my pussy with his wide palm. *Shit.* He slowly glides down until I gasp as I yank my hips off the bed. He corkscrews two fingers into my wetness and I close my eyes to savor the naughty play. *Christ.*

"You're so deliciously wet, Ali."

"You're turning me on like the engine of a Ferrari." Every sense in my body is alive like never before. Every part of me screams for more.

"I've barely touched you. Wait until I really get started."

Seriously? I can only imagine what state I'll be in when he pounds me with his big cock.

"Oh," I pant.

"Absolutely. We have all night and I intend on enjoying every second. I look forward to seeing you lose it, Ali."

"Good Lord."

"Oh, you can count on it because I'll make sure that before the end of the night you'll see Jesus," he mocks. "I'm going to make you come so hard, you'll think you've crossed heaven's gates and when you think it's as good as it will ever get, I'll make you come again and again and again."

Thank you, God.

Jake is spreading my knees wider and slips his hands beneath my ass, hauling my body toward him. He drops his head until he's a few inches from my impatient pussy. He looks up at me from between my legs with his blue eyes, his pupils dilated, his lips parted and sexy. "I bet you must taste real good."

His words are raising my temperature and I don't know how much of this I can handle. Honestly, if you were to strike a light underneath me, I'd probably combust. I'm out of my depth here. Foreplay has never been Clark's forte. He's a sloppy kisser compared to Jake and what my ex calls foreplay is nothing more than sucking my boobs for few minutes—for his enjoyment, not mine. Clark always came first. What a contrast with the man now giving me more pleasure than I thought I ever deserved. I'm lost again between ecstasy and euphoria when Jake's smooth voice brings me back to this moment.

"If you taste nearly as good as you smell, I'm in for a treat." His words are sweet, but the rawness I read in his eyes suggests he's not the type of lover to take things nice and slow.

He gets up and takes a step back before stripping out of his clothes in a flash. I blink when he stands in front of me eating me up with hungry eyes. He's so freaking gorgeous. He's looking down at me in all his naked glory, stroking his very long and very thick cock. I've never seen a man hold his erection in his fist like this. It's unbelievably hot to see his stiff penis in his hand. *Wow.*

"Open wider," he says, walking back towards the bed without ever letting go of his cock.

"I'm already so exposed," I protest.

"Perhaps you didn't hear me the first time, Ali. Open. Wider." Jake waits for me to give into his command.

Shyly, I open my legs as I cover my face with my hands to hide my embarrassment. I've never done anything this bold, this dirty, this daring before. The man is so domineering.

"Damn, this is too pretty for words," he says, stroking himself even faster. "As much as I enjoy stroking my dick as I take in every inch of you, I'm sure I'll find even more pleasure inside your wet slick pussy, feeling you all around me," he says, following my gaze to his cock.

In one swift movement, he lets go of his cock and drops down to his knees in front of me. Jake grabs my hips, pulling me to the edge of the bed before lowering his head.

"Oh, God," I exhale. This is the best sex I've ever had and he hasn't even been inside me yet.

Gwyn constantly raves about how hard she comes when Gaven goes down on her. I've never been so lucky. Clark used to boast he was the type of guy who always went down on a woman, but the reality is he had no clue what he was doing. Yes, he'd use his tongue, but he had no aim and he was incredibly impatient. I never once came.

"Please." I silently pray Jake will taste me and make me come. I'd love for once in my life to understand what Gwyn means when she says a man going down on you is the best out-of-body experience—ever. During the time I stayed with my best friend and her boyfriend, I could always tell when Gaven had performed oral sex on her because Gwyn always walked around in the morning humming and grinning like a lottery winner.

"Have your past boyfriends tongue-fucked your pretty little pussy until you thought you were going to pass out?"

I shake my head. I'm too lost in the raunchiness and rawness of his words to answer. I didn't realize I had closed my eyes to give in to my reverie until they spring wide open when the tip of Jake's tongue slips inside my pussy.

"Arghhh," I gasp, raising my hips and undulating in ecstasy. "Jake, please."

CHAPTER NINE

JAKE

Hearing her beg only arouses me even further. I've wanted to taste her pussy all evening, but I never imagined it could be this sweet. When I stroke the tender crease between her legs, she shivers. I know I'm taking her to new heights and I'm enjoying every one of her moans.

Leaning forward, I nibble on her stomach, my breath warm against her skin. I barely caress her clit, but my touch makes her quiver with delight.

"Yes," she whispers.

"You want more, sweetness?"

"I need more," she pleads.

She's insatiable. I'm still shocked she'd have such a hard time believing I could be attracted to a beauty like her. She doesn't get it. Why in the world would I settle for fucking a shapeless girl when I can grab her hips from behind and ride her like a thoroughbred stallion? It's like choosing filet mignon over Hamburger Helper. In my world, she's a feast fit for a king.

"You want it so badly it aches, doesn't it? Come on, tell me you want it as much as I do."

I know I've hit a nerve with my question when her legs close around my head as she yanks up her hips in the air. I considered for only a minute taking things slow with her since it's our first time together, but I decided Ali can take it. She might come across as young and innocent but by the way she purrs, I know she likes things raw and dirty—just like I do.

My hands close around her thighs, holding her as tightly as I can before dipping my head again. I poke my tongue out and lick into her.

"Oh, oh, oh," she cries out in surprise.

I circle her clit in teasing little flicks and her breath nearly stops with each tiny touch.

"Jake, you're killing me." She's nearly sobbing, thrusting against my tongue.

I don't bother responding. I'm too busy devouring her juicy pussy. As I lap at her wetness, my erection grows hard as a rock. I already know I'll fuck her until we both pass out.

I slide my fingers inside her and she screams out again. "Ah, ah, ah." Her legs are shaking under my torturous play and there's no going back now. "Your fingers and your tongue are going to make me lose it."

Good. "You love it when I finger-fuck you?" I pump my fingers in and out. One finger at first, followed by two, and then my mouth settles on her clit.

My eager tongue strokes her nub, soft at first and then harder and harder.

"Don't stop," she pants in little hard breaths.

"Hmmm," I groan against her.

"More, more, more."

I know I have her where I want her. Fueled by her sobs, I close my mouth over her clit and I suck hard as I plunge my fingers in and out of her.

"Jesus Christ," she screams out as her entire being spasms.

She's close. I suck harder in a slow circular motion.

"Jake!" She yells my name so loudly, I'm sure some folks in Denver heard her.

She's panting in short, stifled breaths and suddenly she convulses into an orgasm as her hips jerk up uncontrollably, taking me with her. She's wailing now, sobbing as I draw from her a climax she's unlikely to forget anytime soon.

She's spent. I slide my body next to hers on the mattress and I watch her as she comes back to life. She slowly opens her eyes and it's as if she only now remembers I'm still in the room.

"I think you liked the way I tongue-fucked you." My gaze is steady on her face, taking in every expression.

"I don't know what to say."

"You're speechless in a good way, I hope." I chuckle.

"That was out-of-this-world amazing," she lets out.

"That good, eh?"

"Nothing has ever felt like this before. I've never come so hard—not with a guy and not with my fingers. What you did to me is like comparing an afternoon sprinkle to a tropical storm."

"I hope you understand now how attracted I am to you. I wanted to give you pleasure before I take mine."

"Oh."

"You're blushing again. I hope you didn't think it was over?"

"You made me come so hard I don't even remember my own name."

"I can assure you, you'll come again in a few minutes."

"Impossible," she says, shaking her head fervently. "There's no way I can come twice in one night. It's never happened before. I mean, it's a miracle I came at all. Half the time I never do."

"Baby, who are these losers you've been fucking?" I can't believe she'd accept being with men who couldn't pleasure her.

"It's a long story."

"Let's write a new one then. I'm ready to sacrifice myself right now to ensure you come at least two more times tonight."

"You want to make me come three times in one evening?" She seems amazed by my bold predictions. "This I have to see."

"Ali, don't challenge me. You'll always lose. I guess in this case, you'll win once I leave you breathless." I wink.

"I'll be careful what I wish for."

"That's a good idea. Because I'd love nothing more than to help turn every single one of your sexual fantasies into reality."

"Whoa. You're serious, aren't you?" She widens her eyes, shocked by my promise, and I crush her lips against mine to make sure she knows I'll always give her more than what she thought possible.

"I'm as serious as the erection I've been sporting since you walked into the house for dinner with your mass of hair flowing down your back. My cock is aching badly to be inside you and I don't think I can wait a minute longer, beautiful."

I roll to my side and reach out to the night table and pull open the drawer. I rummage until I land on a condom. After ripping open the packet with my teeth, I slowly roll the shield over my cock without leaving her gaze.

"I never imagined watching a man put on a condom could make me wet like this."

"You're too easily impressed." With a swiftness that contrasts with my earlier unhurried movements, I grab Ali by the knees and pull her down until she's flush with me. I hoist her legs up and fold them behind my back. *Oh, yeah, open up wide for me.* I grin as I move on top of her and reach down for her pussy. The minute I touch her she trembles as I tease her clit and her lower lips. "It doesn't take you much to get you going again."

"It's as if I can't resist you."

"Don't. I promise you it's going to be way more pleasurable if you give in fully."

I run my cock up and down her slickness and she rewards me with desperate moans as my dick sets off little spasms inside her.

"Look at me, Ali," I command and she obeys. *Good girl.*

I stare into her eyes as I thrust slowly into her. Being between her thighs is the ultimate aphrodisiac for me and having her legs wrapped around me is such a turn-on, I pound into her hard, hot and hungry, filling her completely. She slides her legs a little higher up against my back and I fuck her even deeper. She wriggles underneath me, struggling for breath, but I ram into her with even more determination. Every one of her moans pushes me to satisfy her even more.

"Fuck, your pussy is too sweet, Ali." I don't usually do the missionary position, but goddammit, it feels so good right now, I have to focus in order to avoid shooting my load too early.

My heavy balls thud against her ass and her body jolts as I slam into her mercilessly.

"You're so big," she whispers.

"Too big?" I hope I'm not too much to take for the first time.

"Nah. Your thickness is impressive and you're so long. You make all the other guys I've been with so far seem tiny." She giggles.

"I guess that's a compliment?"

"Oh, yeah." She smiles.

"I want to make sure this is as enjoyable for you as it is for me."

"Trust me, I'm not complaining."

She raises her hands to caress the back of my head, inviting me to continue. When she shifts her body upwards, her huge breasts brush against my chest and I let out a low groan. *Fuck.* I lean down to nibble her succulent peak and she winces, anticipating the pleasure. I'm not going to lie, I'm a sucker for large tits, but Ali's are beyond anything I've ever seen. I could suck on these babies for the next year and I still wouldn't get enough.

Ali's pussy clenches around me as I suck on one of her perky nipples, then the other, toying with them until her body responds the way I want her to—with ravenous desire.

"You want more, baby."

"Yes," she hisses, tilting her hips forward.

"I've got so much more to give. I intend on pounding your little pussy to erase the bad memory of all those clueless fools you've fucked in the past who didn't know how to please you." I angle my body so each stroke, each slide of my body brushes against her delicious clit. I want her to rub herself against me as I fuck her with my hungry cock to the point where she loses her senses in the most mind-blowing climax she's ever had. And then I'll fuck her some more.

Ali trembles under me and I know her pleasure is mounting. Her moans are desperate, her hazel eyes feverish. *Fuck.* She's greedy, almost voracious now. She's like a woman who's been suppressing her sexual fury for far too long and the thrill of unleashing this blazing heat is intoxicating. *How far can I push her?*

I pump her hard and controlled, dictating the cadence, and she holds on to me tight like a drowning swimmer. She slides her hands over my arms and her fingernails dig into my biceps as I double the pace and force of my thrusts.

"Yeah," I let out. I love the sweet pain she's inflicting on me and I reward her by pumping harder.

"Oh, God," she wails. "Oh, my fucking God."

"I was worried you wouldn't be able to handle me, but you're a dirty little one. Your pussy stretches perfectly to wrap me in your warmth and you like how I take you hard and rough."

"Jake… You… Ah…" Her breathing is fast and shallow, broken with tiny whimpers.

"You're close, baby?" My eyes sweep over her body, taking in every part of her.

Damn, I love hearing this sound of submission in a woman.

"I'm going to come," she screams out, shaking her head from left to right against the mattress. Her glorious mane is stuck to her face as a telltale sign of our hedonistic interlude.

"Ali, come for me. Don't hold back." I reach down and slide a finger over her clit. Her scream fills the room and her tight pussy spasms around me.

"Yes, yes, yes," she chants as she climaxes against my dick.

"Jesus," I scream out, letting myself go inside her, releasing myself inside the shield. "Ah, shit." Each intense jerk of my cock sets her off and she clenches against me with a flurry of quick strong pulses and I think I'm about to come again.

When I feel her body come down from the pinnacle I set her on, I lower myself to lay my forehead against hers, a little shocked at how overpowering my release has been. Ali's response to my cock had me coming with such force I thought I was going to lose my mind.

"Let me get off of you. I'm too heavy."

Without protesting she unwraps her legs and her arms, freeing me from her embrace. I lie next to her and admire her lingering with eyes half closed in a delicious post-orgasmic state.

"Sweet Ali. I love fucking you. I might get used to this. Are you okay with that?"

Her body contracts at my admission and I bury my grin in her beautiful long hair. *Angelical Ali is back.*

"I... Well... Hmmm..." Her shyness is such a contrast to the woman who was begging for more and giving herself freely to me a few minutes ago. After ravishing her I know firsthand her modesty hides a fiery volcano. It's disarming and utterly charming.

"I don't want to pressure you or make you feel uncomfortable, but when was the last time you came screaming?"

Ali tucks her face against my chest rather than answer.

"Oh, no, you don't. You can't pretend to be demure after the way you were wailing and begging for more." I pinch her nipple and the pain catches her breath. "There's not a lot to hide from each other after what we've shared."

She peeks up at my face and bats her eyelashes like an innocent soul. "Well…"

"Well what? Either you've come screaming like this every time a guy has fucked you in the past or you and I are good together."

"I told you earlier. No man has ever made me come like you have with your mouth and I've never had an orgasm while a guy was inside of me. What you do to my body is addictive."

"Are you saying you wouldn't be opposed to more?"

"God, I feel so exposed. It's as if you're reading me like an open book."

"Maybe I am. Maybe I know exactly what your body craves and maybe I'm more than willing to give it to you." My hand runs down her cheek and neck.

"You're so in control."

"Is that a bad thing?"

"No," she whispers softly. "It's a major turn-on."

"Good, because I promised to make you come three times and we have one more round to go." I smile devilishly, knowing full well I've caught her off guard.

"What?"

"I always keep my promises. Not to mention I love hearing you purr and I love watching your face as your orgasm takes over."

"I don't think my body can take anymore."

"Really?" I say, lowering my head towards her tits and licking her left nipple before biting. "Let's check."

"What do you mean?"

I slide my finger inside her pussy and I can't help but smile when I retract a slick finger coated with her juices. "You're wet again, gorgeous," I say, holding her surprised gaze as I bring my finger to my mouth to lick her off. *Oh, yeah, she's ready.* "You want more?"

She nods her head obediently with eyes wide open in anticipation. She has me so wired up I could fuck her all night long, but I'll take it easy on her tonight.

Three mind-blowing orgasms in one night should ensure she'll be begging for more before breakfast.

ALLISON

Why is my body aching all over? I'm desperately trying to understand why I can barely move. I peel open my eyes when I hear a rooster in the background and I'm totally confused. *Where am I?*

Suddenly it all comes back as I stare at the Rocky Mountains. It's as if I'm watching the scene-by-scene playback from my first night in Colorado. Yeah, it actually did happen.

What a difference a day makes.

Yesterday evening I was complaining to Gwyn about how lonely I felt and how I was dying for some attention and here I am still sore from Jake's very large cock.

I don't even have to turn my head to know Jake is sleeping beside me. His deep breathing is an instant reminder of our passionate night. *I slept with the sexiest man I've ever met.*

Jake may come across as a gentleman, but he's the raunchiest lover I've ever had in my short life. I can't believe this happened to me. I smile to myself, thinking of how shocked Gwyn will be when I tell her about my first day in Denver.

Oh, gosh. Suddenly a sinking feeling hits the pit of my stomach and my joy is short-lived when I register this hot guy is my new boss' older brother and I'll be living with him on his ranch for the rest of the summer. *What have I done?* I panic when a scary thought crosses my mind. *What if he wakes up and thinks all this was a big mistake?* What if he sees me in broad daylight and no longer finds me as attractive as he did last night after a few too many beers? God, have I screwed up the best opportunity of my life just to get laid? *I have to get out of here before Jake wakes up.*

Slowly, I move the heavy arm cradling my naked body and I slide off the bed. I grab my clothes and make my way to the same bathroom I used yesterday to freshen up on my arrival. I quickly jump into my jeans and pull on my shirt. I take one look at myself and shake my head while scorning myself for being so impulsive. I quickly comb my fingers through my hair so I don't look too disheveled, hoping this ruse will erase last night like a kid erases childish scribbles from a magic board.

Who the hell are you fooling? You look like a royal mess.

I open the door and tiptoe down the wooden steps, praying they don't squeak under my weight.

I'm so afraid to wake Jake up, I hold my breath trying to be as quiet as a mouse as I make a run for it.

How am I going to face him later today? Thousands of unsettling thoughts collide in my head with each step I take. My eyes are glued on my feet to ensure I don't trip because the blood rushing from my heart to my brain is nearly blinding me. I'm halfway down the stairs when I think I'm home free and I start rejoicing silently.

I lift my eyes and stop, frozen.

Please God, this can't be so.

I blink a few times hoping my mind is playing tricks on me, but no, I'm face-to-face with Isadora.

Shit. I didn't realize she starts her day at Jake's house. The woman standing in the kitchen raises her hands and puts them on her hips before lifting her eyebrow.

"Allison, did you just come from upstairs?" She asks the obvious question while bouncing her gaze from the top of the stairs to my guilty face.

"Uh…" I'm paralyzed with fear at the idea I've sabotaged the perfect job within twenty-four hours of my arrival in Colorado. I open and close my mouth like a goldfish in a tank, but nothing comes out.

"What are you doing here in Jake's home so early in the morning?"

Crap. I'm so screwed. How do I explain to my boss' nanny-slash-housekeeper I've spent all night being thoroughly fucked by a man who's given me more orgasms in one evening than I've had in the eighteen months I spent with my ex?

PART 2—BILLIONAIRES' INDULGENCE

Pure Lust

Chapter One

My mind is racing so fast it's not even funny, but for some reason I'm still unable to find the words to get me out of this mess. I've been caught creeping downstairs the morning after sleeping with Jake. I'm as guilty as if Riley's nanny-slash-housekeeper found me with my hand deep into the cookie jar and the fear consuming me has robbed me of my ability to speak.

I mean, how do I explain why the hell I'm standing in the middle of Jake's house at the crack of dawn attempting to sneak out like a thief? It's not as if I can confess to her that after a night of unbridled sex, I just left the comfort of Jake's warm body because I was freaked he might think last night was a mistake when he rolls over and sees my imperfect naked body lying there? Once he's sobered up, maybe he might not think I'm all that attractive. How do I divulge to this woman looking at me for answers that last night I came so many times I thought I was going to lose my mind? There's no way I can put into words how my desperate need for attention and affection turned me into a sex-craved kitten willing to submit myself to Jake's naughty desires. It's impossible.

In less than twenty-four hours since arriving in Colorado I've flirted with my boss' super-sexy older brother, accepted the advances of his hunky and equally delicious business partner and allowed myself to do unmentionable and downright dirty things with the most gorgeous man I've ever known. *Holy shit.* I've been so uncharacteristically bold, I barely recognize myself and now I'm paying the price for my newfound sassiness.

"Allison. Is everything okay?" Isadora presses me and I blurt out the first thing that pops into my mind to save my ass.

"I thought I left my iPhone in the upstairs bathroom," I say, pointing to the ceiling above me. We both follow my pointed finger before locking eyes again. *I'm in so much trouble right now.*

"Oh," she responds carefully. It's as if she's trying to assess if she should trust my lie or not.

"I fell asleep on Jake's sofa last night after dinner and I guess he didn't want to wake me up." The words come out choked since the fear of being caught is pressing against my vocal cords. "I wanted to call my best friend before she left for work to let her know I had safely arrived, but I realized my phone wasn't in my crossbody bag so I thought it was in the bathroom." As embarrassed as I am for lying, I don't see any other way out. Riley would freak out if she found out I spent last night in the arms of the most formidable lover I've ever had—her brother. There's no way for me to tell the truth and hold on to my dignity, let alone this job.

God, did she buy it? Isadora is still looking at me suspiciously.

Granted, it's the crack of dawn and it's quiet as can be, but the heavy silence in the room as Isadora takes me in is overpowering. I try my best to hold her inquisitive gaze, but I've never been bold enough to maintain eye contact with someone for this long. I ready myself to plead my case when she speaks again.

"I can't understand your generation. My kids are the same way. They can't live without that stupid phone glued to their hands. The scary thing is this phenomenon is hitting even the young ones. My grandkids are already addicted to that thing." Her genuine smile melts some of my fears away.

Relief washes over me like a spring shower when she laughs and I let my tense shoulders fall. I take another tentative step down the stairs to join her in the kitchen, but her next question stops me in my tracks. "Did you find it?"

Okay, I guess she won't back down.

"Oh, you mean my phone?"

"Of course, child."

"No. It wasn't upstairs and it's not in my handbag. I'm sure I'm a bit all over the place since I just arrived and I might have forgotten it in my other bag in my bedroom."

"You better find it quick because knowing kids your age, you'll die if you don't." She laughs again and I allow myself to join her.

"My life is in that phone."

"So I've been told many times by my own offspring. I still have a simple flip phone. I know it's old-fashioned, but I hate these miniature things that run on swoops and swipes and taps on buttons that aren't really there."

"I totally get it, but once you start using them, you can't go without." I'm so thankful the mood in the room has shifted.

Get out while you're ahead.

"Why don't I go back to my house and see if I can locate it," I say in an attempt to escape this uncomfortable situation.

"I can't believe you're up so early. I mean the roosters are barely up." She chuckles. "You must be struggling because of the jetlag. No wonder you can't remember where you put your phone."

This is certainly not my ideal way to get introduced to Isadora. "There's a two-hour time difference with New York and the city must be already bustling."

"It's a quarter past five here," she says, looking at the big silver-framed clock on the wall. "I'm sure some New Yorkers already have a full day's work under their belts. Everything moves so fast out there."

"You're right. It would already be seven-fifteen in the morning and I'm usually up and about by this time along with ninety percent of the city."

"If you can make it there…"

"Exactly. It's always go, go, go in the Big Apple."

"I couldn't survive more than a day. I love the peace and quiet I can enjoy out here."

"I've only just arrived, but I can understand why you'd prefer living here." The tense conversation has turned into a pleasant one and I can see why Riley is so fond of this tiny woman.

"I wanted it to be a surprise, but since you're standing here, you might as well know I'm preparing a special breakfast this morning to welcome you. Miss Riley won't be up for a while and then she'll be busy for a little while with her rambunctious kids since it's summer vacation and school is out. I'll go over there in a few hours to help out, but I thought a hearty breakfast would be a good thing to ease into your first day on the ranch."

I'm touched and her kindness makes me feel guilty for lying to her. "I didn't expect this much. You're so sweet."

"I prepared a few things last night before I left, so if you run back to your house and get ready, I'll treat you to my signature breakfast."

"This sounds amazing."

"You don't even know what I'll be serving," she teases.

"You're right, but something tells me I'll have seconds."

"Oh, I can guarantee that much, child. No one can resist Isadora's home cooking. The folks out here think they know food, but I'm from the South, where we take food real seriously. Now, go on," she says, waving me towards the door. "Breakfast will be ready in thirty minutes. You better get yourself back to your house, take a quick shower and rush back over here. Trust me, you don't want to be late because I don't know how long I can hold off Mr. Hunter and Mr. Jake from devouring the feast I'll prepare in your honor."

"Even though Riley's dinner was insanely delicious, I'm starved."

"Good. I'm glad to hear it. What I'd give to be your age again. You burn off calories just by sleeping. God knows, my appetite isn't what it used to be."

The fact that I'm so famished has little to do with a goodnight's sleep and everything to do with the fact that Jake made me come so many times last night, I have nothing left this morning.

"I'll grab my bag in the living room and I'll be on my way." I rush to grab my crossbody bag. I slip back into my shoes and I turn on my heel.

"I'll see you soon, and make sure to bring your appetite." Isadora winks at me as I head towards the door.

"Don't worry, I will." I wink back.

I wave goodbye to Riley's nanny-slash-housekeeper, who has already started pulling out pans from cupboards on my way out. I only allow myself to breathe once I shut the door behind me.

That was way too close for comfort. Thank God it's over.

My short-lived relief turns into worry once I realize I'll have to confront Jake at breakfast in front of Hunter and Isadora.

Crap. What have I gotten myself into?

"Maybe I shouldn't have left without so much as a goodbye," I tell myself aloud as I walk away from Jake's house.

I surely would hate it if he thought last night wasn't amazing, but from my experience, the morning after changes a lot of things when a man sees you in broad daylight with all your flaws exposed.

CHAPTER TWO

JAKE

I'm fast asleep when voices from downstairs wake me up. A part of me knows full well I have to get up and get started with my day, but the horny man in me just wants to stay in bed and fuck until lunch. Two months of jerking off don't come close to fucking a sensual woman.

I reach out to caress the suppleness of her body, but as far as I can reach, I'm unable to touch her. I peer open my eyes, but to my surprise my bed is empty. *Where is she?*

I sit up, rub my eyes and look around the room for traces of the woman I devoured with such satisfaction last night. *Her clothes are gone.* Intrigued by the commotion below, I flip back the sheets and jump out of bed to grab a robe to cover my nakedness. I open the door to my bedroom as carefully as I can to avoid raising any attention and I tiptoe to the hallway all the way to the top of the stairs. I angle my body to remain hidden while listening in on the conversation.

I can't make out the words because they've lowered their voices to a near whisper, but I do hear the warm laughter of my housekeeper and I also detect Allison's sweet voice. *Was she trying to sneak out? Did Isadora accidentally walk in as Allison was leaving?* I lean in to hear better, but as I do, Ali leaves my house without so much as a goodbye.

What the fuck? Did I push her too far last night? I know I should have exerted some restraint, but how was that even a consideration when Allison's body left me weak in the knees? I pounded her so hard last night after going without for so many months. I didn't think she'd be able to sustain three rounds, but to my pleasure and hers, she managed fine. I swear, she screamed so loud, I thought for sure Hunter would come running to save her. She made me come so hard it was as if all the blood in my body hit my brain all at once as I released myself between her thighs.

Yeah, things moved fast last night, but there was no denying the raw attraction we shared. She wanted me as much as I wanted her.

After pacing my room for a few minutes, I decide I'm not going to get any answers standing here and I might as well jump into the shower to start my day. I know the household can be a bit loony at times with Riley's young kids, Isadora's effervescence, Hunter's presence and everything else that goes on around here, but I'll have to corner Allison before I leave for the city to get an explanation from her. *She's the first woman to share my bed since I moved out here.*

Hunter and I made a pact. We didn't want to parade different women in front of my nephews, so we usually end up spending the night at a woman's home or the hotel where she's staying. I didn't even invite Lindsay over while we were dating. But there's something about Allison that made it so natural for me to take her up here.

I want more of her. Heck, I want her in my bed right now. I would have loved to wake up with her sexy body wrapped around me and there's no way I would have started this day without fucking her again just to hear her squeal and beg for me to make her come like she did last night. But I'm not going to force her hand. She has to want this as much I do.

* * *

When I open the door to my bathroom, I'm greeted with the aroma of bacon. The sweet smell has seeped under the gap below my door, tantalizing my nostrils and tempting my tummy. I'm so starved I could eat a whole cow this morning. Isadora must have prepared one of her famous Southern breakfasts to greet the newcomer. I jump into my work clothes and sprint down the stairs, skipping every other step, to my kitchen.

"Well, good morning, Mr. Jake."

"Good morning to you, Isadora. Even when you cook up a storm, you manage to keep this place spotless... unlike someone we both know." As I look around, I marvel at how she was able to tidy up my kitchen after Riley left such a mess last night. We'd all be lost without this woman.

"When your sister cooks, you'd think the house got hit by a tornado." The beautiful black woman rewards me with a complicit smile.

"You got that right. I honestly don't know what I'd do without you."

"Ain't that the truth?" She grins at me before winking mischievously.

Isadora Bennett has been part of this family for four years now and without her, we wouldn't be able to tell our right foot from our left. I remember how I bumped into her—not that she'd ever allow me to forget it.

Riley had just moved in with three active boys and a tiny little baby girl and she was desperate to get her life back in order. She'd gotten married young when she found out she was expecting at the tender age of sixteen. Unfortunately, her scumbag of a husband walked out on her, stating he was too young for this domesticated life and he had stopped loving her and the kids. Single, penniless and humiliated, she had been heartbroken for months after she'd arrived, but eventually she found the strength to rebuild herself and her life.

One afternoon, she left me with my nephews and my niece to go to an interview to find a job to feed her kids. No matter how many times I reminded her I had enough money to last us five lifetimes, my stubborn sister refused to rely on me. I've known her since she was in our mom's tummy and I'd die before leaving her to fend for herself. Since Riley's marriage

started unraveling when she was three months pregnant with Erika, we spent a long stretch of time
without seeing each other because she was consumed
with damage control. She devoted herself heart and
soul to saving her marriage, but to no avail.

By the time she moved in, I was rusty in my
role as uncle and I was doing a shit job disciplining
the boys. I was at Albertsons grabbing some food and
pleading with Zack and the twins, Brady and Perry, to
behave when this woman with a beautiful ebony
complexion approached me. After telling me I was
doing a poor job at letting the boys know who was in
charge, she went on to explain she had dedicated her
life to being a nanny to help parents who couldn't
handle it all on their own.

I was no fool—I knew I was in way over my
head. After hearing of her credentials, I summoned
her to the ranch that same afternoon to meet my sister.
After a series of grueling interviews and thorough
background checks, we hired her. The fact she keeps
my house and the rest of the ranch as clean as she
does is an added bonus. I couldn't ask for more.

"Speaking about the truth, you know I'm not
one to hold my tongue."

"No, you're not. What's troubling you this
morning?"

"You look as tired as Miss Allison does."

"I do?" I ask carefully, worried I might tip
Isadora off.

"Yeah. I came in early to get everything ready
for the surprise I had in store for her, but she's the one
who surprised me when I saw her crawling down

from upstairs." Isadora waves her finger in front of her.

"Really?" I don't want to add more than I have to because I don't know how much Isadora knows. I haven't got a clue what the two women discussed before Allison ran out. "What was she doing upstairs?"

"Apparently she fell asleep on your couch and you, being the perfect gentleman you are, allowed her to rest for the night. Poor thing, she must have been exhausted with this new adventure. This morning she wanted to call her friend in New York and thought she had left her phone in the bathroom upstairs."

"I didn't hear her."

"No wonder. She was tiptoeing like a mouse trying to steal a big ol' piece of cheese without anyone noticing." Isadora laughs. It's amazing how such a deep laugh can come out of such a tiny body. "She looked like she hadn't slept a wink last night. I doubt your couch is comfy enough for a good sleep. In any case, like all of you kids nowadays, she was more worried about her iPhone than anything else."

"Did she find her phone?" I attempt to find out if there's more to this story.

"Nah. She said she might have gotten confused. I'm sure it's the jetlag. I sent her off so she can freshen up before breakfast."

Good on Allison for being so quick on her feet. Had Isadora found out she had spent the night in my bed, there would be no way of downplaying this level of drama. I really have to straighten things out between Allison and I before I drive to Denver later today. We'll be living in such close proximity for the next few months, there's no room for any awkwardness.

"What are you cooking that's making me so hungry?" I say, wrapping my arms around the petite woman, hoping to change the subject.

"Oh, nothing much. A little something to welcome Riley's new assistant," Isadora says coyly.

"In other words, you've prepared a meal Allison will remember forever." I kiss her forehead.

"I'm simply showing her a little Southern hospitality."

Eager to find out what Isadora has cooked up, I walk towards the gas stove and lift the lids on top of the pans. "With all this food, we'll be way too full to get any work done around here." I catch her smiling eyes.

"You boys work like dogs. You need a little something in your stomachs."

As I prepare to peek inside the oven to check out what's hidden in there, the front door pulls open and my best friend walks in.

"Good morning, everybody."

The tall cowboy barely sets foot inside my house before Isadora runs to greet him. "Good morning, Mr. Hunter."

"I can't believe I get to kiss the prettiest woman in Colorado."

"Stop your flirting." Isadora pounds her fist against Hunter's massive chest and we all laugh. "You're being fresh with me because I'm an old woman and I gave up on love and sex a long time ago."

"Isadora, I adore you, but that's too much info," I say, feigning being scandalized.

"Yeah, buddy, she keeps saying that, but I bet you she's got them lined up."

"Stop your silliness and sit down. Miss Allison will be here any minute now and I know you boys have to get started with your day by six-thirty."

The mention of Allison's name stirs up something inside. I feel Hunter's eyes on me, but I avoid his stare. I'm the one who demanded he keep his distance from the blonde and I'm the one who ended up balls deep inside her pussy last night.

"Jake, did you sleep okay? You look exhausted. Did you wrestle with a bull all night?" Hunter chuckles and Isadora joins him.

"I'm good. I had a great sleep."

"I was just telling Mr. Jake that—"

Isadora is about to let the cat out of the bag, but luckily, Allison pulls open the front door. One second more and I'd be standing here explaining to my best friend why I went against my own advice.

My housekeeper is so delighted to see the newcomer, she loses her train of thought and opens her arms to greet the New Yorker.

"Come on in, child. I was afraid I was going to have to rope these two on those stools to prevent them from eating all the food."

"Good morning, Isadora."

Allison is more beautiful this morning that she was last night. There's a glow about her. *I guess three mind-blowing orgasms in a row will do that to a woman.* I place my hand over my mouth to hide my own amusement.

"Morning. You're up bright and early. I thought you were going to stay in bed a little longer." My best friend smiles brightly when he sees Allison arrive.

He'll kill me for asking him to back off when I fucked Allison without restraint last night.

"Good morning, Hunter. I wanted to get a headstart on my first day here. I guess I'm excited to dive right into things."

"One thing is certain, you look more awake now."

Allison's eyes shift nervously to mine as Isadora's comment floats in the air.

"More awake now? What do you mean?" Hunter looks at Isadora, perplexed, and I intervene quickly to prevent things from unraveling.

"Good morning, Allison," I say, ignoring my friend's inquisitive stare. Even though my attention is focused on the beautiful woman who entered my house, I can see from the corner of my eye Hunter frowning.

"Good morning, Jake." Her voice is higher than I remember. She looks up at me shyly and I hold her gaze for a second, trying to read her state of mind.

Her long hair is pulled back in a ponytail, revealing her bright hazel eyes, and for some reason her porcelain-white skin is more luminous this morning than it was yesterday. She's wearing a black button-down shirt with her sleeves rolled up to the elbow. I peek at her curves and smile when I recognize the same hip-hugging jeans I peeled off her body last night before taking her. *Hmmm, I wonder if she's wearing another pair of those sexy lace undies.*

"Nice shirt, but by noon, you'll be roasting." Hunter takes in Allison from head to toe and I'm sure he's dying to see her in something more revealing that would allow him a better glimpse of her body.

"Oh, really?" She looks down at her shirt.

"It's not the same heat as Manhattan. Am I not right, Jake?"

I follow Hunter's gaze. He zeroes in shamelessly on Allison's huge tits. *Bastard.*

"It can get pretty hot during summer months," I respond absent-mindedly. "Your black shirt will attract the sun and make it uncomfortable for you."

I can't believe I have issues with him openly admiring her beauty when I'm the one who took things too far by seducing her.

"You'll see for yourself later. As Jake's sister promised last night, our cowboys will be walking around shirtless before lunch—isn't that right, Isa?"

"I wouldn't know. Remember, I'm an old woman. I don't notice men anymore."

Isadora's joke lightens the mood and suddenly Allison isn't as preoccupied by her fashion choice.

"You won't believe the feast this one over here prepared to welcome you to our ranch," I say, pointing my chin at my housekeeper.

"Okay, I might have gone overboard," Isadora says, pulling Allison towards a stool. "Since I don't know what you Northerners like to eat in the morning, I prepared three different recipes."

"Isa, you do know we're all Northerners in this household except for you." Hunter is grinning ear to ear.

"Hush, child. Now, as I was saying, Miss Allison, sit down so you can taste some authentic Southern cooking."

"I hope you brought your appetite, because I'm starving. I'm running on empty. It's as if I ran a marathon all night long," I say, rubbing my stomach and flashing Allison a mischievous smile.

She blushes and lowers her eyes at my innuendo. "I'm hungry as well."

"What's up with the two of you? You're acting mighty strange this morning."

"Hunter, have you been drinking before breakfast again?" I tease, hoping to steer the conversation away.

"You're funny, buddy." My best friend stares at me intently and I can read the questions in his eyes. "In any case, my stomach is growling like a black bear who's waking up from hibernation. Come on, let's eat."

"Men." Isadora rolls her eyes. "Let me serve the food before this one over here dies of hunger."

A few minutes later Hunter and Allison are sitting in front of a hearty Southern breakfast, but I'm still standing to be better able to admire the blonde.

"My God, I can't believe you prepared all this for me." Allison brings her hands to her cheeks. *I love seeing her turn rosy like this.*

"Nonsense. Dig in."

"Isadora, what are we eating?"

"Yeah, Isa, you have to tell us what's on the menu."

"As if you boys care. As long as it fills you up, you're usually happy," she scorns. "Miss Allison, as I said earlier, I didn't know what you like, so I prepared a few things. First on the menu is my famous praline-pecan French toast. Girl, you'll have visions of God when you bite into this delectable sweet treat."

I'm pretty sure I took care of that a couple of times last night.

"Riley has this recipe on her site." Allison sits up a little straighter in her chair, taking in the sugary starter.

"Yes, Miss Riley does, but mine is a little different. I top mine with a sweet praline mixture and a hint of cinnamon and vanilla. She fancies things up by using croissants and I use plain white bread. It's a family favorite."

"That sounds divine."

"It is. If you prefer something savory, you can dig into my sausage-hash brown breakfast casserole."

"My favorite dish," my best friend chimes in. "Isa combines sausage, eggs, cheddar cheese and hash browns in her casserole, making it one filling and delicious dish. I always have seconds."

"The last time Isadora made this you nearly polished off the plate on your own. I had to fight to get a bite." I laugh.

"Ignore those two." Isadora waves us away with her hand before returning her attention to Allison. "Now let me tell you about my third dish. If none of these options are to your liking, you can sink your teeth in my mouth-watering buttermilk pancakes with buttered honey syrup."

"I don't know if I can choose. It all sounds too tempting."

"Have a little bit of everything. Jake and Hunter eat like wolves. Whatever you don't finish, those two will have inhaled before you're done with your first cup of coffee. Right, boys?"

"Yes, ma'am." Both Hunter and I jump in on cue.

"I've also prepared a big ol' plate of crispy bacon, which goes well with whichever option you choose. I mean, everyone loves bacon, right?"

"Oh, I love bacon. Isadora, this is better than anything I've seen in my food porn magazines."

"Your what, child? It's way too early to be talking dirty."

"I'm sorry. I didn't mean to offend anyone." Allison flushes and nervously bats her eyelashes a few times. "Back in New York, food magazines are often referred to as food porn because you can salivate over each glossy page."

Since I'm leaning against the kitchen sink right behind Isadora, Allison finishes her explanation by locking eyes with me. The sultriness I read in her gaze makes me want to fling her over my shoulder and climb those stairs two by two all the way to my bedroom without caring what Hunter or my house-keeper may think. *Damn. I'd forfeit food to have her again this morning.*

"I guess you learn something everyday. Up to now, I've only known of one type of porn." Hunter's comment has us all rolling our eyes.

"Food porn? I like that expression, but then again I'm an old lady and anything gets me excited."

We all laugh.

"Jake, you look like you're standing guard, boy. Sit down and start eating. You and Hunter have to get to work soon. Miss Allison will have time to linger before Miss Riley is ready for her."

I stride to the granite kitchen island and I take a seat across from Allison. Since I'm sitting right next to Hunter, he won't be able to catch me staring at Ali. He's been glancing my way since Allison walked in, hoping to read my expression, but I've been very careful to remain as stoic as possible.

"Oh, Jake, before I forget, yesterday your sister and I stocked up your refrigerator—the same goes for you, Miss Allison and Hunter, your fridges are also full. You won't lack choices when lunchtime comes around, but since I'll be in town with Miss Riley and the kids, I've prepared my grandma's overnight coffee crumble cake. It's cooling over there on Jake's counter. You can heat it up later or eat as it is. Whichever option, it's going to be crazy good."

"Oh, my God. I can't believe you went through all this trouble on my account."

"Allison, get used to it. Both Isadora and my sister spend half their lives cooking." I laugh.

"Let's dig in. Jake, buddy, it's already five to six and we're going to have to get our day started soon. The guys will be arriving in half an hour."

"You're right."

"And I'd love to have a few minutes of your time after we wolf down this food. There's something I want to talk to you about."

"You got it."

I know I'll have to tell Hunter I broke my own vows. I guess this morning is as good a time as any to get it out in the open. It's not fair for me to ask him to ward off his desire for Allison while I tongue-fuck her and then make her come with my dick lodged deep inside her.

We have to talk man to man.

CHAPTER THREE

ALLISON

I'm so grateful Isadora didn't mention in front of Hunter that she caught me escaping Jake's house like a thief in the night. That would have been embarrassing and it would have prevented me from enjoying an out-of-this-world breakfast.

Everything is insanely delicious and we all devour the food. Isadora is so pleased with my reaction to her cooking, she packs the leftovers in a few plastic containers for me to take to my own kitchen. I don't realize how starved I am until I take a bite of the buttermilk pancakes. I've never tasted anything so fluffy and so decadent. Those put to shame New York's finest.

As much as I try to focus on food, it's nearly impossible to avoid glancing in Jake's direction. He looks so gorgeous freshly shaved. I have to force myself not to linger on how his jeans hug his ass like a kid glove. He looked good in the chinos he wore last night, but they didn't showcase his assets as well.

The fact that I have eyes for Jake isn't a surprise since the man made me come with such force for the first time in my life, but during breakfast I find myself mesmerized by Hunter. I catch him a few times looking at me so intently I have to lower my gaze because he's stirring something incredibly raunchy in me. How can I be sitting across from two of the most handsome men I've ever met and want both of them with so much fervor? I'm sure it's the dry spell talking. I know Gwyn was teasing, but there's no way I can have sex with two best friends. I'm not bold enough.

We're all enjoying a second cup of piping-hot coffee when all of a sudden Jake and Hunter's manager, Dirk Edwards, comes running into the house seeking help to deal with two unexpected early-morning crises. It seems Betsy, the pregnant cow, is having a very difficult birth and Romeo, a young horse Jake bought a couple weeks ago, is being unruly again and scaring the other horses. Without hesitation, Jake and Hunter grab their hats, jump into their boots and run out of the house to save the day.

As tempted as I am to run out after the three men to catch all the excitement, I have an important meeting with Riley, so I sit idly in Jake's kitchen and chat with Isadora until my new boss is ready for me.

After a two-hour intense briefing session about my new duties and responsibilities, my boss hops into her BMW SUV with her kids and nanny in tow, heading to Denver to conduct a special cooking class for a bunch of executives. After adding photos for this week's recipe on my boss's blog, answering readers' comments and taking care of social media updates, I run to Riley's massive organic garden to fetch the vegetables she needs to start testing a few new recipes upon her return later in the day. Since she's left me a set of spare keys, I place everything in her fridge and check off another item on my list.

Once I've crossed off all the pressing tasks for the day, I grab my trusted Nikon camera to start taking a few practice shots. It's nearly ten in the morning when I'm finally able to wander around the ranch hoping to catch both Jake and Hunter in action.

I'm desperately trying to capture the birth of the baby calf on camera, but my timing is way off. Jenkins Williams, one of the workers, and Dirk have delivered the newborn a long time ago under Hunter's watchful eye and they are already busy with their other chores.

"I'm such a city girl," I whisper to myself, walking away after Jenkins has burst my bubble. The young cowboy was still cleaning the stable when I peeked my head in with my camera ready to snap hundreds of shots of Betsy and her baby Poppy, but he explained the newborn had already taken her first steps.

After venturing around the ranch for half an hour, I decide to head to the fenced-in pasture where Jenkins said I'd find Jake training Romeo, but I find myself stopping every five minutes to admire the spectacular scenery. Everything is so green and so wide open. There's a sense of freedom you simply can't find in a crammed city like New York. I've always lived in a large metropolitan city and nothing surrounding me seems familiar—no smog, no tall buildings, no incessant honking, no one begging for change and no impatient drivers shouting at pedestrians. It's peace and quiet as far as the eye could see. *What a change of pace.*

Even before I get close, I make out Jake's muscular frame from afar. As I approach him, my heart skips a beat and I falter, nearly tripping over myself. The man who worshiped my body and who gave me incredible pleasure last night is riding a spectacular black horse like a rodeo king.

He's clad only in his tight-fitting jeans, his cowboy boots and his hat. He's discarded his shirt and his sun-kissed chest is fully exposed. *Oh. My. God.* I blink a few times because the imagery is so darn lascivious before taking another shaky step forward.

He's doing laps inside the gated area, holding a rope and forcing a smaller white horse to obey his command. *It must be Romeo.* "Lord," I say under my breath as I take Jake in. He's the complete package— a successful businessman, a strong man who can wrangle a wild horse and a seducer who can sweep you off your feet.

With him riding shirtless under the beaming sun, I can see how powerfully built he is. I try to turn away, but my eyes are glued to his incredible physique. The man is oozing testosterone that's making me as dizzy as I was last night when he first kissed me.

Both Jake and his black beauty cut imposing figures against the Rocky Mountains. *This would make quite the photo.* I'm tempted to pull up my camera and capture this moment in time, but I'm worried I might distract him.

It must have been a trying morning for Jake, because every time he calls out Romeo's name to get him back in line, his jaw tightens as he grips tighter on the reins of his own horse. Damn, he's so sexy, so commanding and so utterly fuckable right now.

Down, girl. He's your boss' brother. Not a random hunk at your disposal. Last night was a forgivable indiscretion, but it can never happen again.

I know he says he's not a cowboy, but he surely rides like one. As I observe Jake moving like a prize rodeo winner on his black beauty, I can't help but think of how profoundly he affects me. When Isadora sent me back to my house to take a shower before breakfast, I did something unfathomable to me until a few hours ago and just thinking about it now brings fire to my cheeks and my pussy. Fueled by the longing I still had for Jake after crawling out of his bed in a hurry, I touched myself under the cool running water, reliving every moment from last night.

I was on the verge of dissolving over my own finger when Hunter's face flashed in my dream out of nowhere. Tall, cocky and handsome as hell, Hunter joined us in Jake's large California king bed and there I was trapped between a pair of sexy studs. Two hunks. Two hard cocks under my tongue. Two men worshiping me. My fingers had quickened at the thought of being possessed by these two men and as my arousal mounted, I slid my fingers eagerly in and out of my slick pussy as images and sensations flooded over me. I came so hard, I had to hold on to the shower wall in order to avoid collapsing.

I've never touched myself like that in my life. Flashing back to that moment forces me to close my eyes as I bite my lower lip. *Damn, that was hotter than hell.* These two tempting guys are going to make it hard for me to keep focused on my new job. Sex with Jake was out of this world last night. Hmmm, I wonder if Hunter is as good as a lover?

As soon as the thought pops into my consciousness, I squash it. *Seriously, Ali?*

Suddenly Jake is staring right at me and his glance sends warmth all the way down my pussy. He looks away when Romeo rears up on his back legs and waves his front hooves in a menacing way. Freaked out, I back away from the wooden fence and I resume my little exploration. *I need to let Jake do his job.*

I walk a while from where I left Jake towards a remote barn ahead of me. Intrigued, I follow the path leading to the shack.

I don't know what I expected, but when I push open the door, I'm greeted by an empty space that looks like it's been arranged by a Hollywood set designer. There are stacks of hay, empty crates, a few antique pieces of furniture, piles of crocheted blankets, an old pinball machine and a vintage jukebox that looks like it's jumped out of the movie *Grease.*

I tilt my head back, astounded by the wooden beams in the ceiling. The cracks between the wooden planks allow a beautiful late-morning light to seep in. *Gosh, this is perfect.* I take a few steps inside the empty space, trying to angle myself to capture the perfect shot. When I turn around, I face an area that resembles an exposed attic.

"Seems like they stock surplus hay up there," I say aloud.

The old ladder leaning against a plank leading up to the little nook only adds to the montage. This looks so vintage compared to the other more modern buildings on this ranch. I grab my camera and start snapping, hoping one of my pictures will depict the beauty I see.

"You should have taken photos of Romeo when you were watching us out there."

Jake's voice startles me and I spin around so quickly I nearly drop my camera. "I didn't want to distract you. You were so focused," I babble.

"Yeah, it takes patience and concentration to calm down an excited horse."

"It was impressive to watch."

"Romeo is young, strong-headed and impetuous. He likes to give the guys a hard time, but he knows he can't intimidate Dirk, Hunter or I. Since none of the men could handle him this morning, I decided to give it a shot. Dirk would normally be the one taming Romeo, but he already had his hands full."

"Well, from a spectator's point of view you looked like a pro."

"I learned how to ride a horse like a cowboy by taking lessons from the best riding coach in Colorado when we bought the ranch, but thanks for boosting my confidence." He grins.

"For some reason, I doubt you need my seal of approval." Jake is the most self-assured man I've ever met.

"You changed your shirt? Yellow looks good on you."

His presence is so overpowering, the words choke at the base of my throat. "You guys were right. Black attracts too much heat." I fan myself to emphasize my point and to hide my nervousness.

"Told you it could get pretty hot out here. Half the time, we don't even bother wearing a shirt."

Thanks for pointing out the obvious. I'm unable to peel my eyes away from his tanned and well-defined pecs. His six-pack is calling for my touch and his muscular biceps are begging for my kiss. I'm about to turn away, but a pearl of sweat trails down the middle of his powerful chest and slides along his defined abs. The glistening drop only stops when it reaches the belt of his Wranglers. A line of dark hair extends from his belly button down into his jeans. *Fuck.* I fold my lower lip into my mouth to avoid gasping at the sight of his half-nakedness. My pussy pulsates as my eyes run down the sides of his sculpted V. I have no doubt God was a clever one. He must have conceived the tongue just to allow us to brush up and down that erogenous zone on a man's delicious body.

Mother of God, this man is ripped.

I'm sure I'm ogling him so intensely he must see the drool dripping from my mouth.

He pushes off the doorframe, closes the heavy door behind him, flings his cowboy hat on the floor and crosses the barn towards me.

"If you're going to stay with us for the next few months, you'll need proper cowgirl boots," he sneers. "These New York City sneakers won't do around here for long."

"I know," I say, looking down at my feet, which are so tiny compared to his. "Boots cost a fortune in Manhattan and I figured it would be easier to buy an affordable pair out here." I stare down again to avoid what I read in his eyes. His scarred cowboy boots are firmly planted on the ground and his tight-fitting jeans do little to conceal the muscles in his thighs or his bulging erection. This is a powerful man. Not one of those idiotic boys I've been dating so far who pretend to be grown up.

"You should get Riley to take you shopping."

For some inexplicable reason my Nikon feels like it weighs a ton. I take a few steps towards a stack of hay and drop the camera I've been clutching since he walked into this place.

"I will." I turn around and muster the courage to look up and meet his lustful gaze.

The conversation between us is tense, as if both of us are trying to find the words to justify last night. *I still owe him an explanation.*

"I wish you hadn't left my bed so early."

Once again, his words catch me by surprise.

"I'm sorry," I say. His gaze lingers on my boobs, bringing a rush of heat to my cheeks. The air is stifling inside the barn and since I was alone until a few minutes ago, I allowed myself to undo a few buttons to cool down. It was a good idea at the time, but now I feel completely exposed. "I didn't mean to… You know…"

"No, I don't. Why don't you tell me why you refused to allow me to taste more of you when I woke up?" He takes a few steps closer to me and he's now towering over me. I know I'm only five-two, but I'm so small next to his enigmatic presence.

"Jake, we were both in a trance last night and I thought maybe this morning…"

"A trance? Is that how you feel? It makes it sound like you weren't wholly present last night. Were you holding back on me?"

My eyes widen and I jerk my head back as if his question hit me across the face. "I wasn't."

"Ali, I was very much aware of what I was doing."

"You don't have to soften the blow." I prefer giving him a way out now than getting hurt later.

"I'm not. If only you knew how much you made me lose my mind last night."

"But you said things…"

"Did I say anything bad?"

"On the contrary. You said things no man had ever said to me. You used such dizzying words to describe my body… I figured maybe you'd wake up and realize I look differently in broad daylight…" I let the words trail off.

"You're right, you do."

I knew he'd have a change of heart once he was well rested.

"You're more beautiful than last night. Your pale skin is radiant under the sunlight. I took in every part of you while I was fucking you, Ali, and I could gorge on you all day long."

"Oh." His rawness leaves me speechless. I didn't expect he'd still want me.

"I love everything about you. Why is it so difficult for you to accept this?"

"Men don't usually react to me this way," I confess.

"I had to contain myself this morning at breakfast not to clear off the granite counter with one hand and take you right there in front of Hunter and Isadora—I wanted you that much."

Pure lust rages through me like a blazing incandescence and I can't stand the distance between us for one more minute. Judging from the carnal look in his sparkling blue eyes, neither can he. He closes the gap between us and we're so close I can hear his heartbeat.

"I know we haven't spent too much time getting to know each other before jumping in bed together, but this kind of attraction isn't something you fake—I can't, anyway."

"Jake," I exhale.

The intoxicating scent of sweat and leather emanating from his sinful body only makes his plea more irresistible.

"If you want out, now's the time to say so, because once I kiss you, I'm not stopping until I come gushing between your thighs," he says, his breath tickling my chin.

I can't believe this virile man wants me so much. The last thing I want is out. *I want all of him.*

"I'm in." Before I even finish my sentence, he leans in, cups my head, pulls me so close to him it's as if we are one, and gives me a kiss so smoldering hot it puts a raging California fire to shame. When he releases me, I gasp for air, raising my hand to my lips. *And here I thought he might have felt last night was a mistake.* Damn, no one has ever touched me the way Jake does—no one. I break our embrace and look up at him, panting. My head whirls like a spinning top as I lose myself in his blue eyes. "You're an incredible kisser."

"Your lips respond so well to mine," he says before leaning in and taking my lips again. His hand slides around my waist and he presses me closer to him—against his erection.

I stand on my tiptoes to respond to his embrace. *God, this is insane.* My hands are compelled to explore his muscular body and my skin tingles with every touch. A combustive heat builds up inside me that had pretty much died until he revived it last night and I allow myself to believe he is my reward for all the shitty boyfriends who have crossed my path. When Jake slides his hand down my back, I lean into him, too far gone in our kiss to care about any of the silly little rules I set for myself earlier this morning in regards to our relationship during my stay at the ranch.

Jake caresses the length of my body all the way to my boobs. My breath catches at the back of my throat and I remember how he grabbed my breasts as if he owned me last night.

"I like your hair up, but when it's down, it's so much sexier," he says, pulling the elastic out of my hair, freeing my mane. "Now, that's much better." He combs my waist-length hair with his fingers before he fists it, forcing me to look up at him. "Do you know how much I want you right now?" He smiles slowly at me as I quiver in his grasp and I already know he has me where he wants me.

"I want you so badly, Jake."

"I can see that." His cheeks crease with his smile and it's only when he runs his finger over my lips that I realize my mouth is open. I'm breathing fast.

"I shouldn't have said that." I blush at my own forwardness.

"You give me a hard-on every time I see you," he growls, pressing himself harder against me. "If we walk back to my house, one of the workers will catch us and we'll raise suspicious looks and unnecessary gossip. In here, I can take my time exploring you intimately."

"What if someone walks in and catches us?"

"The workers know better than to come out to this barn. Riley, Isadora and the kids are gone. Even if the kids were here, this is a no-play zone to them. Not even Isadora is allowed in here."

What if Hunter were to walk in on us?

The thought pops into my mind and a particularly raunchy scene of the two men kissing and caressing every part of my body flashes in front of my eyes. *What has gotten into me?* I've gone from the queen of vanilla to an insatiable vixen who gets turned on by the thought of being with two men—at the same time.

His right hand curves around the swell of my boob and lightly squeezes.

"Argh," I whisper as my nipples harden under his touch and my pussy clenches, desperate for relief.

A rush of excitement travels through me and I bite the inside of my right cheek when his fingers find my erected nipples and begin to tease them thought the fabric of my bra and shirt. I'm so hungry for him, I kiss him harder as he sweeps his thumbs over my sensitive peaks, nearly driving me to moan out loud.

CHAPTER FOUR

JAKE

When she purrs like this, I could give her any-thing she wants.

I hadn't planned on fucking Allison in the barn like this, but when I was breaking Romeo and I saw her approaching, I couldn't keep my eyes off of her. I don't know what was going on through her mind, but when she closed her eyes, the expression on her face made my cock so hard it made riding an un-comfortable experience. When she walked away, I instinctively followed her from a distance.

When I felt the young rebellious horse had had enough for the day, I asked Ross Tilworth, one of our newest recruits, to take over. I don't know what I was thinking, but when I caught a glimpse of her swaying hips, all bets were off. I had to have her again.

Once is an accident, but twice is deliberate seduction and I know it's going to be challenging for me to justify my salacious actions to my best friend.

He has the right to give me a hard time about what I've done. *But how the hell am I supposed to resist her?*

"I'm pretty sure you've never had sex in a barn in the Big Apple." I chuckle against her lips.

"I've only had sex in a bed."

"What?" I pull away to make sure I've heard her correctly. "You mean, not even on a couch or in the shower?"

"No. My ex-boyfriend, and the ones before him, liked it in the bedroom. Since I haven't been with that many men, I just assumed it was normal," she continues shyly.

"Fools," I say, undoing the buttons to her yellow shirt. "Keeping it solely in the bedroom is so old-school. I thought younger guys would be more adventurous." I slide my hand under her bra and cup her firmly. The startled way she inhales makes me smile. "Do you want to discover more?"

"What do you mean?"

"I'm not sure how far I can push you, but there are things I want to explore with you... if you're willing to be open."

She stares up at me for a few seconds and I can see her pondering my offer. The twinkle in her eye is a dead giveaway, but when the sides of her lips curl up, I know she's willing to take this ride with me.

I've been dying to live out a kink of mine and I know Ali is the only one who can satisfy this naughty fantasy.

"Take me there."

Her vulnerability in this moment is like a drug. Without wasting one more precious minute, I grasp her wrists and elevate her arms above her head. She looks up at me and she sees I'm waiting for her reaction.

"Are you sure?"

She nods and her lips part. Her glimmering hazel eyes catch the light peeping between the planks in the ceiling and they sparkle like gemstones.

"I want to take your body to new heights. I would never hurt you. Do you trust me?"

What I have in mind might rattle her at first, but I know she'll lose all her senses once I'm gorging on her ravishing body.

"Uh-huh." She nods, but I need to be sure.

"I want to hear the words, Ali."

She sucks in a deep breath as if she's about to jump off a cliff straight into the deepest part of Cache la Poudre River that flows through Fort Collins. "Jake, I want more. I trust you."

"Good girl." I crush her lips, satisfied with her answer and excited by the thought of unleashing more of the bad girl who came out to play last night. I bring my legs closer together, trapping her between them, and I continue unbuttoning her shirt. "Hmmm, matching bra?"

"Yes. I told you last night. I have a thing for lingerie."

"I'm very grateful you do." It's been a long time since I've been with a woman who takes so much care in the selection of her naughty underwear. Sure, it was a common occurrence in Silicon Valley and nearly a rite of passage in New York, but women from Colorado don't seem to obsess as much over the lacy and frilly underwear that breaks down my resolve. As for Lindsay, she had a tendency to go commando, which could be practical, but it robbed me of the pleasure of casting my eyes on delicate lingerie.

"I gather you like them?" Allison asks with a touch of disobedient defiance.

"What's not to like? I can't wait to see the matching panties."

As I move from one button to another, she holds her breath.

"Is everything okay?"

"Yes."

"If anything feels strange or uncomfortable, just say lemon and I'll back off. Is that clear?"

She nods.

"What's the word you need to use if things aren't pleasurable anymore?"

"Lemon."

"Very good."

I quicken my fingers, consumed by my own desire to lose my cock deep inside her warm pussy. When I finish undoing the buttons on her shirt, the yellow fabric opens and she stands beautifully with her arms stretched above her head half-naked. In this empty barn. In broad daylight. She flinches and looks away from my gaze, but I tighten my grip.

"What are you trying to do?"

"Jake. It's so bright in here." She blushes.

"You say that as if it's a bad thing."

"I don't… I mean it's… Well…"

"Are you hurt?"

"No," she whispers.

"Then what's the problem?"

"There's nowhere for me to hide." She fixates her gaze on my boots and she bites her lower lip like a child who's delivered the wrong answer to a strict teacher.

"Why would you want to hide from my eyes? I've already seen you in all your naked glory, Ali."

"But you haven't seen my body under the sunshine like this."

"If you knew what you do to me, you'd know you have no reason in the world to worry. I'm enjoying every glimpse I catch of your sultriness—especially under the bright sun."

"You are?"

"Abso-fucking-lutely."

She laughs.

"Can I go back to ravishing you now?"

"Yes, please."

"For the next hour or so, your body is mine. Are we clear?"

"I am."

I reward her by caressing her tits and when a shudder runs through her, I bite her lower lip to intensify the pain-pleasure factor. I push her backwards until we reach a little alcove right under the ledge of the exposed attic that was originally built for extra storage by the former owners. The wooden beams hang lower here than in the rest of the barn and the gap between the beams and the ceiling is wide enough to fit a thick rope.

"Don't move."

I walk to the other side of the barn and fish through one of the wooden crates until I touch the rough finish of a large rope. I search a little more before finding a few thinner ropes. I pull all four out and turn around to face Ali.

She frowns at first as if she can't believe what she's seeing. Her gaze bounces from my hands to my face, searching for answers. I can tell she's taken aback.

"You can't be serious. You want to tie me down?"

"You said you trusted me."

"Yeah, but I didn't think you were going to shackle me like a prisoner."

"If your hands are restrained, you won't have a choice but to savor the pleasure I intend on inflicting on your body, sweetness."

"I don't know about this, Jake."

"It's all about pleasure, baby. Yours and mine." I cup my cock with my free hand to show her how much I want her. "You know what to say if things get uncomfortable?"

She nods. "Lemon."

"You have nothing to worry about then." I smile, moving back to where she's still standing docilely. "If you didn't trust me, you'd already have run out the door."

She opens her mouth to respond, but nothing comes out.

You're dying for me to push you past the limits of your vanilla sex life.

"Take off your jeans and your shoes."

"What?"

"Get. Undressed. Now."

She closes her gaping mouth and kicks off her sneakers before fiddling nervously with the zipper of her jeans. I guess I could turn around and give her a few minutes of privacy, but I'm enjoying the sight of her too much to afford her the luxury of disrobing without me staring.

"Now take off your bra and slide out of those panties before I rip them off of you," I growl, conscious of my hardening erection.

She unhooks her bra and drops it to the floor. She shimmies out of her panties and tosses those to the side with her foot. *God, she's delicious.* She covers her breasts and her pussy, causing me to smile, amused by her attempt to conceal herself.

"Your shyness only turns me on even more. You do realize that, don't you?" I lick my lips, anticipating how sweet her tits will feel inside my mouth.

She looks up at me from under her lashes and something in her has changed. Perhaps my commands are turning her on or maybe my rawness is making her wet, but I read the same lust I'm struggling to repress in order to control my feral nature.

I shove the ends of one of the thinner ropes inside my jeans, dropping the other two on the floor before flinging the thicker rope over the beam above me. I pull one end and tie it to a metal ring plunged in a side beam. I turn on my heel to face her.

She's gorgeous and the submissive way she's batting her eyelashes at me is so freaking hot.

"Give me your wrists."

When she hesitates, I wait patiently, my eyes on her.

She trusts me, but she's not doing as I ask.

"Remember, we can stop this at any time." I take a few steps closer until I'm dominating her with my presence again.

"I want to continue," she says, holding out her arms while staring straight into my eyes. She places her hands into mine and I can't help but smile in approval. I lift her hands over her head and I lean forward, putting my weight against her, anchoring her in place.

"Form two fists in the air with your hands, but keep them above your head."

She obeys. I grab one of the thin ropes and wind it around her wrists. I wrap each end five times and then I cross the ropes beneath the handcuffs-to-be.

"Ahhh."

"Are you okay?"

She nods. I grab the ends of the rope and wind them around before lifting the last loop and tucking the end of the rope through the resulting circles from one side to the other. I gather the remaining rope dangling from her wrists and pull them tightly together. I lift her arms a little higher and I tie the ends of the thin rope to the larger one that's hovering from the beam over my head.

I've been fantasizing about this for a few weeks now, but I didn't expect to be able to play with someone so soon.

Once I secure her, I lower my gaze to make sure she still trusts me. "Is this too tight? I left enough give to avoid any numbness in your arms. You should be comfortable for the next little while."

Ali looks up at her handcuffed wrists in awe. She inhales sharply and yanks as if to test my roping skills.

She's a feisty one.

"You're restrained. You're not going very far, baby."

Tilting her head a little further as if she doesn't believe me, she stares at the handmade cuffs encircling her wrists, securing her to the thick rope that's been lassoed over the wooden beam. She tugs as if she's going to plunge over the edge of panic before bringing her eyes to mine.

"Jake? I don't know about this." Her voice shakes. She squirms underneath me.

I grab her face between my hands in an effort to calm her frantic movement. I caress her face, but I'm still holding on to her. "Ali, look at me." My command forces her to focus her attention to me. "You know I'm not going to hurt you. You do believe me, don't you?"

She hesitates a few seconds, but finally she looks into my eyes and she nods.

"You have my word, I'm not going to leave you here alone roped up like this. Your job is simply to enjoy the ride. Can you do that?"

She gives me a tiny nod.

"Good girl." I lower my head and kiss her with hunger. The cadence is fast and furious—just like I like it.

"More," she whispers between my kisses.

"Don't worry, I'm just getting started."

I needed to be certain she really wanted to be pushed further and I was willing to take as much time as necessary to make sure she was comfortable with our naughty play, but being so close to her naked body is going to make me lose my fucking mind.

I can't wait any longer.

Bending my head towards her tits, I lick sensually over her right nipple. She jerks.

"I've wanted to suck on these since I woke up this morning."

She tries to pull her arms down, but she stops fighting with the rope when she accepts she can't escape.

"I can't touch you," she laments as if this is the first time she fully realizes how in control I am right now.

"No, you can't, baby."

"But I want to touch you," she pleads.

"For now, let me touch you where I want, how I want."

Her eyes are almost begging me to free her, but when I cup both her breasts into my hands, stroking her hard nipples with my thumbs, she bites down a moan and forgets all about her need to touch me. Her head thumps back as she closes her eyes, finally allowing herself to submit fully to me.

"It's not so bad is it?" A soft moan escapes her lips as she gyrates her hips in circular motions. "I guess you agree with me," I murmur in her ear. "When I play with your nipples like this, do I send a charge all the way down to your wet pussy?" I bite on her right nipple and she gasps. "That's what I thought."

"You're going to make me forget my name if you keep this up for an hour."

"I intend on making you forget way more than your name by the time I'm done fucking you."

She lowers her eyes to me and instead of the worry I read a few minutes ago, what flickers in her gaze hardens my dick.

I kiss her, taking her mouth slowly and passionately, letting my hands wander over her full breasts.

"Your tits are every man's dream."

She laughs and shakes her head, unwilling to accept my compliment.

Her nipples are surely going to make me mad. They are pale pink like cotton candy and they are velvety soft. I please myself for a while, licking and sucking until the hard peaks turn into a vibrant shade of red, indicating she's as turned on as I am. Her body slowly turns hotter than the beaming sun peering through the cracks of the roof's wooden planks. Under my touch, her body eases slightly.

She must think this is as far as it goes. She's in for a big surprise.

I kneel down in front of her and reach out for the other two ropes I dropped to the floor a few minutes ago. I caress her stomach and travel sensually all the way down to her painted toenails. I grab her left ankle and I'm amused by how she's desperately trying to keep her legs together in protest.

"You don't want to spread your legs open for me? You seemed to enjoy it last night."

"You can't possibly be going to shackle my ankles with these ropes."

"Do you want partial pleasure or full-on heart-stopping pleasure?" I know it's devious to answer her question with such a daring one, but I'm about to take her to a place she never thought existed.

She closes her eyes in agreement and I tie her left ankle securely before pulling the rope towards a beam. I knot the rope to another metal hook and I open her up to ensure her leg is angled outward. When I do the same to her right ankle, I hear a whimper of worry.

"You'll be whimpering with joy in a few minutes, sweetness," I say, standing back up. I take a step back and I nod, satisfied. She's perfectly exposed, her sweet pussy awaiting my touch.

Taking a step closer, I lean forward and I run my hand up and down her restrained arms until her breathing eases and she stops pulling at the ropes.

"You're getting used to this, aren't you?" I whisper in her ear. "I can't explain what a turn-on it is to see you like this. I'm going to do things to your body you'll never forget. You're mine in every way now."

She looks at me with dilated pupils and she can't conceal the quivering of her body at the rawness of my words. I take a few steps backwards before grabbing a small stool and I return to where Ali is roped. I plop the seat in front of her and I sit down right in front of her pussy.

"Jake, what are you going to do to me?" she pants, looking down at me.

"Nothing I haven't already done to you last night. This is going to be a little... let's say, edgier."

"Edgier?"

"It's a different level of enjoyment for both of us when I'm fully in control."

"Oh," she exhales.

"Ali, my cock is so fucking hard looking at you. You're like a feast with your arms over your head and your big tits jiggling freely with your breathing. You might be asking questions, but your hardening nipples betray your arousal, sweetness," I say, reaching out and pinching her rosy peaks.

"Jake." Her cry sounds like a plea and it only fuels the alpha in me.

"You like it when I tease your tits, don't you?"

"Yes, please don't stop."

"I love hearing you beg for more."

I kiss and caress her body until I reach the lower part of her tummy.

"I bet you if I were to slide my finger inside your pussy, you'd drip all over my hand."

"Argh," she pants. "You're going to make me come without having to fuck me if you keep talking like this."

"It wouldn't be the first time I've used my mouth to pleasure you. I never pegged you for a girl who would sport a landing strip, Ali. Were you trying to deceive me with your stories of tame past sexual encounters? Because your pussy exposed like this under the sun says otherwise."

"Oh, oh, oh." She swings her hips forward hoping to touch my hand, but I move it back to tease her further. She's so turned on now, I could light her up like a bushfire just by blowing on her pussy.

"You want me to touch you, don't you?"

"I need you to touch me, Jake."

"I'm not ready yet. I'm too consumed by admiring how the light glows against the little patch of your pubic hair."

She moans an inaudible sound and folds her lower lip into her mouth in hopes of calming her mounting desire.

"I've got to tell you, with your legs widely spread like this and your inner lips peeking out begging for my tongue, I really don't know how much longer I'll be able to hold it together before I need to fuck you and shoot my load inside you. You make my cock extremely hard."

"I do?" she pants. I run my finger through her pussy and I smile. "Jesus."

"Naughty girl, you're so very, very, wet." I slick her pussy with her moisture and I stroke over her clit, enjoying her high-pitched whine. I taunt her further by sliding my finger over one side of her engorged node, over the hood and down the other. "You like that?" Her body convulses and I ignore her gasp of pleasure as I ruthlessly drive her right to the edge of climax. "Are you close, baby?" She nods helplessly, too consumed to even bother answering. When I lift my hand, her hips try to follow. Her eyes are half closed.

"You can't possibly stop now."

"I have no intention of stopping until I make you squirm." Under her watchful eyes, I lean forward and I lick right over her clit.

The second my lips touch her pussy she bobs her head backward, fighting the overpowering sensation.

"Christ, your wet tongue is going to drive me completely out of my mind."

"I haven't even started licking you properly yet, baby. Save your prayers for later."

A soft cry escapes her lips and she attempts to lift her hips closer to my mouth, but the ropes I used to restrain her legs are too tight for her to move freely. She resigns herself to quivering, realizing she can only take pleasure from me. She can't return the favor. From the way she's rocking her hips I'd say she's very close. The more I lick her, the more her legs tremble.

"Don't stop, don't stop, don't stop," she begs.

"You like what I'm doing to you?"

Lick.

"You're dying for me to take you there."

Lick.

"You want me to make you come screaming out my name."

Lick. Lick. Lick.

"Or would you prefer for me to lick you so hard you pass out when the blood hits your brain from the powerful climax?"

"Jesus."

I continue to tease her, increasing my cadence, pushing her further. Her body tightens and her hips push forward as far as the ropes allow. *She still wants to believe she can control this dance.*

"Are you being impatient again, Ali?" I lift my head and I stop pleasuring her.

"No. You can't do this to me." She's flushed with passion like a woman on the verge of losing all reason.

"I decide when you come," I warn her.

"Please, Jake, I'm begging you to make me come," she pants. "Now."

"Force my hand again and I'll untie you right now, grab my hat and I'll walk out of this barn."

She slowly lifts her head and looks down at me with pleading eyes. "This isn't funny."

"I'm not trying to amuse you. My goal is to bring you the type of unbridled pleasure that will make you think you're free-falling through the crack of an abyss."

She frowns and I can tell her body is responding beautifully to my sensual touch. I'm ready to give her what she craves, but hearing her beg so desperately only intensifies my own arousal. My bulging cock is pressing so hard against the zipper of my jeans, I'm sure it won't take much to burst it wide open. Her eyes are still on me as she watches intently, and I'm still trying to determine if my words have appeased her or not.

"Damn you," she spits out, yanking at her restraints in protest

"You're still fighting this, Ali."

She opens her mouth to say something, but I shut her up. I circle her opening before plunging my finger inside her—fast and hard.

"Fuck."

I lower my head and set my mouth on her, licking her pussy mercilessly along the sides of her clit. Again and again and again.

"Hoo... Haa... Ohh..." she chants deliriously.

"God, you taste so fucking good," I tease before thrusting my finger in and out of her wetness, scraping against her inner walls. I flick my tongue over her swollen nub while I finger-fuck her until she quivers. Each one of my calculated touches gets me the reaction I want from her.

"Help me, God," she cries out.

"You're close, Ali. I can feel it."

"I'm losing it."

I wrap my mouth around her clit, pressing her little node firmly between my lips, heightening the frenzy by swirling my tongue on top of her nub even as I thrust two of my fingers in her with the same force I would use if I were fucking her with my dick. Her whole body is shaking like a leaf on an oak tree and when I slide my free hand up her back, sweat coats my palm.

"This is too much," she screams out. Her eyes widen and I can tell from lifting my gaze to her that her loud voice startles her.

I press my lips down once, twice and three times before holding her clit captive inside my mouth and she explodes.

"Mother of God."

She shuts her eyes the second her pleasure crashes through her, bucking her hips against my mouth as if she wants more.

"It's not over yet."

Before she can respond, I close my lips tighter against her clit. She lets out a wailing cry that rivals the one that escaped her lips a few minutes ago and she spasms against the fingers thrusting inside her. When I draw out my fingers, she pops open her eyes, moaning. Rising back to my feet, I cup her face and I take her lips tenderly, wanting her to taste her climax.

"Do you taste that?"

"Uh-huh."

"I told you I'd bring you more pleasure than you thought possible if you were willing to trust me... and you did, sweetness."

She blinks at me with her long lashes, trying to find her ability to speak again. "Jake... That... God... You... Shit..." Her voice is husky with her own lust and desire.

"It was that good, eh?" I tease between kisses.

"How can I go back to what I was used to before knowing you?"

"You shouldn't. While you're here, there's a lot more I'm dying to explore with you. Your untouched rawness is a big turn-on to me. You're so submissive and so passionate."

"Me passionate?" She frowns at me. "Are you sure?"

"You respond to me without holding back. I couldn't ask for more."

"You're so..." Her eyes shift from left to right, searching for the appropriate word. "You're very certain."

"You mean dominant?"

"Yeah." She blushes. Shy Ali is back.

"I like taking control. Making you quiver, moan and scream gets me off so much. The intoxicating sound of your voice yielding to my sexual hunger tightens my balls to that sweet point where pain meets pleasure."

"Oh."

"What can I say? I know what I like. And I always get what I want." I gently tap her nose with my index finger.

"Your words are going to turn me into a puddle of messiness."

I tilt my head and I let out a laugh that fills the barn. Her innocence is disarming.

"Well, you should know by now, I only say what I mean." I hold her stunned gaze before kissing her again. "I like kissing you."

"So do I," she pants inside my mouth.

Our lips lock and I grip the back of her head and I pull her closer to me to suck more of her tongue into my mouth. When I open my eyes I can read the question burning her tongue.

"What are you dying to ask me?"

"Are you going to unshackle me now?" The fact that she leans forward while squinting her eyes and scrunching her nose makes her even more adorable.

"Are you worried I'll leave you here like this?"

"No, because you promised you wouldn't. It's that…"

"What?"

"What about you? I mean shouldn't I… reciprocate?"

"I'm not done yet, but I'm not going to let you go."

"Why not?"

Instead of answering, I take a few steps away from her while still holding her gaze. I kick off my boots and strip out of my jeans. Her eyes widen in amazement when she sees the extent of my arousal.

"You're huge."

"Wasn't that obvious last night?" I mock.

"Yes, but under the brilliance of the sun, you seem so much bigger."

"I'm extremely turned on." I squat to fish through my pockets in search of a shield. I tear open the packet with my teeth and cover myself before standing again. "It's been a challenge for me to contain myself as I watched you dissolve while I tongue-fucked your pussy."

"You make me lose control, Jake."

"It's just the beginning. I'm going to fuck you hard like a raging bull with your hands still handcuffed." Allison gasps, taken aback by the crudeness of my words. "I'm sure it won't take me much effort to get you wet again since you're already spread open for me. All you can do is take it." I grin.

"You can't make me come twice in such a short period of time." She almost sounds panicked.

"Why not? I did last night. In fact, I made you come three times, if you remember."

"This kind of mind-blowing stuff has never happened to me before."

"From what I can tell, there are a lot of things you've never experienced before that you seem to enjoy immensely."

"You're going to make me blush again."

"Good. I like you with rosy cheeks." I smile. "I'll free your legs, but you still won't be able to touch me."

I walk towards the first rope and I untie it from the post before walking to the other side and doing the same to free her right leg.

"I wonder if I'm going to make you scream as loudly as you did a few minutes ago." I place the palm of my hand on her chest and the other against her back before licking her lips. I slide my hands sensually down her body and when I reach her hips, I travel down one leg until I reach her ankles and I unshackle her before freeing her other leg. I get back up and circle her body until I stand behind her with my erect cock brushing against her back.

"Ahhh," she lets out, surprised.

"Ali, from what you've shared, I gather you've never had sex standing up?"

"Jake, I've never experienced anything like this before in my life. Since you touched me last night, you've shattered my world."

"Why don't I rattle your golden cage a little more?"

I bend my knees just enough to reach under her thighs in order to lift her legs up until they touch her tits.

"The only unfortunate thing about this position is that I won't be able to see your luscious pussy fully spread out as I fuck you." I lean my body forward, pressing my weight against hers, and I push my cock inside her pussy from behind.

"Oh, my God," she wails. She yanks her body up by pulling down against the rope, but I hold her firmly in place.

"Where do you think you're going?"

"I can't do this. It's too good."

"I've taken things slow so far, Ali, but now my appetite for you has turned into feverish need." My voice is so deep and coated with desire, I barely recognize myself. I'm desperate to lose myself inside her wetness and I need to shoot my load so badly, my balls ache.

"Oh, Christ." Her breathing turns ragged.

I swing my hips back and forth, sinking in deeper with every thrust. The sound of my balls slapping against her ass only intensifies my carnal instinct. I hammer into her without restrictions and without asking permission. I drive my ravenous cock with such force I fear the pressure from her hands pulling at the rope above our heads will cause the wooden beam to collapse.

"Touch me, please," she begs.

"Where do you want me to touch you, sweetness?" I know perfectly well what she craves, but I'm determined to make her beg.

"You know, Jake," she responds shyly.

"I don't. You tell me. Your wish is my command."

"Please don't make me say it. This is already too much."

I chuckle. "All right. You win. I think you've had enough frustration and surprises for one morning." I close her legs together and I grab both of them and cradle them in my left arm, holding them firmly, freeing my right hand to pleasure her at will.

"Is this what you want from me?" I whisper in her ear.

I slide my hand under her ass and I squeeze her cheek. She squirms—desperate. I continue to torture her by sliding my middle finger over her asshole. I pause a few seconds before circling her tightness.

"Oh, no, oh, no, oh, no." She's gasping and I can't tell if she's excited by the idea of my finger exploring her backside or if she's frightened. "You can't do that to me."

"Don't worry, you're here for a while. I have plenty of time to fuck your asshole."

"Holy hell. You can't just take me like this without asking."

"You can't say I didn't warn you in advance. Consider it my way of asking." I reward her spunkiness by slowly sliding my finger over her hard clit, teasing her mercilessly.

"Oh, Lord."

"You asked me to touch you. I told you, your wish is my command." I toy with her, taunting her clit as I jerk my hips forward, ramming into her inch by inch. "Jesus Christ, Ali. Your pussy is going to be the end of me," I grunt, feeling my own orgasm looming.

I pump her faster and harder once, twice, three, four times before pulling out, allowing only the tip of my cock to remain lodged inside her. She frantically shakes her head against my bare chest, fighting what's going to explode inside her and jolt her to the core.

"Don't hold back, baby." I tilt my hips back slightly and I thrust inside her so hard the slapping of our skin grows louder and louder until it drowns our own moans.

Shit, this is so intense. I can't hold it much longer.

"Oooh," she coos.

"You know what's hotter than you coming?"

"No."

"Both of us coming at the same time."

Her body is convulsing so much, I know she's about to combust. I circle her hard clit with enough pressure to make her scream out my name.

"Jake."

I'm coming.

"Ali, come for me," I whisper in her ear hoping to send her over the edge. I press her clit one last time, knowing I've already lost all control.

Fucking shit.

My balls tighten as my come gushes inside the shield and I grunt in a low guttural voice, doing my best not to scream aloud. I throw my head back as my orgasm bursts through my body like a rocket and I swing my hips one more time to set her off.

CHAPTER FIVE

ALLISON

"Ahhh," I cry out as my climax hits me like a thunderbolt. "Uh, uh, uh," I continue to chant, dizzy. My heart is thumping against my chest so quickly it threatens to jump out of my body for relief. My legs tremble uncontrollably in his hand as my orgasm charges through my body like an electric current.

Jake's last thrust nearly sent me to Nirvana. *Mother of God.* He's grunting against my ear, panting heavy, and I can only assume his climax hit him as hard as mine did.

I've never come like this before in my life. It was earth-shattering. It came from so deep inside me. It was unrecognizable. Jake hit something inside my womb and unleashed a flurry of unfamiliar emotions.

Oh, my Lord, is that what Gwyn has talked about? Is this my elusive G-spot?

Jake has broken me, forcing me to bend to his will without ever asking for my permission. *Fuck. That was hot.* I'll never be happy with predictable sex for the rest of my life. Jake's need to control me when we have sex is an unexpected aphrodisiac. *Damn, I love every part of it.*

After a few minutes of quiet Jake whispers in my ear. "Are you okay? I hope I didn't push it too far." He's still holding me tightly in his arms and my hands are still shackled above my head, but this moment feels so intimate and so perfect I never want him to let me go.

"You…" I'm lost for words. I try to catch my breath, but my heart is still pounding like a drum. "Your cock…"

"Too small?"

"Certainly not." I widen my eyes, shocked.

"Too big?"

"Maybe."

"Should we never do this again?"

"You're mocking me, aren't you?"

"A little."

"No, I was trying to say that your cock brings out something foreign in me. It's as if there's another person living inside me who comes alive when you penetrate me."

"You do the same to me."

"I do?"

"You bring out an animalistic rawness that makes me want to be unyielding until you come undone and you dissolve into my arms." He kisses my cheek. "Let me put you down before your legs go numb."

"You've been holding me up for so long I might not remember how to walk."

"Trust me, it's like riding a bike, you never forget." Although I can't see him because I'm still roped, I can hear the amusement in his voice. "I'm going to put you down slowly, but you're going to have to take it slow or you'll collapse."

Jake unfolds my body. When I finally land back on my feet, I falter. It's as if all the blood has vanished from the lower part of my body and is rushing back.

"Careful." Jake grabs me in his strong hands to prevent my fall. "Don't rush. I'll admit it was a peculiar position to fuck you in, but it allowed me to slide so deep inside you."

Once I steady myself, he circles me until we're face-to-face again. He reaches up to free me from the makeshift handcuffs that have held me captive since I agreed to play along with his naughty game.

"You're shaking, baby," he mocks, flashing a victorious smile. "Look at the dazed look on your face."

"Stop teasing me. You know perfectly well you nearly made me lose my mind."

"It can still be good even if you're not touching me?"

"It was amazing."

"I'm happy you allowed me to take my own pleasure by giving you an insane amount of pleasure." He grabs me by the shoulders and forces me to look up at him. "Listen, I hate this, but I have to go, sweetness. Let's get dressed and then I'll put the ropes away. I'll leave first and you can follow a few minutes after me. This way we won't attract any un-wanted attention from the workers."

"You have to go already?" I snuggle closer to him, refusing to let him leave.

"I have an important meeting in the city at two. We've been here for over an hour and it's al-ready twelve-thirty," he says, glancing at his watch.

"I understand. In any case, I should get some work done as well before..." I bite my tongue when it hits me that I've had sex with my boss' brother for the second day in a row since arriving at the ranch yester-day afternoon.

"Before Riley gets back?" He sweeps a strand of hair behind my ear before kissing my forehead.

"Yeah." I instinctively move my hands to his firm torso and skate them down his chest, tracing eve-ry single line of his clenched-tight six-pack. It's the first time I've been able to touch him since he hand-cuffed my hands. "I can finally touch you."

I love how his body tenses up under my flirta-tious touch. "Yes, you can, Ali."

"I like being able to do that, even if what you just did to me was toe-curlingly good." I'm so capti-vated by his perfect body.

"Ali, look at me." I'm still stroking his wash-board stomach, but I resign myself to peeling my eyes from his Adonis body to meet his gaze. "Remember, this is our little secret." He waves his finger between our bodies. "My sister doesn't have to know a thing. It's not as if having my cock inside your sweet pussy is going to affect your photography skills." He chuck-les.

"It depends."

"On what?"

"If you keep making me come like this, it will be increasingly more challenging for me to focus on work during the day." I smile.

His laughter fills the barn and I can't help but join him.

"My sister and Isadora will be gone until later tonight, since all the kids have sporting activities and Riley usually takes them to Totally 80's Pizza to eat before coming back. The workers will be off by three-thirty and you'll notice how quiet the place will be. I'll make sure Hunter checks up on you."

"When are you back?"

"Both Riley and I should be back around six. Why don't you and Hunter come over my house for a late dinner? I can't promise a repeat of what Riley served last night, but I can whip something up quick. How about burgers?"

"That sounds good."

"Great." He crushes my lips again. His mouth is so hot and so needy. It's hard to believe he's been all mine for the past hour and he still can't seem to get enough of me. I swipe my tongue across his lips, responding to the urgency in his passionate kiss.

"Come on, get dressed now."

It takes no time at all for Jake and I to jump back into our clothes. I'm bent over one knee, lacing up my sneakers, when he addresses me.

"I'll make sure to talk to Hunter before I leave so he's aware you'll be manning the ranch for the rest of the afternoon." He winks.

"I like Hunter. He's a little forward, but he seems like a good guy." I get up and take a few steps closer to Jake.

"He's forward because he likes what he sees as much as I do."

Jake's words catch me off guard. "What do you mean?"

"I think I'm pretty clear. Hunter and I both have a thing for women with hourglass figures and heavy tits."

What is Jake saying? "Oh."

"Don't blush, sweetness. We're all adults here. I have eyes and I saw how my best friend looked at you over breakfast and I could tell you weren't unaffected by his stare."

Shoot, I can't believe I was that obvious. "I didn't mean to…" *God, I feel like such a promiscuous woman.*

"Don't worry. I'm not upset. It gets lonely on a ranch and your arrival has piqued his attention as much as it has mine."

"But—"

"But nothing. This afternoon, you'll have a chance to get to know him better and hang out with him."

Is Jake suggesting I be open to Hunter's flirtatious ways?

I'm confused, floored and turned on all at the same time. It's as if this incredibly hot lover is pushing me to get to know his utterly lickable best friend a little more. *Here I was thinking I had come to Colo-*

rado, but it seems more like I've crossed Heaven's gates.

"I like you, Jake," I blurt out, worried I'm making him feel like he's not enough for me.

"I like you as well, Ali. So does Hunter. I've known my best friend long enough..." His words linger in the barn and he leans down to kiss both my cheeks. "I hope you'll share my bed tonight."

"Uh..." I'm still stuck on this whole idea that two dangerously desirable men think I'm attractive. I mean we're talking about me here and not supermodel Kate Upton. I have to focus to answer his question. "Of course, I'd love to be with you tonight."

"Good. Give me your mobile phone and I'll punch in my number so we can text each other. It's a less conspicuous way for us to communicate." He winks.

I fish into the back pocket of my jeans and I hand him my phone, still shocked he likes me so much he'd want to continue what we started.

"There you go," he says, handing me back my iPhone. "Enjoy your day, Ali."

"I will. I hope your meeting goes well."

"I'm sure it will." He pauses for a few seconds before speaking again. "Hunter's a great guy."

"I'm sure he is, but I like you, Jake." I'm repeating myself, but I don't know how else to make him understand how important what we've shared so far is to me.

"You're too young to restrict yourself, sweetheart." Jake casts on me a longing glance, letting his gaze caress my body so seductively it's as if he's feathering my skin with the tip of his fingers.

"I'm still not quite sure what you mean."

"I'll see you in a few hours." He leans in to brush my lips with his. The contact instantly sends shivers of desire down my spine and back. *How does he do it?* One touch and I'm willing to strip out of my clothes and get down on my knees. *Damn, I'd allow him to rope me again as long as he makes me come like he did.*

He flashes me a cocky smile before heading towards the door.

"What the hell?" I ask myself. Since when have I been the object of desire of drop-dead-gorgeous men? Gwyn is going to think I'm making all this stuff up when I share the last twenty-four hours with her. It must be this heat because I'm unaccustomed to falling hard for a near stranger like this. I don't think I can ever get enough of this man who fills me and sets my whole body on fire. If I'd known sex could be this sweet, I'd have begged Riley to take me on as her assistant ages ago. New York will never be the same when I get back home.

Do I even want to go back to an empty bed after these toe-curling sexual interludes with a hot, dominant alpha male?

CHAPTER SIX

HUNTER

If you'd told me five years ago, when Jake and I were the kings of Silicon Valley and we made history when we became instant billionaires, that I'd be overseeing the delivery of a baby calf before eight in the morning, I would have laughed hysterically. We've gone from CEOs of one of the hottest tech companies to ever exist to successful ranchers in a matter of a few years.

As incredible as it might seem, both Jake and I love our lives out here in Colorado. The fame that followed such a monumental buyout was more than either of us could handle. We never signed up to become overnight celebrities. We just like writing code that creates addictive apps and cool programs. Colorado is paradise compared to warding off paparazzi and reporters.

Well, nearly paradise. A rancher's life can be a lonely one. Since Allison's arrival yesterday, this brutal reality has hit me hard. It was impossible for me to take my eyes off of her over breakfast and although it was only six in the morning and I had already jerked off in the shower, I found myself sitting across from Allison completely aroused. Thank God the granite counter concealed my desire for her. With a ten-inch cock, it doesn't take much for me to become totally improper.

I really wish Jake and I could've connected before we started our day.

It's been such an insane morning, Jake and I had to forfeit our usual early-morning meeting at our office. Jake was so weird during breakfast, I wanted to confront him about it. I know he's doing his best to fight this attraction we both have towards Allison, but I honestly don't know how long I can control myself.

It's no secret he has way more willpower than I have when it comes to women. I thought I was being paranoid, but I saw how he and Allison were exchanging complicit looks this morning. She kept blushing every time he spoke to her. I'm dying to know what's making her turn beet red every time Jake opens his mouth.

I knew my best friend had a meeting in the city and I was hoping to talk to him before he hit the road, but Betsy's newborn wasn't adapting well to the other cows and the new mom become protective of her baby calf and things become chaotic in the stable. We needed to intervene fast to restore peace. As I was making my way to meet up with Dirk and Jenkins, I saw Jake walk in the direction of the office and told him I wanted us to talk before he left. Since he nodded, I figured he'd wait for me. Unfortunately, by the time I was done, Jake was driving away in his truck. He didn't bother saying goodbye and he didn't even send a text.

Weird. It's like he's avoiding me.

I swear, something is up between those two and I intend on getting to the bottom of things when my best friend comes back home.

This morning has already drained me. I need a break.

As I make my way to the office to make a fresh cup of coffee, Jake finally texts me.

Sorry, buddy, I couldn't wait to talk. I didn't want to be late for my meeting with Benjamin Russell given he owns the most important chain of restaurants in Colorado and he's very interested by our Angus beef. I'm at the gas station filling up and I wanted to text you real quick.

I really wanted to talk to you.

You know how things go on the ranch. Listen, everyone will be gone. Make sure to keep an eye out for Allison, it's her first day and she doesn't know the land very well.

No problem.

I don't want her to wander off too far in her quest for the perfect photo.

I'll keep her company.

Thanks.

What's up between you and Allison?

What do you mean?

I'm no fool, I have eyes.

It takes Jake a few minutes to respond and I'm not sure if it's because he's stalling or if it's because he's busy pumping gas in his vehicle.

Let's just say you might be right about her.

In what sense?

She could be a sweet indulgence for both of us to share.

I nearly choke when I read his response. *Seriously?*

What makes you say that? Yesterday you were singing a different tune.

Why don't we talk when I get back? I need to hit the road now because you never know how heavy traffic will be in Denver.

```
I'll see you later.
```

```
       I'll be back around six. Riley
should  also  be  back  at  the  same
time.
```

I'm staring at my iPhone, rereading our short conversation, unable to believe the words scrolling up on my screen.

Is Jake saying what I think he's saying?

Less than twenty-four hours ago he was telling me to stay away from Allison and now he's saying he thinks she'd be open to being with both of us? *How did that conversation come about?* "Hey, Allison, I know you've just arrived, but my buddy Hunter and I would like to fuck you at the same time. Would you be okay with that?"

I laugh at my own reenactment, but I'm still confused by my friend's message.

Is he speculating or did something happen last night that would explain the complicit looks between the two of them over breakfast?

I brush the thought from my mind because I have a pounding headache. *I really need a cup of coffee.*

* * *

After I take care of a few last-minute chores and give instructions to Dirk so he can oversee the workers for the rest of the day, I make my way to Riley's office to check up on Allison. It doesn't take me long to realize the blonde is nowhere to be found. I'm about to wander off when my eye catches a Post-It note stuck to the door.

Hunter, if you're looking for me I'm having a late lunch at my house—Allison.

I turn on my heel and make my way to the guest house where Allison will be staying for the rest of the summer. As I stroll by the green pastures, I can't help but look up at the blue sky that outlines the majestic Rocky Mountains. The scenery is so magnificent, it's as enchanting as a work of art from a famous landscape painter.

From time to time, when I'm not too bogged down by our many responsibilities, I allow myself to be in awe of what Jake and I have created. My best friend's idea to build smaller homes on our land in order to maintain our privacy while living in such proximity was pure brilliance. Although it was supposed to allow both Jake and I to invite home a few female companions, we made a decision a while back that it wouldn't be a good example to flaunt women in front of the boys. So we've kept our naughtiness off the premises, but I must say the full bushes and the tall trees are perfect to conceal what could happen behind closed doors between consenting adults.

Since I've taken a back road, I have to circle the guest house to reach the front door. I hope Allison likes her new home. As I approach the porch, a voice drifts out. *Allison?* I stop in my tracks to listen in on the conversation.

"I don't care about your stupid lease. We're no longer together and your problems are no longer my business. I can't believe you'd have the audacity to call me after everything you've put me through."

Is it her ex-boyfriend?

"I'm not signing any papers. Get your business partner to step up. I don't give a flying fuck if Jasper is still digging himself out of student loans. You and I are a thing of the past."

Ouch.

"Then why don't you ask your precious little Paula to help you secure that outrageously priced office? Since you seem to enjoy her company so much, maybe she'll be eager to come to your rescue. After all, she's been the one relieving a lot of tension in your life in the last six months of our relationship. You have no morals for calling me and demanding such things of me. I'm not going to allow you to manipulate me like you've done in the past."

Holy shit.

"Whatever. I don't give a fuck. Clark, this conversation is over."

I can't believe that creep would upset her like this.

I push myself off the wall I was leaning against and take a few steps towards her porch. She's just sitting there, staring at her iPhone as if it's fascinating.

"Allison, is everything okay? Jake wanted me to check up on you. I didn't mean to eavesdrop, but that conversation didn't sound too pleasant."

She looks up at me with teary eyes before hiding her face in her hands. "I'm such a mess."

I climb the steps to her porch and kneel in front of her to comfort her. Nothing breaks my heart more than a woman in need. "Nonsense. We all have bad days. I don't mean to pry, but you were shouting. I assume it was your ex-boyfriend."

"Yeah, it was."

"Is there anything I can do to help?"

"The idiot is beyond help."

"I wasn't interested in helping him. I'm more concerned about you."

"Thanks, Hunter, but like with everything else in my relationship with that guy, it's complicated."

"Try me," I say, sitting on the bench near her.

She looks at me, unsure if she should reveal more. I caress her back to let her know she can confide in me. She flashes a weary smile before speaking.

"Clark called because of some stupidly expensive lease renewal on an office he's been renting in downtown Manhattan for nearly a year."

"If he's your ex, why is he calling for lease renewal papers?"

"Eleven months ago, he passed an important exam that catapulted his trading career. He got an incredible promotion that doubled his salary and he was also set to receive eye-popping annual bonuses. After this milestone in his career, he declared he was starting a side business and he needed to lease a space to look legit."

"So you did go into business with him?"

"Nah. He started Venture App with a co-worker. That said, I was desperate to hold on to our fraying relationship. I was willing to do anything. When the big money started rolling in, Clark quickly distanced himself from me, so when he asked for me to co-sign some papers since I had a steady job and we were living together, I didn't hesitate. So no, we're not business partners per se, but I did help him secure the office he's been renting, hoping my good-will would spill over into our relationship."

"But it didn't."

She doesn't have to answer my question. It's clear her attempt at saving her relationship failed.

"I came out here to escape the turmoil of my life in New York. I needed a fresh start. Clark's call sucked me right back into reliving the eighteen months I wasted on his sorry ass."

"You stayed a long time in a relationship that wasn't fulfilling you."

My words must have taken her by surprise because she seems stunned. "My best friend Gwyn says the same thing."

"So why did you stay so long?" I hope I'm not being too forward, but I'm genuinely interested in knowing more about this woman.

"I didn't want to be alone," she responds shy-ly. "New York can be a cruel dating jungle. I got tired of being single and when Clark seemed to be fairly normal and seemed interested in me, I jumped into the relationship and I made sure not to create any unnecessary drama in order to keep him."

Her comment takes me by surprise. "Huh? What are you talking about?" Instead of answering she lowers her gaze and fumbles nervously with her interlaced fingers. "If I didn't know better, I'd say you're completely oblivious to the beautiful woman sitting in front of me."

"You're just saying that."

I exhale, trying to find the words to let her how much she turns me on. "No, I'm not. I mean it." She looks up at me and bats her long eyelashes before rewarding me with a wide smile. "I know I've only met you recently, but from what I know about you, I'd say you've been selling yourself short. Your ex didn't deserve you."

She curls up the corner of her lip and shakes her head. "It took me a while. Maybe too long. It was only when I left my ex and moved into my best friend's basement that I was able to take an objective look at my eighteen-month relationship with this guy and realize how much of a fool I had been."

"You're right about one thing."

She furrows her eyebrows. "What?"

"Fort Collins is the perfect place for a fresh start. So I'm going to suggest something and it's up to you to accept my invitation."

"I'm all ears."

"I think you and I should go on a nice long walk to clear your head. Cache la Poudre River isn't too far and the scenery surrounding the river is so breathtaking I'm sure it'll make for some incredible photos and it'll allow you to forget all about your ass-hole of an ex-boyfriend."

She weighs my proposition for a few seconds and I can see the wheels churning in her mind. "You know what, Hunter? I think you're right. I'm not much of a hiker, but I'm willing to take you up on your offer."

"If you prefer, we can always horseback our way to the river."

She widens her eyes and brings her hand to her mouth. "I grew up in Chicago and I've been living in New York for the past few years. The closest I've ever been to a horse is this morning when I was watching Jake train Romeo." The mention of my best friend's name make her blush. "I've never been on a horse in my life."

"You'll sit behind me and hold on to me and we can ride together," I say with a sly smile.

I can already imagine her huge tits pressing against my back. I shift slightly in my seat to relieve the tension growing between my legs.

"I'm sure my nervousness will distract the horse." She laughs.

"I doubt the horse will be half as distracted as I'll be," I whisper, locking eyes with her. I bring my hand to her cheek and caress it. She flushes.

"Hunter…" My name hangs so sensually on her lips.

We need to get going or else I might get on my feet, fling her over my shoulder and march right into her bedroom to fuck her senseless.

"Come on, let's go for a ride before I betray myself."

She laughs.

CHAPTER SEVEN

ALLISON

I don't know what to make of Hunter's comment. To my surprise I found Hunter's presence overwhelming. I should have moved away from him when he scooted closer to me on the front porch given what I shared with Jake a few hours ago, but I couldn't. It's as if I'm drawn to him like a magnet. At first I thought he was just being nice, but the fire burning in his eyes brought back the conversation I had with Jake a few hours ago.

"He's forward because he likes what he sees as much as I do."

How can I possibly elicit this kind of attention from two incredibly gorgeous men when I could run down the streets of Madison Avenue naked and not even get one blink from the typical New Yorker?

I can't possibly want two men with such ardor. Hunter is hard to resist. He's oozing charisma and let's face it, he's a deliciously yummy sight—his brown eyes are mesmerizing, the line of his jaw commanding, and when he hugged me to comfort me after Clark's upsetting phone call, I had to take a step back to keep from running my tongue along his collar bone to the hollow at the base of his throat. *Holy hell, the man is hot.*

I'm happy I've accepted Hunter's invitation to ride with him all the way to the river. Although I'm a little freaked out at first, Hunter puts me at ease. He's a formidable rider and after a hilarious twenty minutes of me fighting my way onto his beautiful chocolate-brown stallion and Hunter's unwillingness to allow me to call it quits, I have to say the view out here is priceless. The open land before me is so picturesque under the bright mid-afternoon sun, I can't help but soak it all in. There are wildflowers in an assortment of vibrant colors wherever I look and when I feel brave enough to look up, I blink in awe at the fluffy clouds hanging from the sky.

I've never been a fan of old Western movies, but sitting behind this sexy demi-god with my arms wrapped around his muscular chest, I can understand why a woman would lose her head over a cowboy. This was only supposed to be an innocent horseback ride, but Hunter's closeness makes it hard to breathe. I'm so grateful he's wearing a tee shirt to cover up his sinful body because had he been bare-chested like Jake was a few hours ago, I don't think I could have contained myself.

What's wrong with me? How can I lust over two men like this? A guilty voice reminds me of my little interlude inside the barn not long ago with Jake where I dissolved in his arms. I screamed so loudly I was certain one of the workers would come and find us, but there's another part of me yearning for the man sitting in front of me.

I'm taken by the moment and Hunter's voice surprises me.

"We're going to be galloping faster, so make sure to hold on to me a little tighter... for security reasons, of course."

From where I'm sitting, I can't see his smile, but I know it's there.

"Ah, of course. Safety first." I laugh.

"We don't have too far to go so it will be a short ride, but it will be a bumpy one."

We take a left fork in the road and I inhale at the sight of the river raging beneath us. Hunter positions the horse near the edge of the cliff so we can have a good view without getting off.

"The landscape is simply stunning. I can see why you moved out here."

"Yeah, it's pretty close to perfect."

"My God, Hunter, I'm dumbfounded by the beauty of the water," I gush, looking at the river running beneath us.

"It's pretty incredible, isn't it? This part is the most tumultuous and this is usually where whitewater rafters come for an afternoon of fun. We can get off the horse and we can walk around for a few hours, or we can continue riding and I can show you a little private spot Jake and I built when we first moved to this ranch."

The idea of walking under the blazing sun isn't nearly as appealing to me as riding behind this hot guy with my body nestled so closely against his. "Can I still take photos?"

"Yes, ma'am. Your camera is in the bag right behind you. You can take photos along the way. The little hideaway where I'm taking you is nestled between tall trees and full bushes and surrounded by tons of colorful flowers. There are a lot of great picture opportunities there as well. I'll be honest, I have a feeling you'll be too dazzled by what I'm about to show you to care about taking photos."

"Really? Now you've piqued my curiosity."

"Trust me, it's well worth it."

There's something extremely suggestive in the way he says those words, and perhaps I should be more cautious given the fact I fucked his best friend twice since arriving yesterday, but honestly, my feet aren't touching the ground—figuratively or literally. If a good-looking guy wants to flirt with me, so be it.

"Take me there, you fearless cowboy."

We both laugh and Hunter yanks at the horse's reins and before you know it we take off like a rocket.

CHAPTER EIGHT

HUNTER

The faster we gallop, the more my cock gets uncomfortable under these tight jeans. Riding hasn't been this painful since I took my first lesson five years ago and I can only blame the presence of the woman hugging my chest.

Damn, she makes me horny as hell.

My initial intention was to walk along the Cache la Poudre River and allow her to take photos. I knew the scenic view would get her mind off of her worries, but for the last couple of hours that we've been riding, I couldn't focus on much more than the bulge of her tits pressed firmly against my back. Jake was very explicit in his message and if he thinks there's a slight possibility Allison might be interested in having both of us at the same time, I don't see why we should waste anymore time finding out for sure. This little hideaway is a perfect place for me to discover how far I can push the sexy blonde.

When we first moved out here, we built a small wooden cabin that contains a hot pool. We used the examples of hot springs we've visited so many times in Santorini, Greece. The water there is usually about ninety-one Fahrenheit and it's so soothing to the skin stress melts away like snow melts off the mountain peaks in the middle of summer.

Our hot pool isn't as warm as those Greek ones, but it's pretty close. Jake and I keep this place under lock and key because we've decked it out like those fancy day-spas we've visited in San Fran and New York. The cabin has everything imaginable—lounging chairs, a couple small glass circular tables and chairs, surround-sound speakers, a mini-bar and a large shower made with natural limestone imported from Italy. There's even a massage table, which neither of us have ever used since we've never bothered to hire a masseuse.

Let's face it, this is as close as we'll ever get to having our own man cave on this ranch and we spared no expense. The exterior blends with the rest of the buildings and conceals our little hideaway.

Once I secure the horse to a post, I help Allison off. "Careful, cowgirl."

"I'd hardly call myself a cowgirl. All I had to do was hold on to you for dear life. You did all the hard work."

I take her in my arms to help her down, doing my best not to brush my erection against her. "That's it, nice and slow."

"It feels so strange to be on firm land again."

"If you continue riding, you'll get used to it."

"My ass is burning from sitting on this horse," she says, contorting her face as she rubs her bum. "Whatever you're hiding behind this wooden cabin better be worth it."

Her wit catches me off guard and I find myself laughing at her response.

"You're laughing, but I'm a city girl. I swear, I won't be able to walk tomorrow and I'm pretty sure when I regain use of my legs, I'll start walking bowlegged."

Wait until you ride my cock, then you'll have something to complain about.

"Are you still curious to see what I want to show you?" I ask her with a huge grin.

"Of course."

"You won't be disappointed. In fact, I have the perfect cure to heal your sore bum."

"Now we're talking."

When I finally compose myself, I look down at her. Her yellow shirt is drenched in sweat and her matching bra is showing through the damp fabric. It's like an open call for me to unleash my carnal fury on her. *Fuck.* She must have caught my gaze because she lowers her eyes.

"Great. My ass is hurting like hell and I'm sweating like a pig."

"Don't be so hard on yourself. I'm sweating as well," I say, pulling at my wet tee shirt.

"Yeah, but you're a guy. There are no chances of you exposing yourself indecently like I am now."

"If it makes you feel better, I'm not complaining. It's an incredible view."

"No, you're not. In fact you seem pretty amused."

"What's there not to like? A gorgeous woman with ample breasts is having a wardrobe malfunction? Bring it on."

She turns beet red so quickly, I can't help but laugh.

"Okay, I'll stop teasing you. Let's go inside. We'll take care of your tits and your ass at the same time. Oops, did I say that aloud?" I grin from ear to ear at my own joke and Allison rewards me by punching me in the arm. I can tell from the electric charge in her eyes she's not very offended by my forwardness.

I grab her hand in mine and I take her inside the hot pool to show her around and to spend a little private time with her.

"Welcome to our little cabana," I say, flinging my cowboy hat off before shutting the door behind me.

She steps forward and I follow her. When we walk inside the cabin, I turn on the heater to steam up the pool. I switch the lights to a dim setting and I select a playlist of songs sure to get her in the right mood.

"My God, Hunter, you were right," she says, spinning around in circles, soaking in every inch of the place. "This is a fantastic spot. I can't believe you can come here whenever you want."

"I agree, it's surreal. Jake and I end up here at least three times a week to unwind."

"You even have music," she marvels, looking up at the encased speakers in the ceiling.

"It's the ultimate way to melt your trouble away."

Allison takes a few more steps forward and trails her hand over the massage table while admiring the stone wall surrounding us and I see a vision of the future—Allison riding my cock like pioneer women used to ride in the Old West. I'm talking about long blonde hair flying back in ecstasy, heavy tits bouncing in rhythm as I grab her ass, guiding her up and down my loaded missile like a specially trained army officer. If Jake thinks she'd be willing to do both of us, it's only fair I warm her up to the idea by giving her a preview that will make her think every man she's had before me was an inadequate teenager.

My boxer briefs could use a few extra inches right about now.

"I can't believe you guys get to enjoy this kind of luxury at will."

"Guess what? So can you for as long as you stay on the ranch. In fact, you can start enjoying it right now."

"Riley didn't tell me about this, so I didn't pack a swimsuit."

"This is a private pool. You don't need a swimsuit."

"You mean…?"

"Strip out of your clothes and jump into the pool." My voice is so deep, it's impossible for her not to hear how much I'm yearning for her.

Her sparkling hazel eyes widen and she gapes in shock at my audacious suggestion. "You can't possibly be serious. I don't make a habit of exposing myself to men I just met."

"Lucky for you we've already known each other for nearly twenty-four hours." I wink.

"You're a clever one."

"If you'd like, I can dim the lights even more and I can turn around to give you a little bit more privacy until you're in the water," I say flirtatiously.

"And you're going to stand at the door with your back turned to me while I enjoy a relaxing swim in your hot pool? Is that the plan?" She has both hands on her hips like a woman who means business.

"Well, it depends," I respond, closing the gap between us.

"On what?" She tilts her head backward and she meets my lustful gaze.

"On you."

"Me? You're the one making outrageous propositions."

"I'm not. I'm simply giving you options. The choice is yours."

"Choice?"

"Yes, Allison. Do you want me to stand guard at the door or would you prefer I join you in the pool?" I might be pushing my luck here, but so far she's not resisting me.

"Hunter…" Damn, my name hangs on her lips so seductively.

I step back, dropping my voice to a low growl. "I have to confess, just in case it wasn't clear yet, I might be a bad influence on you. You see, Jake is the good one. I, on the other hand, I'm a little bit more unpredictable. More dangerous."

"Oh. You're trying to shock me."

"Not at all. I'm just warning you of things to come."

"I see. You're a first-class charmer, aren't you?" She's obviously mocking me. Unfortunately for her, she doesn't realize I'm as serious as my hungry cock.

"I prefer seeing myself as the masterful seducer."

Her jaw drops, but the twinkle in her eye suggests she might be willing to take me up on my offer. It's just the two of us for the next few hours and I intend on taking full advantage of this opportunity.

"And you think you can seduce me?"

Her bold repartee surprises me, but I'm so up for the challenge. *She wouldn't have asked this question if she wasn't interested.*

"I think I already have."

Nothing would turn me on more than to watch Allison get undressed so I can peek at her yellow lingerie before she discards it to dip into the hot pool. I can already imagine her naked body shimmering under the ripples of the steamy water like a dream—her huge tits floating and inviting me to a whole lot of naughtiness, her beautiful long hair flowing like she's falling from the sky. I've wanted to fuck her since I laid eyes on her yesterday afternoon and this secluded cabana is the perfect location to devour her wholly.

"Forgive me for being so forward, but your plump lips make me wonder what the rest of you tastes like."

We stand there, watching each other. I run my eyes up and down her body to let her know how serious I am. She follows my gaze and even in the dim lights I notice her cheeks flush. *She's not opposed to me taking her.* Her lips part, like she wants to say something but can't. I take that as my cue to continue seducing her.

"I want to do unimaginable things to you. Things that will make you blush when you think of me," I take a step towards her and our bodies are so close it's as if we're one.

"God."

Our eyes are locked together and the passion in her gaze is unmistakable.

"Allison, are your pouty lips as sweet as your pussy?"

"Jesus Christ." There's a brief moment of silence before she tilts her head back and offers me her mouth.

I crush her lips with mine and I unleash the pent-up hunger I've been suppressing since meeting her. My lips are firm and demanding, teasing her desire. I nip at her lower lip, forcing her to open her mouth for me, and I plunge in, my tongue stroking hers.

"Everything inside me is melting," she pants.

"Good, or else this is an utter waste of your time." I smile into her mouth.

With a low laugh, I grab hold of her wrists and slide her arms around my neck, forcing our bodies to collide. Nudging her legs apart with my knee, I move between them. We're so close to each other, I can nearly hear her heartbeat. I grab her butt cheeks as if she already belongs to me and I slide her closer until her stomach rubs against my thick dick.

"You're so hard," she gasps.

"Everything about you is driving me crazy, Allison."

She yanks herself up on her toes and I take her mouth with more determination. After a few minutes of passionate kissing, she presses her palm against my chest. She's flushed and her hair is a mess, but she still looks delicious.

"Good Lord, Hunter, I don't know if we should do this."

"Why are you fighting this attraction between us? The way you were checking me out over breakfast hasn't gone unnoticed. Trust me. There's nothing wrong with two people giving into their mutual desire."

"This can become complicated."

"There's nothing complicated about this." I silence her doubt with another ravenous kiss and she melts in my arms. I pull off the elastic holding her mane and her gorgeous hair cascades all over her shoulders. "What did I tell you last night?"

"You said a lot of things last night."

"It should be a crime for you to pull your hair up," I whisper.

"Your words are an aphrodisiac."

"Wait until I slide my cock between your legs, then you'll truly understand the meaning of the word *aphrodisiac*."

"You're so sure of yourself." She laughs into my mouth.

Yeah, I'm cocky, but I know what I'm packing. I've yet to meet—or should I say fuck—a woman who hasn't begged for more once I've dipped my monster dick into her pussy. I push Allison slightly backward and bring my fingers to her blouse, unbuttoning her as quickly as humanly possible. When the fabric parts and reveals her heavy tits in her bra I gasp in anticipation.

"Damn, you're beautiful."

"Hunter," she begins. "I really need to tell you something—"

"Shhh." I hush her with my finger against her lips, too eager to explore her body to allow her to protest. "What matters is us right here, right now. I'm enjoying this moment with you immensely and if you're not, that's cool, we can walk out the door right now. It's your call. Do you want out?"

She hesitates a few seconds before answering. "I'm enjoying you as well."

"Good. I'm happy we both agree." I help her out of her shirt and before the fabric even hits the floor my hands are already moving to her back to unhook her yellow bra. "As dangerously hot as this is, it's preventing me from sucking on your tits."

"Lingerie is my guilty pleasure," she says from under her lashes.

"And it's certainly mine now." I grin.

I slide the satin and lace fabric off her body slowly, unwilling to rush the moment. When I take in the sight of her magnificent tits, I step back, astounded. "Holy shit. These are more unbelievable than I ever imagined."

She shyly attempts to cover her big boobs from me, but I extend my arms to prevent her from doing such a foolish thing.

"Please. Don't," I beg.

She looks up at me as if she's inebriated and lets her arms fall to her side.

"Good girl." I run my finger down her side, grazing her nipple. She moans and closes her eyes and she finally lowers her defenses.

I've seen my fair share of huge tits before, but these are the most incredible pair I've ever held in my hands.

I caress her breasts and I squeeze her nipples before sucking them into my mouth. She wiggles in my arms at the sweet sensation of the warmth of my tongue over her erected peaks, sending shivers of desire down my spine. *Damn.* My hands travel to her waist and I wait to see if she'll try to stop me before tugging at her zipper. I unbutton her jeans and push the cotton fabric down to give me enough room to slide my fingers inside her panties until I reach her pussy.

"Oh, you're ready for me." I pump my fingers a few times inside her wetness, enjoying the slickness of her juices on my hand.

"Argh."

Enough. I need to taste her.

I latch on the belt loops in her jeans and I squat in front of her, pulling them down to the floor with me until she's forced to step out of them. She kicks off both her sneakers and the denims with such impatience, I allow a little smile of victory. *She's turned on.*

"Let me help you with these lacy panties." Slowly I remove the last piece of fabric preventing me from having free access to her pussy. *Finally, she's fully naked.*

When I get on my feet, she shamelessly reaches out for my buckle and fumbles with it with eager fingers.

"Someone's in a rush."

"It's hardly fair I'm the only one who is totally exposed here."

"You're right." I brush her hand to the side and I pull my tee shirt over my head and throw it behind her. I sit on the massage table and remove both my cowboy boots at the speed of light before pulling down both my jeans and my boxer briefs in one swift movement. When I get back up, Allison frowns and blinks a few times as if she's witnessed an apparition.

"Oh... Wow... I've never..."

I follow her gaze to my aroused dick. *It seems like I'm bigger than usual.* "What can I say? Your naked body turns me on."

"Hunter, there's no way... I mean..." She's fixated on my cock, waving between my erection and her pussy. "Shit."

"Don't worry, it'll fit." I reach out my hand to her and she grabs it, her eyes still darting to my dick. I slam her against me and fist her hair, forcing her to tilt her head back. "Trust me, your pussy will stretch to take me in fully."

"You sound so certain of yourself," she whispers, giving me her lips.

"I am."

I lower my head slowly, prolonging the tease, and when she's on the verge of frustration, I crush her lips with an ardent kiss.

"Damn, your lips are even sweeter than I imagined. If this is an appetizer to your pussy, I'm in trouble."

Allison moans and pushes her tongue further into my mouth. My tongue tangles with hers, swallowing her tiny whimpers, sending another charge of pleasure all the way to my cock.

Suddenly I break the kiss, incapable of appeasing the burning need to get down on my knees and tongue-fuck her pussy. I swing her around until the backs of her thighs touch the edge of the massage bed.

"Drop your hot ass on this table." I place my right palm against her chest until she sits down.

She's still cooing at my command when I pin her hands at the side of her body and I lower my head until our eyes meet. I want her to know I'm about to turn her world upside down. I lock eyes with her for what seems like an eternity, studying how her lust has taken over her entire being, before speaking again.

"Open wide for me, Allison."

"Huh?"

"Your legs," I say, waving my hands at her trembling thighs. "Spread them open so I can play with your clit."

"Oh, my God, your words are going to make me lose it."

"Honey, my words, as dirty as they are, can't rival what my tongue is about to do to you. I'm going to make you come so hard you'll stop breathing." I drop to my knees in front of her and trap her with my hands. "Lean back, hold on to the edge of the table and put your feet on my shoulders," I order, pressing lightly on her chest to make her fall back slightly so I have better access to her pussy. She obeys and I reward her with a cocky smile.

I gently stroke her opening, never once leaving her gaze.

"Christ," I let out in a huskier voice than I've ever heard come out of my mouth before. "You're dripping all over my hand. Do you want me to wrap my mouth around your perky little nub?"

"Ah, please, yes," she grunts.

"You don't have to ask twice."

I slip a finger inside her wetness and I bring my lips to her pussy. I blow warm air, preparing her body for the assault I'm about to subject her to, and when I can't handle it anymore, I stick out my tongue and lap at her clit. I'm gentle at first, but this urgency burning inside me transforms me into a wild animal. I alternate between light strokes with my tongue and using my full lips. I pick up speed as I press her bud more firmly with my lips.

"Shit, this feels incredible," she hisses, closing her eyes and tilting her head back as I explore her body.

I chuckle at the way she's giving herself to me, digging my finger harder and pumping inside her a little faster.

"Your pussy is intoxicating, Allison."

"Ahhh, Hunter," she pants.

She tastes so good, I could shoot my load just by making her come without ever even stroking my cock. I lift the hood of her pussy to intensify her pleasure. I press my tongue even harder, hoping to make her squeal.

As I take pleasure from making her feel like she's about to lose her mind, I'm reminded of Jake's words. If he really thinks Allison will warm up to the idea of taking both of us at the same time, one of us will have the pleasure of fucking her ass. *I wonder if she's ever allowed a guy to take her to the dark side.* I know I should be patient and refrain from asking the question burning my tongue, but I need to know. If both of us are going to take her, one of us will be deep inside her asshole. The best way to get anything out of a woman is to take her to the brink of reason.

"Damn, you're a luscious little one with a sweet pussy and you're spread open in front of me for my enjoyment. Fuck, this is so hot."

Lick.

"Oh, Jesus," she pants between heavy breaths.

Lick.

"Have any of your past boyfriends licked your asshole as well as they've licked your pussy?" My lips are still on her wetness, but I lift my eyes to catch her reaction.

"Wh-what?" She drops her head forward, pops her eyes wide open and stares down at me as my finger slowly trails down her crack. "No, you can't touch me there." She reaches out and fists my hair, attempting to protest.

"Why not? I am right now," I respond defiantly.

"Well…" she starts and then pauses, looking for her words. "No one has ever licked me there. It's private," she babbles.

Is she really opposed to this?

"Your hand may be on my head, but you're not pushing me away." I continue circling her hole, waiting for her to ask me to stop, but she doesn't. "You might not be willing to admit it, but your body loves the way I'm teasing it."

"Hunter…" Although she looks startled, raging lust is burning in her eyes. *I got her.*

"It's okay, Allison. Good girls are allowed to be bad."

"But it's so wrong."

"Not when it's done right."

"It sounds so dirty."

"It's supposed to, baby."

"Ahhh." She slides a finger in her mouth and bites down slowly, consumed by my words and by the way I'm playing with a part of her she's never given to a man before. She's too dazed to even come up with a repartee.

"If you allow me to lick and finger-fuck your asshole, you'll think you're having an out-of-body experience—it's that good."

"Sweet Mother of God."

"Don't worry. I have a feeling you and I will meet at this little hideaway a few more times this summer and at some point, you'll not only beg me to lick you down there," I say, lowering my eyes between her legs, "but you'll be dying for me to fuck you." I've always had a foul mouth when I'm with a woman, but something about Allison unleashes a ferociousness I didn't know I had. I lower my head, eager to taste her pussy again, and I stop a few inches from her wetness.

"Would you consider my naughty proposition?" I don't give her time to answer. I poke my tongue out and continue to tease her mercilessly.

Lick.

"Fuck, I'm about to lose my mind. Right now, I'm willing to give you anything as long as you make me come." She's gyrating her hips against my lips, desperate to climax.

"Anything?"

Lick.

A sensual woman willing to take my dick up her ass? What a wish come true.

Instead of answering me, she bangs the palm of her hand against the massage table and grips the sheets so hard the color drains from her fingers.

"Hunter, I'm going to come."

"You can't come yet."

Lick.

"I can't take this dirty talk anymore."

"I'm not done tasting your pussy."

She pulls my head close to her while letting out a guttural sound. I'm glued to her so tightly, I can barely breathe.

I know it's wishful thinking, but you can't blame a guy for dreaming. As much as I'd love to be the one claiming her, there's no way I can ease her into this. I'm way too big and my monster cock threatens to scare her off anal sex for the rest of her life. Jake will have to be the first one to take her virginity. *She might have been surprised and even shocked by my filthy proposition, but she didn't say no.*

I give her an indulgent break by licking her slowly, allowing her to catch her breath before I push her over the edge.

"Oh, Hunter."

I stroke, changing my touch to hard licks with longer pressure at first followed by my lips wrapping tightly around her hard nub. The way she wiggles under my mouth, I know she's close. I slide my hands against the massage table to lift her hips, stabbing my tongue into her core, lapping at her juices. With each lap, I bring her higher and higher until she cries out so loudly, I doubt the stone walls surrounding us are thick enough to muffle the echoes of her climax.

"Ahhh, ahhh, ahhh." Her thighs spasm as she squeezes them around my head.

Good girl. I pull my head away from her and I stick out my tongue, licking my lips, unwilling to allow any drop of her sweet juices to escape me. I get back on my feet and I admire her as she's still enjoying the ripples of the orgasm. I move my eyes to my throbbing erection and I swear my cock has grown by another ten inches. I fist my dick and stroke myself in front of her in an attempt to appease my voracity. She's still panting with her head back.

"Allison, I can't wait any longer. I need to be inside you now." My voice is strangled by the weight of my own yearning for her. "Turn over on your stomach. I want your beautiful ass slapping against my stomach every time my dick thrusts inside your juicy pussy. I'll also be able to tease your clit and make you come again."

"Hunter, I don't know if I can take more."

"Inexperienced boys make a woman come once. Real men make you come over and over and over. Now flip your body over. My cock is hungry." She obeys and settles her forearms against the massage table and she yanks her beautiful naked bum towards me. *Goddammit.* I fumble inside the pocket of my jeans in search of a condom. I sheathe myself quickly, ready to lock and load. "Look at this fine ass." I stroke Allison's behind as I lick my lips with each stroke. *This is going to be one sweet ride.*

I love everything about fucking a woman, but those first few seconds when I penetrate her by pushing in every bit of my ten-inch cock all the way in makes me grunt like an animal. It's such a rush because I know I'm dominating her so completely, she's not going anywhere until I release myself inside her.

I lean down and fold my body over hers before moving two fingers between her pussy to play with her clit. "You're still so wet. Even after coming, you're dripping."

"Lord," she exhales.

"Honey, we've only just begun. When I'm done with you, I'll have to carry you out of here because you won't be able to walk."

I swing my hips back before thrusting into her, ramming her so hard we both take a step forward.

Fuck.

CHAPTER NINE

ALLISON

Hunter pulls me closer so he can enter me with more force and he releases my hip to fist my long hair. He pulls my head back until he reaches my ear. I expect him to say something raunchy to get me off, but to my surprise he puts his wet tongue inside my ear. My heart is pounding like a drum and I'm sweating from being so turned on. He reaches down to caress my clit again, alternating between soft and urgent touches. With each stroke it seems like he enters me deeper and deeper. I scream with pleasure as my pussy pulsates from his sensual touch.

"Jesus," I choke. The tall hunk fucking me from behind looked huge before sliding into me, but now his cock is dominating me fully. Each swing of his hips is so overwhelming it's as if he's crucifying me to this table.

"Allison, every time your ass slaps against my stomach, I swear my dick grows by an inch."

"Hah," I pant.

"Your sexy body leaves me begging."

"Christ." The pleasure is so intense. Too intense. I thought Jake was hung like a horse, but Hunter's cock is indescribably massive. He's longer and his girth is impressive. Honestly, I never thought he'd fit without ripping me in half, but to my surprise he's pounding inside my pussy and making me lose my mind.

How the hell did I end up in this position with Hunter lodged inside me when a few hours earlier Jake was fucking me to the point where I forgot my own name?

Who is this woman I've become?

How can I let two men I just met yesterday fuck me in the same day? I blame years of neglect for unleashing this dormant vixen in me.

Hunter picks up the pace and ravishes me with even more urgency now. I sob with each swing of his hips and I respond to each one of his grunts with a desperate moan. Every time I think my body can't sustain any more pleasure, Hunter takes me to another level.

"Oh, oh, oh," I chant, trembling under the weight of the man who has me pinned down, completely submissive to his will.

"Jesus, this is so fucking good," he groans, thrusting harder and faster. "Are you going to come again for me, Allison?"

I'm so close to another orgasm, I can't think straight enough to answer him. My eyes are closed as if I'm lost in prayer and I'm gripping the sides of the massage table for dear life as Hunter rams into me inexorably. The only thing consuming me right now is the need to climax again. I yank my ass up and I sink deeper onto his cock to allow him to pound me to ecstasy.

I'm so fucking close.

Suddenly everything stops.

"If you're not going to answer me, I'm not going to make you come again."

He can't be serious?

I'm certain Hunter is teasing and I continue gyrating my hips provocatively in a circular motion, hoping to entice him to keep ravishing me, but when he withdraws from me, I cry out. Like an addict in withdrawal I'm already yearning for him to fill me up again.

"Please, I'm too close. You can't do this to me." I hear the plea in my own voice, but I have nothing to lose anymore. An orgasm is my only salvation.

"I love hearing you beg." He slides back into me and I exhale, relieved by his thickness. I steady myself for another round of skin-slapping sex, but he does it again. Hunter withdraws himself almost completely, leaving just enough of his cock in to torture me while he waits for my reaction.

What the fuck? I press my palms against the massage bed and swerve my head to the right so quickly I fear it will snap off of my neck. I breathe heavily through gritted teeth as I lift my eyes towards him. *He better finish what he started.*

"Are you trying to kill me?"

Hunter holds my gaze without even blinking. He leans on top of my body, his weight pressing my belly against the table and forcing me back on my forearms. He gently pulls my hair back and kisses my cheek. I gasp.

"You're rushing me. I'm the one controlling this ride, baby." I catch his mischievous grin from the corner of my eye and it says it all. I know that if I don't submit, I'll have no hope in hell of coming again.

Slowly, I turn my body away from him and wait for him to decide when I'll climax.

After what seems like long, cruel minutes, Hunter enters me again. He thrusts inside me deep, forceful and hungry. Groans and grunts echo around us as he moves fluidly inside me, hitting the same spot Jake hit a few hours ago.

"Help me, God," I wail.

He grips my hips harder and thrusts.

Oh, yeah, I'm there.

My body convulses and my legs tremble underneath me. Were it not for this table and Hunter's strong hands holding my hips so decisively, I would collapse from the waves of ecstasy rippling through me.

I'm going to lose it.

"I'm coming." My voice is barely audible.

"Don't hold back, baby. Come for me," he whispers in my ear.

"Shit. Oh, God, right there."

Yes.

Hunter's words detonate the delirium of carnal ecstasy I've been trying to contain. I'm screaming my head off when the door to the cabin flies open unexpectedly and someone enters.

What's going on? I turn my head, but Hunter's impressive frame is hiding my view. I lean in further by pulling myself against the sheets, determined to catch a glimpse of the person who's entered the room, but the man fucking me has me pinned down as he rides me to his own climax. I'm desperately trying to think straight, but my heart is in my throat as I recover from Hunter's sweet punishment.

I listen for someone to approach, but after a few minutes, I don't hear a thing. I allow myself to believe perhaps I was delirious and the noise was all in my head. I breathe a sigh of relief, but suddenly I distinctly hear feet on the stone floor.

Who the hell is it?

****

Get Your FREE SECRET Chapters!

Thank you for purchasing this romance book!

I'd love for you to lose yourself in more
sultriness, sexiness and steamy passion!

When you sign-up today, I'll send you the following
Secret Chapter for Part 2 of this serial:

*Riley and Jake Drive Back To The Ranch After Their
Day In Denver*

*** <u>PASSWORD FOR</u> Secret Chapter Part 2:
Barn-Hot-Pool

Note: the password is case sensitive!

Sign-up TODAY!

www.RomanceBooksRock.com

***If you've already signed-up to my list from previous books, you can visit the same page to download
the Secret Chapters for this romance***

****

PART 3—BILLIONAIRES' INDULGENCE

Wicked Pleasure

Chapter One

Hunter has me pinned down as he's fucking me senseless in this secluded cabin. I've just come so hard, I'm certain I'm going to pass out from all the blood rushing to my brain. I'm bracing myself for Hunter's final blow when the door to the cabin swings open. Once the mystery person takes a few steps forward, I know we're busted.

It's a challenge to focus because I'm caught between sheer panic and the need to climax again, because just like Jake, Hunter is a formidable lover. I try to detect if it's a man or a woman approaching to find out if my new boss has walked in on me in a compromising position with her brother's best friend, but I can't tell. It's my own damn fault for thinking I could allow myself to get fucked by two strapping and handsome guys in the same day and get away with it.

What was I thinking?

That's the problem. I wasn't. I was feeling. For the first time in my adult life, I've felt depths of emotions I never knew existed. Now God is punishing me—He gave me the most mind-blowing orgasms of my life today at the hands of these two hunks and now He's taking it all away from me.

Whoever walked into the room is witnessing this wanton debauchery. There's no hiding what's happening here—I'm folded over a massage table and Hunter's massive cock is pounding me.

I'm certain Hunter has heard the footsteps against the stone floor, but he's done nothing to slow down his cadence. On the contrary, he's grunting louder and from the way this massage table is squeaking underneath me, he's fucking me with more determination.

The steps are getting closer and closer. I close my eyes, hoping I can ignore the pending storm that's about to erupt inside the cabin, but the feet stop moving and I feel a presence hovering over me. I peek open one eye and immediately recognize the scuffed cowboy boots.

Oh, no.

"Ja-Jake?" I call out his name in a feeble voice, scared I've betrayed a man who's worshipped my body, made me feel beautiful and given me more pleasure than all my past lovers combined... except for the man fucking me now.

My first instinct is to shut my eyes and pretend it's still only Hunter and me in this room, but I know I'm only fooling myself. I'm caught red-handed. I'm screwed—literally.

"Jake?" I call out his name again, but he still doesn't answer.

Hunter pauses mid-thrust as if it's the first time he realizes we're not alone anymore, but he picks up where he left off, unbothered by Jake's presence. As my heart races, I realize as much as I hope Hunter will stop pounding me, there's another part of me wanting him to continue ravishing me under Jake's watchful eye. *What's wrong with me?*

Jake doesn't move. He's just standing there and in this position, it's impossible for me to contort my body to meet his eyes. I can only assume he's shocked and angry as hell.

He must think so little of me now.

How could I do this to him? How could I be this selfish? A few hours ago he was fucking me and now I'm allowing his best friend to have his way with me. *Shit.* I'm certain Hunter is going to stop pounding me since Jake is standing in front of us and they must be face to face, but to my great surprise he continues ramming into me, totally unaffected. I want to scream out to Hunter to wake him from this trance he's obviously in, but I can't. I'm way too consumed by the moment—one stud is fucking me while the other one watches.

"Fuck, yeah, Allison," Hunter grunts, thrusting into me fast and furious. He smacks my ass cheeks and picks up the rhythm. I moan, lost to my own twisted kinkiness. Suddenly, Hunter fists my hair and pulls my head back until I meet Jake's dark stare.

I'm completely freaked out right now, but still I'm unable to ask Hunter to stop. Jake squats in front of me, extends his large hands and cradles my face. We lock eyes and I struggle to keep focused, conscious of another looming orgasm. I can't tell from his expression if he's upset, disappointed or angry.

"Jake... I'm... I'm sorry,"

"Tsk, tsk, tsk," he says, shaking his head. "Look at you, Allison. I'm gone for a few hours and you find a clever way of entertaining yourself. You're such a libertine."

Jake must be crushed I've allowed another man to fuck me like this. There's so much going on right now in this room and thoughts are bouncing around my head like the steel ball trapped inside a pinball machine.

"I'm coming," Hunter growls. "Christ." Hunter slams me harder.

There's a part of me dying to come again, but there's another part petrified to lose control in front of two men. I do my best to suppress my orgasm, but Hunter has other plans in mind. He slides his hand between my stomach and the massage table and finds my pussy. He presses his middle finger against my clit with such precision, I lose it and I come screaming again. The whole time I'm freefalling into the abyss of ecstasy, Jake interlaces his fingers into mine and he squeezes tight, heightening this naughty moment.

"God, God, God," I pray.

"Come for me, Allison." Hunter sounds as desperate for relief as I do.

"Are you going to dissolve all over his cock, naughty Allison?" *Holy hell.* Jake's question hits me at my core and sends my body shaking under the weight of a heart-stopping climax. I gasp for air with my gaze fixed on his electric-blue eyes.

The next thing I know Jake crushes his lips against mine and he kisses me. Not a peck, but a full-blown tongue-to-tongue kiss as the waves of my sweet orgasm shake my entire being in the most earth-shattering way.

I'm baffled by his unexpected passion and I'm at a loss for words. Jake is still kissing me when Hunter grunts again as he pulls back and drives into me one last time before screaming, "Fuck, yeah." His animalistic cry bounces off the walls and echoes throughout the room.

Jesus.

Knowing Hunter has given into his own orgasm with his cock inside my eager pussy while Jake's tongue is dancing with mine is pure euphoria. It's forbidden. It's wrong and yet so right. *God.* If this is a dream, I never want to go back to reality.

Jake's hands slide off my face and he gets back up. Hunter's weight is pressed against my body and I can't lift my head high enough to see Jake's face. I can only hear his voice.

"Well, well, well. Allison is kinkier than I ever suspected." He chuckles. I may not be able to see the expression on his face, but I can see the bulge between his legs. His jeans are so tight they leave little to the imagination. Instantly, I flash back to our earlier interlude in the barn and I instinctively reach out and cup his crotch.

I'd love to take him in my mouth.

The thought surprises me. It's as if it belongs to someone else. Someone I don't recognize. How can I be fucking one man and get turned on by the idea of sucking another? What's happened to me since I landed in Colorado?

Jake remains silent for a few long minutes. I'm unable to tell if he's surprised by my action or if he's infuriated by my boldness. Slowly he brings his hand up and covers mine. He gently caresses the back of my hand before pushing his hard cock against my palm. He brings his hips forward and grinds against my hand suggestively. I moan, completely overtaken by his salacious move.

"As much as I'd love nothing more than to unzip these jeans, which are threatening to rip open because my cock is pressing uncomfortably against the seams of the fabric, and stick my throbbing dick inside your warm mouth until you make me come with such force I fear I'll pass out, I need to have a heart-to-heart with my best friend about what I walked in on," he says, pulling my hand away from his cock. "Hunter, I'll wait for you on your front porch. We need to talk, buddy."

"Uh-huh," Hunter responds between heavy breaths.

I'm expecting Hunter to try to justify our actions or at least plead with Jake to listen, but he doesn't. He simply caresses my ass without ever removing his cock from inside me.

"Allison, why don't you get dressed and go to your own house. I'll come for you later. Hunter and I have a lot to discuss."

I'm breathing hard, trying to regain my composure to beg for mercy if Hunter won't do it.

"Jake, I'm... God, I'm so sorry." The words come out sounding so awkward and so desperate, but I don't know how else to grab his attention.

"I didn't ask for an apology, Allison," Jake interrupts. "I told you to go back to your house and wait until I'm ready to talk to you. Is that clear?"

"Yes," I answer in a meek voice.

"Good."

The next thing I know Jake is walking towards the door, leaving me there lying on my stomach, still clenching Hunter's cock. Jake slams the door so hard behind him, I jump.

Shit. I've messed up everything.

CHAPTER TWO

HUNTER

I'm still trying to figure out if Jake was upset or turned on. When he circled the massage table and locked eyes with me as I was pounding Allison, I recognized that feral glee I've seen before when he's watched me fuck another woman. I've known him for too long and I'm certain he took pleasure from that kiss he planted on Allison's lips as my whole body was overtaken by my own orgasm. When he was squatting in front of her and he lifted his eyes to me, I swear I saw him lick his lips.

I was so far gone shooting my load inside Allison's pussy under my best friend's lustful gaze, I figured he was okay with the fact I went ahead and tasted the sexy blonde before he did. Heck, he even confessed to having a major hard-on, but the stone-cold look he shot my way before exiting the cabin leaves me perplexed. It's as if there's more to this.

Okay, I should have waited for him to come back to talk things out after his epiphany about Allison being a sweet treat for both of us to share, but I couldn't wait. Now I have to go face my best friend and I know his wrath will be difficult to endure since I promised him I'd stay away from Allison and I broke my word—which I never do. It's true we agreed if she seemed interested to let nature run its course, but let's be honest here—I allowed my horniness to do the talking and I pushed her hard into submitting to me. I guess I didn't play fair.

Allison is still lying under me as if she's waiting for my cue to move. After a few minutes trying to predict how my impending meeting with Jake will unfold, I finally break the heavy silence as I pull out of her. "We should get dressed."

She stands up and turns to face me. Her eyes are clouded with worry and I'm afraid my eagerness might have caused her more harm than good. "Allison, are you okay?" I slide my hands up and down her arms to soothe her.

"I don't know, Hunter." She seems so shaken by Jake's dramatic entrance.

"Don't worry about him. My best friend can act like a grizzly bear sometimes."

"Jake is going to be so upset with me."

What is she talking about?

"You're making too much of it," I say, trying to defuse the situation.

"Hunter, he walked in on us and there wasn't anywhere to hide."

"He'll get over it."

"Yeah, but I might not. I tried to explain something to you earlier, but you were in such a hurry and I was so turned on I didn't bother, but now I regret not forcing you to listen."

"What did you want to tell me?"

She lowers her eyes and shifts from one foot to the other.

What can possibly be so bad?

"I guess it doesn't matter anymore."

"Listen, I'm sure once we talk it out, Jake and I will have made peace in no time. You don't have to worry your pretty little head. You did nothing wrong. I'm the one who wanted you so badly I couldn't even wait."

"Yeah, but I'm not innocent in this story. I allowed you to seduce me and to be honest, I wanted you as much as you wanted me."

"You did?" I smile. "I couldn't tell from the way you screamed your head off." I wink, trying to lighten the mood.

"You're funny," she says, hitting my arm, and I reach out to embrace her. "I had many opportunities to walk out that door, but I didn't."

"I'm sure everything will be fine. Jake and I will have a long conversation and later we can all laugh it off over a few drinks and some dinner."

I do my best to hide my concern over Jake's reaction. There's no point in worrying her because after all, I'm the one who dragged her into this. I really have no one to blame but myself. I'm going to march back to my house and take it like a man.

"I don't want to come between the two of you," she blurts out.

"What makes you think you're coming between us?" I squint, surprised by her confession as I lower my head to meet her eyes.

"Nothing. Forget I said anything. Let's just get dressed and get out of here. You have to go straighten things out with Jake and I need to go clear my head."

* * *

I take my sweet time getting back to my place, rewinding Allison's words in my mind. I'm still not sure why she thinks she might come between Jake and I... unless something happened between the two of them.

When I'm about to shoot my load, my brain goes numb, but I distinctly heard Allison apologizing twice to Jake. *I don't get it.* Is Jake hiding something from me? Is that why they were exchanging such complicit looks this morning? I was going to tell him I went ahead and fucked Allison when he got back. It might have gotten me into some hot water, but I was going to finesse things in such an irresistible way we were guaranteed to have our first evening sharing the sexy blonde tonight. I figured the cabin would be the best spot since it's remote enough from Riley's home to ensure privacy. The tall trees and full bushes surrounding the cabin are an ideal shield from prying eyes and the stone walls are soundproof, which makes them perfect to muffle carnal moans.

This is only the second time a woman has joined one of us at the cabin. Although we've dated a few women, we've been careful not to bring them to the ranch unless the relationship was getting serious. The funny thing is since we built this place, I've only been here with Nina Dallion during a weekend when Jake and Riley were away in LA visiting their parents with the kids. When Riley is away for a long stretch of time, Isadora usually follows.

I dated Nina, a busty brunette, for two months, but things fizzled out fast when she started putting too much pressure on me. I couldn't stand hearing about her biological clock ticking. It was always the first thing out of her mouth after we had sex and we were both lying on my bed catching our breath. In the end, she sounded like a broken record and I had to end things. Let's face it, I'm just not ready for marriage. Heck, after Nina, I doubt I can ever be exclusive with one woman ever again.

Other than Nina, this place has been our little oasis. Jake hasn't yet met a woman he wanted to take here when his sister was away. Both of us have been coming around solo when we need to get away from all the busyness. When he was seeing Lindsay Corbin, he made sure to keep their sexual interludes to a hotel in Denver when she came to Colorado. He never wanted to bring her anywhere near the ranch.

Riley hates these elevated temperatures, so she never sets foot here and she's been pretty strict at preventing her kids from trying to sneak in while one of us was in here. Yup, this is as close as we'll get to having our own man-cave on this land.

Damn. Jake caught me red-handed.

I shake my head, flashing back to the way Allison submitted herself to my will and my cock hardens, but when I lift my eyes and I see Jake sitting on my front porch, I'm brought back to reality—fast.

"It took you a long time to get dressed." He doesn't even allow me to reach my house before he goes for it.

"I wanted to make sure Allison was okay."

"Isn't it a little late to take her into consideration?" His words hit me right between the eyes.

"Whoa, buddy, calm down. You're jumping down my throat before even allowing me to defend myself."

"You looked pretty guilty to me."

"The last time I checked, this was America and I'm entitled to plead my case." I'm still trying to understand why Jake is fuming so much.

"How are you going to get yourself out of this one, Hunter?" Jake leans back against his chair, tips the brim of his cowboy hat upward and folds his arms over his chest, waiting for my answer. "Are you going to tell me your cock accidentally fell into her pussy?"

I open my mouth to respond, but I'm still shocked by his reaction and I'm not certain how to approach this. I climb the few steps up my porch and take a seat next to my best friend.

"Listen, Jake, I'm sorry."

"You're not sorry. You've been hinting at this since the first time we talked in our office yesterday and you wait for me to leave for a few hours on business concerning *our* ranch before having your way with Allison. You couldn't even wait for us to talk tonight."

"You're the one who texted me to let me know you thought she might consider having both of us at the same time. So why on earth are you so angry at me? I was simply warming her up to the idea. Is it because I had her first?"

I'm expecting Jake to pounce on me for my bold answer, but to my surprise he looks away. *What the hell?*

"Wait a minute. Wait a minute." I shake my index finger as the lightbulb goes on. "You're not upset at me because I had her first. You're upset at me because I had her before you gave your blessing. It all makes sense to me now. I understand why Allison apologized so many times while I was coming inside her and why the two of you looked like you were keeping a secret this morning." *I can't believe he's playing me like this.* "You've already had her."

Although he's shaking his head, the slight grin on his face indicates I'm right. Jake has already fucked our guest.

"I'm right, aren't I?" I pressure him into giving me an answer.

"Yeah, I did. I've been trying to find a way to confess to you all morning, but I allowed myself to use my business trip to Denver as an excuse. I should have come clean before getting into my SUV, but instead I covered it up by telling you she would be a sweet indulgence for both of us to share."

"We never hide this kind of stuff from each other, Jake. Why start now?"

258 · SCARLETT AVERY

"Remember, I'm the one who told you to keep it your pants and I was the first one to break that oath. I don't know why I got so upset seeing you with her inside the cabin, but I did. I guess it's because after scouring the land for an hour looking for both of you and then suddenly having a thought pop into my head that was impossible to shake off, I allowed my emotions to run the show. Before I even made my way to the cabin and I saw your horse roped outside, I already knew your cock was inside her."

"I'm glad we have this in the open. Our friendship is way too important to fight over a woman—no matter how intoxicating she is. That said, I still don't understand what makes you think she'd be willing to be with both of us at the same time. Did you ask her?"

"Nah, it's not the kind of question you ask a girl like Allison. She seemed way too innocent to have ever explored anything that risqué."

"So what was it?"

"Before I left for Denver, we had another interlude inside the barn—"

"This morning?" I interrupt.

"Yeah. I had her last night and this morning again."

"Jeez. You're ahead of the game," I mock.

"As I was saying, I asked her if she'd allow me to push her boundaries further. She didn't hesitate. Without even knowing what I had in mind, she agreed. And when it became clear what she was going to submit her to, she still didn't run away."

"What did she agree to?" I ask, curious to find out what kinky game Allison was willing to play with my best friend.

"You know I've been going on about my fantasy about tying a woman up and having my way with her?"

"No way," I blurt out, shocked. If I didn't know better, I'd think Jake was lying.

He nods. "Oh, yeah. She not only allowed me to shackle her hands above her head, but I also roped both of her ankles. She was completely mine for the taking and she didn't complain once. I gave her a safe word, but she never used it. I knew then she could be ours. I was going to tell you about it tonight."

"So we've both had her. What now? How do we bring up sharing her?"

"I think we've already crossed that line." Jake looks at me from the side and raises an eyebrow that speaks volumes.

"God, you're right," I say picking up on Jake's unspoken words.

"The scene inside the cabin was almost like an introduction for her. She didn't flinch when I took her lips as you were coming inside her. On the contrary, I think she relished it as much as we did."

"But how do we know for sure?"

"Why don't both of you come over to my house later tonight after Riley has gone to bed and we can figure things out—together."

"Listen, this isn't going to be a comfortable conversation for Allison. This is most likely something she's never even considered. She may not be ready to give us an answer on the spot. It's more complicated than, 'Would you like to be trapped be-tween the two of us or would you rather go for ice cream?' I think we need to give her some space so that we're certain she wants this as much as we do."

"What are you suggesting?"

"I think I have a really great idea."

CHAPTER THREE

ALLISON

I need to get a grip on myself. Fast.

As I walk back to my house, in a brief moment of lucidity I try to chastise myself for my recently acquired bad-girl attitude, but it's impossible. I'm still extremely confused by everything that happened inside the cabin. I mean, one minute Hunter was riding me and the next Jake walked in on us, but instead of being angry, he claimed my lips in a passionate kiss as Hunter was climaxing like an animal behind me. It was so intense, I nearly lost my head. But once he got back on his feet, everything changed. It was as if the magic spell had been broken and Jake realized I had betrayed him.

Although Hunter tried to reassure me, I can't help but feel guilty about my actions. I don't know if I could live with myself if I came between those two. Before I showed up at the ranch, they shared a tight bond and now there's tension between them. Tension I caused.

Thankfully it's only a short walk from the cabin to my house. It seemed so much further earlier because we came from the Cache la Poudre River, which is several miles away. Once I close the door behind me I allow myself to exhale. I shut my eyes and lean against the door, hoping to compose myself. After a few brief moments, I decide to take a shower to calm down. I head to the bedroom and slip out of my clothes before running to the bathroom. I'm so worried about how things will unfold between the two friends, I feel the need to wash away my sins. I need to get rid of the guilt weighing so heavily on my shoulders.

What an insane day.

As the water drizzles all over my body, I flash back to when Jake squatted in front of me while Hunter's big cock was buried deep inside me, pounding me relentlessly. *I'm certain I saw lust in his eyes. Even if he was able to fake that, he can't fake an erection.* I shake my head, still trying to make sense of everything, but I can't. *I need to speak to Gwyn.* At this rate, I'll go nuts replaying every scene in my head.

I turn off the water, towel off, put on some clean clothes and dial my best friend's number. There's no way I'll be able to figure this out on my own.

"Am I calling at a bad time?" I ask when Gwyn picks up.

"Not at all. It's only ten here and Gaven is totally engrossed in his TV show. You sound stressed. What's up?"

Gwyn is always able to read me so well.

"I might have done something really bad."

"Did you screw up a project Riley gave you?"

"Oh, no. My job is the easy part. It's about Jake and Hunter."

"Men trouble? Already? You just got there," she mocks. "Which one of the two billionaires makes you weak in the knees?"

"Both."

"That's my girl. Why lust over one sexy stud when you can fantasize about two of them?"

"Gwyn, it's more than lust and it's more than a fantasy. Jake and Hunter seduced me and I've been so deprived of any attention from a man, I…"

"What are you saying, Ali?"

"Remember you joked about me having both men?"

"I wanted to push you out of your boundaries. I know full well you'd never go through with it, but I was hoping thinking about the possibilities could put you in a different frame of mind."

"Yeah, well, my boundaries were pushed really far today." I bite the inside of my mouth, trying to find the courage to spit out the words that will change my friend's perception of me forever. "I… It sort of happened unexpectedly…"

"Oh, for the love of God, Ali, just say it."

"Gwyn, I had sex with both men today."

"As in the same day?" I can hear the shock in her voice.

"You won't believe everything that's happened to me since I set foot on this ranch."

For the next hour I explain everything to Gwyn. Between recounting my saucy tales and her gasping for air at everything I say, it becomes clear how perverted this day has been. *But would I change anything if I could?*

There's a heavy silence on the other end as my best friend takes in my words.

"Am I still speaking to my best friend, Allison Randall, or is this an impersonator?"

"Gwyn, if you had asked me to bet on anything this surreal happening to me, I would have lost. I could never have conceived of these rapturous interludes in my wildest dreams. Everything about what I shared so far with both Jake and Hunter feels so right."

"Honey, I don't know about right, but it all sounds dangerously naughty," she says in a fake British accent.

"These two hunks are going to make it impossible for me to have sex with anyone else for the rest of my natural life. They've broken me and there's no going back." *My God, they're both equally delicious.*

"You actually have a thing for Jake and Hunter?"

"I can't deny my attraction to both men. When I'm around them, I'm completely powerless and I'm more than happy to submit myself to their will. Jake is intense, domineering and decisive. Hunter is playful, spontaneous and unpredictable. They're both amazing lovers."

"What a far cry from the guys you've been with so far."

I haven't been with dozens of men, but I'm no virgin. "I know, right? The men I've been with, including Clark, have been fairly clueless in the bedroom and until last night, I thought there wasn't much more to expect from sex. Sure, some were willing to take a little bit more time to satisfy me, but for the most part they were in such a hurry to get off, they forgot about my needs."

"Didn't you mention that by the end of your relationship, sex felt more like a chore than a thrill?"

"Tell me about it. On nights when Clark came home late exhausted from work, sex felt more like a machine-gun than a slow amorous exchange. After playing with my boobs, he'd usually poke around my pussy for sixty seconds with his tongue or his fingers and somehow he'd always manage to be about an inch lower than where he should've been. Then poof, he'd shove his cock in me and come before I even had time to ease into it."

"You already know how I feel about your whole relationship with your ex. You should have demanded more."

"I can see it now, but back then I was always too insecure to ask for what I wanted. What I needed. Most times, sex with Clark and the few boyfriends I've had was so cold, detached and uninviting—fast, fast, fast and then it was over. I was always left wanting more."

"Sounds like you're having the sex of your life."

"Let's just say I finally understand what you meant when you told me about the toe-curling explosion of a G-spot orgasm."

"There's absolutely nothing like it in the world." She laughs. "So, what next?"

"They're at Hunter's place now debating everything and I'm a nervous wreck. I have a feeling I've caused a rift between them by sleeping with both of them."

"From what you described, Jake wasn't too upset about seeing you with Hunter," she mocks.

"Waiting to find out how my actions affected their friendship is making my stomach turn."

"Sweetie, you need to stop racking your brain and wait to have an open conversation with Jake and Hunter about today. You're just going to end up giving yourself a headache."

"You're right."

"Not to mention, maybe there's an opportunity for you to sample both... at the same time."

I can hear the amusement in her voice and I'm not certain if she's joking. "Gwyn, I'm not that kind of woman. Today was a mistake and I have to get my act together. I'm here because Riley selected me as her assistant, not to engage in unspeakable sexual interludes with two of the hottest men I've ever known."

"All I'm saying is keep an open mind. Why limit yourself?"

She's officially lost her marbles.

"You're right about one thing, I should stop trying to figure this out and just wait to speak to them," I say, trying to veer the subject to something a bit safer.

"I agree."

"When it comes to your other suggestion, I think you and Gaven have been watching too much porn lately." I laugh.

"Don't knock it till you try it. It's opened up a whole new world of possibilities in our relationship."

"Okay, I'm going to pour myself a glass of wine and unwind before the verdict comes in. Thanks for being such a great listener and a good friend."

"Seriously, honey, why have just one stud when you can have both?"

We both laugh.

Hunter and Jake have given me more pleasure than all those inadequate past lovers combined. My climaxes were as exhilarating as reaching the peak of the Rocky Mountains. *What a high.*

No matter how many deep-seated emotions these two have stirred up in me, I can never allow myself to go there with either of them ever again. I know Gwyn sees things differently and she's pushing me past my own boundaries, but I can't see myself going there. *I guess it's going to be a long summer.*

"Oh, one more thing before I go," Gwyn says. "I'm sorry to bring back unpleasant memories, but it's about Clark. He dropped by looking for you a couple days ago. I guess you never told him you were leaving NYC."

"What an asshole. He called me earlier today and I told him off."

"Yeah, he seemed pretty adamant about some kind of lease the two of you share on a downtown office."

"Yes, it's the stupidly priced office I've told you about. He wants me to sign for the renewal and I told him it was no longer my problem. I even suggested he ask Paula to help him, given they're so close and all," I snarl, disgusted.

"Oh, you didn't! Good on you for putting him in his place."

"I don't owe him anything anymore."

"He became very pushy when he was here. Luckily, Gaven was around and after a few minutes of insistent pestering, my fiancé told him to get off of our property or else he'd call the police."

"Wow! It got that out of control?"

"He had a crazed look about him and it seemed like it was a do-or-die situation. In any case, as you said, it's no longer your problem. Aren't you happy he's no longer in your life?"

"Happy doesn't even start to describe it, Gwyn. He's part of my past and that's exactly how I want to keep things "

"Why fret about a crappy ex-boyfriend when you can have a little fun with two sexy billionaires?"

"You kill me, but I love you to pieces."

"Love you right back."

* * *

It's already quarter past eight. They've been talking for a long time now.

I've been sitting nervously in the living area waiting for Jake to call or text me, although I've been checking my phone every five minutes he's still not been in contact. I wish he or Hunter would come over and put me out of my misery. I need to make sure everything is okay between them and I also want to straighten things out with Jake.

This waiting game is torturous.

I get up on my feet and start pacing the living area hoping to pass time when my phone rings. I run to the coffee table where I left it and Jake's number flashes on my screen.

"Jake?"

"Hey, Allison, I know I said I was going to come by for you later tonight, but something came up."

My heart sinks to the pit of my stomach. *Shit, he won't forgive me for this afternoon.* "Are you still upset at me? I wish we could talk this out."

"It has nothing to do with me being upset with you. Originally, I intended for us to sit down with Hunter to iron things out, but I just got off the phone with Riley. Her SUV broke down and since her phone was low on battery, she hadn't been able to call earlier. She's been out in the middle of nowhere for hours now."

"Oh, my God, is she okay?"

"She's fine. My sister is a tough woman. The only problem is she's stranded between Denver and Fort Collins with an SUV full of hungry and tired kids."

"I can only imagine, since the kids left with her early this afternoon. Doesn't Isadora have a phone?"

"Isadora, bless her heart, hates modern technology and left her phone in the glove compartment of her car. So Isadora is stranded out there with my sister, but her phone is sitting right outside my door." He chuckles.

"It's good to hear you laugh."

There's a long silence between us and I can hear him breathing on the other end. "I really wanted us to talk, but it's already getting dark and it's going to be a challenge to get Riley out of this mess. I wanted to call you to let you know you're most likely going to be on your own for a few hours."

"What about Hunter?"

"I'm taking Hunter with me. I'll take care of Riley, Isadora and the kids while he takes care of her truck. He'll drive in with our friend Brewster Wilson who owns a garage in town and they'll take care of towing Riley's truck back to Fort Collins."

"I see. Well…" I hesitate, unsure if I should be bold and request this of him, but there's a force inside of me pushing me to ask the question. "Maybe if you don't come back too late you might consider coming over and we can talk. Even if Hunter can't join the conversation, I'd love to make sure you and I are still okay."

"I can't promise I'll be back early enough for us to talk, but you don't have to worry. You and I are okay. I had a great conversation with Hunter."

"Really?"

"Really. I have to go now. If I get back at a decent time, I'll text you when we're approaching the ranch. Since it's nighttime, it will be easy for you to sneak back into my house without raising any suspicions. Once you're here, I'll ask Hunter to come over. Does that sound good?"

"It does." I nod, knowing he can't see me, but reassuring myself everything is still okay between us.

"I'll see you in a few hours."

CHAPTER FOUR

HUNTER

Last night was a nightmare. As if Riley's SUV breaking down in the middle of nowhere wasn't bad enough, we had to deal with a raging storm. It rained so hard it was nearly impossible to see even a foot in front of us. Had it not been for the three guys who came with Brewster and I to take Riley's truck back to Fort Collins, we would have been in big trouble. I know I'm built, but Brewster's cousins are beasts.

By the time we got back to the ranch it was late and we were all exhausted. I stopped by Jake's place to find out if he had talked to Allison, but although he got back at a decent time, the blonde's eventful day did her in. Jake tried to reach her by texting her and calling her, but he didn't hear back. After a few failed attempts, he strolled down to her house to make sure she was unharmed. Luckily, she fell asleep on her couch with her curtains still open and Jake was able to confirm she was okay.

We decided over a couple glasses of brandy that we'd find time today to put our cards on the table. Since Riley will be heading back to Denver for another culinary training with a few executives, we'll have plenty of time to seduce Allison over to the idea of taking both of us at the same time.

It's going to be another scorching hot day.

Jake and I have been at it for a couple of hours already and even though it's only nine o'clock in the morning, I can already feel the heat. I was tempted to swing by Allison's house an hour ago to see if she was awake, but since Jake and I agreed to talk to her together, I had to find work to preoccupy my mind. I must have jerked off three times last night before falling asleep—not even a crazy night and a physically demanding evening were enough to prevent me from relishing the memories from my raunchy afternoon at the cabin with her. I woke up this morning with an impressive boner begging for relief, dreaming of sharing her with my best friend. I know it's only a matter of hours now, but I'm so impatient I can barely contain myself.

I hope she agrees to being with both of us.

I'm in the barn with a couple of our guys assessing which of our prime cows we'll reserve for one of our biggest new clients. Jake's meeting with Benjamin Russell went better than expected and the owner of all twenty-one of Benny's Grill restaurants in Colorado wants our Angus beef on his menu. He made an irresistible deal with Jake in record-breaking time. Obviously meeting my best friend was simply a formality.

I'm busy with Justin and Michael, two of our workers, when Jake approaches. I do a double-take at the worried look on his face. "Hey, buddy, is everything okay?"

"I just got off the phone with Riley."

"What's the problem? I thought Brewster did a good job of fixing her SUV. I mean, he had that thing parked in front of our ranch by six this morning."

"No, the truck is fine. She's heading back from the market with Isadora and she asked for an urgent meeting at her house in fifteen minutes."

"Urgent?"

Jake's eyes darken as he nods in agreement.

I look over at the two workers. "Justin and Michael, why don't you guys continue without me for a few minutes? I need to step out and have a word with Jake. Call on Dirk if you need help."

"It's not a problem, boss." Justin is the first to answer.

"Yeah, Justin's right. We've already done a lot and there's not much left to do."

Once I'm confident our two workers can take over, I step out with my friend.

"Why don't we take a walk, it'll be more private."

I look at Jake, surprised by his suggestion, and I follow him. Once we distance ourselves from our workers, I inquire about what's gotten him so rattled.

"Talk to me. Is it that bad?"

"Well, she said it was an important matter that concerned all of us—you, me and Allison. Given what happened between Allison and I and the fact Isadora caught her sneaking out of my house yesterday morning, I have a feeling the nanny might have spilled the beans on me."

"But you said Isadora didn't suspect a thing."

"Yeah, but it doesn't mean she didn't innocently mention to my sister what she witnessed."

"Shit."

"We don't know anything for sure, but when was the last time Riley called for an urgent meeting?"

"That's a good point. I think we have to brace ourselves for the worst. Let's head over there right now," I say, slapping my friend on the back to comfort him.

Allison arrives at Riley's office at the same time we do. And from the worried look on her face, I can tell she's as nervous as Jake.

"Good morning."

"Good morning, Allison," we both chime in at the same time.

"Well, you look well rested." I can't resist. She looks absolutely radiant this morning.

"I am. I think it's a combination of the fresh air and this new adventure I'm on, but I can't remember the last time I slept so well."

I'm sure getting fucked by two incredibly well-hung men in the same day had nothing to do with it.

"I texted you when I got back last night, but I didn't hear back from you," Jake says. "I came over your place to check up on you and I saw you had passed out cold."

All three of us are making idle conversation trying to pretend yesterday never happened when Riley makes her presence known in her booming voice.

"Don't just stand out there. Come on in, you guys. There's a lot to talk about."

Jake's sister breaks our casual chitchat and forces us to face the fact we may all be in trouble. Although no one else knows I gorged on the sexy temptress yesterday afternoon, Riley is well aware of my sexual appetite and she'll be quick to reprimand me and warn me to stay away from her new assistant.

"Did you have to call a group meeting like this? What's so important you couldn't text? We've got a busy day in front of us." I can't tell if Jake is irritated or anxious, but he dives right into his sister.

Riley shakes her head. "Don't we all, big bro. I wanted to look you in the eyes when I deliver this news."

She's usually so cheerful, but this must be serious, because her face is closed.

She grabs hold of Allison's hand and drags her inside her house. "Honey, come sit next to me." Jake and I follow right behind. "The two of you can sit over there." Riley points at two gray armchairs. My friend and I remove our cowboy hats and take seats right across from Allison and his sister. "Isadora took the kids out for a walk. She already knows what's going on."

Uh-oh.

"I'm still struggling to accept it all, so I'm just going to do my best to remain as calm as possible while we have this little conversation this morning."

I know Riley is one for theatrics, but I'm starting to think my best friend's right. His sister's nanny might have inadvertently handed her his head on a platter.

"You're worrying me, Riley. What's going on?"

Jake is fidgeting with his hands and when our eyes meet I see the same worried look he must read in mine.

"Well, here we go. I thought I was going to spend the summer at the ranch training my new assistant," she says, squeezing Allison's hand and smiling at her warmly. "But yesterday a few major events occurred that were only brought to my attention a few hours ago. We're talking about colossal circumstances that have forced me to change my plans."

Shit. Did someone catch me at the cabin fucking her assistant?

Riley pauses and I swallow hard. I furtively glance in Jake's direction and I catch him raising his eyebrows. *This isn't good.* Although Allison is still focused on Riley, I can tell she's as anxious as we are because the color has drained from her face.

"Thank God my faithful nanny was with me this morning when I found out or I think I would have fainted. I mean I couldn't believe any of it."

We're so busted.

The tension in the room is so thick you could cut it with a butter knife.

In an attempt to push Jake's sister to drop the axe so we can get it over with, I ask a question. "Riley, these events have to do with all of us sitting here?"

Riley nods. "Hunter, we're talking epic proportions here."

Yikes. She definitely knows.

Riley turns to face Allison and cups her hands. "I'm so sorry to do this to you, Allison."

Oh, no. She can't fire her like this.

"I don't understand, Riley. Have I done something wrong or have I dropped the ball?"

"I'm as confused as Allison. Jake, what is your sister talking about?" I look at my best friend for support.

"Beats me. She's talking in riddles. Riley, what is it that you're not telling us?"

Bless Jake for cutting to the chase.

Suddenly, Riley lets go of Allison's hands, jumps to her feet and paces around her house clutching her stomach. *Is she pregnant or is she going to be sick?* The blonde looks at me for answers. I just shake my head to let her know I'm as stumped as she is.

"I don't know how to share this news calmly."

"Well, don't. Just blurt it out and get it over with, Ri." Jake's impatience is bordering on annoyance.

"If you'll just give me a minute," she retorts, "I was trying to say Allison will be on her own. I won't be able to train her like I'd wish because..." Riley pauses again and all three of us lean in waiting with bated breath for her to continue. "You're looking at the new judge for the Food TV show *Iron Skillets!* A few hours ago Food TV asked me to step in at the last minute for Chef Rick Bateman who can't finish the season as a judge because his wife just gave birth prematurely two days ago to triplets. Since he already has two other toddlers, he's back home taking care of his family and I'm flying to Cali to replace him. I'm leaving tomorrow late afternoon with the kids and the nanny for LA. Can you believe it? I'm going to be on a major TV show!"

Riley delivers her news at such a speed I look around the room, bewildered. When Jake raises his eyebrows, surprised, and Allison gapes, I know I'm not alone.

What?

It takes me a second to get it but when Riley starts screaming her head off and crying with joy it hits me—we're safe.

* * *

As we leave Riley's office, Jake slaps my back as if we just won the Larry O'Brien NBA Championship Trophy for basketball team of the year and I can't help but return his grin.

"Can you believe this? I don't think we could have planned this better if we had tried."

We bump fists like two winners coming off of a life-changing Vegas poker-winning streak. Soon we'll be able to possess Allison fully.

"Your sister is leaving for the next ten days and she's taking her kids and her nanny with her. You realize we have the ranch all to ourselves? When was the last time she left for that long?"

Given the thousands of responsibilities Allison will have to take over during Riley's absence, she stayed behind, but Jake and I snuck out the second we could. It was obvious we were both elated by the fortuitous turn of events.

"I'll be honest, I stopped breathing for a minute. I mean, with the way she was looking at Allison, I thought for sure she knew, but when Riley started to scream and jump up and down like a schoolgirl, I quickly realized her big news had nothing to do with us fucking her assistant. My sister is going to become an instant celebrity. Her food blog is already doing really well, but being called in to replace a judge who couldn't sit in on a new food show will skyrocket her popularity."

"I know. This is going to be a mind-blowing year for her. I guess it makes sense that she takes the kids."

"As rambunctious as those kids are, she can't leave them behind. It's way too busy here at the ranch during the day and let's face it, Riley would miss them like crazy."

"It's a good thing Isadora will also be in LA or the twins might burn your mom and dad's house down." I chuckle. "Those two are a handful."

Suddenly Jake stops walking, pulls off his cowboy hat and flings it in the air. "Yahoo!" he yells in the middle of the open field.

"I guess we're thinking the same thing." I look at my friend with a huge grin on my face. "When it became clear Riley would be away for the next little while, I came up with a master plan to seduce the goddess we both shared yesterday and entice her to have both of us at the same time."

"You can tell me all about it while we walk. Let me text Allison now and get her to come to our office when Riley leaves for Denver. This is a golden opportunity. We get the entire ranch to ourselves and if Allison says yes, it promises to be a wild ride."

"Wait. Ask her to come around at the end of the day. Let's say around six. We can't just ask her to take one of us up the ass without preparation. I'll make a quick a trip to Pleasure Principles and I'll buy a few toys."

"You're going to drive to a sex shop this afternoon?" Jake asks, shocked. "I was hoping to keep this as low-key as possible, but obviously you have other plans in mind."

"Hear me out. Once the workers have left for the day, I'll jump in my SUV and I'll go buy a few things to ease Allison into it. Let's not kid ourselves. We're both well hung and it doesn't matter which one of us claims her ass, since she's a virgin we might as well make sure she's ready."

It takes Jake a few minutes to accept my suggestion. "You know what?"

"I'm brilliant, right?"

Jake nods. My suggestion makes a whole lot of sense. Truth be told, I have a knack for turning any uncomfortable situation around—even anal sex.

"If we're going to do this, we might as well do it right. Make the trip and get everything we need."

"Now we're talking. I'm glad we see eye to eye on this one."

"Let's have a barbecue at my house and see how the evening unfolds."

I haven't seen Jake's eyes sparkle like this in months.

* * *

"It's nearly six o'clock." I've been looking at my watch every minute since I returned from my little shopping expedition at Pleasure Principles. Jake is sitting behind his iMac computer pretending to work, but I'm too excited to sit down or to focus on anything other than the woman who's been occupying my thoughts.

The energy flowing through my veins is intoxicating. If there was a way of convincing Allison to take both of us together tonight, I'd jump at it, but I do know my patience will pay off. We need to make sure Jake's sister has left town tomorrow and we also need to make sure that her assistant is comfortable with the idea of us pushing her boundaries.

"She should be here any minute now." When our eyes meet we grin from ear to ear. The truth is we haven't come down from our high since Riley announced she would be away for a few weeks.

The second his sister jumped into her SUV, my best friend texted Allison and asked her to come to our office at the end of the day when all the workers had gone home. His sister will be in Denver teaching one of her executive cooking classes until four o'clock this afternoon, then she'll take her kids to their sporting activities. Since last night's storm put a damper on their plans, Riley intends on making it up to her kids and her nanny by taking them to Totally 80's Pizza for dinner before she comes home. This should give us more than enough time to seduce Allison to the idea of allowing two men to worship her at the same time.

"I've got everything ready," I say, looking around the room for the twentieth time. "I hope she likes the desserts I selected. Since most women love sweets, I'm hoping this might ease her into it." After I left the sex shop, I made a special trip to Cakes, Cakes and More Cakes to grab a few chocolatey treats we can enjoy with wine.

"Well, I have to hand it to you, you went all out, buddy. I don't think I would've thought of all of this, but considering she's most likely a virgin, I think your setup will make it easier for her to say yes."

"I really hope so."

"So do I."

Suddenly we hear a knock and we both lock eyes.

Damn, am I ever excited.

"Hunter, wait," my best friend whispers as I take a few steps towards the door.

"Yeah?"

"Don't lay it on too thick. We don't want to scare her."

"You don't have to worry, Jake, I'll handle it with kid gloves."

When I open the door and catch sight of her beauty, the first thought that pops into my mind is to yank her over my shoulder, walk towards my desk, drop her there, unzip my jeans with one hand while holding her down with the other and fuck her once again under my best friend's watchful eye. I blink a few times before shaking my head. *Focus. Get your mind out of the gutter.*

"Allison, you look absolutely radiant. The pink shirt looks so feminine on you and I'm happy to see you're taking my advice to heart by letting your hair flow seductively over your shoulders." I wink at her and extend my hand to invite her in.

Hmmm, I wonder if her no doubt provocative underwear matches the color of her shirt.

"It was another steamy day and I had to take a shower before coming over."

I wish I were able to join you. There's nothing quite like shower sex.

"Hunter's right. The soft shade brings out your features." Jake gets up the second she walks in the room.

I'm glad to see I'm not the only who zoomed in on her ample breasts.

My best friend's compliment flushes her cheeks and my dick twitches.

"Why, thank you, Jake." I'm dying to lick the lower lip she's biting. "Wow. The two of you sound like you're buttering me up for something." Allison immediately focuses on the generous assortment of cakes and the bottles sitting on the filing cabinet.

"Now that cuts real deep," I say, holding my chest. "You say that as if I haven't been tripping all over you since you arrived here."

"I have to agree with Hunter. That hurts." Jake winks.

"Forgive me if I'm wrong, but when a man resorts to decadent sweets and wine, there's often more to it than what meets the eye."

"Who says those are for you?" I cross my arms over my chest, pretending to be offended.

She takes me in for a few seconds before bursting out laughing. Jake and I join her.

"Okay. You win. Those are for you. I hope you like chocolate?"

"Are you kidding me? Is there a woman on this planet who'd say no to chocolate?"

"Glad to hear it. Sit down and I'll grab you a plate and a glass. White?"

"I'll be honest, after the eventful morning and the busy day, I couldn't ask for anything more than some cake and a glass of chilled white wine."

"That's music to my ears." I take a step towards the filing cabinet, but Jake raises his hand to stop me.

"Why don't I bring Ali the treats and the wine while you sit down with her?"

I pick up on my best friend's not-so-subtle way of telling me to start talking.

"Oh, God. Jake, you are very mysterious, and you didn't give me much to go by in your text message."

"I hate to quote my sister, because that would imply she's right for once"—Jake chuckles—"but there are certain things that are best said in person."

"I hope you won't have me on pins and needles holding my breath too afraid to make the slightest sound like this morning in Riley's house." Allison's freaked expression has both of us bursting out laughing. "That was a bit too dramatic for me."

"Well, we are talking about Hunter."

"Ignore him." I roll my eyes before focusing my attention on the blonde. "Similar to our meeting this morning, what I want to discuss with you does involve all of us in this room, but I can't promise I'll be able to match Jake's sister's theatrical delivery... even if my best friend thinks otherwise."

"Good. One of those a day is quite sufficient." She grins.

"Since Jake and I had to go rescue his sister last night and the storm made things complicated, we got home after you had already fallen asleep. Jake didn't have the heart to wake you up, so we were never able to talk about what happened inside the cabin."

"But I thought Jake said we were okay." Her big, beautiful hazel eyes search Jake's for confirmation.

"Ali, I meant what I said. You and I are okay. My relationship with Hunter remains unscathed and that's what's most important to me. My best friend wants to talk about an idea we've been bouncing off of each other and we'd like your input." Jake hands Allison a plate of sweets before handing her a glass of wine.

"That makes me feel so much better because I was afraid you'd be upset by what you witnessed, or worse, that I had come between you two."

"I won't lie, I was surprised and I was even a little irritated watching you take so much pleasure at his mercy, but once I was able to calm down, I realized this opens the door to a lot of possibilities for us."

"What do you mean?" Allison frowns while shaking her head.

"Why don't I let Hunter explain."

"I think both Jake and I have been quite forward about our attraction to you. And a few days ago, you were able to experience firsthand how much we want you."

"Oh." She blushes so much the color matches her shirt.

"You don't have to be shy about it. You're a gorgeous woman with sensual curves and you're so passionate. It shouldn't come as a surprise that you've seduced us and that we've fallen under your spell."

"I have to agree with Hunter. The way you respond to me when we're together nearly drives me mad."

"If the two of you keep showering me with compliments, I'm going to demand you lower the temperature on the A/C because I'm burning up here."

I smile before continuing. "Do you remember when Jake walked in on us?"

"How can I forget?" She lowers her eyes to the plate on her lap.

"Having him in the room didn't stop me. On the contrary, it fueled me. When he was watching me take you with such unrestricted fury, it only made me want to fuck you harder."

"Hunter." She says my name with so much lust.

I reach out for her plate and drop it on the desk next to her before cupping her hands into mine. "I also noticed you didn't ask me to stop even when Jake was squatting in front of you kissing you with such ardor I could feel your body quiver under his touch." My voice is so low the tremor hardens my dick.

"I... Well... I mean..." She stops, trying to regain her composure. "I really don't know how to respond to this." Her shyness is endearing.

"It's okay if you enjoyed having me inside you while my best friend watched." I bring my index finger to her face and trace the contour of her jawline.

"It is?"

"Absolutely. We both enjoyed it as well, didn't we, Jake?"

"You definitely seemed to enjoy yourself more than I did, buddy, since her pussy was clenched around your dick, not mine, but I took a lot of pleasure from watching Ali submit to you." His voice is coated with desire and I can just imagine that his cock is as hard as mine.

"My God," she exhales, wiping her forehead with the back of her hand as if the cool temperature isn't enough to tame the fire burning inside her.

"Allison, we were hoping you'd consider doing it again."

"You mean us together," she says, waving her finger between us, "while he watches?" Her eyes bounce from mine to Jake's and it's clear she's shocked by my proposition.

"It would be a little different…"

"How so?"

"In the sense that this time Jake would participate fully."

"Huh?" Her jaw drops.

"It's more fun when we're all naked." I grin.

"Hunter, what do you mean?"

"Allison, have you ever had two men worship your body at the same time?"

"Until a few days ago I had never had two different men in the same month, let alone the same day. What you're suggesting is so far out of my comfort zone, it's not even funny."

That might be the case, but she isn't making any effort to run out the door.

"Hunter, may I?"

"Jump right in, buddy."

Jake takes a step towards us and I scoot my chair back a little to give my friend some room.

He kneels in front of the blonde and takes her hands into his. "Ali, when I took you in the barn, you trusted me implicitly." Allison nods and shifts her eyes to me. I smile and she returns a shy grin. "And you were more than open to the idea of me giving you more pleasure than you've ever experienced in your life. Am I right?"

"Yes, but—"

"Ali, neither of us would ever do anything to harm you. You believe me?"

She nods. "I know you wouldn't, Jake." She turns her attention to me. "The same goes for you, Hunter."

I extend my arm and caress her cheek with the back of my hand to reassure her.

"What Hunter is suggesting is another way for us to take your sexual awakening to a whole other level... one that's unparalleled by anything else you've ever even dreamt of. I can promise you, when two men yearn for you as badly as we do and focus their insatiable hunger on your heavenly body, it can be mind-blowing."

"Gosh," she whispers.

"Sweetheart, when you climax sandwiched between the two of us, you'll think you've seen God."

"Oh. Your words are going to make me lose it, Jake." She's fanning herself profusely with one hand and I can't help but focus on the other hand slowly travelling down her chest. *Damn.* I'd pay good money to have those tits in my hands right about now.

Snap out of it. "Jake's right. It wouldn't be much different than it was a few days ago inside the cabin, except for the fact that we'd all agree in advance to give and to take as much pleasure from each other as we possibly can."

She lowers her eyes and squeezes Jake's hands. "Do I have to decide right now?"

My buddy shakes his head. "Both Hunter and I feel it would be unfair to force you to make a decision on the spot, since this is most likely very new to you."

"It is. Until a few days ago, I had always assumed I needed a bed in order to have sex." She flashes a wry smile.

"I guess you know differently now?" I couldn't resist.

We all laugh.

"Talk about bursting my bubble."

"What we're suggesting will make everything else you've experienced so far tame and predictable, but it's well worth the ride," I add.

"That it is, but we don't want to pressure you. We want you to be comfortable with the idea and let our conversation sink in." My best friend chimes in.

"And if I did accept, what would this look like... between the three of us?"

Allison might not have said yes yet, but everything about her demeanor suggests we've piqued her curiosity and she could be open to exploring more naughtiness at the hands of two alpha males.

"Since my sister is leaving tomorrow mid-afternoon, why don't you come over to my house at about seven o'clock for a barbecue and you can let us know your decision then? You'll have plenty of time to ponder the idea of being with the two of us. You'll either be aroused by it or not." Jake stretches back up, pulls up a chair and sits next to Allison.

"If you decide you want both of us as much as we want you, I have a gift for you," I say, getting up and walking to my desk. I grab the little sex toy I hid at the bottom of my drawer and walk back to Allison. "This is for you."

"Wow. You're giving me a gift before I even make a decision?"

"If you say yes, this will come in handy."

"What is it?" She reaches out, drops the little silver bag on her lap and impatiently fumbles through the star-printed tissue paper.

"If you decide you want to know how heavenly it feels to be fucked by a man while you suck another guy's cock, this will make things much more pleasurable for you."

Allison's eyes widen so much, if they were to get any larger they'd take over her whole body.

"Hunter." Jake scowls. "Didn't we talk about you not shocking Ali?"

"I thought you meant at the beginning." *Jeez.* "But why be shy about it now?" I grin from ear to ear.

She pulls out the purple silicone toy and brings it up to eye level. After a few long seconds, she flashes me a perplexed look. "What is this?"

"It's a naughty toy."

"As in a sex toy?"

"Yup," I respond.

"Have you ever bought anything to enhance your pleasure before, Ali?" Jake asks the question that's been on my tongue since I left Pleasure Principles.

"Oh, God, no."

"You're going to enjoy this a lot." Jake's half-closed eyes speak volumes.

"And what am I supposed to do with it? Do I bring it with me if I decide to take the plunge?"

Her innocence is such a turn-on.

"Yes and no." I know I'm being vague, but I'm enjoying seeing the puzzled look on her face as she tries to figure this out.

"Huh?"

"Ideally, you should use it as soon as possible." Jake raises his eyebrows and Allison flushes.

"I don't follow."

"Ali, it's a butt plug." My best friend delivers the news with such calmness. Had it been me, I would've surely turned this into a raunchy moment.

"A wh-what?" The color drains from her face like it did earlier today right before Riley delivered her big news. She opens her mouth a few times, but nothing comes out. I'm tempted to speak, but I decide to give her a minute to digest everything.

"Does this go where I think it does?"

Her reaction is priceless.

"As smart as I am, I'm no mind-reader. You're going to have to speak your mind, girl," I tease.

"Hunter, give her a break." Although he tries to adopt a stern tone, Jake is obviously struggling to bite off a smile.

"Let me jump in before my friend scares you. This is simply an option if you decide you want to explore... your darker side."

"Good Lord, I didn't even know I had one of those," she huffs before rolling her eyes.

"We all have one. Yours is simply untouched," Jake adds.

"Will this… you know… hurt?"

"You mean the butt plug?" Jake asks.

Smooth.

"Yeah."

"No. It shouldn't hurt one bit. Hunter bought you a smaller size. So it should be very comfortable. We assume this is your first time…" Jake lets his sentence hang and we both lean in, awaiting her answer.

"Oh, definitely. I've never had this kind of conversation with any man before and I certainly didn't know you could insert objects up there," she says, wiggling her nose and pointing to her bum.

That's not quite what Jake wanted to know, but I guess there's no point in freaking her out too much.

It takes all my will not to laugh and when I look at Jake, he's also struggling to keep a straight face.

"Gosh, this is so much," she says, placing the toy back into the bag.

I really hope she agrees.

"I like being with you, Allison," I say to make sure she understands how important this is to me.

"I do as well, Hunter."

Jake gets up from where he's sitting and drops a soft kiss against Allison's cheek. "And I could gorge on your celestial body every day and never get enough."

"Jake…"

"Seriously, Ali. I haven't enjoyed being with a woman like I have with you in a very long time."

"I love being with you as well."

"You see, you like both of us and neither of us can get enough of you. That's why we're hoping you'll take us up on our proposition."

"I have a lot to think about, I guess."

"Take your time. We're meeting tomorrow night at my house," Jake says, caressing her long silky mane.

"I have a suggestion in terms of letting us know which way you decide."

"Oh, there are options?"

"Of course, baby, this isn't black and white, there are a few wicked shades in between," I mock. "You have full say in this. One, you may want to be exclusively mine. Two, you might want Jake to keep taking you in the barn while I slave like a dog manning the ranch." I grin. "Three, you might be willing to take both of us at the same time."

"Whatever you decide, we'll respect your choice, Ali."

"Jake's right. I have a clever idea that will make it easier for you to let us know which option you're most comfortable with. Do you want me to share it?"

"I'm all ears."

CHAPTER FIVE

ALLISON

This must have been the craziest day since I arrived on the ranch. Scratch that, this was the craziest day of my life.

When I received Riley's text message calling us all in for an urgent meeting, my heart sank. I thought for sure Isadora put two and two together and I was going to get fired. Imagine my surprise when I find out Riley got presented with an amazing opportunity. As if that wasn't excitement enough, the chat I had with Hunter and Jake at the end of the day left me dumbfounded. After a frantic afternoon with Riley, who was desperately trying to give me a list of to do's, I received a text message from Jake the second my boss got in her vehicle to head to Denver.

Although Jake said he had discussed things with his best friend, I expected the two of them wanted to talk to me about what Jake had witnessed when he caught me inside the cabin getting my brains fucked out by his best friend, but I was dead wrong.

Of all the things they might have suggested, I surely didn't see that one coming.

I mean I've had dreams about both men pleasuring me, but it's very different when you have the opportunity to it live out. Let's be honest, that's a whole other ball game—one I never thought would present itself to me.

I've been replaying the conversation in my head as I leave their office and race to my house to call my best friend. My heart is still beating so fast from all the emotions rushing through me as I fumble with my phone. After a few frustrating minutes, I finally compose myself enough to dial Gwyn's number. Lucky for me, she picks up.

"Hey, Ali, I was thinking of you and I was going to call you after work."

"Oh, is this a bad time?"

"No, not at all. I'm walking to Mocha Heaven to grab a coffee so I can keep awake this afternoon. This has been such a grueling week for me."

"So you can talk for a few minutes? Because I really—"

Gwyn interrupts me by yelling. "You stupid idiot. Don't you have eyes? That's my light. Red means stop."

"Is everything okay?"

"Jeez. New York drivers, I tell ya. Damn, I bet you don't miss any of this mess."

"I'll be honest, I don't. I thought I was going to get bored, but—"

"Are you freaking kidding me?" She lowers her voice. "You're having mind-blowing sex with two hot guys. How the hell did you expect to get bored?"

"I was talking about missing the Big Apple's energy. But from your reaction, I gather you think I do one thing all day long?"

"If I were single and I was caught on a ranch with the two delicious men you've described with such unrestricted lust, I'd be fucking twenty-four seven." She laughs.

"Funny. Talking about Jake and Hunter, I need your guidance."

"Trouble in paradise—again?" she mocks.

"Not quite. It's more complicated than that."

"Shoot. I'm all ears."

"Well, you already know what's been going on."

"Oh, did you sort things out between the two of them?"

"I guess you can say that."

"What do you mean?"

"The strangest thing happened today—"

"Give me a sec, it's my time to order," she says before moving the phone away from her mouth. "I'll take an extra-hot, extra-tall, skim-milk latte with a touch of your hazelnut syrup, please. And don't pour too much of that stuff because there's like a gazillion calories." I wait patiently on the other end, realizing the one thing I do miss about Manhattan are those complicated coffee drinks. "Okay, I'm back. What's going on over there?"

I had planned on being cool and somewhat casual about it, but the enormity of it all hits me. "Jake and Hunter asked me to…"

"I'm listening," she presses.

"They want the three of us to be together… you know, intimately," I blurt out in one shot before I lose my courage.

A few very long seconds pass before Gwyn speaks again. "Huh? Come again?"

"You heard me."

"I did. I just refuse to believe you said what you said."

"I never thought we'd ever have this type of conversation."

"The last time we spoke, I was kidding around when I said maybe you might sample both guys. I never imaged it could become a reality."

"Same here."

Suddenly I hear commotion on the other end.

"I got my coffee in hand. I'm going to walk to a park nearby and you're going to spill your guts, girlfriend."

During the next half hour, I fill her in.

"Gwyn, I'm really nervous and I don't know what to expect. What if I do everything wrong and ruin the night?"

"Honey, you're selling yourself short. If those two didn't like being with you separately, there's no way they'd want to share you. I think you've been doing a lot of things *very* right." I can hear her holding back a smile.

"You and Gaven are into a lot of this spicy stuff. I've always been too much of a chicken to even consider any of it. Not to mention most of my ex-boyfriends were as conservative as I was. You've always been way more daring than I've ever been in the bedroom and I was hoping you could... you know... tell me what I'm supposed to do so I don't look like a complete newbie."

"I'm going to go out on a limb here and say these two know you've never done this before, right?"

"Yeah, I told them. But doesn't sharing two men sometimes involve... you know..." God, I can't bring myself to say it.

"I think you being a newbie is part of the attraction for them. Men love taking your virginity. Since we aren't saving ourselves for marriage anymore, most guys view anal sex as the ultimate way of claiming and dominating us. And it's not all bad, you know..." Gwyn lets her words trail off.

"You mean..." I struggle to find my words. "You and Gaven?"

"Uh-huh."

"You've never said a word to me before. How can you keep something so monumental from me? I'm your best friend."

"I already know you think we're wild animals in the bedroom. Scratch that, we are." She chuckles. "I didn't want to freak you out."

"How long?"

"He took my virginity when we were on vacation last year in Puerto Rico."

"And you've been doing it ever since?"

"Not all the time, but yes, we do it and I really like it."

"Didn't it... hurt?"

"As long as he's very gentle and patient, you'll be fine. Once he's fully in and you start to get into it... it's pretty hot."

"Wow," I gasp, amazed by her confession. "I guess that's why they gave me this butt plug."

"Whoa. They did?" I hear the shock in her voice.

"Yup. I nearly passed out when they explained what it was." I blush. "Did Gaven buy one of these for you?"

"Uh-huh. I wore it for a few days before he took my virginity. It makes a huge difference, Ali."

"I can't believe I'm even considering doing this."

"But you want this, right? They're not pressuring you?"

"I don't think I would have put it into words like they did, but I've been having wet dreams about giving myself to these two for a few days now."

"You've been holding back on me."

"No, I've been too scared to share my fantasies with anyone. I thought there was something wrong with me for wanting two men at the same time. But now I see how naïve I've been."

"What do you mean?"

"Between the conversation I had with them and your revelation, it's clear I've been playing it way too safe."

"You're being hard on yourself again."

"I'm not. You're not afraid of going after what you want. You're so much worldlier than I'll ever be."

"Sweetie, what these two men are proposing is way more exciting and way more daring than anything I've tried. Having two men adore every part of your body is the ultimate fantasy for most women. And you know what? Amongst all my friends, you're the only one who'll be lucky enough to experience it."

"Really?"

"Honey, it's good to be bad sometimes. Go with it and enjoy it. Oh, you better call me the next morning and share every salacious detail or else I'm cutting you off as my BFF."

"Deal."

We both laugh.

CHAPTER SIX

JAKE

My sister's departure is like a whirlwind. I know she has to pack for herself and her four kids, but you'd think they were leaving for the entire year with the amount of luggage I saw lined up at her place earlier today.

While Riley was deliberating over what to bring and what to leave behind, Isadora besieged my kitchen. The tiny black nanny decided she couldn't leave for ten days without stocking our fridges with pre-made food. I know I'm no celebrity chef like Riley, but I can cook half-decent meals. When I told Isadora we were planning a barbecue, she took it upon herself to get everything ready. I could have managed fine, but since I've been preoccupied by a certain blonde, I was grateful my sister's nanny took over.

After Hunter got back from Pleasure Principles, we all met at our office. Hunter's idea was a clever one to allow Allison to let us know if she'd agree to take both of us. I'll admit she was a bit freaked out when Hunter gave her the bag containing the butt plug, but to our surprise, she seemed to warm up to the whole concept once we had explained how the little silicone sex toy would open her up to new possibilities. We really want this to be pleasurable for her as much as it will be for us. She listened intently to everything we had to say and she agreed to let us know if she wanted to share both of us or if she'd rather only be with one of us when she comes over for dinner in a few hours.

I won't lie, the last twenty-four hours have been excruciatingly painful. I've been walking around with a hard-on and no matter how many times I jerk off, I still can't satiate my desire for Allison. Hunter and I have had many conversations throughout the day trying to figure out if Allison will accept or not, but it's impossible to be inside a woman's head.

Finally, at two o'clock, my sister, her four kids and her nanny hit the road and Hunter and I start counting the minutes until all three of us meet at my house. As much as I want her all to myself, it would be an incredible experience to share her with my friend.

Only one more hour to go.

It's six o'clock and if I continue pacing around my house, I'll wear out my floors. I decide to put this pent-up energy to good use by getting ready for our barbecue. Since Isadora took care of the food, my job is easy. Although I only learned to appreciate country music since moving to Denver, it's the perfect background for this evening. After fiddling around with my playlists, I decide Thomas Rhett's *It*

Goes Like This is the best selection to take my mind off of things.

I know I'm eager, but I start setting the table at the back of my house and I get the grill going. I'm about to walk back into my kitchen to grab more plates when Hunter walks in.

I smile and look up at the clock. "You're an hour early."

"I'll be honest, this must have been the longest day of my life."

"I hear you. Since I couldn't figure out what to do with myself, I decided to get started. Now that you're here, why don't we have a couple of beers while you help me get things set up? This way we can both pretend we're not dying to find out if one of the hottest women we've come across in a long time has decided to take us up on our proposal."

"Yeah. We might be embarking on a pretty thrilling ride if she agrees."

"Is that why you're all dressed up?"

"I'm not wearing anything fancy."

"Hunter, those jeans are obviously new and your grey shirt is ironed so perfectly there isn't a wrinkle in sight."

"Look who's talking? I don't think I've ever seen these boots before and your Wranglers are as new as mine. Don't even think of denying that you spent as much time ironing your blue tee shirt as I did my shirt."

We both laugh.

"Man, you selected some good country music for tonight," he says, grabbing the bottle of beer I hand to him.

"You're the one who said if we're going to do it, we might as well do it well," I respond, twisting the cap off of my bottle before clinking my bottle against Hunter's and taking a long gulp.

"So you do listen when I talk?"

"Only when it suits me." I smile.

Over the next few minutes my best friend and I busy ourselves as best as we can as the time ticks away. By seven o'clock, we're ready for the evening and we're only waiting for Allison's arrival. My head is stuck in the fridge while I search for mustard, ketchup and relish when Hunter hits me so hard on the back I nearly collapse.

"What?" I say impatiently when I get back up. "You almost made me drop all of these bottles."

Instead of answering, Hunter stares right past me as if one of the dinosaurs from Jurassic Park is parked in front of him. His eyes are bulging out of his head and his gaping mouth is a clear indication some-one has entered my house. When I turn around to see what's gotten him so freaked out, I nearly take a step back and slam my back against the fridge when I see her standing there looking more breathtaking than ever.

"Ali." Her name comes out in a near whisper.

"Hello, big boy," she says flirtatiously and then it hits.

Holy fuck.

Hunter was a true master planner. He gave Allison three options. One, if she wants to only be with Hunter, she's to wear her hair up in a ponytail. Two, if she wants to only be with me, she's to come to the barbecue with her hair cascading over her shoulders like when she came over at my house for dinner the first night she arrived. Three, if she wants to share both of us, she's to arrive with a flower in her flowing blonde hair.

I blink a few times with my eyes fixed on the dainty purple and white Rocky Mountain columbine looking at me.

She's agreed.

Just seeing her in a magnificent red-orange dress that accentuates her sensual body makes my dick twitch, but knowing she's ready to take both of us makes me want to bypass dinner and run straight up to my bedroom.

Jesus, this is going to be a night I'll never forget.

* * *

We spend the evening enjoying a superb dinner and making casual conversation. Isadora outdid herself. I could have managed a basic meal, but I would never have been able to prepare this spread—juicy prime Angus steaks from our ranch marinated to perfection, succulent barbecued chicken, buttery corn on the cob and the best potato salad I've ever tasted in my life. We've just polished off a second slice of Isadora's heavenly chocolate and caramel tart and we all look satisfied.

Of all the desserts in Isadora's repertoire, this one is a masterpiece. I think it's the layering—a dark chocolate crust layered with sweet caramel topped with a bittersweet chocolate ganache—that does the trick. It's simply sinful.

The evening is full of lustful energy. We're all laughing, trying our best to pretend we don't already know how the night will end. There's something about sharing a woman with Hunter that's unbelievably magical. But patience is key here. We don't want to push the object of our desire too fast. When my best friend reaches for the bottle of white wine ready to top up Allison's glass, instinctively I stop him.

"It's best if Allison is fully aware of her decision."

An awkward silence passes between Hunter and I before she speaks.

"How is this going to work?" Allison's question catches us off guard.

Both Hunter and I look at each other before I break the heavy silence.

"I guess from the flower in your cascading hair flowing so seductively over your shoulders, you've agreed…?"

She nods and her cheeks turn bright red, instantly hardening my dick.

"Are you sure?" Hunter presses.

"Yes, I am. I decided a few hours ago. I was very curious when you initially made the suggestion, but I was too much of a goody-two-shoes to agree on the spot."

"I know we haven't talked about this, but you're okay with the fact both of us are older?"

"How much older?" She bounces her eyes from me to Hunter with a worried look.

"I remember you telling me you were twenty-three. Jake and I are both twenty-nine."

"I've never been with anyone who was older than twenty-four. I mean, all the guys I've been with were my age."

"But have any of them made you come the way we have since you've arrived?"

Ali flushes at Hunter's cocky question.

"If I can speak on behalf of Hunter, I can say we're both really excited about tonight. You already know we're both extremely attracted to you and all three of us together will be mind-blowing."

"Yeah. What he said," Hunter adds with a huge grin.

We all laugh.

"I have a question," she says shyly.

"Shoot. We want you to be comfortable."

"I agree with Jake. Don't feel there's anything you can't ask us."

"Will you, you know... I mean... Do you..." She waves her index finger between the two of us, unable to ask the question burning her tongue.

"You're going to have to speak your mind, because right now it's all Greek to me," I tease.

"Yeah, Allison, I'm as stumped as Jake is."

"Okay, here we go," she says, looking up as if to give herself courage. "If we do it all three of us together, will the two of you also... you know... touch each other?"

"God, no," we both answer at the same time before bursting into laughter. "Not that there's anything wrong with being bisexual. But we're not. We'd much rather play with you."

"We get off by giving you pleasure," I say. "I'll be honest, I love watching. When I walked in on both of you inside the cabin, I had to contain myself because the only thing I wanted to do was strip naked and join the two of you. I also love telling Hunter what to do when we share a woman. It takes my kink for voyeurism to another level."

She's gaping, and I realize I might have been too raw in my explanation.

"I'm sorry. Maybe it's too much. Am I shocking you?"

"Everything has been too much since I've arrived, but at the same time I want to keep pressing on the gas pedal."

"I'm glad to hear you say that." I've known my best friend for long enough and I can read the insatiable lust in his eyes. He's going to take her hard and he's going to come screaming like an animal.

Since Allison doesn't seem to mind my frankness, I continue. "We've done this before and we've never touched each other. There might be some unintentional rubbing here and there, but that's as far as it goes."

"He's right, we get turned on by watching you submitting to the other one. Not to mention a woman's skin is far softer than his—not that I'd know firsthand, of course."

Hunter can always find a way to lighten up any conversation.

"Have you been wearing the butt plug, Ali?"

"I have," she answers shyly. "Are you going to... you know?"

"We can't wait to claim every part of you, but let's ease into things. Do you have any other questions?"

"Well, what do you want to do to me?" Her voice is so deep and so low, I cup my hard cock.

"What do you want us to do to you?" Hunter's flirtatious suggestion gets us all twitching in our seats.

Her eyes sparkle and she leans in closer as if to share a big secret. "Since I knew little about being with two men at the same time, I did a search online and..."

"And?" Both Hunter and I lean in towards her, drinking up every word, eager to find out what she's discovered.

"I landed on a few porn sites." She lowers her voice to a near whisper, even though there's nobody other than the two of us to hear her for several miles.

Shocked, I rest my chin against my closed fist to prevent my jaw from hitting the table. *She was watching porn?*

"Hmmm, you did? So now you know there's more than food porn." Hunter's eyes are sparkling.

"Turns out porn sites can be as tempting as food porn ones," she says with a devilish smile.

We all laugh.

"Did you see anything that turned you on?"

"I saw a lot. I was so wired up, I had to… you know."

"No, we don't." Once again Hunter and I respond in unison.

"Relieve myself."

"You mean, you touched yourself while watching porn?"

Instead of answering she lowers her eyes and stares at her fumbling hands.

"Why don't you describe what you saw that got you so worked up?"

I hit my best friend on the arm for pressuring Allison.

"What? If we know what she likes, we can indulge her and fulfill all of her deepest and wildest fantasies."

"I don't mind sharing," she says boldly and we both arch our eyebrows, surprised by this vixen sitting across from us.

"Well, I do," I say, getting up from my seat. I pull down my tight jeans, hoping to relieve the pressure between my legs, to no avail. I walk towards the sexy seductress who's trying to make me lose my mind by telling us how she wants us to pleasure her. There's no way I'll be able to survive this cruelty. This whole evening has already been a painful waiting game. "We've already been talking way too much for one evening."

"Did I say something wrong, Jake?"

I don't even bother answering. My arousal is making it impossible for me to think straight. I take a few steps forward and I'm standing over her. I reach out my hand to her and when our skin touches, I close my hand over hers and pull her up.

"Get your sweet ass over here."

"Jake…"

"Watching Hunter fuck you the other day was enough of a tease. Instead of telling us what you want us to do to you, why don't we start having a little fun?" I slam her body against mine and I take her lips voraciously without asking for permission. Thrusting my tongue inside her mouth, I sweep my thumb across the swell of her full tits and she moans, pawing at me like a desperate soul.

"God… You… You're turning me into this reckless woman I don't even recognize," she says, pushing herself away from me.

"If you're not living on the edge then you're not living at all." I put an end to any more chitchat by kissing her with urgency.

She reaches out and runs her hand up my chest before fisting the hair at the back of my head. She kisses like she's been waiting for it all night and I'm hit with the energy of her tongue, the raw need of her mouth, the impatient way she gropes at me.

Suddenly, I feel a presence and without even opening my eyes I know Hunter is standing right there.

"Oh, God, Hunter." Ali's cry is intoxicating. My best friend presses into her back as he grinds his hips against her. From the way Allison moves towards me, I'll bet his erection is wedged between the cheeks of her ass—hungry and demanding. With me all over her tits and Hunter behind, she's trapped. The little blonde is sandwiched between two very horny and very eager alpha males. "Ahhh," she moans when I slide my hands up her sides and I cup her heavy tits, swirling my thumbs over her hard nipples until they pucker.

"What's wrong? You've never been dominated like this by two men who want you desperately?"

"I think you're right, Jake. By the way she's losing it, I'd say our sweet little vixen is more than ready for us to rock her world."

Both Hunter and I lock eyes. I'm certain the cocky grin on his face matches mine. "Fuck, yeah," I mouth to my best friend and he nods, raising his eyebrows suggestively.

"You know what?" Hunter says.

Ali turns her head to the right, trying to look at my best friend. "No. I don't." She shakes her head and she licks her lower lip.

"I bet you you're completely wet right now. What do you think, Jake?"

Ali is gaping, unable to reply to my friend's raunchy question.

"I'm sure she's soaking through her panties at just the thought of my tongue dipping inside her while she sucks on your cock."

"Jesus." She squirms.

"I bet you can't wait for me to taste you again and make you come the way I have many times since you've arrived at the ranch," I say as I slip my right hand down her thigh before pulling up her red-orange dress, shamelessly exposing her.

"Jake, I think one of us should check and make sure she wants us as badly as we want her." Hunter's eyes are half-closed and the desire I read only intensifies the dirtiness of the moment. "I think you should do the honors, my friend."

Neither of us wait for Allison to respond. Frankly, she's so far gone right now, the only thing she can do is submit herself fully. When two domineering horny men want you, it's game over.

"Mmm, I think you're right," I whisper as my fingers trail over the satin fabric of her underwear until I wedge my fingers between her warm thighs.

"The two of you are going to kill me," she pants.

"Yeah, but you'll die a very happy woman." I grin. "Oh, honey, you're dripping for us." My best friend sweeps her hair to the side before unzipping Allison's dress. I take a small step backward so I can capture every salacious movement. He helps her shimmy her beautiful body out of the fabric and she doesn't even resist. She pulls out one arm and then the other and before you know it, she's standing there with her heavy tits begging to be sucked.

"Hot damn," both Hunter and I say at the same time when we take in her outrageously sexy lingerie. Her massive tits are trapped in a lacy bra that matches the color of her dress and they're squeezed so tight they look bigger than the last time I had them in my hands. Although everything about her breasts is pure sin, the tiny little yellow bow nestled between her tits makes me so hard I could come right here.

"I've already warned both of you I have a thing for expensive underwear," she says provocatively.

"Holy shit." Hunter's eyes nearly bulge out of his head as he admires her from head to toe.

I drink in the lines of her sensual body like I'm witnessing a miracle. *Goddammit. Everything about her leaves me weak in the knees.*

Hunter reaches out and strokes her tits. As his thumbs circle around her nipples, she spreads her legs, giving me just enough room. I step closer to her with a huge grin on my face and I pull down her dress all the way to the ground.

I get back up, lean in and whisper in her ear. "This is getting in the way. Why don't you step out of it so we can have full access to your gorgeous body."

"But… I can't."

"Why not?"

"I'm going to be fully naked and we're outside under the lights of all of these lanterns."

"Technically, you're already fully exposed." I grin. "Secondly, we're in the middle of nowhere on an early weekday evening. You don't have to worry, sweetness, no one will come to your rescue as we ravish you." Resigned to being ours for the taking, she obediently steps out of her dress, removing yet another barrier. *Finally.* "I'm dying to rip these panties off of you and lick your clit like a starved man."

"Christ," she whimpers.

"Hunter, this dance has been going on for long enough. I'm horny as hell and I need relief. Now. You hold her while I tongue-fuck her."

My best friend doesn't waste a second. He steps behind Allison and grabs her by the shoulders.

"Wh-what? We're staying out here? In your backyard?"

"Not for the entire evening. Just until I've made you come. Then we'll go up to my room and Hunter and I will take turns at making you lose your head. All. Night. Long." I curl my lips up in a half smile.

Right on cue, Hunter unhooks her bra and she brings up her hands to cover her breasts protectively. *She's playing hard to get.* Without giving her another chance to protest, I drop to my knees in front of her and I bury my face against her stomach as I caress her hips.

"I'm tempted to make good on my word and rip your panties to shreds, but I think it would be far better to keep them on and use them in my naughty play."

"Buddy, I haven't seen you this hungry in a long time." Hunter casts dark eyes on me and I can tell from his half smile he's enjoying being a peeping Tom.

"Oh, God," she hisses when I push the fabric of her panties to the side before sinking two fingers into her slippery wetness.

"I can't get enough of your sweet pussy."

It's as if my words put her into a trance. Her arms fall helplessly to her sides, giving Hunter the opening he needs to pull her bra off completely. She's too preoccupied by what my fingers are doing to her to do anything more than to lock eyes with me, dazed. *That's it, baby. I've got you where I want you.*

"Ali, you're even more drenched now than you were a few minutes ago."

"Jake, please." She squirms.

She reaches down as if to stop me, but I brush her hand to the side. "No, you don't. From now on, we're in control of your pussy, your tits, your ass and pretty much every other part of you. Do I make myself clear?"

She opens and closes her mouth to say something, but nothing comes out.

"It's way more fun to enjoy the ride and stop fighting me on this."

She closes her eyes and tilts her head back until she's leaning against Hunter's chest. *Good girl.* My best friend takes advantage of her free-falling at my mercy to capture her mouth as I zero in on her clit. I stick out my tongue and rub her around and around, ramping her up, pushing her towards an explosive orgasm.

"I'm going to lose it," she cries out as she bucks her hips into my mouth while pushing on the back of my head. I'm trapped between her thighs and there's nowhere else I'd rather be. "Oh."

"Don't hold back," I order before clamping my lips around her throbbing clit.

She arches her back, pushing herself towards me even more, allowing me to tease her mercilessly. *Fuck, this is hot.* I'm grunting like an animal, Allison is panting like a desperate woman and Hunter is groaning like a beast. We're all lost into this deliciously decadent moment. All consumed by one thing—seeking and taking pleasure.

"Good Lord, your nipples are so hard, I don't know how long my cock can take this."

Although I'm solely focused on tongue-fucking her, I can still hear the impatient tone in my best friend's voice. Suddenly, Hunter steps away from Allison and the next thing I hear is him sucking and lapping at her tits. The harder he sucks the more Allison shivers, and the more both of them moan the more turned on I become.

"Oh, yeah. I could lose myself between your tits and never come up for air for the rest of my life."

Hunter's words set me off and I increase my cadence, flicking her clit over and over again. I grab her round ass with both hands and I spread open her cheeks before slapping them back together.

"Yes, yes, yes. Do it again."

I nod before repeating my kinky play, but this time I up the ante. I lick and suck and kiss her pussy with such carnal desire while I repeatedly slap her ass cheeks together. *Damn.* It's as if it's the first time I've tasted her. I swirl my tongue around her clit, toying with her, torturing her little nub. *Oh, yeah, you're going to come hard for me.* She nearly loses it when I push my tongue inside her wet pussy, thrusting in and out. She moans and cries and bucks into my mouth as I devour her inexorably.

"Jake... Please... Please... Don't stop."

I ease the pressure to give her time to catch her breath. When her body slumps into my hands, I pick up where I left off. I trace around her pussy with my finger, rimming the edge of her needy hole until I dip two fingers deep inside her. *Holy Christ.* Ali's muscles clamp around me as if she has no intention of ever letting me go. *She's close.*

"I know you're about to lose your mind."

"I can't take this anymore," she begs, shaking her head as if that will deter me.

"Jake, make her come so hard she forgets her own name." Hunter has been so busy claiming her tits, it's as if he's lost his power of speech until now.

Not that I need any encouragement from my friend, but seeing how lost he is in the moment doubles my determination to give Ali the most mind-blowing climax of her life. I slide my free hand up her stomach, caressing the suppleness of her skin until I reach the back of her waist, pulling her forcefully towards me as I deliver a final blow—I press her clit between my lips and I squeeze hard. Her whole body convulses and she screams out my name as her orgasm takes over her body, sending waves of spasms throughout her entire being.

She's trembling so hard I wrap my arms around her hips to calm her down.

"It's okay, baby, it must have been really good," I tease as I lick my bottom lip, still glistening with the juices from her climax.

"You... You... I can't believe you did it again."

I don't even need to look up to know she's come undone, but my raging erection is begging for relief and it's high time for me to fuck her and to watch my best friend take her. I get back up on my feet and flash her a victorious smile. Hunter is still angled to the side sucking hard on her left tit, but obviously, his impatience is growing as much as mine. He's rubbing furiously at his exposed cock while his tongue flickers the peak of Allison's nipple. *When the hell did he whip it out?*

"Why don't we take this inside? If we continue out here, we might get in trouble."

"But I thought no one would walk in on us."

"Yeah, but if you continue to scream your head off, your voice will be heard at the next ranch several acres away." She rolls her eyes when she realizes I'm teasing her. "Come on, Hunter, zip it up and let's go inside." Reluctantly, my friend unwraps his lips from her breast and when he does, Allison falters backward, nearly falling. I grab her before she loses her balance. "Are you okay?"

"All of this is making me dizzy," she says with a smile.

"We don't have to continue if it's too much."

"We don't? Buddy, maybe we should make these types of decisions together." Hunter is shoving his cock back into his jeans and flashes me a panicked look that suggests I've lost my head.

"Remember, we want this to be as enjoyable for her as it is for us. If it's too much, we should slow things down."

"I want to go all the way. I don't want to stop now," she blurts out.

"Are you sure?"

She nods emphatically. I smash my lips into hers, forcing her to taste her climax still lingering on my mouth, and she purrs.

I'm doing my best to seem cool and collected here, but her words unleash something so raw in me. I simply growl before lifting her and throwing her over my shoulder.

"Wait. We can't leave my underwear and my dress outside as telltale signs of our evening. What happens when your workers come in tomorrow?"

"You're right. Let's not take chances." I march towards my house and turn to face Hunter. "What are you waiting for? Grab Ali's dress and her underwear before coming upstairs. She wants both of us," I say, smacking her ass and kissing her round ass cheek.

CHAPTER SEVEN

ALLISON

Jake kicks open the door to his bedroom and marches straight to his large California king bed. He tosses me on to the mattress so hard I squeal as I bounce, my hair whipping into my face. I brush my mane back to see Hunter walking into the room and standing next to Jake. His eyes zero right between my legs, which are spread wide open.

"Hot damn. Are you ready, girl?" he asks, removing his cowboy boots.

Without even waiting for my approval, Hunter strips out of his shirt, his jeans and his boxer briefs while holding my gaze. He leaps onto the bed like a superhero and lands right next to me. He rolls to the side and folds his arm under his head, caressing the side of my body.

"I love every curve on your body."

"You're just saying that." I laugh.

"I think both Jake and I have proven time and time again how much we can't get enough of you, but if you insist, we're more than willing to show you again." He smiles.

"Well, I wouldn't say no," I tease.

"I'm happy to oblige." He flashes me a cocky grin before climbing on top of me, covering my body with his own. "I think it's my turn now to taste your pussy since that one over there," he says, pointing his chin at Jake, "has already gorged his fair share."

Hunter slides his body down before settling between my legs. Heat radiates through me as he crushes my swollen boobs under the weight of his muscular physique. Jake casts upon me a dark and lustful glance. Even though Hunter's large frame hides his erection, I'm pretty certain he's extremely turned on.

Hunter must sense my moment of distraction because he cups my chin in his strong hands, forcing me to look at him. "Don't worry about him. He gets off from watching me do dirty things to you. And you know what?"

"What?" The word comes out so softly I'm surprised Hunter hears it.

"I enjoy doing the most unspeakably raunchy things under his watchful eye. It gets me extremely turned on to know he's observing me while I give you pleasure."

"Oh, he's really going to just stand there?"

Although I'm speaking to Hunter, my eyes are glued on the tall, silent hunk in the room.

"Uh-huh. He may be so inclined to boss me around a little bit, because it also turns him on when he uses my tongue, my cock or my fingers as an extension of his own. I'm sure you're going to enjoy hearing him command me as much as I'll get off from doing all the stuff he's going to ask me to do to you."

As if to prevent me from asking any further questions, Hunter works his way down my neck and he moves lower, capturing one of my boobs in his mouth and circling my hard nipple with his tongue, sending delicious shivers of anticipation through my body.

"Ahhhh." I close my eyes, savoring the moment, enjoying his body and his mouth on me.

"I want you to suck her tit while you grope the other one and make her moan. Loudly."

My eyes pop open with Jake's first command. He's looking down at me with a side grin on his face. He's so in control.

"Jake, come here." I reach out for him but he's too far for me to touch him. I guess he'll decide when he's ready to come closer. "It's not fair if Hunter and I are naked and you're still fully clothed."

"Sweetness, don't worry about me. Focus on what I'm about to tell him to do to you."

My mouth gapes open at his answer. No matter how much I rack my brain, it's impossible for me to come up with a reply. *Damn.*

"Oh, God," I squeal when Hunter pinches my nipple with one hand and bites down against the peak in his mouth.

"Good." Jake's mouth curls with satisfaction.

"Allison, I can't tell you how hard I was watching Jake eat your pussy. It was so fucking hot," Hunter whispers, kissing his way down my stomach.

The closer he gets to my pussy, the more I ache for him.

Suddenly, Hunter pulls me down the bed until my ass meets the edge. He slides my legs over his shoulders and hoists my bottom into the air. *Shit.* I watch in amazement with my lips slightly parted as he spreads my lips and lowers his mouth to my throbbing pussy.

"Jesus…" As his tongue skates around my wetness, I'm shocked by how ready I am for another orgasm. The pressure gathering between my legs is uncomfortable. *How can these men keep doing this to me?*

"Make her squirm even more." Jake delivers another command. I turn my head towards him to catch him fumbling with his belt. *He wants to come and play with us.*

When Hunter's tongue runs along the length of my slit I cry out, closing my eyes and arching my back. *This is too good.* At that moment, I realize how wholly at their mercy I am. Jake is throwing out one salacious command after another, and Hunter is only too happy to satisfy his best friend's kinks.

"Flick her tight little nub. I want to see her ass yank off the mattress as she's unable to withstand your teasing."

Right on cue, Hunter continues torturing me, this time pausing to inflict more pleasure and pain by flicking my hard node, sending a surge of electricity throughout my entire body.

"Holy mother of—"

"Look at you, you're enjoying Hunter's mouth on you. You like how he's lapping at your clit, teasing it, squeezing it."

It's nearly impossible for me to think straight, especially now that Jake is removing his tee shirt before pulling down his jeans, revealing a monster erection. *He's huge. Much bigger than I've seen him so far.* He stands there with a devilish grin plastered across his face like a modern god expecting me to worship him. Instinctively, I reach out my hand, desperate to feel his fullness in my palm, but he simply looks down at me, shaking his head.

"Tsk, tsk, tsk, not yet. I've told you before, you're too impatient."

"But…"

"But nothing. Enjoy the ride for now. I'll fill you up soon," he says, raising his eyebrow.

I'm still whimpering at Jake's refusal to indulge me, but Hunter's voice pulls me back to him.

"Come in my mouth, Allison."

"Ohhhhh." I close my eyes when Hunter squeezes my clit gently between his lips.

I have little say in this. Hunter will do whatever it takes for me to come undone all over his face.

"Will you do that for me?" His voice is laced with restrained hunger as his eager tongue probes at me before he thrusts it in.

"Don't make her come just yet, buddy. I have other plans for her first."

I turn my head in the direction of Jake's voice and I exhale at the sight. He's a magnificent man.

"No problem. I'll keep pushing her further and further until she thinks she's about to explode and then I'll take it all away from her." Hunter's unmistakable bad-boy smile suggests he wouldn't hesitate one second to torment me like this.

"I like the way you think. I want to fuck her mouth with my cock and have her come all over your tongue while she's swallowing the creamy load I'll shoot down her throat."

"Mmmm." Hunter hums against my clit and my eyes nearly roll into the back of my head.

Jake's words and Hunter's grunt detonate something inside me and my short-lived worry about being with two men at the same time vanishes. Greedily, I want it all—Hunter's cock inside me, Jake's in my mouth, their hands all over me and me screaming as I free-fall into ecstasy. If they want to claim my ass, I wouldn't object. I can't. I belong to both these hunks.

My eyes are fixated on Hunter's bobbing head when I notice from the side Jake's hand moving rhythmically with his best friend's movements. When I turn, I gasp, stunned. I can read in his glee the same carnal desire I saw in his eyes a few days ago when he last ravished me and pushed me off the cliff of reason right into the total abandonment of a sweet climax. Hunter yanks his body up and instead of his tongue, he glides the tip of his cock up and down my pussy. *Shit, shit, shit.* Feeling his slippery dick against my hard node is a new and surreal experience for me.

"Your pussy is so warm and sweet," he growls.

The intensity is so heavy that I try reaching for his shoulder to slow things down, but Jake steps forward and grabs my hand and holds it. "No, you don't, Ali. I'm the one who decides when you've had enough. Hunter will keep at it until I decide otherwise," he orders.

He steps back and his best friend picks up where he had left off. I close my eyes, hoping I can block out the wave mounting in me, but it's impossible. *Too much. God, this is too much.*

"Oh, shit," Jake growls.

I peer open my eyes and I turn my head in his direction. There stands the other Adonis who's about to rock my world, stroking his thick and long shaft while holding my gaze. Watching him play with his perfect cock while Hunter's dick is skating around my clit is more than my body and my mind can bear. My body trembles and just as I'm about to come, Jake approaches the bed with his eyes locked on me, still gripping his cock.

"Move down, I need to fuck her mouth."

Oh God.

Hunter lets go of his dick and grins at me before sliding down to his knees. My eyes are still focused on Jake, but Hunter breaks the trance.

"Allison, has one of your teenage boyfriends ever fucked your mouth?"

Hunter's question instantly makes me blush. Sure, I've given awkward blowjobs, but I had never seen a man fuck a woman's mouth until last night when I was surfing porn sites. There's something so submissive, so wrong and so dirty about how powerfully a man can thrust in and out of your mouth. I still remember how wet I was just watching a woman on her knees with a man fisting her hair and forcing his huge cock in and out of her mouth. She sobbed with joy, at the mercy of her lover.

"No," I let out shyly.

"Have you ever swallowed before?"

Jake's question shifts my eyes to him and I simply stare, unable to answer. At this moment, I realize how inexperienced I am with men. The boys I've dated so far never had the brazen attitude these two hunks have. They're both walking sex gods and they know it.

"We've got a virgin on our hands. Fuck her good, buddy."

Jake nods at his best friend before crawling onto the bed and positioning himself at my shoulders. He sits on his knees right above my boobs. He leans his body towards me with his already erect shaft bobbing a few inches from my mouth, taunting me.

I never take the lead when it comes to blow-jobs. I always let the guy dictate what he expects of me, too afraid of screwing things up, but Jake's cock is so magnificent, I reach out unabashed and grasp it in my hand and I begin to stroke him from base to tip.

"You're so eager, sweetness."

Instead of answering, I circle my lips with my wet tongue, already anticipating the moment he dominates me.

"I can't wait for your pout to be wrapped around my cock."

"Uh-huh. Me too, because I can't get enough of your cock," I respond suggestively.

"Watch out, the vixen is out and she wants to play," he says, smiling at me. Even in this dim light, his hungry blue eyes are sparkling.

I shut him up quickly when my thumb skates over the head of his cock, smearing a bead of moisture along the tip. Jake moans softly, tilting his head back. He rewards me by rocking inside my hand. I've never seen a man look at me the way he does now—unrestrained, passionate and ravenous.

My attention is pulled from him to Hunter as he pumps two fingers in and out of me, taking me voraciously. "Fuck, it's so hot seeing you on top of her like this," he grunts, as he increases the speed of his thrusts.

"Keep working her pussy while I keep her mouth occupied." One dirty-talking man is one thing, but the two of them together are an outrageous turn-on.

As difficult as it is to focus my attention on Jake's cock again, I grip him tighter.

"Open wide, baby," he commands. I part my lips and I gently urge him closer to me by pulling his dick towards me until it's in line with my mouth. "Come on, take me in."

I lift my head and I stick out my tongue and circle the head of his cock. *Oh, yeah.* I flick at the tip and I lap at the moisture dripping down his shaft. Jake moves his arms behind him and cups my boobs possessively. He alternates between caressing me and pinching my nipples tight.

"Argh," I let out as the intoxicating waves of pleasure and pain pulse through me.

Hunter is still playing with my clit and when he clamps his lips around my throbbing nub, I know I'm close.

"Come for me, Allison."

The murmur of Hunter's smoky voice acts like rocket fuel. I nearly scream when Hunter's tongue thrusts into me while his fingers are still pumping in and out of me, but Jake pushes his shaft deep inside my mouth, his cock muffling the sound of this exquisite sexual gluttony.

Fucking Lord. One of them is controlling my orgasm while the other is forcing me to give him pleasure. Everything about these two men is so carnal, so sexual and so raw. Hunter's hands are all over me, touching, caressing, groping, bringing me closer and closer to my breaking point. This is so overwhelming I'm barely able to focus on anything else.

"Hunter is so good you almost forgot about me?"

A tinge of guilt washes over me and I steady myself, shifting my attention to the man rolling my nipples between his fingers. I work harder to please him, one hand at the base of his shaft tightening around him and working in unison with my mouth as if I'm begging Jake to come gushing down my throat. *Oh, yes.* As Jake rocks against my mouth, I began to buck against Hunter's thrusting tongue, the three of us unified in an unspoken commitment to reach the peak of orgasm together.

"Ali, baby, do you want me to come in your mouth?" Jake looks down at me, searching my eyes.

I squeeze his cock hard and pull him deeper into my mouth. When he touches the back of my throat, I shut my eyes, surprised, but I never let go. I slide my free hand under his balls and cup them tight. His cock throbs before a warm explosion erupts, hitting my tongue with incredible force. I struggle to swallow him, since this is my first time, but I manage. He watches me with eyes half closed as I lap the last few drops of his orgasm that had escaped and he smiles at my enthusiasm.

"For someone who's never had a man come inside her mouth, you're enjoying yourself a lot," he mocks.

"Mmm-hmm."

I would have done just about anything to avoid having a man come inside my mouth, but Jake's cum leaves me begging for more.

My victorious moment is short-lived. As I scoop up the last few drops of Jake, Hunter's tortuous combination of tongue and fingers pinching my clit contribute to my demise.

"Ahhhh. I'm coming," I whisper, closing my eyes and tilting my head back against the mattress. "Oh, God, I'm coming." I fist the blanket under me, hoping to tame the mounting wave, but I'm only kidding myself. As my orgasm takes over, Jake scoots down my body before lowering his head and sucking at my left boob while Hunter pushes me further and further. My mind goes blank and there's only one thing that matters—the frenzied climactic pulsations rippling through my body.

My eyes are still shut, but Jake's weight shifts off of me.

"You got her good."

"I did, didn't I? Seems like she made you come real hard as well."

"Yeah. Ali gave me a core-shaking blowjob. She's not as innocent as she looks, buddy."

I can't put my finger on it, but there's something so perverted about the two of them talking about me as if I'm not here listening to them plot their next naughty move.

"I agree." Hunter groans as he still laps at my pussy before slowly sliding my legs from his shoulders and laying them on Jake's bed. I'm trying desperately to regain my breath, but the minute Hunter's lips claim mine as his rock-solid cock slides between my legs, I know this ride isn't over.

His naked dick is teasing at my drenched pussy, probing at the opening, begging to be let in. He slips his tongue inside my mouth, inviting me to taste my own juices. Until I started having sex with these two, I had never tasted myself, but now I find it strangely salacious.

"Hmmm," I hiss when he releases my lips.

"Hunter, sheathe your cock and fuck her. I'll watch."

Both Hunter and I turn over. Jake is staring down at his growing erection. "Take her now or else I will."

Holy shit, the man is commanding.

Hunter shakes his head and moves his attention to me. "Don't worry. I'll take care of her." He places two fingers under my chin, forcing me to look at him. "You heard the man."

"Uh-huh," I manage to answer, still stunned by Jake's dominating nature.

Hunter catches the condom Jake throws at him with one hand, unwraps the packet and slides the rubbery shield on. I brace myself, but Hunter is still teasing me. I'm not sure if he's trying to tempt me further or if he's hoping to flare up Jake's impatience, but he slides his cock along my wet slit and any hesitations I might have about him taking me as Jake watches dissipate like morning fog under the rising sun.

"So you're ready to become a bad girl?"

"I think I already crossed that line a few days ago." I wink.

"Look at you."

I return his smile and I shrug, proud of my daring repartee.

"You're right. Jake's already seen me bring you to orgasm and I could tell he loved every minute of it," Hunter responds as he plunges his very large cock inside me. In this position, he seems even bigger than he did when he had me on my stomach.

"Oh."

"Am I going too fast?"

"You're so…"

"Big? I know." He grins. "We'll take it slow."

Hunter pushes himself in inch by inch. With every thrust a soft groan escapes his lips. His face is unrecognizable. When I was on my stomach a few days ago inside the cabin, it was impossible for me to catch every sinful expression on his face, but lying on my back with him on top of me like this engrossed in taking pleasure between my legs is a powerful aphrodisiac. *I never knew a man could react this way to me.*

He eases himself into me while still locking eyes with me. And although we're staring at each other so passionately, it's impossible for me to forget the other handsome guy in the room. At some point, Jake moves, but I'm too taken by this moment to look away. Hunter's slow cadence is driving me nearly insane and I buck under him in an attempt to force him to fuck me harder and deeper.

"No, you don't." Hunter shakes his head, refusing to allow me to control things. "Why are you in a rush? I want to feel every inch of me slide inside your warm pussy."

"Hunter, you're killing me here," I grumble.

"Hunter, why make her suffer any longer?" Jake is sitting on a large chair in the corner of his room fully naked, his legs spread open, his cock fully erect and his eyes on me.

Hunter slams the rest of his long cock into me, making me scream out. *Shit.* My nails dig into his lower back in an attempt to curtail the pleasure. "Oh. My. God."

"What? I gave you what you wanted, didn't I?"

I open my mouth to respond, but anything I was going to say gets cut off when his lips crush mine. I lose myself in his kiss as he devours me ravenously. I begin to follow Hunter's cadence, our bodies rocking in unison, giving and receiving unbridled pleasure.

"I don't know what's more mind-blowing, my tongue inside your pussy or my cock pounding you."

His words detonate a combustion within me that would put any volcano to shame. Hunter picks up his tempo and Jake chokes off a groan. I shift my eyes from the man fucking me to the other one and gasp. Jake is vigorously stroking his cock with his right hand. *Sweet baby Jesus.* I'm so turned on, I squeeze my legs around Hunter's waist and I press down against his cock, clenching hard as I grit my teeth.

"Christ, Allison." Hunter tilts his head backwards when the jolt hits him.

"I don't know if I can handle any more," I sob.

"Oh, I know you can. I fucked you harder inside the cabin and I'm only getting started here." He puts his weight on me as if to trap me in place and he rams into me as if he's on a mission.

I gasp for air, reaching over my head to cling onto the blankets, but Hunter's frantic pounding is so overwhelming I find it impossible to hold on. "Dear God."

"I can't even begin to tell you how amazing it is to watch Hunter fuck the hell out of you. Take her harder, Hunter."

The words are still hanging thick in the room when Hunter doubles his efforts at making me lose my mind while his best friend gives out another dirty command.

I pivot my head to meet Jake's stare. *Mother of God.* Watching Jake stroke his cock while Hunter rides me heightens the fire burning inside me to unbearable heights. Jake is sliding his tight fist from his balls to the tip of his cock, squeezing just enough to allow a few drops of his pre-cum to escape. He reaches to a side table and grabs a small bottle and pours a translucent liquid all over his cock. *Oil?* Jake's eyes are dark and impenetrable. He strokes his cock with one hand while squeezing his glistening balls with the other, all the while grunting and yanking his hips up in the air.

"Oh, God, I'm so fucking hard," he lets out in a low growl.

Everything about this moment is so hedonistic that if I could extend my hand far enough while Hunter is still lodged inside me and scoop a few drops of Jake's cum running down his shaft, I would. For now, I can only content myself by watching him pleasure himself as I near the edge of reason.

"Ahhh." I clench my pussy tight around Hunter's cock as Jake's words send a current through me. "Fuck, I'm going to come."

"Argh," Hunter grunts, turning his focus onto his best friend.

These two are going to make me lose my mind.

"Oh," I let out as the buildup that precedes a mind-blowing orgasm takes over my body. "Fuck, this is it."

The room is filled with the sounds of our carnal debauchery and each grunt takes me closer to the edge. *This is a surreal experience.*

"I'm coming, I'm coming, I'm coming," I chant, my eyes still glued on the blue-eyed lover sitting in the corner of the room.

"Don't hold back, Ali," he says, stroking his hand up and down his shaft.

"Allison, I'm close." Hunter is panting on top of me, trying to slow down his breathing with every thrust.

I turn my attention away from Jake and lose myself in Hunter's lustful eyes.

"God, this is too much."

"Allison, come with me."

As if Hunter's words aren't potent enough, Jake roars like an animal as he strokes his cock faster and faster. His eyes are half closed and he's biting his lower lip with such force I fear he'll draw blood. He strokes his cock rhythmically, matching Hunter's thrusts, and he comes screaming and convulsing all over the chair he's been sitting on. He slides his fist, pressing down against his balls, and he squirts out his cum halfway across the room.

Unable to withstand any more raunchiness, I close my eyes and I succumb to a climax so powerful it's as my heart stops for a split second as my pussy clenches around Hunter's cock.

"Jesus!" I scream aloud as my pussy throbs violently from the most powerful of my three orgasms of the night.

Hunter yanks up my limp body closer to his and he pounds harder into me one last time.

"Fuck, Allison." Hunter screams out my name as he collapses on top of me.

All the grunting, pounding, moaning and yelling stops. I'm breathing heavily, trying to slow down my heart rate. Even though I'm lying on my back, I'm so dizzy from this mind-blowing orgasm, if I wasn't holding on to Hunter so tightly, I would most likely have fainted.

These two have claimed every part of me… well, almost.

CHAPTER EIGHT

HUNTER

Allison's head is resting against my chest and her legs are sprawled across my best friend's legs. Her arms are wrapped tightly around my waist and I can feel the warmth of her breath against my skin. Her long magnificent hair is all over the place and even though I'm dying to stroke her mane, I resist because she's sleeping so peacefully.

Since Jake has passed out in a coma-like post-climactic sleep on his stomach, I can't see his face, but I'm pretty sure he has the same grin of blissful satisfaction plastered across his face as Allison does.

Damn, we worked her hard last night. I'm surprised at how far she was willing to let us push her boundaries. Both Jake and I were feral last night and we didn't allow her inexperience to slow us down.

After a few minutes of watching both of them sleep, I carefully roll to the side to look at the clock near Jake's head, conscious of not waking anyone up. *Five-thirty.* The workers will start in about an hour and Jake and I will have to go and join them. As much as I'd love nothing more than to spend the whole day taking turns at fucking Allison and also engaging in a few naughty sessions where my best friend and I take her together, we still have a ranch to manage.

Running my hand up and down Allison's side, I coax her back to life. I brush her cascading hair away from her face and I gently kiss her forehead. The contact of my lips against her skin immediately wakes her up from her stupor and I can tell from the lethargic way she's moving her body must be aching badly.

"Good morning," I whisper.

"Morning," she answers with her eyes still closed.

"Are you okay?"

"I'm not sure yet, since every muscle in my body hurts like hell." She sounds so groggy.

"Aren't you happy we took it easy on you last night?"

"Seriously? Is that what you call taking it easy?" She opens her eyes halfway and tilts her head back to look at me.

"I hate to burst your bubble, but we showed you a lot of mercy." I wink. "As much as both of us wanted to take you at the same time, we thought it would be a better idea to ease you into it. We wanted to give you a chance to discover how amazing it is to have two men be solely devoted to giving you as much pleasure as possible before taking things to the next level."

"I can't imagine what the next level feels like because right now, I feel like a steam train ran me over."

"Don't worry, you'll find out soon." My best friend rolls over with a devilish grin on his face.

"Jake, you're awake."

He nods my way. "As Hunter said, last night was a warm-up."

"So you mean next time... one of you..."

"Let's just say Hunter didn't buy the butt plug for decoration. Since you've been using it, next time one of us will claim your ass. Don't worry, we'll be gentle, we'll use lots of lube and we'll take it slow at first, but it's only when both of us take you at the same that you'll be able to really appreciate how out-of-this-world it feels when two men worship you."

"You could have at least waited for me to have my first cup of coffee before laying it on so thick."

We all laugh.

"Can you blame me for being eager? You were amazing last night." Jake turns to me. "Wasn't she?"

"She was more than amazing. Were it not for the fact we have a business to run, I'd already be inside her."

"Business? Yeah. Good point. What time is it?" Jake doesn't wait for my answer. He flips back onto his stomach and pivots his head to check out his alarm clock. "We still have time."

"I'm famished. I need a proper breakfast or I'll starve to death or worse, I'll pass out."

"Especially since this one had us all worked up last night," Jake says, pointing his chin at the siren cuddled inside my arms.

"I'm hungry as well," she says, bouncing her gaze from Jake's face to mine. "I have an idea. Since my job isn't nearly as physically demanding as yours, why don't I run downstairs? I'll get some breakfast ready for all of us."

"That sounds great," I say. "But I'm a bit disappointed. I was hoping to take a shower with you..."

"I thought you were hungry," she says with a twinkle in her eye.

"Yeah, but..."

"Hunter, look at the clock and look at the size of your dick," Jake says. "There's not nearly enough time for a proper breakfast and a proper fuck before the workers show up."

"Jeez, enough with all this dirty talk, you two," Allison says.

"You didn't seem to mind last night when we were making you come." Jake lowers his head and kisses Allison passionately while her head is still resting against my chest.

"I guess it's a little different in the morning."

"Get used to it. Neither of us are shy in expressing how we feel about you or your heart-stopping body." Jake looks up to meet my gaze and I nod in agreement.

"He's right, you know. It's just the three of us on the ranch for the next nine days and you should expect a lot of dirty-talking and a lot of sex." I grin.

"And during the day be prepared for either of us to take you whenever and wherever we want. Needless to say, nighttime is when we all get together to play at my place or at Hunter's."

"Oh, God, you are going to make me blush so hard. Okay, I have a feeling if I stay in bed sandwiched between your rock-hard bodies, you guys will start your day late."

"You're right. I know that one over there is famished, but I'd be content feasting on your ass and I'd gladly skip food." Jake swipes his tongue over Allison's lips as he gropes her tits and my cock twitches. *Damn.* Were it not for the workers showing up so early, I'd definitely go for another round after breakfast.

She gently pushes Jake away. "Why don't I run downstairs and prepare some food for all of us? What about a simple breakfast—eggs, bacon, bread and lots of strong coffee? Would that fill your stomachs and take your mind off of sex?"

"Yes to all of the above. Not sure about the last part, though." My stomach lets out a loud grumble. Both Allison and Jake look at me and I shrug apologetically. "I told you I was starved."

"I agree with Hunter. I'm all in except for the last part. With your tempting body, there isn't enough food to replace how satisfying it is for me to gorge on your juicy pussy and your heavy tits." Jake slides the sheet off his body, exposing a hard-on that puts mine to shame. Allison has such a potent effect on both of us and we're lucky that for the next few days, we get to fuck her when we want and how we want.

CHAPTER NINE

ALLISON

Since I've arrived, every morning on the ranch has been glorious, but this one is particularly spectacular. Although my body is aching and I feel like an old lady coming down Jake's staircase, I wouldn't change a thing about last night.

Sitting at Jake's island eating, laughing and joking around seems as natural as if we've been doing this every single morning for months. It's hard to believe just thirty-six hours ago Hunter presented me with a little gift and a proposal that would change me in such a transcendental way, I still struggle to find the words.

After a quick and gratifying breakfast, my two lovers pull on their rugged boots and grab their hats before running out the door to start their day. Once I've tidied up Jake's kitchen, I run back to my place to take a shower and to have a little me time. I need to be alone in my cocoon to try to make sense of how I went from having the worst luck in men to scoring big time.

Everything that's happened in the past few days has been so surreal I have to keep pinching myself to believe this is actually happening to me. My dating life has never been this exciting and it's surely never been this satisfying. Let's face it, in New York I'd have to be on the verge of a cardiac arrest to have men as strapping and handsome as Jake or Hunter look at me twice, let alone touch me, but last night I shared the most mind-altering, blissful experience of my entire life with two sex gods. Until I landed in Colorado, an orgasm was a rare occurrence, but the last few days have been one epic climax after another.

My best friend Gwyn will think I'm lying when I tell her I took her advice to heart and I did go after both heartthrobs. She'll fall off her high heels when I tell her how amazing it is to have two men solely dedicated to bringing you pleasure and I'm pretty sure her beautiful brown eyes will pop out of her skull when I share how incredibly aroused you get when you're in a room with two other people grunting. She'll definitely pass out when I explain how dirty it was when all three of us came in unison.

It's not as if she has anything to complain about because from what she's candidly shared, her fiancé is quite the stud in his own right and the times we've discussed size, it's clear Gaven is a very big boy. That may be so, but I now have a leg up on her. *I'm Miss Vanilla Sex no more.*

* * *

Around mid-afternoon, Jake drives back to Denver to meet with Filipe Moura, the owner of Churrascaria Steak House & Cellar, a prestigious high-class Brazilian steakhouse with a head office in Denver. This location is only one of many since the restaurant chain boasts a fleet of twenty-five extremely popular addresses across the country. He's confident that since this is their third meeting, he shouldn't take too long and he should be back in Fort Collins before six. Apparently Mr. Moura is extremely interested in doing business with him and Hunter. Obviously, my two guys are super excited about this opportunity because it represents another very lucrative deal—the second one in a week.

Hunter has been busy all morning with the workers. A few hours ago, he waved me goodbye from the office door before jumping on his horse and riding alongside his cattle, accompanied by Dirk Edwards, his manager, and Jenkins Williams, one of his cowboys. Most of the other workers have left for the day, but Hunter asked Dirk and Jenkins to stay behind since it's been a busy day and the animals need some exercise. I'm so grateful I had the presence of mind to run after them with my camera to capture quite a few extraordinary photos as I watched them ride a herd out in the pasture to allow the cows to roam freely.

Once I can no longer see the three men on the horizon, I turn on my heel and head back to the office. Since Riley left me so many projects to complete, I diligently work my way down this long list of priorities for the next two hours until my phone rings. I grab it from the desk hoping it might be Jake checking up on me, but it's my mom.

"Sweetie, finally. I'm able to get you on the phone."

She's been trying to reach me for a few days now, but we've been missing each other because she's in Australia with my dad visiting my brother Peter and his wife Katie. The second my brother met his wife, he knew she was the one. He fell so hard for her during his last year of college that he packed his bags and moved to the other side of the planet when it was time for her to go home to Australia. My parents visit them every couple of years and this year is particularly important since Katie gave birth six months ago and my parents have yet to meet the firstborn grandson. My oldest brother Josh's daughter Kimberly is so special to all of us, but contrary to Josh, we can't see Pete or his son at will. The only way to bond with little Samuel is to go and visit him Down Under or via Skype video chats.

Mom and Dad left before I got the big news about this incredible opportunity to work with Riley, so my mom has been getting my updates via text messages and I've been leaving really long voicemails packed with rich details about my new life.

"Mom, it's three-thirty in the afternoon here. What time is it over there? It must be the middle of the night."

"No, it's already five-thirty in the morning in Melbourne and since your little nephew wakes up before the roosters I've been up for a bit helping

Katie. The poor thing is exhausted. Being a first-time mom is hard work." My mom laughs. "Honey, I can't wait for you to meet the baby. He's perfect. He laughs all the time and he has huge green eyes like your brother. He's bald like an eagle and he's a riot. Your dad is totally in love."

"Oh, I can't wait to go to Australia either, but after the past few months, I'll need to save before I can even entertain that thought."

"Your brother's business is doing very well and he said he'll fly you over here. Not to mention, your dad is sitting on a lot of air miles. I'm sure it wouldn't take you much to twist his arm."

"You're funny. I'm sure Dad would easily cave in if I bat my eyelashes at him. Would Pete really pay for me to come visit?"

"You're his baby sister and he wants to see you. You haven't seen him for three years now."

"I know," I sigh, heavy-hearted. Since my ex wasn't much of a traveler, we stayed put in New York unless we were visiting our parents. Not to mention that Clark's expensive studies didn't leave much of a fund to explore the world. "How's Pete?"

"He misses you so much. The two of you are only ten months apart and you've grown up like twins. As much as he loves Katie and baby Samuel, he adores you."

"I miss him so much as well. We talk and we have video Skype chats, but it's not the same. If he's willing to fly me over, I'll jump on the next flight."

"He'll be thrilled when I share the good news with him. So tell me about this exciting new job of yours. I've read all your text messages and I've listened to your voicemail messages. You sound giddy. Life on a ranch must be treating you well. I haven't heard you this excited in ages."

For the next half hour I tell my mother as much as I can about the last few days since moving to Colorado. As I share my new adventure, I can't help but be in awe of all the amazing things that have happened to me. As if I weren't lucky enough, the added bonus of hooking up with two hotter-than-hell hunks is more than any girl can wish for.

"Honey, I knew you would get back on your feet after that adulterer betrayed you."

"You mean Clark?"

"Of course. What an awful man who lacks morals. Don't get me started on that woman you caught him with. You haven't heard back from him, I hope."

The vision of Clark pounding Paula in my bed flashes across my mind and I feel a twinge of fury creep up in me.

"He's been trying to catch my attention since I left him, but a few days ago I caved in and spoke to him. Unfortunately he's been bombarding me with pesky text messages today. It got so bad I was almost tempted to change my number, but then I remembered I'd have to contact everyone I know to inform them of my new number. Honestly, he's not worth it. I'll keep ignoring him. Had it not been for all of his melodrama, I would've had a pretty amazing day."

"Is he still bugging you about that ridiculous downtown office you co-signed last year?"

354 · SCARLETT AVERY

"Yup. I told him off a few days ago, but he's still at it today—with a vengeance."

"Why can't he get someone else to co-sign?"

"I haven't got a clue why he can't understand his problems are no longer mine. He's been trying to convince me to pick up my phone all day with his fake-alarming subject lines insinuating I'll regret it if I don't get back to him pronto, but I've let all his calls go to voicemail and I've deleted his text messages. I don't care if it's a matter of life and death, as he puts it. He can get support from his current girlfriend, Paula, or his business partner, Jasper."

"Good on you for moving forward. Don't let him drag you down or manipulate you like he used to."

"Nope. Don't worry. I'm done with Clark and his drama-filled life for good."

"Honey, you don't have to deal with either of those traitors for the rest of your life."

"You're right, Mom. Thank God for small favors."

"Listen, I didn't call all the way from the other side of the planet to talk about you know who. How's your day? Is it sunny out in Denver? How is it to work for a celebrity like Riley? I can't believe you're staying in a house instead of a small room. Do you like it?"

"Mom, that's a lot of questions in one sitting. And for the record, it's Fort Collins, not Denver. I'm about an hour north of the big city. It's hotter than New York here and Riley is amazing, but she's away currently."

"So you're on your own like a big girl," my mom mocks.

"Yup. I'm pretty proud, considering it's my first day managing things on my own since Riley left for LA."

"Doesn't Riley have any help on the ranch? I mean, you said she had young children."

"She has a manager and a few workers who come in daily."

Yup, I'm bypassing the handsome brother and his dangerously hot best friend who I've been fucking since I arrived. My mom and I don't have the kind of relationship where I tell her about my intimate life.

"That's good. It must be so hard on her... you know, being alone. She sounds like a strong woman. I remember you mentioning in a text she was off to California to become a judge on a reality cooking show, right?"

"Yes. She had to leave in a hurry to sit as a replacement judge on the popular TV show *Iron Skillet*."

"Wow, impressive. I love that show. I can't believe my daughter will have a link to such a prime-time show. It's too bad you couldn't go with her. Maybe you could have made a cameo appearance."

My mom sounds so excited. Had I even had the smallest part in that show, she would have contacted all of Chicago press to let them know that one of their own was on TV.

"She already has to deal with her four kids and her nanny, not to mention she put me in charge of a very important project."

Of course, I omit to tell my mom that travelling to the West Coast would have been a real bummer since it would mean being far away from Jake and Hunter and that would have prevented me from having the most mind-blowing orgasms of my life.

"Oh, do tell." My mom sounds so thrilled for me. She's never been the cool mom, the hip mom or the fashionable mom, but she's always been so supportive of all of us. I love her so much for that.

"It's never been like this in New York. I spent most of the morning taking care of emails and social media, but the last few hours have been the most exciting so far because I had to edit a series of photos for Riley's upcoming holiday cookbook. Her last holiday cookbook sold like crazy and she told me her editors have even bigger expectations for this new edition. At this rate, I'll end up editing about eighty percent of the photos since her last assistant had barely started when she decided to go on her missionary trip. Mom, I lose all track of time when I'm immersed in photography work and Riley has already declared it will be the most important part of my responsibilities."

"It sounds like you like your job."

"Mom, I don't like my job, I love it."

"Oh. my God, honey, I'm so proud of you. Do you think you might be lucky enough to find a nice young man while you're at it?"

"Mom, I'm here to work, not fall in love."

"You know what they say…"

"No, but I'm sure you're going to tell me," I say, rolling my eyes at the phone.

"It's when you least expect it that it hits you right between the eyes." I hear her slap her forehead and I can't help but laugh. "That's exactly what happened to Pete and Katie. Remember—"

"Yes, Mom, I know their love story is textbook perfect. You've recounted their fairytale so many times I know it by heart, not to mention I was there."

"Well, no need to get upset at me. I'm simply suggesting you keep the door open, because you never know. Since you seem to have the worst luck with New York men, maybe a change of scenery could be good for your career and your love life." *I don't know about my love life, but it's doing wonders for my sex life.* "I want you to be happy. After Clark and all those other losers, you deserve the best."

"I didn't know you felt that way about the guys I've dated. Why is this the first you've mentioned it?" My mom has always listened attentively to my heartbreak stories, careful to never judge.

"I never wanted to bring it up. You keep saying you're unlucky in love, but I suspect you've been doing what I did my whole life until I met your father."

"What's that?" I ask, knowing the answer before it leaves her lips.

"Settling, because you're afraid no one will want you just the way you are."

There's a heavy silence between us. My mom has told me many times she had dated the worst men hoping one of them would like her even if she didn't have a perfect body, but they never stuck around because of her own deep-seated insecurities. After she caved in and had sex with them, most would leave her. She had just about given up on love as a single woman in her early thirties when her girlfriends were married with growing families until she bumped into my dad at a wedding. She never expected my father would call her after they had exchanged phone numbers, but he invited her out for a date the very next day and the rest is history.

"When I met Michael—"

"I know the story by heart, Mom," I interrupt. "You've told me a million times about how you and Dad met."

"Fine, then. Since you seem to know it all, why don't I let you go and you can go about your day."

I'm immediately hit by a pang of guilt. "I'm sorry. I didn't mean to snap at you."

"I wasn't going to tell the whole story, Ali. I know you've heard it before. I wanted to remind you of the reason why your dad noticed me."

"Isn't it because you got smashed and you became this wild free-spirited vixen?" I tease.

"Very funny," she answers, unimpressed. "You know I can't handle more than a sip of alcohol before having a terrible headache. The reason I met your dad is because that night I didn't care anymore about impressing a guy. I went to the wedding with one intention—to have fun. I hadn't changed anything about myself and I hadn't lost a pound. Since I wasn't expecting anything, my whole demeanor changed. Your dad noticed me well before I caught him staring at me. He said he was instantly attracted to my self-confidence. I laugh every time I tell this story." She chuckles. "It wasn't confidence. God, I couldn't spell that word with Google's help. It was because I had decided to throw caution to the wind that night. You've been too serious since leaving school and then you locked yourself in a relationship by moving in with Clark. I think Colorado spells new beginnings and you should be a little more of a wild child for once in your life. You never know who's watching."

"I can't believe you said that." My mom has told me this story so many times, but today it really hits me.

"I shared that because I love you and I see myself in you, honey." Suddenly a wailing infant interrupts us. "Oh, gosh, Samuel is up again and he's not happy. Katie hasn't slept in days because your nephew is teething. Let me go take care of my grandson before he wakes up the whole neighborhood. I'll call you back later this week, but before I go, promise me you'll live more while you're in Colorado. I'm sure not much happens on a ranch located in the middle of nowhere, but maybe there's a chance one of those workers you talked about might turn out to be a flame or maybe you'll be invited to a barbeque and something magical will happen."

If you only knew.

"I promise, Mom. Kiss the baby, Dad, Pete and Katie and call me back soon. I love you."

"I love you too, honey."

After I hang up with my mom, I stare at my phone, fascinated. It's so funny she would say I need to step outside my boundaries since I never expected Jake or Hunter to live on the ranch and I surely never expected to give myself to both men. The only question eating at me is can I really like two men at the same time?

I shake my head and dive back into my work. *Everything is so good now. Why rock the boat?*

* * *

It's only when I take a break to unwind the tension building up in my shoulders from hunching over my screen and being so laser-focused that I look at the time on my iPhone. I'm surprised to see it's already five o'clock. *I need to get out of here and get some fresh air.* Instead of remaining cooped up in Riley's office behind this iMac computer until Hunter, Jake and I get together for dinner at seven-thirty, I decide to go grab a few vegetables from Riley's garden. Since she's delegated the responsibility of testing the recipes she hasn't yet tried out, I figure I should get started now because there are a lot of new recipes that will be included in the upcoming edition.

I lean down to grab my bag when my stomach reminds me I've not eaten anything since breakfast. I've been living off of ice tea, coffee and a few random snacks Riley keeps in the office since I sat my butt in this chair. Other than the few occasional bathroom runs, the short photo session when Hunter left and the call with my mom, I've been diligently focused on my work.

Yikes, I need some fuel. Fast. Before I start taking care of these new recipes, I decide to run back to my place for a quick and light snack. As much as I love cooking, the way Isadora has been pampering me since arriving is heartwarming. Before she left with Riley, she packed my fridge with enough food to last me a year.

I get up from my desk and grab my keys, my phone and my iPad. The minute I step outside, I'm reminded of the difference in temperature between the air-conditioned office and the outdoors. Even this late in the day, it's still scorching hot. I nearly sprint to my house—I'm that hungry and I want to ward off the beating sun.

When I get back to my place, I thank my lucky stars Hunter and Jake grew up in Cali and insisted on installing central air-conditioning in every one of the houses on the ranch. After rummaging through my fridge, I prepare myself a chicken salad sandwich and to be good, I add a few of the veggies Isadora packed in my fridge. It's not that I don't like vegetables, it's just that there are so many other things I prefer eating, like chips.

I pour myself some of Isadora's homemade lemonade and I grab my plate and my glass, determined to make the most out of this beautiful day by eating outside on my shaded porch. Since this is a luxury I'd never have in New York, I've made a point of sitting out here as often as I can since arriving.

When I take the first bite, I realize how hungry I really am. *God, this is the best chicken salad sandwich I've ever had.* I'm enjoying my delicious food with my eyes glued on my iPad as I catch up on my latest food porn when I notice someone moving around from the corner of my eye. At first, I ignore the person, thinking it must be one of the workers who came back, but a female voice peels my eyes away from my screen.

"Yoohoo. Oh, yoohoo!" she chants as she waves both hands above her head at the same time as she walks towards me.

I drop my sandwich, bring my right hand up to shield my eyes from the sun and squint to catch sight of the woman trying to catch my attention. *Who is it?* I stand up to get a better view. A very thin woman wearing ridiculously high heels and an impossibly short skirt is approaching my house.

Neither Jake nor Hunter mentioned a visitor, so I'm a little bit confused. *Maybe she's lost.* As I rack my brain trying to remember our early-morning conversation before my two studs started their day, I can't help but wonder if this stranger isn't trying to get directions to a nearby bed-and-breakfast.

As she gets closer, she trips and nearly falls. I bite my tongue to avoid laughing. I know it's not funny, but everything about this woman seems over the top. She must be one of those high-maintenance fashionistas who even takes a shower in her heels because she's not dressed for a vacation out in the country.

"Oh, God, it's so hot." The stranger stands at the base of the stairs leading to my porch, fanning herself and breathing heavily. "I nearly melted walking from the limousine around the premise to find someone. It's almost like a ghost town here."

No, seriously, who is this?

"May I help you?"

"Gosh, this heat is getting to my brain. I'm Lindsay. Are you Riley?" Although she's shared her name, she makes no effort to extend her hand like most people do when meeting someone new.

"No, I'm not." I guess I could make it easier on her by revealing my identity, but there's something that irks me about this woman.

"Then who are you?" Obviously my answer is displeasing to her because she looks me up and down as if evaluating a strange specimen.

For the record, you're the one who just arrived on this property. I was here first. "My name is Allison and I'm Riley's new assistant."

"Of course you are," she says, avoiding my eyes and scanning around the ranch. *What is she looking for?* She squints at the bright sun before focusing her attention back onto me again. "Which one of these belongs to Jake?"

Excuse me?

"Is there a specific reason why you're asking?" I tread carefully. "Jake hadn't mentioned I should be expecting anyone later this afternoon."

She huffs impatiently before speaking again. "You know what, it would be much easier if I spoke to him directly instead of his sister's assistant. Can you go get him?"

What? Do I look like the maid?

If she was trying to get on my good side with her snarky remarks and her demeaning side glances, she's failing badly.

"Jake is at an important meeting in Denver." I could be more accommodating and let her know he'll be coming back shortly, but I don't like anything about her and I have no intention of making her life easier. Everything about her is pissing me off right now.

"What about Hunter? Is he around?"

"He's in the field with a couple of the workers."

"Well, is there any way to get in touch with either of them?" She raises her voice slightly and puts her right hand on her waist. Her body language suggests she's utterly unimpressed by me and I'm trying her patience.

Condescending bitch! "I can certainly text both of them. Who may I say is looking for them?"

She perks up her collagen-injected lips before answering. "I guess you must have only started your job very recently, since you haven't heard about me." *Oh, no, she didn't.* "I'm Jake's girlfriend and I need help with all my luggage over there." She points a bejeweled hand at the five large suitcases sitting in the middle of the ranch baking under the sun.

Girlfriend? Is she high?

"I'm sorry, but there must be some kind of confusion."

"Honey, there's no confusion whatsoever," she retorts as quickly as if we're playing table tennis.

"I would remember if Jake had told me a visitor was coming." I carefully avoid calling her the "g" word.

"Obviously you didn't understand the first time. I'm no visitor. I'm Jake's girlfriend," she snaps as I take stock of the bright red suitcases, trying to make sense of it all. "And I'm moving in."

****

Get Your FREE SECRET Chapters!

Thank you for purchasing this romance book!

I'd love for you to lose yourself in more
sultriness, sexiness and steamy passion!

When you sign-up today, I'll send you the following
Secret Chapter for Part 3 of this serial:

Allison discovers porn sites for the first time.

*** <u>PASSWORD FOR</u> Secret Chapter Part 3:
Ali-Discovery

Note: the password is case sensitive!

Sign-up TODAY!

www.RomanceBooksRock.com

***If you've already signed-up to my list from
previous books, you can visit the same page to
download the Secret Chapters for this romance***

****

Craving More

Chapter One

I'm staring down at the blonde standing at the foot of my porch stairs who's interrupted my delightful late lunch on a splendid sunny afternoon. I'm still trying to wrap my head around her preposterous claims.

A few minutes ago, I was basking in the afterglow of an incredible day that started in the arms of two of the most seductive men I have ever met in my life and now I'm staring into the furious eyes of a woman who's come out of nowhere and says she's Jake's girlfriend. To make matters worse, the over-dressed, over-sexualized and over-the-top woman whose red luggage is sitting in the middle of the ranch declares she's moving in.

I've been here for several days and there's never been talk of any Lindsay—not once.

I try my darnedest to remember if I had the girlfriend talk with Jake and Hunter, but for some reason I've been under the impression they were both single. Isn't that what Riley was lamenting when I first arrived? Now I'm faced with the fact I wasn't inquisitive enough before jumping into bed with two strapping hunks. *Is she really Jake's girlfriend? And is she moving in?* Surely Jake or Hunter would have mentioned something this morning before going about their day.

I'm sure I'm gaping in shock and I fail to find the words to continue this ridiculous conversation. I guess I really have no right to claim either man, but after last night's toe-curlingly raunchy ride where I shared both men, standing here in front of this brash woman who's looking to put an end to a good thing, I can't contain the wave of jealousy inside me.

I need to compose myself. Fast. I don't want to give Lindsay the satisfaction of knowing her words have crushed me. How stupid could I have been? How could I have believed either of these men could be mine, let alone both?

Since I arrived at the ranch, my life has been a rollercoaster of hedonism. On my first night, Jake seduced me and I simply couldn't resist him. The next day, although I had promised myself it would never happen again, I allowed him to take me in a secluded barn with my arms and legs shackled in ropes—bound like a dirty girl. To make matters worse, I had sex with Jake's best friend on the same day inside the cabin.

I blame years of neglect for my promiscuous actions. It's as if my body was dictating and my mind simply gave in to my sexual urges.

Then how do I explain last night since I gave myself freely to both of them? My God, Jake stroked his cock while watching Hunter fuck me and I enjoyed every second of it. I could've walked away at any time after the men made their intentions clear, but deep down inside I wanted both of them—together. Does it mean Lindsay is here to sabotage my perfect life?

She purses her lips before speaking again. "I'm sorry, are you just going to stand there staring at me or are you going to get your phone and text either Jake or Hunter? I'm melting out here and I need to get off my feet. Not to mention I'm thirsty and I'm starving."

The bitchy blonde's remark wakes me up from my shocked state and forces me to pay attention to her again. I look Lindsay up and down with an expression that's one part surprise and one part may-I-vomit-now, but I decide to keep my feelings to myself.

"I apologize. It's been a very long day. I'm sure you must be tired. Why don't I text Hunter and Jake to find out when they'll be back," I answer in a softer tone. "Perhaps I can take you to Riley's office and you could wait there while one of them gets back to me. It's cooler and you'll be able to sit."

I turn on my heel and approach the table where I was eating to grab my phone. I could invite her to sit on my porch, but there's no way I can be next to this woman without dissolving. She'll see right through me and she'll know her arrival is causing me grief.

I furtively look at her from the side and bite my lower lip. I'm nothing like her, but Jake said the most incredible things about my body.

Confusion and worry creep up as I'm faced with the brutal reality Lindsay might be here to burst my bubble. I grab my iPhone and search for Hunter's name. *Thank God we exchanged phone numbers yesterday.* I could text Jake instead, but I'm hoping Hunter might be able to make sense of things before my drop-dead-gorgeous blue-eyed lover comes back from his business meeting in Denver.

Lindsay is still fanning herself and I'm just about to dial Hunter's number when all of a sudden he strides towards my house. When the thin blonde follows my gaze and sees him approaching, she throws her hands up in the air and starts running towards him like a child greeting a loved one.

"Hunter, it's me."

I haven't got the slightest clue how that woman is able to run in her five-inch heels in such a skin-tight skirt, but she meets Hunter halfway. She jumps into his arms, but something is off. Usually when you're happy to see someone, you greet them with open arms before embracing them. Hunter is standing with his arms pinned at his sides as Lindsay twines herself around him like a koala bear hugs a tree. The way she's squeezing him, it almost looks like he's choking. His eyes are bulging and when he meets mine it's as if they're saying, *What the fuck?*

"Lindsay. What are you doing here? And why is there bright red luggage in the middle of our ranch?" he says, frowning down at her.

Since I'm frantically trying to understand who this woman is and if she's telling the truth, I take several steps closer to be in earshot of their conversation. I know I might be a bit neurotic about this, but I just can't help myself. I have no intention of sharing either Jake or Hunter with this woman.

"Hunter. Seriously, you didn't think it was over between Jake and I. I understand he doesn't want to move back to San Francisco, and I respect that. So after a lot of soul-searching, I decided to quit my job and give up my apartment. I put most of my stuff into storage and I packed a few belongings to move in with him. Before we take our relationship to the next level, we have to at least live in the same city, right?" She looks so smug and so proud of herself. Honestly if I could bitchslap her right now, I would.

"I'm really happy about this newfound sense of direction, Lindsay, but did you discuss any of this with Jake before arriving?"

"You look as dumbfounded as Riley's new assistant," she says, pointing at me." *I hate her.* "Sometimes you have to take the bull by the horns in order to get what you want in life. Right now, I want Jake and I want us back together as a couple. Scratch that, I need us back together again."

Oh, God. I think I'm going to puke.

CHAPTER TWO

HUNTER

I'm approaching the ranch with Dirk and Jenkins in tow when a limo drives off.

Jake and I asked both men to stay later tonight since we have another cow about to calve. Jezebel, the expecting mom, has been very temperamental all day yesterday and all day today. It's only a matter of time before she calves and having my manager and an extra worker on staff for a few additional hours will make my job much easier.

My intention is to go back to the office, but when I see that long black limousine, I'm curious to find out who's arrived. Since we aren't expecting any visitors, I tell the boys to come get me if Jezebel gives any signs of calving while I go to check up on things. Since Allison is still a newcomer, I want to make sure she doesn't have to deal with any unforeseen situations.

I don't know whom I expect to see, but I sure as hell never imagined Lindsay would be standing there chatting it up with Allison.

The minute I see her bright red luggage parked in the middle of our ranch, I know we're in for trouble. Don't get me wrong, Lindsay is a charming woman in her own way. I wouldn't say we're friends, but the few times I've hooked up with her and Jake in Denver to party, I had fun. When you get a few drinks into her, she even lightens up. She's extremely sexy and from what Jake has shared she's pretty hot in the bedroom, but she's a handful. I'm sure one day she'll meet the perfect guy she can walk all over, but at the best of times she acts like a prima donna and at her worst, Lindsay can be a real bitch.

Jake always met her in Denver when she came to visit him, at a hotel not far from the airport. He most likely talked about our ranch during the time they were seeing each other, but he's been careful to never bring Lindsay around. He was afraid once she set foot on our property, she'd cling on to him for dear life, never wanting to leave.

Now she's holding on to me as if she's drowning and I can tell from Allison's unimpressed gaze the two women aren't likely to get along. I push Lindsay slightly away from me so I can breathe again.

"How did you find the ranch?"

"Oh, that was easy." She takes a step back and looks up at me with a beaming smile. "When I got into Jake's truck to go for dinner a few months before he decided he needed a bit of space"—a whole lot of space, to be exact—"I noticed some documents on the dashboard while he was getting gas. I casually opened them and I saw the name of your ranch and the address. I made a mental note and I took a snapshot with my phone for good measure. And here I am."

Sneaky. "It might've been a better idea for you to give him a heads-up before showing up."

"Perhaps I should've warned him, but I think my being here will help us make some decisions about the direction of our relationship."

I think Jake is very clear where this relationship is headed. "Lindsay, you must know Jake well enough by now to know he's not a fan of surprises."

"He hasn't been returning my calls and my text messages. I got fed up, so I decided drastic measures would force him to listen. We were a great couple and I know if I'm close by we'll be able to rekindle our romance. After all, he can't keep ignoring me if I'm right in his face."

Wow, is she ever in for a rude awakening.

The last thing Jake expects is a possessive ex-girlfriend desperately trying to weave her way back into his life. When he sees her, all hell will break loose.

"I was telling Riley's assistant over there," she says, pointing at Allison, who still has this bewildered look on her face, "that my feet are hurting, I'm starving and I'm dying of thirst, but she's been very unhelpful. I had to press her twice before she finally made the effort to let you and Jake know I'd arrived. Why don't you show me to Jake's house and I can wait for him there," she purrs, sliding her hand up my chest. "Maybe I can wait for him under the covers… if you know what I mean." She flashes a grin and when I catch Allison's nauseated expression, I nearly burst out laughing. *Nope, these two aren't going to be best friends—ever.*

There's no way in hell I'm going to get in trouble with my best friend. I'm playing it safe until I get him on the phone.

"I'm happy you met Allison. She's a fantastic new addition to our little family and she's been a god-send to Riley. To be fair, she didn't expect you and neither did we. Why don't I take you to our office and you can cool off while we wait for Jake to come back? He should be back from a business meeting in Denver any moment now."

"That one said the same thing," Lindsay me-ows, pointing at Allison again, "but the way she delivered her message made me think she was brushing me off with some bullshit story."

To this day, I have no idea how Jake managed to date Lindsay for five months. I would've strangled her within five hours. She's way too high-maintenance for me and I think the only reason my best friend stayed that long was because her pussy was lethal and she was open to just about anything. It's not entirely Jake's fault since Lindsay played her cards right. She didn't reveal her catty side until Jake started to think there might be a future with her. The second she had any leverage on him, she turned like the wind.

"Let's seek shelter from this sun and I'll get you some ice tea to quench your thirst."

"That sounds absolutely wonderful," she says, wrapping her arm around mine. "Wait, what about my luggage? Can you bring my suitcases to Jake's house?"

I'm not your manservant and furthermore Jake would kill me with his own two hands.

"Your luggage is safe right where it is. I'd rather Jake make that decision once you speak to him."

"What are you saying? Jake won't be happy to see me?" She looks alarmed and I backtrack.

"It would be presumptuous of me to speak on his behalf, that's all."

There's no way I'm touching that question with a ten-foot pole. Lindsay is manipulating her way into Jake's bed and knowing him, he'll be extraordinarily ticked off. I turn around and call out to Allison, conscious of the fact she's been witnessing this whole conversation without a word. I'm sure it must come as a shock to her given what we shared last night. While Jake and Lindsay duke it out, I'll have to explain things to her so she knows Jake hasn't been playing her for a fool. "Why don't you join us?"

She jerks her head back as if my question hits her across the face and points at her chest, as if someone else is standing next to her. "You want me to follow? Oh, I still have so much to do before dinner."

I can tell from her expression she's lying and I can't help but smile. "I think your work can wait," I say, gesturing at her to tag along. "While Lindsay cools off, maybe you and I can talk?"

She grabs her keys and her phone. "Fine. I'll come," she lets out like a very pissed-off teenager.

382 · SCARLETT AVERY

We're making our way to the office when
Jake's Range Rover comes raging down the road. I
can tell from his expression how annoyed he is by our
unexpected visitor. *This isn't going to end well.*

Lindsay immediately lets go of my hand and
races to meet my best friend. *Holy hell, that must be
the shortest skirt in history.* I didn't appreciate how
revealing her skirt was when I first approached her
because I was too puzzled by her presence on our
land, but now, watching her run away from me, I'm
sure if I cock my head to the side, I'll catch a glimpse
of her panties... or lack thereof.

Jake comes to a screeching stop, cuts off the
engine and gets out of his vehicle. The minute he
slams the door shut behind him, Lindsay starts cam-
paigning like a politician seeking more votes.

"Oh, snookums, I've missed you so much,"
she says, jumping in my best friend's arms.

Jake is so taken aback he doesn't react when
the blonde slams her chest into his. One would think
it's a joyous reunion, but the fact that Jake's arms are
still wide open instead of embracing the woman nestled in his arms speaks volumes.

"What the hell are you doing here, Lindsay?"

Before she can answer, Jake turns his attention to Allison and when I pivot my head to look at
the blonde standing next to me, I'm surprised by her
indignant stare.

"I don't want things to end between us, Jake,"
Lindsay pleads, dropping kisses along Jake's chin.

"I'm pretty sure I was quite clear about us
ending things a month ago, Lindsay. You think show-

ing up here unannounced on my property will change things?"

Jake's voice is deceptively calm, but I know him well enough to know he's raging inside. Lindsay's manipulative ways will only end up distancing them. I've seen Jake in the toughest negotiations and you can't break him. Jake is able to keep his composure under any situation. Lindsay can storm as much as she wants, but there's no way she'll ever see Jake's bedroom.

"Why don't we go inside your house and we can talk about things... in private?"

I watch in shock as Lindsay slides her hands between Jake's legs and grabs his cock. She squeezes his dick, closes her eyes, tilts her head backwards and moans as if they're behind closed doors. *Holy fuck.*

The next thing I know, Allison turns on her heel and races back to her house. Jake looks at me as if to tell me I need to go after her, but before I can even move my feet, Dirk comes seeking my help.

"Hey, boss, one of you needs to come real quick."

I hesitate, bouncing my gaze from Dirk's worried face to Allison walking away from us.

"I think we're losing Jezebel. She just went into labor and something's not right. Jenkins is by her side helping, but it's more than he can handle. She's in pain. We need your help."

I meet Jake's concerned stare and he gestures with his chin for me to follow our manager. "Are you serious? I hope we don't lose her."

"Unfortunately I am. She's bleeding pretty badly."

I'll have to deal with this emergency first and then I'll have to talk to Allison. She deserves to know what's going on.

CHAPTER THREE

ALLISON

I slam the door to my house behind me so hard, I'm surprised it's still standing. I'm furious at myself for not having been more careful. Of course Jake and Hunter would have girlfriends. I mean, who do I think I am? It's not as if these two sex gods were waiting for me, their perfect partner. I'm just a plaything. A toy. I was too stupid and too cowardly to ask questions. *Way to go, Ali.*

Now I'm the one who's hurt and humiliated. If Lindsay talks her way into moving in with Jake, there's no way I'll be able to remain here to witness this trainwreck. I won't be able to bear watching her grope him as indecently as she did in front of Hunter and I. Jake didn't even try to stop her. *God.* I shake my head, reliving all the events of the past hour since this woman burst into my life, and I bristle at the realization that her long tanned legs, size-zero figure, Barbie hair and perfect painted face make me feel beyond insecure. Why would Jake want someone like me when he can have someone like her? My sudden pang of envy surprises me, but it only gets stronger when I remember once again Lindsay's desperate attempts at claiming Jake. *Bitch.*

After half an hour consumed with resentment towards the intruder in my life, I realize if I don't speak to someone, I'll combust. I pull out my phone from my back pocket and dial Gwyn's number. I pace around my house waiting for her to answer, but after four rings, it goes straight to voicemail. I try again, but when it happens a second time, I throw my phone on the couch, defeated. *She must be in a meeting.*

I'm sure all this wouldn't be so hard to digest if I was willing to admit to myself I've fallen for Jake. It's not that Hunter isn't amazing, it's just that there's an undeniable pull towards Jake I've never felt with any other man before. Gwyn's picked up on how much I gush over Jake. I don't think I was aware of it until she pointed it out. I was baffled. I tried to deny it, but Gwyn knows me well. I was hoping the torrent that builds inside me every time I'm near Jake was just a passing thing, but Lindsay's arrival is turning my world upside down. *I've never seen Jake look so polished and so freaking hot.* As I walk around my place trying to calm down, I can't help but flash back to the moment Jake stepped out of his vehicle. I swear the air got sucked right out of my lungs. I mean, he was so dashing in his tailor-made navy-blue suit that made him look even more dangerously handsome than usual. *Damn.* His crisp white shirt accentuated his tanned skin and when I looked at his laced-up black shoes, I knew they had to be expensive. He was oozing something so powerful, so commanding and so arresting, I licked my lips, he looked that good.

Since I arrived in Colorado, I've only seen him in tight-fitting Wrangler jeans, casual chinos, t-shirts, cowboy boots and a cowboy hat... unless of course he was naked. Seeing him today looking so dashing reminded me that before owning this successful ranch, Jake was a Silicon Valley king. *What would he want with the likes of me?*

When it becomes clear I'll have to deal with this crisis on my own, I walk to the fridge in search of salvation—alcohol. In a fit of jealous rage at my own delusions, I swing open the kitchen cupboards in search of a wine glass. *Thank God Isadora stocked up.* I grab a bottle and pull the cork out before pouring a very generous amount in my glass. If I numb my emotions, I can pretend I'm not feeling as crappy as I am right now.

I lift the glass to my lips and tilt my head back, taking one big gulp. *Sometimes wine fixes everything, especially when you're trying to lie to yourself.* I grab the bottle ready to pour myself more liquid liberation when there's a knock at my door. I'm tempted to disregard the intrusion, but Hunter is calling my name so loudly, it's impossible to ignore him.

"Allison, I know you're in there. Please open the door. I need to talk to you."

"Hunter, I'm busy."

"I have a spare key to your house. Either you open this door or I'll let myself in. Your choice."

Great, I have no privacy. I resign myself and set down my wine glass on the table before walking to the door.

When I catch sight of Hunter, I gasp in horror. "You're bleeding. Are you hurt?" I fix my eyes on his soiled t-shirt.

He looks down before smiling at me. "No. I'm fine. We had a false alarm with one of the cows that was giving birth. When you stormed back to your place, Dirk came to get me to help with Jezebel, but by the time I ran to the barn, nature had taken over and our cow was well on her way to calving with Jenkins by her side. I stuck around to make sure everything was okay, but when a cow calves, there's blood everywhere."

"God, you scared me."

"The minute I knew Jezebel was going to be okay I came running over here. I need to talk to you about Lindsay, but my clothes are too dirty for me to come in. Let's sit on the porch instead."

"It's okay, Hunter. You don't have to make excuses for Jake. I get it."

"Jake's a big boy and he doesn't need me to air his dirty laundry, but Lindsay is something else and you need to understand that. Hear me out."

I hesitate, but I'd be lying if I said I wasn't curious about the witch of Eastwick who's turned my world upside down.

"I'm willing to listen."

For the next twenty minutes Hunter shares the intricate detail of Jake and Lindsay's former relationship. I listen intently and can't help but realize that my feelings about her weren't too far off. It was clear from the first second I laid eyes on her she was impossible to handle.

"I hope things make more sense now and that I've shed some light on Lindsay."

"Where's Jake now?" I'm grateful Hunter came over to explain things, but I would have preferred it if Jake had done it in person.

"He's on his way back to Denver with a very pissed-off ex-girlfriend in the passenger seat. He texted me while I was in the barn to let me know he was putting an end to things once and for all by checking Lindsay into a hotel. He's dropping her off and driving back."

"Really? He wasn't going to let her stay the night? She could've stayed at Riley's place." I'm not entirely unhappy to know Lindsay is gone, but since it'll be nighttime soon, it might have been easier to keep her here until the morning.

"No. You don't play Jake. He wanted me to talk to you because he was worried this ordeal might make you think…"

"He was cheating on his girlfriend with me?"

"Exactly."

"So Jake is really single?"

"He's as single as I am. We'd never do anything like this. It's not worth the aggravation. We like our drama-free life. When things don't work out with someone we're seeing, we break things off and we move on, but Lindsay… she's a special case."

I look at him from the side, still unsure if I'm willing to voice my feelings. "Everything about her made me uncomfortable and groping Jake in front of us was distasteful. She looked so desperate it just turned my stomach and I couldn't bear to watch any longer. Not to mention she was very rude to me from the minute she first met me."

"I could tell and that's why I wanted to talk to you. Now that everything is out in the open, let's go enjoy the rest of our evening."

"What did you have in mind?" I say, excited to put this drama behind us.

"Why don't I go take a shower, change into some clean clothes and let's go to the cabin? Let's have a few drinks and we can unwind before dinner. What do you say?"

"Sounds like a really great idea."

"Give me thirty minutes and I'll be back for you. I'll text Jake so he knows where to find us when he gets back."

* * *

The second Hunter turns on the lights inside the cabin, I realize he's been planning this moment since before he even came to speak to me to straighten things out. He's thought of everything—stainless-steel buckets of ice filled with beer and wine bottles sitting near the edge of the pool, a selection of scrumptious-looking appetizers, refreshing ice tea, water with slices of citrus fruits floating on the surface, one of Isadora's signature loaf cakes and relaxing music. *Wow*. I turn around to look at him, but he speaks before I do.

"With all this Lindsay drama, it's late and by the time Jake gets back, dinner will be the last thing on his mind." Hunter winks.

"The spread is a nice touch, but I'm surprised by the slices of oranges and lemons floating in the water," I mock. "Where did you learn that? I'd never imagine a guy would pay such attention to details."

"Isadora," he says with a boyish grin. "She claims it's a Southern thing and it makes for a much more refreshing drink. Riley claims every spa in America serves this type of fruity water. Personally, I think it's a heck of a lot better-tasting than plain water, right?"

"Point well taken."

"Let me adjust the pool's temperature and we can climb in." Before I can answer, Hunter is playing around with the thermostat. I take a few steps towards the bar and lean back, watching him set the perfect mood for our evening. He turns around and stares at me, gesturing up and down my body with his index finger. "What are you still doing fully dressed?"

"Why do I always have to be the first one naked?"

"Because I never get tired of seeing your delicious body and although my best friend isn't here yet, I'm pretty sure he'd agree," he says suggestively while striding towards me, cornering me with his large frame against the edge of the stainless-steel bar.

"You're just saying that so you can have your way with me."

"Of course I am. What did you expect?" Hunter laughs before speaking again, this time in a much deeper voice. "This eventful evening has interfered with my well-laid-out plans," he says, sweeping a strand of hair behind my shoulders.

"Did those plans involve your cock and my pussy?" I swear, since I set foot on this ranch I've been transformed into a woman I barely recognize. There's no way I would've ever had the guts to ask such a bold question before, but around Hunter and Jake, it's safe to let go of my inhibitions.

"You read my mind. I intended on being buried inside you by now while Jake watched me fuck you, but I guess I'll have to get a head start and hopefully he'll join us well before I come gushing all over your velvety-smooth stomach." He leans down and drops a soft kiss against my lips while he unties my robe.

Hunter surprised me when he showed up at my place a few minutes ago to take me to the cabin holding a white terrycloth robe. He brought the same one in a larger size for himself and he suggested I slip into mine instead of the casual clothing I was wearing. Secretly, I suspect it's his way of speeding things up.

"You're in a rush," I pretend to protest. "Why have such a delicious assortment of food if it's just to ignore it?"

"Because I'd rather have you as the appetizer and keep the food for later. Once I'm done with you, I'll need to refuel," he says, parting his own robe and revealing a raging erection.

"Hunter, you're so—"

"Huge?"

"I was going to say big, but sure, let's go with huge," I tease.

"Being around you is such a turn-on."

"What about me? I'm famished. I wouldn't mind nibbling on a few appetizers."

"Don't worry, I'll pump your mouth and you can suck on my dick instead. That'll be plenty for you to handle."

"You're so self-assured."

"You're not fooling anyone, Allison. The way you sucked our cocks last night, I know you're dying to drop to your knees, wrap those lips around my dick and swallow every last drop of me."

"Damn, you have a dirty mouth, Hunter."

"You say that as if it were a bad thing. You can't get enough of the way my raunchy words make your pussy wet. You pray for my lips to suck on your heavy tits. And I know you lose it when my tongue flickers against your hard clit. Admit it, you love everything about this mouth."

"Crap, am I so transparent?"

"Your desperate moans, your slippery wetness and the frantic quivering of your body when I'm with you betray you."

"Oh." I can't think of anything right now because I'm too focused on enjoying his hands all over my body.

"I knew you'd be open to sharing both of us the second I laid eyes on you. It took my best friend a little bit more convincing."

"Really?" I push him slightly away from me to meet his gaze. "So you looked at me and thought,

'Yeah, she'd be willing to take two cocks at the same time?'"

"Pretty much," he mocks. He leans down and claims my lips, silencing me and preventing me from making any further smart remarks. He slides his hands down my back until he reaches the roundness of my ass and he squeezes me closer to his erection.

"Argh."

I'm so aroused by the idea of being with both men again that my clit throbs uncontrollably, already seeking salvation. I slide my hand behind his back and I hold him tighter, grinding myself against him. *Shit.*

"Shouldn't we wait for Jake?" The second the question leaves my lips I regret it.

"Ah, Jake," he says, kissing my chin and pushing my robe off my shoulder before cupping my breast. "You like him, don't you?"

"I… I like both of you," I hiss, closing my eyes with excitement when he pinches both nipples.

"You know what I'm talking about," he says, lowering his head to take my right boob into his mouth. "I've noticed the way you look at him."

"What are you talking about, Hunter?"

"You don't look at me in the same way."

"You're being silly," I respond, trying to re-route this conversation.

I like both men and not only because they worship my body and make me come to the point where I can barely remember my name. I genuinely like being around them, but there's something about Jake. I'm shocked and somewhat embarrassed Hunter would pick up on that. I guess I've never been very good at hiding my true feelings. "I look at both of you as if you're sex gods." I attempt to make up for my faux pas. I know I'm skirting the issue, but I can't allow Hunter to know how I really feel about Jake or I'll threaten what we share.

"So you like when we're both fucking you, or would you—"

"I sure as hell hope she likes it because tonight, we're both claiming her at the same time. I have no intention of sitting back and watching you fuck her pussy."

When did he get in? I didn't even hear him open the door.

Jake's entrance prevents Hunter from finishing his sentence and buys me the time I need to get out of this uncomfortable conversation. Jake's also clad in the same kind of white robe that's wrapped around me and when I look down, I can see the outline of his hungry erection.

"You're back." The words escape my mouth in a whisper.

"Of course, baby girl. You didn't think I was going to let him have you all to himself tonight?" he says, pointing his chin at Hunter.

"Damn, and here I thought it was my lucky night alone with Allison."

"Sorry to burst your bubble, buddy."

"That must be the fastest time on record. Did you fly to Denver to drop Lindsay off? Because there's no way you could have had time to drive there and back."

I was just thinking the same thing. Suddenly I'm aware I'm half naked and I pull up the robe to cover my exposed breasts.

Jake answers Hunter's question, but his eyes are glued on me as he watches my every move with a sly smile. "Ten minutes down the road she threw another hissy fit. I put my foot on the brake so hard she nearly flew out the window. We had another fight and at that point, I had had enough. The idea of staying stuck in my SUV with her for another forty-five minutes nearly gave me an ulcer."

"Did she end up walking all the way to Denver carrying her five pieces of luggage on her back?" Hunter pulls away from me, chuckling.

"That would have been quite the scene, but nothing that dramatic. I called a limo to come pick her up. I waited and made sure she got in the car before driving back to the ranch. I even gave the chauffeur a hundred dollars so she wouldn't have anything to complain about. She's out of my life for good and there's no more room for her to think we're still together when we're not."

"Good. No more drama."

"I should thank her, though."

"For what? Being annoying?" Hunter looks horrified, but I'm too mesmerized by how handsome Jake looks to do anything more than stare in his electric-blue eyes.

"Lindsay's brash nature was a blessing tonight."

"Okay, you've lost me."

This story with Jake's ex-girlfriend is so layered, it's not my place to share my opinion, so I just listen as the two men debate.

"The long drive to and from Denver would have prevented me from being here to enjoy the blonde you were about to ravish." His comment takes me by surprise and I bring both hands to my mouth to hide my smile. His eyes are still on me when he speaks again. "Hunter explained everything?"

It takes me a few seconds to find my composure. "Yes, he did."

"We're good?"

"Of course we are."

He flashes me a wide smile. "Hunter's idea to unwind in the hot pool is a brilliant one, but I thought we might add a fun element to up the stakes."

"What do you mean?"

"Yeah, buddy, what are you talking about?"

"Since one of us will have the honor of claiming Allison's ass tonight, I thought that instead of tossing a coin, we might let her decide who she wants. But of course, it wouldn't be nearly as thrilling for her to pick one of us as it would be for one of us to win the honors."

"Oh." I blush. It's true the steam is rising above the water inside the pool, but I'd be fooling myself if I blamed the temperature for the warmth against my cheeks.

"You almost sound surprised," he teases. "You didn't think we had forgotten? Yesterday was a warm-up. Tonight you'll discover what it's like to be dominated by two men who worship you." Jake's gaze is so intense I bring the back of my hand up and wipe a few pearls of sweat running down my fore-hand.

"You want us to duel over who takes her vir-ginity?"

"You're funny, Hunter. I have something a little more civilized in mind," he says, pulling a blind-fold from the pocket of his terrycloth robe.

Oh, my God. First he shackles me with a rope in a remote barn and now he wants to blindfold me? Is there no end to this man's kinkiness?

"I don't know what you have in mind, but what's dangling from your hands is making me nerv-ous."

"There's nothing to be worried about," Jake responds, taking a few steps towards me.

"If we're going to blindfold her, should I run out and grab a collar or handcuffs?"

"Hunter," I say, scandalized.

"Well, if Jake wants us to battle it out, I want to make sure I have a chance of winning." Hunter grins from ear to ear.

"Ali has already been with both of us sepa-rately and we shared her last night. Let's see how well she knows her lovers."

My lovers? I like the sound of that.

"I still don't follow." Hunter is as perplexed as I am.

"Yeah, I don't think it's fair for me to have to choose between the two of you blindfolded." I don't know what he has in mind, but knowing Jake his naughty experiment will leave me panting.

"Once you can no longer see, your other senses will kick in. The more you allow your senses to guide you, the more this game will turn you on... and it should do the same to us as well."

"My cock's already fully aroused." Hunter is grabbing his crotch with a devilish smile.

I doubt either of them will spare me tonight.

"Hold your horses. I need to lay down some ground rules."

"Good idea. I can already see Hunter cheating." I wink.

"How can you assume I'd cheat to have a chance at fucking your ass?" Hunter's fake innocence is endearing, but I know first-hand the kind of passion this man is capable of.

"Here's how it's going to work. We're all going to get into the pool and I'm going to blindfold Ali. Ali, your job is to enjoy the warmth of the water and to be a willing participant in my little game. You need to guess which one of us is touching you. The one you recognize by touch the most often is the one who will have the honor of claiming your ass."

"That sounds easy enough, I guess."

"Oh, there's one more thing."

"What?" I ask nervously.

"Every time you're right, we drink. If you're wrong, you'll have to take a little sip of your wine. I won't let you get drunk, but if you can't figure out who's who, you'll surely be a little tipsy by the end of this game."

"I'm loving the idea," Hunter cheers.

"It's easy for you to say. You're not the one who's losing their virginity tonight." I frown at him.

"You want this, don't you?" Jake reaches out for my cheek and I press my face against his strong hand. "We're not forcing you to do anything against your will?"

"No," I respond without hesitation. I know what I agreed to when I accepted the butt plug Hunter bought for me. I want both men and I'm not about to run away now.

"Good," he says holding my gaze while he pulls at the sash around my waist. "Loose the robe so I can cast my eyes over your heavenly body." It's not a suggestion. Jake pushes open the robe, exposing my nakedness, before I can even respond. He leans in and takes my lips with his. I close my eyes, savoring his lingering kiss, and I extend my hand behind me, calling my brown-eyed lover to join in the action.

When Hunter presses his muscular body against my ass and I realize I'm sandwiched between my guys, my clit swells and chafes against my lower lips as I anticipate both men putting their hands all over me and pleasuring me.

After a few minutes of kissing, Jake whispers close to my ear. "Come on, let's start this game. My cock is hungry." Hunter pulls away and lets Jake guide me to the pool.

I climb down the stairs and squat to dip my whole body into the warm and soothing water. I look up and both men are standing side by side, eating me up with their gazes, as they remove their robes, revealing the two very big cocks I'll be riding tonight.

Sweet mother of Lord have mercy. The scalding heat emanating from both of them makes the temperature of the pool seem icy. *I will never be able to walk again after tonight.*

Hunter jumps in first, followed by Jake, who approaches me holding the blindfold over his head to prevent it from getting wet. When he gets close enough, he pulls it down over my eyes.

"Remember, no touching," he says, securing the blindfold so I can't see a thing. "No cheating." He places my left hand on the edge of the pool, forcing me to lift my boobs higher. "No talking." He trails his finger over my lips. "No hesitating. You blurt out the first name that comes to mind."

Once everything is pitch black around me, it hits me. *How on earth am I going to tell which one of them just touched me?* I thought this would be easy, but now I'm not so sure.

The water ripples, lapping around my exposed breasts, teasing them remorselessly. Without having to look, I know my nipples peek above the waterline because the contrast between the ambient air flirting with my rock-hard peaks and the warmth of the water sends shivers down my back. Thankfully the pool is shallow.

"When you said no talking, did you mean I can't ask questions? What if—"

A pair of lips silence me. *Who is it?* I don't know how, but this lover isn't touching me anywhere but on my mouth. The touch is so delicate, I barely feel it, but it's still incredibly sensual. *Shit.* A tongue brushes against my lower lip and just when I reach out to touch the face of the man taunting me, he eludes me. *Damn.* Whoever it is moves, licking the corner of my mouth and sending me into a passionate whirlwind. I lean forward, hoping to capture his lips, but he laughs softly before moving away.

Gosh, I haven't got a clue who it is. "Hunter?"

One of my lovers grabs the hand that's on the edge of the pool and places a glass in it. I take a sip. Okay, so it was Jake.

"I don't think it's fair. The two of you are plotting to get me tipsy and have your way with me."

Instead of an answer, the water shifts again and I feel a body moving behind me. *Focus.* I breathe deeply and try to take in the cologne of the man behind me. I'm out of luck because everything around me smells like pool water and the scented candles surrounding me.

"Jesus," I sigh.

One of them flicks my left nipple with his tongue. I raise my boobs out of the water, breathing heavily when lips, a tongue and teeth pull at my swollen nipple before moving on to the left. As much as I try, I'm still stumped and I can't tell if it's Jake or Hunter assaulting my boobs. I'm still convinced they're trying to trick me and I flash back to one of our passionate interludes and for a moment I'm certain I know who's latching at my boob, but when I whisper the name of the stud I think is responsible for leaving my legs feeling like Jell-O, my wineglass returns.

Two for them and zero for me. I'm losing in a big way and they'll both still be sober by the end of this. I brace myself for the next touch, fully prepared to ace it, but I lose all my resolve when a hard cock brushes against my back under the water. *Not fair.* "Jake?"

Both men chuckle and my wine glass returns. This time, instead of wetting my lips, I take a big gulp.

"There's no way I can win this," I say, aggravated, fully aware I'm breaking one of Jake's cardinal rules. The two of them are so different, so how can I be failing so badly at this game?

A pair of hands wrap around my boobs. *I know those hands.* I open my mouth to blurt a name, but a finger slides against my sensitive clit. I'm about to complain about the fact Jake never said anything about both of them touching me at the same time when the man behind me grabs my hips, lifting me and placing my body against the edge of the pool.

Fuck. I reach out with both hands and I hold on tight to the towel laid out in front of me. *Where did the other one go?* I don't have time to wonder because the man holding me pushes me forward, bending me over and exposing my ass to the open air. *Oh, God.* I'm still unable to predict their next move.

Then one of them spreads my ass cheek open with his hands and his mouth closes in, tonguing me from behind.

"Holy Christ," I cry out, shocked. He grips me firmly, preventing me from escaping. He's incredibly strong, but then again both of them are strapping demigods. "Holy Jesus." The tongue sweeps me from my asshole to my eager clit, lapping ravenously. There's no way I can tell if it's Jake or Hunter, but who the hell cares at this point because that tongue against my pussy is threatening to make me lose my mind.

The man behind me moves away and I grunt in frustration. "No. You can't get me all worked up and leave me like this." I've barely finished protesting when he returns. I steady myself against my hands and I yank up my ass higher, but instead of a tongue, a man's cock butts up against my slick pussy, teasing and torturing me.

"Oh." I'm so consumed by the cock gliding against my wetness that I don't notice when the other lover lies down on the towel I'm still clutching with both hands. He slides his long legs between my arms and fists my hair possessively. He pulls my head towards him and punishes me with an urgent kiss before pushing me along his lean, athletic body until my lips brush against his dick.

This game is getting dirtier by the minute.

"There will be no winners because you two are going to kill me tonight and neither of you will get to fuck me," I bark.

The man in front of me pushes my head down until my lips touch his shaft as if to silence me. I stick out my tongue and I graze the tip of his cock, licking his moisture while the other man slides the tip of his shaft against my impatient clit.

"Hmmm," I moan against the cock inside my mouth as I gyrate my hips to encourage whoever is behind me to never stop what he's doing.

Jake was right. The fact that I can't tell who's doing what to me heightens my arousal to no end.

Both of them grunt at the same time and it drives me fucking insane. Since I've already broken the rules by talking, I reach for the man in front of me and caress his thighs, hoping to be able to put a face to the body. When it becomes clear I'm enjoying this moment way too much to care about naming the man fucking my mouth, I grab the base of his cock while I bob my head up and down along his length, matching the rhythm of the man now plunging his tongue in and out of my ass. I raise my head, still gripping the big cock in front of me, and I let out a raw, throaty moan when the man behind me plunges two fingers inside my pussy while still lapping at my ass.

"Aaaah." This game is maddening.

Frustrated by being unable to see the two guys assaulting my body in the sweetest possible way, I rip the blindfold off and fling it in the water. I blink a few times at the man in front of me and I gasp.

"Hunter?"

"Damn, Allison, why did you have to stop sucking my cock? I'm nearly there. Come on, baby, wrap your pouty lips around me again," he says, yanking his hips up towards my mouth, holding his dick as an offering. His deep brown eyes are heavy-lidded and provocative. I can read the desperation in them.

I turn to the lover behind me, but I know exactly who it is before I meet his dangerously seductive blue eyes.

"Jake?"

He lifts his head and smiles without removing the fingers inside my pussy. "Who else did you expect?"

"Are you going to be the one to claim me?" I'm surprised by my own forwardness. I realize I willingly gave myself to him with my question.

"Why don't we take this to Hunter's place? His house is the closest to the cabin. We can continue what we started in a much more comfortable setting. Your first time shouldn't be in a pool. We should take you on a bed."

"You didn't answer my question," I press boldly.

"No, I didn't," he says, holding my gaze. "Hunter and I decided his girth might be too much to handle for your first time, so I'll do the honors." He stands up behind me and presses his cock against my back as he grabs hold of my boobs. I close my eyes, feeling his hands all over me as I grind my bum into him.

"I'll take you from the front while Jake introduces you to the dark side, but don't worry, we have all night… there's plenty of time for you to get accustomed to my size." My eyes pop open when Hunter speaks and I can tell from his cocky grin my two lover boys decided a long time ago who was going to take my virginity. I never had any say in the matter and this little naughty game was purely for their enjoyment—and mine.

"Buddy, help her out of the pool." Jake has barely finished his sentence before Hunter stands up and pulls me out of the water. Once my feet are firmly planted on the ground, he picks me up and flings me over his shoulder.

I squeal with delight. In their arms, I'm as light as a feather. "What are you doing?"

"You heard the man. He said we needed to finish you off at my place." Hunter chuckles and slaps my ass for good measure.

CHAPTER FOUR

HUNTER

Luckily my house is only a few steps away from the cabin and all three of us are able to make the short journey butt naked without having to worry about being accused of indecent exposure. I climb the stairs all the way to my bedroom, kick open the door with a carnal grunt and turn on the lights. I walk decisively to my bed and throw the sexy blonde's body against my mattress, impatient to ravish her.

I take a few steps backward to admire Allison's glistening body under the soft lights. When she falls backward, her long hair fans out like a crown around her face. Her arms are raised above her head, letting us appreciate her best assets. Her heavy tits fall toward the sides of her exquisite body and the only thing I want to do is reach down and cup them. In a shy attempt to conceal her nakedness from our eyes, she folds her legs closer to her body and plants her feet against the mattress as she wiggles her painted toes. *She's absolutely beautiful.* It doesn't take long for Jake to come join me and we stand shoulder to shoulder looking at the woman we're about to brand.

"Fuck, your beautiful curves are glimmering under these dim lights." I'm unable to peel my eyes away from her.

"Hunter is right, you're absolutely glowing, Ali."

"I'm going to enjoy watching you get taken by both of us, Allison." My thick and swollen cock jerks when she bites her bottom lip, bouncing her eyes from my hungry dick to Jake's.

"And I'm going to take a lot of pleasure from seeing you climax with both our cocks buried deep inside you while you scream your head off."

"I want this, I really do, but there's a part of me that's scared shitless because I've never had two men inside me at the same time." Allison blows out a tense breath and I can tell she's still a bit nervous, although we've been preparing her for this moment for a few days now.

"Don't worry, we'll be very gentle and we'll use a lot of lube."

"Promise?"

"Remember what we've said to you from the beginning. This is supposed to be as enjoyable for you as it is for us."

She swallows and nods jerkily as she soaks in Jake's words.

"I'll prepare your ass while Hunter has a little fun with you. We'll make sure to ease you into it so you don't have to worry about a thing."

"O-okay."

Jake walks to my night table and grabs the bottle of lube and a couple condoms from the box I pulled out before going to get Allison to take her to the cabin. The truth is, we've both been planning this moment with a great deal of anticipation. My best friend strides back towards me with a huge grin on his face as he throws a packet my way, which I catch with one hand. *Greedy bastard.* I already know he's going to come like an animal up her ass while I pump her pussy hard. This is a night our gorgeous little blonde is unlikely to forget for a very long time.

Jake climbs onto the mattress next to Allison before leaning in and kissing her lips. I watch as he licks her face until he reaches her earlobe, which he sucks into his mouth until she squeals with contentment. As much as Jake loves watching me take Allison as he masturbates, I derive as much pleasure if not more from watching her succumb to him. I fist my cock and choke it, stroking up and down as my friend feasts on her supple skin. He nibbles along her neck until sweet shivers travel through her body. When he draws away, Allison reaches out for him, already begging for more.

"I'm not going too far, baby, but I can't wait any longer. I need to find out how tight you are," he growls. "Get on all fours, Ali."

She sucks in a breath, glancing in my direction for support, but she quickly realizes I'm as eager as Jake is when she sees me taking pleasure. She smiles at me and obeys, turning her body around until her round ass is pointing at me.

Christ, how sinful. The sight of her pussy and asshole only adds to my enjoyment and I stroke my cock harder, grunting with every thrust. Jake turns in my direction and casts me a complicit stare before positioning himself right behind Allison's rear, ready to claim her. His half grin lets me know he sympathizes with me and he understands it's impossible for me to contain myself any longer.

Allison wiggles her ass impatiently, stealing his attention away from me.

"Did you enjoy my tongue up your ass when we were all in the hot pool?" Jake squirts the gel in his hands.

"Uh-huh. I did."

"Good. You're going to like this even more."

Allison sucks in a breath as a heavily lubed finger slides against her tight asshole. "Oh," she gasps. My best friend presses his finger past the ring of muscle and she hisses while gyrating as he slides it in deeper.

The pressure builds at the base of my balls, tightening them, and the sensation mounting is overpowering. I'm trying to ward off the inevitable, but watching her in this position with Jake dominating her like this is intense. I won't lie, it's intoxicating to watch another man finger a tight, virgin asshole before he fucks her.

Jake's husky voice breaks my trance. It's as if he can tell I'm close. "Hunter, save your climax for Ali and get your cock over here so she can keep busy while I work her from behind."

There's no doubt we're both dominant alpha males, but there's something so unapologetic and so unrepentant about Jake when we take a woman together. The way he uses my tongue, my fingers and my cock as extensions of his own with each one of his commands is extraordinarily dirty.

I climb onto the bed in front of Allison and slide under her until I cup her huge hanging tits. When I look up, all I can see are her heavenly breasts, nearly suffocating me. When I shift my eyes behind me, I see my friend working her ass and I can't help but smile. *Damn, this is going to be mind-blowing.*

I cup her left tit and suck her right nipple into my eager mouth. *Fuck.* She moans when I wrap my lips around her peak and she pants when I nibble and lap at her large areola. From this vantage point the weight of her tits sits nicely on my face and I swear I could stroke my cock and come while biting down on her erect nipples.

Behind her, Jake withdraws his fingers. The loud sucking sound that follows causes her to sob, but suddenly her wailing turns into gasps. Jak*e must have inserted two fingers.* I take that as my cue and I bite gently on her peak and she rewards me with another squeal.

"How is it, Ali?"

"Jesus, Jake," she hisses.

Although I'm still lapping at Allison's tits and pinching her nipples, I notice when Jake withdraws his fingers again. He waits a few seconds before penetrating her again and her entire body contracts, expecting more.

"Fuck, three fingers?" she screams, outraged, when Jake slides deeper inside her tightness. The slurp of the lube follows, but this time her knees wobble as Jake invades her ass once again. "Oh, Christ." Her raspy voice arouses my already rock-hard cock and I slip my hand down her stomach until I reach her pussy. She moans and widens her legs, inviting me to stroke her clit.

"I can't take this any longer."

Jake takes a step back and the condom crinkles. I slide from under Allison and get up on my knees. I pat around the bed in search of my own shield and when I find it, I bring the packet to my mouth to rip it open. With our cocks sheathed, we nod at each other.

"Are you ready for us, Ali?"

"Uh-huh." She folds her lower lip into her mouth.

"No, baby, I want to hear you say the words."

"I want both of you to take me. Now."

Jake and I lock eyes and we share a silent understanding that transcends words.

"Hunter, our little virgin is ready to discover her wild side. Get inside her so I can do the same." Jake's order is precise and I sit back down and glide to the edge of the bed with my dick spearing into the air, grazing Allison's stomach. I hold out my arms to her and she smiles at me as if she can't wait to mount me.

"Slowly," I say, holding her hands as she scrambles to position herself.

I grab her hips as she climbs over me. When my dick's head nudges at her pussy, I struggle not to thrust into her in one quick movement. "Come on, sit on my cock and lean into me."

She obeys and with every inch of me she swallows with her pussy, I grunt at the pressure. Within a few seconds, I'm fully impaling her.

"Oh, fuck," she purrs when I'm all the way in. I groan in response as her pussy grips my dick and her muscles clamp around me. I brush her damp hair from her face and lose myself in her gaze. Her eyes are already glazed over and we've barely begun to rock her world.

"Fucking shit," I say when she begins to gyrate against my shaft.

"You're so deep inside me," she marvels.

"You like being on top?" I tease.

"Do I get to control things?"

"In your dreams, but you do get an A for effort. I'm the one who has the cock, so I'm the one controlling things," I say, playfully sticking my tongue out at her.

She folds her body towards me and laughs into the crook of my neck, but Jake's voice puts an end to her lightheartedness.

"Spread your thighs for me, Ali." Jake's command is strangled and urgent.

Allison shifts her body against mine and she widens her legs.

"Damn, this is a magnificent view. It's too bad you'll miss it, Hunter," Jake mocks.

"Don't worry about me. Enjoy it while you can because it'll be my turn soon enough." I wink at her.

The next thing I hear are two slaps followed by Allison's muffled cry.

"I'm going to enter you now, Ali, nice and slow."

"Okay." She casts me a worried look as she bites down on her lower lip.

"Hold on to me," I say, tightening my grip around her waist. "You're going to be fine."

"Oh." Her body jerks forward. She reaches for me and I lift my head high enough to take her mouth to calm her down.

"Easy, baby. It'll be good once I'm all in." Jake's words reassure her and she rewards me with a weary smile. "Spread yourself further. I'm going to use more lube because you're an untouched little one," he chuckles.

"It's okay, Allison. Breathe, baby," I whisper, nipping at her neck.

"Jesus, Hunter, she's so insanely tight."

"I bet she is."

"Argh," she yelps, biting my shoulder to keep from crying out.

"Where do you think you're going, Ali?" She tries to escape him but Jake will have none of it. He grabs the blonde's hips and pulls her back towards him. "I'm entering you slowly—inch by inch."

"Once Jake is fully in, you're going to lose your mind. You'll have two lovers filling you up."

She closes her eyes and tilts her head back. "Holy hell," she yells out. *He's inside her.* And just like that, the tension leaves her body and she submits herself fully to both of us.

Damn, it's about to get dirty.

JAKE

I've been waiting for this moment since I first laid eyes on Allison's delicious body. She's riding my best friend's dick and I've just entered her very tight asshole.

"Oh, fuck, buddy, she's clenching her pussy around me hard. I'm going to shoot my load in no time," Hunter shouts through gritted teeth.

I have no intention of rushing things. I want to savor every inch of her ass as she swallows me. I pull out slightly before pushing in slowly, stretching her while allowing her to become accustomed to having me fill her ass. When I'm nearly all in, I withdraw again and thrust into her with more determination.

"Is it good, baby?"

"Mmmmm."

"Are you ready? I'm going to go faster now." I brush her hair to the side and kiss the back of her shoulder.

"Yes," she hisses through clenched teeth.

"If it doesn't feel good, what should you say?"

She hesitates for a moment and then remembers the safe word I gave her when I took her inside the barn. "Lemon."

"Good girl."

I slide my free hand to her tits, pinching her tightening nipple, and she bucks wildly against me. I push my dick further into her ass, groaning loudly, bringing both hands back to her hips and holding her in place. Both Hunter and I move rhythmically. We pull out and slam back into her in unison. *Christ.* She can't do a thing but hold tightly to my best friend's shoulders and take us.

I've barely started moving, but already a wave of pleasure rushes over me. "Holy shit, Ali."

"Fucking Lord," Hunter grunts in response to my plea.

"Oh, God," she exhales.

"Ali, I can't even begin to describe how amazing your ass feels around my dick," I whisper in her ear, reaching around her and palming her tits again, pinching her nipples, painfully hard.

"Argh."

"You like that, don't you?"

"This is so raw, so primal and so untamed, I fear I'm tumbling over the edge." Her body convulses and she cries out but neither Hunter or I slow down. In fact her wailing makes us fuck her harder, faster—relentlessly. We're pumping in and out, increasing our speed, pushing her close to the climax she craves.

"I'm so close, baby," Hunter groans. "Make me come."

"I don't know if I can. It's so hard with Jake slamming into my ass."

"Of course you can. Clench your pussy around my dick and milk me for everything I have."

"Ahhh."

"That's it. Focus and let go."

"Jesus, the two of you are going to rip me apart," she grunts, but neither Hunter or I slow down our cadence. "I'm going to die. This is too good."

"Yeah, but what a way to go—with two guys fucking you." Hunter fists her hair and pulls her mouth down to his, kissing her almost violently.

Witnessing both of them unleashed like this only brings out my feral nature. I thrust harder, faster, slamming her into Hunter.

"Damn, Ali."

She moans, jerking her head back, sending her cascade of hair flying in the air. She keens as my thrusts increase in speed, pushing into her and dominating her like no man has ever done before. "Oh, yes, yes, yes."

"Fuck, Ali, you're a naughty vixen." Her ass greedily hugs my dick.

The room is filled with our moans, grunts and groans and slowly the sound of skin slapping against skin takes over. This is sweet debauchery at its best.

"Ah, Jake, you feel so good," she says, turning her head.

"Oh, baby, you want me deeper inside your ass?"

"I want more. Hunter, keep fucking me, please." She bounces her attention between Hunter and me, unable to decide which one of us is giving her the most pleasure.

"Don't worry, baby. I'll give you what you want."

"I'm going out of my mind here." Suddenly she clenches against Hunter's cock, her hips swing forward and her ass squeezes hard around me. With every buck of my hips, I press her harder against Hunter, forcing her clit to rub against his body.

"Oh, God, oh, God, oh, God," Allison cries out. "Jake, please come in my ass."

"I will, Ali."

"Hunter, fill my pussy."

"Shit, Allison, you're going to get it."

I slide my hands down her stomach and pinch her clit between my fingers, pushing her over the edge.

"Mother of God." Allison clenches her ass so tight it nearly cuts my breathing off. *Shit.* My balls tighten and I know I'm done. I'm no longer in control of any of this.

Her climax hits her hard and she's too exhausted to even scream. Her bottom lip is trembling, tears are in her eyes and she's clinging on to Hunter like he's a life jacket to avoid drowning in the sea of her own euphoric rapture. Her body convulses again and she digs her nails into Hunter's shoulders, leaving long scratches as I slam into her a final time. I explode. I'm lost in this moment of sheer ecstasy and I come with a deep growl I've never heard before. I pull out of her ass and quickly remove the condom before choking my dick, spewing my cum all over her back. *Fuck.* Instinctively, I spread the warmth of my orgasm all over her silky skin—I've branded her.

"Argh," I exhale.

My heart is beating so fast, I fear it will stop, unable to withstand the fact that all the blood in my body has travelled to my dick.

I'm still breathing heavily when my best friend screams out his own release. "Jesus fucking Christ." Hunter's cry comes from deep down. I've never seen him undone like this.

Ali collapses on Hunter, panting hard, but with a wide smile on her face despite the teary eyes.

"Are you still alive?" I tease.

"Barely."

"Seriously, how do you feel?" Hunter asks with his eyes still closed shut. "Did we work you too hard for your first time?"

"Maybe a little. I'm exhausted and a bit sore."

"Hopefully not too sore." Hunter opens one eye and Ali looks at him in disbelief.

"You can't be… Already?"

Slap.

"What?" she protests, turning her body to face me.

I gently spank her gorgeous ass and stroke the sting away. "Knowing my best friend, he's very serious. This is only the first round, baby. We're not nearly done with you yet." I grin devilishly.

Fuck, this was even more mind-blowing than I ever thought possible.

CHAPTER SIX

ALLISON

I wake up cuddled snugly against Hunter, my head resting on his shoulder and my leg draped over his as his arm wraps around my shoulders. *Oh, God, my body aches all over.* I try to move, but I'm quickly reminded of our endless binge of sexual depravity and abandonment.

After Jake claimed me, Hunter did the same and my hunks took turns ravishing me until I couldn't take it anymore. Although I doubt I'll be able to walk without a limp for the next few days, if not the next week, I wouldn't change a thing. I've gone from having the worst luck in men to being worshiped by two extraordinarily handsome studs—it doesn't get better than that.

Both my boys are still sound asleep and I take a minute to admire each one. Although taller, Hunter isn't as broad as Jake. That said, his muscles are incredibly lean and sculpted. His high cheekbones are more pronounced and his jaw is elongated whereas

Jake's is strong, well defined and square. I turn my head slightly to glance over at Jake, who is sleeping on his back naked with his arms spread over his head, sporting a semi-erection. *How in the world did I ever get to be this lucky?*

There's no two ways about it, both men are outrageously sexy in their own way and I guess that's why this experience is even more surreal. I know I'm blessed beyond belief and I'm pretty sure Gwyn will remind me I'm the luckiest woman in the world, but my eyes linger on the blue-eyed man who took my virginity last night.

What is it about Jake that makes him so irresistible to me? Perhaps it's the fact that Jake's intense presence makes me feel safe in a way I've never felt before with any other man. It's strange I don't feel the same way with Hunter considering both men are extremely caring. Maybe it's because I've had sex with Jake twice now and I've bonded with him enough to let my guard down before having sex with Hunter.

I know if I stay in bed, my mind will start playing tricks on me and the internal chatter will take over. It would be selfish to rock the boat because things are really good between the three of us. Why ruin things by questioning them? I look up at Hunter, wondering how in the world I'll be able to move without waking him up, when he lets go of me and turns onto his other side. I take this as my cue to slide out of bed and find an activity that will occupy my thoughts.

Ouch. Every muscle screams in protest as I sneak out of bed and try to stand up on my shaky legs.

Before leaving the room, I glance down one last time at the two men who made me come so many times last night, I thought I was going to forget my own name. *I know for sure they won't spare me when their appetite for me reignites.* I need to replenish if tonight will be a mirror image of last night's wantonness.

I tiptoe my way out of the room in search of a bathroom where I can take a quick shower and find something to wear. I'm very aware I'm no model, but I've never felt more comfortable with my own reflection than I have in the last few days thanks to the way Jake and Hunter praise my curves. On the other hand, I can't cook a hearty breakfast with my boobs flying all over the place.

Hunter's bathroom is as luxurious as Jake's. It's more modern and edgier. I don't linger under the water and once I braid my hair and twist it in a tight bun at the base of my neck, I borrow one of Hunter's oversized t-shirts from a small table in the corner of the bathroom and I run downstairs to the kitchen.

This is truly my favorite place in a home. I immediately swing open the fridge and start my inventory to determine which ingredients to use to prepare a breakfast to refill our energy after a night of forbidden passion. Since Isadora stocked up our refrigerators before she left, I already have a few great recipes in the back of my mind that I can whip up quickly.

My head is still stuck inside the fridge when a pair of strong hands caress my naked ass. I squeal, surprised. I quickly pull my head out of the fridge and turn around to meet a pair of mischievous brown eyes staring down at me. "Hunter! When did you get up?"

"Well, good morning to you too, princess. After our intimate night, I was hoping for a warmer greeting, but I guess I'll have to take whatever it is you're dishing out," he mocks.

"I'm sorry. Good morning. I didn't expect you to be up already since you were still sound asleep when I left the room."

"You're right, but the shower woke me up. My first instinct was to roll out of bed and come join you under the water, but you worked us so hard last night my brain couldn't convince my body to move."

"Are you seriously going to walk around naked like this?" It's taken me a minute to notice Hunter is standing in front of me unbothered by the fact he isn't wearing any clothing.

"What? This is my house after all and I usually walk around in the morning in the buff." He grins from ear to ear.

"Yeah, but you're most likely alone. How do you expect me to focus on preparing breakfast when you have a semi-hard cock dangling in front of me?"

"Oh, sweetness, is that the only thing bothering you? I have an idea about how we can take care of my semi-hard cock real quick." He reaches out for the t-shirt I'm wearing and pulls me towards him before crushing my lips.

"Jake is still sleeping upstairs," I breathe into his mouth.

"Who said anything about going upstairs? And who said anything about waiting for Jake? This granite counter will do the trick very nicely. I just have to fling your body on top of it and I can have my morning fuck before coffee." Without any warning, he slides a finger between my legs and I close my eyes when he glides it over my clit. "My best friend is right, you're a dirty little one. We might have worked you hard last night, but it's obvious you wouldn't mind going for another round or two." His dark and intense stare nearly sears me. When I lower my eyes, his semi-erect cock is now fully ready to fuck me again. *Damn.*

"Oh, Hunter," I gasp, surprised how my body responds to him despite the fact I'm still aching from the overdose of carnal gluttony. "We should wait."

"You're right. We should replenish first. If I have more energy, it'll be a lot easier to make you come screaming out my name." My jaw drops when Hunter removes the finger he had inserted in my pussy and brings it to his mouth with the most oh-my-God-fuck-me-now-before-I-die stare I've ever seen. He licks my juices in such a suggestive way I find myself salivating. *Holy hell.* He takes a step away from me with a finger still in his mouth. "Why don't I run upstairs and cover up and I'll come back down to help with breakfast?"

"I wanted it to be something I prepared for the two of you. It was supposed to be my little surprise and now you've ruined my plans."

He walks backwards towards the stairs with his eyes still on me and his wide grin still on his face. "Well, maybe if you hadn't made so much noise in the bathroom while you were taking a shower this morning, I'd still be sleeping. Jake can sleep through an earthquake so it's no wonder he's still snoring."

"So it's my fault I've ruined your surprise?"

He crinkles his nose. "I have a feeling I'm going to get in trouble if I say anything more."

"I definitely would tread carefully if I were you." I smile.

"I will. On a different note, I'm glad to see we didn't work you too hard last night, since you're still able to walk."

"Barely."

"Honey, if you could bend over the way you did when I first walked in the room and caught you flashing your ass at me, you're doing just fine."

"Careful." I wave a finger at him.

"All right, I know I'm pushing it." He smiles. "Give me a second and I'll be right back." With that boyish grin still plastered across his face, he turns around and disappears as quickly as he made his entrance.

I can't help but laugh watching his naked ass wiggle its way up the stairs. After shaking my head, I get back to work. I open the fridge again and pull out the items I didn't have time to grab before Hunter ambushed me.

I'm busying myself in front of the kitchen sink washing the vegetables I'll use for the omelet when Hunter returns. He circles my waist with his strong arm and leans down and drops a quick kiss on my cheek before stepping out of the embrace and surveying the ingredients I laid out on the counter. "Wow. Someone is getting ready to cook up a storm."

"After last night, we're all starving."

"You're right there. So what's on the menu?"

"Nothing too complicated."

"Usually when Riley or Isadora say that, they cook enough food to feed a small army."

"Trust me, my legs can barely withstand my weight given how exhausted I still am from last night. I have no intention of cooking a meal fit for a king. I was going to whip up a Spanish omelet. I was also thinking of slicing some of that raisin bread I noticed at the bottom of your fridge and I was going to make a huge pot of coffee to wake us all up. See, simple and easy."

"In that case, why don't I help you?"

"You're on. You can start by chopping those onions over there, followed by those potatoes, and I'll hand you the green and red peppers once I've washed them."

Hunter and I work in silence. Although I'm focused on the task at hand, I find my mind drifting to the blue-eyed lover who's still sleeping upstairs and I can't help but wonder when he'll be up.

The minutes always fly when I'm doing photography work or in the kitchen. Once the breakfast is nearly done, I turn around and I lean against the counter to face Hunter. There's a question that's been nagging at me for a few days now and I think this is my opportunity to get clarity. "How is this going to work?"

As much as I'd never change anything if it meant I'd forgo the sheer ecstasy I've shared with these two men over the past few days, I can't help but wonder if Riley will see right through me and I'm also curious to find out if all this will die down once she's back.

Hunter drops the knife he was holding and grabs the dishcloth on the counter next to him to wipe his hands before turning around to face me. He crosses his arms over his large chest and meets my gaze. "Oh, I think we're supposed to wait for the food to cook before eating it."

Grabbing a dishcloth, I swat his arm. "Don't be a smartass. You know exactly what I mean. I'm talking about us. Me, you and Jake… How can the three of us still be intimate when Riley eventually comes back? Let's not forget her four rambunctious kids and Isadora, who seems to have eyes everywhere. How do we make it work?"

Hunter clucks his tongue off of the roof of his mouth, exhales a deep breath and shifts his eyes away from mine to focus on a spot above my right shoulder. He ponders on my question for so long I wonder if he's decided to ignore it altogether or if he's trying to come up with a plan just like I've been attempting to do for the last few days.

"Baby, I'd be lying if I told you I knew. I don't think either Jake or I have thought that far out. I know I haven't. I was so elated when Riley mentioned she had been offered an opportunity of a lifetime by being asked to be a judge on the reality TV show and I figured we had ten days of unrestricted fun at our disposal. After that, I haven't got a clue."

My brows furrow. "So where does that leave us?"

Hunter takes a few steps towards me and grabs the back of my neck before lowering his gaze to meet mine. "Well, I love sharing you with Jake. I think we're good together. There's such an intense energy between us when we both take you. And I know I don't want this to end when Riley comes back. I'm sure we'll have to be a little more creative, but I don't see why this wouldn't work as long as we're discreet."

"I guess we'll have to wait and play it by ear."

"But there's still the matter of deciding who you really want."

"What do you mean?" I ask nervously.

"We started talking about this yesterday inside the cabin before Jake arrived. I think you like him far more than you're willing to admit. I'm happy to come along for the ride because I'll never turn down the opportunity to share a woman with sensual curves like yours with my best friend, but if you'd prefer to only be with Jake... I'll gracefully bow out. You just have to say the word."

My mouth drops open. Wow, am I ever transparent to Hunter. His words take me aback and I'm surprised by his admission. I guess for him, this is just fun and maybe he doesn't see this going further than a few nights of kinky sex. In a way it makes things easier for me since I can't get my blue-eyed lover out of my head, but I can't help but wonder if Jake feels the same way as his best friend about what we share.

Hunter is staring at me and it's as if my tongue is frozen. I want to respond but my brain can't concoct a decent answer that won't shatter the perfect relationship I have with these two men. *Fuck, say something.* Taking a deep breath in, I slowly release it before attempting an answer, but a voice behind Hunter echoes in the room.

"Are you guys going to make out down here? You could have at least woken me up so I could've joined you." Jake chuckles as he enters the kitchen.

My eyes are still locked with Hunter's and neither of us speaks, but that doesn't deter Jake one bit.

"I guess we could also take turns with her. I mean, we can't continue to be as ruthless as we were last night, right? She won't be able to walk soon." Jake circles the granite island and stands next to Hunter and I. "What smells so good? I'm starved."

I close my eyes for a second and shake my head, trying to regain my ability to speak. When I open my eyes again Hunter's cocky grin reappears. *Oh, God, what now?*

"I thought of taking her this morning on the counter, but she worked us so hard last night, if I don't eat something there's no way I'll be able to keep it up long enough to make her come. Luckily, our little seductress prepared a hearty breakfast we'll be able to devour in no time." Hunter takes a step back and leans against the counter next to me.

"No need to rush it. Don't forget, there's plenty of time. We still have eight long days and nights to take her whenever we want, separately or together."

Both men are laughing, amused at their jokes, talking as if I'm not even in the room. I wish I could be as lighthearted as they are, but the idea that we might only have eight days of this makes my stomach queasy. I don't want it to end next week when Riley comes back. I don't want to say goodbye to what we have, even if I'm uncertain of how I feel about Jake. Instead of joining them I simply shrug.

Jake looks my way and raises his eyebrows. "You're awfully quiet. Are you okay after last night?"

"Yeah. I am."

"I'm sure Hunter must have asked, but how are you feeling?"

"Honestly?"

"Of course."

"Well... It's..." I hesitate, trying to find the right words to describe all the feelings colliding inside me.

"Come on, Ali. Spit it out. What's going on in your pretty little head?"

"I'm kind of sore all over, but mostly confused."

"What's troubling you, baby?"

"What happens when your sister comes back?" I blurt out before I can stop myself. My question captures their attention and they stare at my worried face. Jake takes a few steps towards me before wrapping me in his arms and he kisses the top of my head.

"Ahhh, I see. You want to have a serious talk before breakfast."

"Not necessarily. I can wait," I backtrack, hoping my question didn't upset him.

"It's kinda heavy for the day after, isn't it?" I pick up on the mockery in his voice and I know he's teasing me. "It's important for you?"

I nod. "It is." I know I'm being a girl about this, but the uncertainty is giving me an ulcer.

"I told her we didn't have the answers and we should just take it one day at a time until your sister gets back. I'm sure we'll figure something out by then."

Jake nods at his best friend before turning his attention to me. "He's right. I'll be honest, we've never been in this situation before. We've never lived on the same land as a woman we wanted to share. This is uncharted territory for all of us. It's going to make things more complicated when my sister comes back with her brood of children and her inquisitive nanny, but maybe we're getting ahead of ourselves."

"What do you mean?"

"Things are changing fast for my sister—in a good way."

"What do you know that we don't, buddy?"

Jake turns around and looks at his best friend. "Since my sister became the host of her own cooking show, she's had to travel to LA a lot more often than she used to and now with this second show, I doubt she'll be spending a lot of time on the ranch in the coming months. In the past, Isadora was the one taking care of the kids while she was away. But now the ranch is far too busy and there's way too much going on for us to become surrogate parents to my nephews when Riley is away."

"Yeah, not to mention all these new clients we keep collecting like trophies mean we need to hire new guys to help out. We're already maxed. We can't add the role of daddy to the list."

"Riley knows that very well."

"Jake, I don't follow. Do you think Riley will have to move to LA with her kids?" A wave of worry washes over me because I have no intention of moving to LA I certainly would hate to lose the job I love so much this quickly.

"We've talked about it a lot since she wrapped the first season of her show. It was an exhausting experience for all of us and her kids missed her a lot when she wasn't around."

"Would she put the kids in school in Cali?" Hunter's question is a great one and I listen in to find out more about my fate.

"Who knows, but at the rate her career's going I have a feeling she won't have a choice but to spend a lot of time in California. Our parents are out there and they can help, but knowing Riley, she'll rent her own place to have some sense of privacy."

"Would Isa move to be with her?"

"Riley said they've already talked about it. Since her nanny is a widow and all of her kids have kids of their own, there's nothing holding her here. We'd have to find someone new to help around the ranch, but Isadora is so good with those kids and she's the only person alive who can handle the twins."

"You're right there. Not to mention, I love your sister like she's my own, but man, she can turn into a freak when she's dealing with deadlines. Isa always calms her down."

"Oh." I'm disappointed by the news. "Then she won't need me anymore."

"What makes you say that?" Jake jerks his head back and frowns.

"If she's in LA, why would she need me here?"

"Riley is very clear about her future. She knows she wouldn't be where she is without her popular blog and the way she plays up her serene lifestyle away from the big city. She's making way too much money with that thing to give it up... even for Food TV. Not to mention, the whole pioneer-woman-living-idyllically-in-the-country-with-her-kids fantasy is her brand, her trademark. Even if she moves back home to La-La Land, she'll still need a talented graphic artist to hold the fort while she's away." Jake takes me around the waist before placing a tender kiss on my lips. "Trust me, she won't get rid of you that quickly."

"You see, Allison, you were getting worried for nothing." Hunter reaches out and strokes my cheek while beaming at me.

"I guess."

"Listen, you guys, all this is speculation. I've talked to Riley since she's left and she's very excited about where things are going, but she hasn't made firm plans yet. Let's enjoy the next few days together and we'll figure things out when she comes back."

"I agree with Jake."

"Are we good, Ali?"

"Yeah. I'll stop worrying, then."

"Baby, I can think of other things you can put your mind to." Jake slides his hands under my t-shirt and cups my boobs. I lock eyes with Hunter and I can't believe how turned on I am from having one man's hands all over me while another one is watching.

"Shit," I hiss. Jake squeezes my nipples so hard he sends shivers down my spine all the way to my pussy. I close my eyes, taking in the sweet pain, before tilting my head back. "You're as bad as Hunter." I punch his arm and hit a wall of muscle. *Damn.*

"I'm way worse."

It's too early in the morning for me to come up with something clever, so I let this half smile hang on my lips, in awe of my good fortune.

"I'm starving. Let's dig in. Allison, everything must be ready by now." Hunter's need for food breaks the mood.

"I'm sure you're right, Hunter. If you guys stopped taking turns groping me for longer than five minutes, maybe I'd be able to serve breakfast." I roll my eyes. Both men smile at me angelically as if they haven't a clue what I'm talking about. "Jake, sit down." I gesture for my two guys to take a seat at the kitchen island and I walk to the stove to remove the lid off of the omelet. It's perfect. I grab a few plates to my right and cut a large portion with a spatula for my hungry lovers.

"Allison, the food smells amazing. What did you make?"

"Nothing complicated, but it will fill you up nicely."

When I drop Hunter's plate in front of him, I notice the mischievous look they exchange.

"Thanks, baby. You know, it's still early and I'm pretty sure we'll have time for coffee and a quickie."

"Oh, come on, Hunter." I serve Jake an equally heaping portion.

"Hunter's right. It'll keep us going throughout the day since we'll be heading to Denver."

"Denver? On a Saturday?"

"Yeah, I have an early meeting with the client I met yesterday to iron out a few last-minute details before he signs the contract. I'd normally push this to Monday, but this is too lucrative. Not to mention I have a second meeting right after that."

"Seriously?"

"When Jake's done with Filipe Moura, the owner of Churrascaria Steak House & Cellar, he'll join me for a mid-morning meeting with a few partners who own Casa Del Mar, a chain of very upscale restaurants across California. They've heard such glowing reviews about the way we raise our cattle and the quality of our meat and they want to talk business. They're in town for the day, so we'll be busy all morning until early afternoon."

"Oh, I'll be here alone?" I sit across from the two hungry wolves attacking the omelet I prepared with gusto.

"Only for a few hours, Ali."

"You don't have to stay here by yourself. Dirk is coming around with Jenkins to check up on Jezebel and her newborn. Why don't you come with us?"

"What am I going to do in Denver by myself?"

"It's a big city and there's plenty for you to do. You can shop or walk around the mall, but since it's Saturday and I know you're as much of a foodie as Riley, why don't you hit the farmers' markets? You can take some great photos and you can even buy a few ingredients we might want to use for dinner."

"That's a good idea, Hunter, but I have a better one."

"You do?" both Hunter and I ask in unison.

Jake smiles like a man holding the winning hand at a poker match. "Tomorrow, Jenkins, a bona fide cowboy, will be one of the riders at the Rodeo Rising Stars event. I bet you our little New Yorker has never attended a rodeo in her life. Since you haven't yet bought your cowgirl boots, I think this is a good excuse as any to get a pair."

"A rodeo?" I'm so excited to experience a typical country event I can hardly contain myself.

"That's a great idea. It's an all-day event and there's lots to see and eat." Hunter winks at me.

"I agree with Jake, this is a pretty good excuse to force me to finally get those boots I've been too busy to get since I got here. I'll go shopping while the two of you are in your meetings. Manly cowboys riding dangerous bulls," I say, rubbing my hands together while grinning. "I'm all in."

"If that's all it takes to get you salivating like this, I'll go out there and ride one of our own cattle with my riding hand firmly on the rein and my left arm up waving in the air yelling, 'Yeehaw!' so you can gush all over me."

We all laugh at Hunter's joke.

* * *

I brought my camera to Denver with me yesterday with the intention of hitting a few farmers' markets and taking some photos, but when Jake and Hunter dropped me at the mall, I got lost in the shopping. I was only going to run in and out of a shoe shop to buy myself a pair of brand-new cowgirl boots, but I became obsessed with a dress I saw in a window. I'm usually shy when it comes to buying new clothing because it's never easy to dress a tiny woman with hips, an ass and huge boobs, but something about this pretty dress caught my attention and made me decide to venture into the store.

It's usually a song and dance when Gwyn and I go shopping in New York—by that I mean she pleads with me to open my horizons and to be more of a risk-taker in my wardrobe selection, and I dance around her suggestions, doing my best to avoid stepping out of my comfort zone. The reality is since I've set foot in Denver, I've been more audacious, more brazen and more fearless than ever before. I guess that's one of the reasons why when I stepped out of the changing room and looked at myself, I beamed with joy at the sight of my body instead of cringing. I couldn't believe I was the woman reflected at me in the mirror. It's amazing how a few rapturous nights with Jake and Hunter have transformed me.

I look at the time on the microwave and I panic. "Shit, shit, shit." I'm already ten minutes late. I was supposed to meet my men in front of Jake's truck at twelve o'clock and I'm still trying to get ready. I guess I got so carried away talking to my best friend and updating her on my latest frolics, I lost track of time. Now I'm scrambling to put the finishing touches to my look before heading to the rodeo.

I barely have time to pull on my new pair of cowgirl boots before I hear a knock at my door. "God, I'm so in trouble now," I say aloud. I run to the door and when I swing it open two extraordinarily handsome men stand in front of me all decked out in their rodeo best—freshly ironed checkered shirts, tight-fitting Wrangler jeans, the obligatory cowboy boots and let's not forget the sexy cowboy hat. *Damn. They may not call themselves cowboys, but they're surely playing the part to a tee.* For one split second, I consider ditching the event and luring both of them into my bedroom for an afternoon of unbridled fun because they look so delicious, but then I remember we still have the rest of the week to ourselves since Riley isn't due back for seven more days.

If I needed validation on my wardrobe selection, the way Hunter is eating me up is more than I could've asked for.

"Come in, ya'll," I say, waving at them.

Instead of walking in, Jake and Hunter stare at me incredulously. They blink so fast, I bite off a laugh.

"Holy Jesus, Allison, you look delectable in that dress." Hunter's expression is priceless. He widens his eyes while holding on to his chest as if he's having a heart attack.

"Wow. I mean wow! What Hunter said." Jake takes me in from head to toe and his gaze is so intense I have to fan myself to cool down.

"You like?" I take a step back and twirl provocatively.

"Like? Honey, if it wasn't for the fact we've already made a promise to Jenkins to come out and support him, I'd sling you over my shoulder and I'd walk straight to your bedroom to take you."

"And I'd be running right behind him." In usual fashion, Hunter is grinning from ear to ear at his own joke.

"Stop it, you're going to make me blush." It's false modesty. For once in my life I'm ready to own this moment.

"Are you also wearing white lingerie underneath that dress?"

"Hunter, if I reveal my little naughty secret, you'll get rock hard and since it's impossible for me to resist your huge cock, I'd have to get down on my knees to please you while Jake watches, but we don't want to be late to support Jenkins, do we?"

Jake coughs as if he's choking when he hears my response and Hunter is so taken aback his mouth opens and closes, but nothing comes out. I wink at them and devilishly fold my lower lip in my mouth.

From their reaction, I'm so happy I decided to buy the cutest little white dress I'd ever seen. It's a lot shorter than what I'd usually wear in New York and it reveals a lot more of my legs than I've ever dared to expose before, but I've found this pool of confidence that has been dormant inside me for so long. For once in my life, I'm willing to be a lot more adventurous.

There are a few details I particularly love about this dress—the embroidery overlaid on the skirt is extremely flattering to my hips and the western-style belt with bejeweled buckle cinches my waist perfectly. Although the neckline hits me close to the collarbone, I have to face the obvious—my double-D boobs are far too big to sport the tiny spaghetti straps without looking indecent. I'm so grateful I followed the sales clerk's advice because I feel much more confident about my breast size. I've paired the dress with a delicate crochet half-cardigan that adds an outrageously flirtatious touch to the whole outfit while camouflaging my boobs.

I wasn't going to get all dressed up without paying attention to my lingerie. Since I'm pretty sure my men will want to have a little salacious fun when we get back, I've donned a virginal white bra and matching panties. I must say this white-on-white look has me feeling particularly naughty.

Knowing that both Jake and Hunter love seeing my hair cascade over my shoulders, I've allowed my mane to flow freely. I've kept my makeup to the basics—one coat of black mascara to elongate my lashes, a little blush to bring attention to my eyes and a light coral lipstick to emphasize my pout. I popped a pair of silver hoops in my ears and a few bangles on my wrists and I'm good to go. Although I've only had a second to catch a full glimpse of myself before opening the door, I must say I feel extremely pretty.

"I'm glad to see you bought yourself your very first pair of cowgirl boots." Jake's eyes are fixed on my feet, forcing both Hunter and I to lower our gazes.

"I couldn't resist." I smile at him. "I've wanted a pair for a long time and this was the perfect excuse to buy them." It was a struggle to choose the ideal color, but in the end I decided to go with a more classic look by selecting a pair of mid-calf brown boots.

"Damn, between the flirty dress and those sexy cowboy boots, you're going to be really popular today."

"You think?"

"Seriously, Ali, every time you take a step, your hips under this dress will cause a poor unsuspecting soul to suffer from a heart attack."

"You guys are just saying that."

"No, we're not," both men answer at the same time with a serious look on their faces.

I burst out laughing.

"Honestly, you look ravishingly beautiful. I'm happy Jake and I will be standing by your side because I have a feeling we're going to have to beat them down with a stick to keep them away from your sensual curves."

"For the record, I don't intend on sharing you with anyone else but Hunter."

"I wouldn't want it any other way."

"That's music to my ear, doll. Let's hit the road, lil' lady." Jake adopts a pronounced Southern accent as he presses his fist against his hip, creating a triangle with his arm. I accept his silent invitation by sliding my arm into his and I follow him to the truck. Hunter closes the door behind me before running to join us. I hook my left arm around his and I'm sandwiched safely between my two men.

Something tells me this is going to be another one of those unforgettable days.

* * *

Nothing could've prepared me for my first rodeo.

The place is packed. It's as if all of Denver is crammed under the roof of this arena. The Grand Entry inside the arena is spectacular and it draws a huge roar of admiration from the crowd. The Native Americans ride their majestic horses, all decked out in their colorful native clothing, proudly waving the American flag.

Although we cheer loudly, Jenkins doesn't qualify in the bull-riding event. He makes a valiant effort, but the bull that was drawn for him is a wild one with a fiery temper. Jenkins nearly makes it, but unfortunately Durango, the bull, is more determined than he is and our cowboy isn't able to ride him for the eight seconds required to allow him to compete in the next round.

I can't believe how steadfast that animal is about throwing Jenkins to the ground. Durango is bucking, kicking, flying and performing vertiginous pirouettes in the air until our friend can no longer hold on. I'll admit I'm very impressed. It takes courage, confidence and craziness to do anything so dangerous. It's thrilling to watch.

After the main event, my guys give me the tour of the outdoor fair. Since I'm wearing white, I'm paranoid about sampling some of the crowd favorites because every food item is either deep-fried, laced with barbecue sauce or drizzling with chocolate— usually I'd be all over them, but I really don't want to ruin my pretty dress. When Hunter and Jake notice I'm refusing everything they suggest, I have to 'fess up. Unwilling to let me go hungry, my two dashing lovers rush me home so I can change into something more casual before they whisk me away to a magical location in Fort Collins where we have a picnic under the stars.

Jake has packed everything we need for a delightful outdoor meal before making a quick detour to grab dinner on our way to the lake. He stops at Texas Roadhouse to allow me to sample their award-winning ribs, slow-cooked in their legendary signature secret BBQ sauce recipe. Jake also grabs their melt-in-your-mouth-delicious pulled pork. He tops off this food madness with a side order of steak fries, green beans and sautéed onions. I can't tell you how grateful I am to no longer be wearing white because I indulge to my heart's content.

The stars are set high in the sky, the food is scrumptious and I have the undivided attention of my two favorite guys.

It's a perfect night.

CHAPTER SEVEN

ALLISON

Six days later

"I can't believe Riley is coming back tomorrow with her kids and Isadora," I say to myself when I take a break from editing photos for my boss' upcoming holiday cookbook.

Wow, this time has flown by so fast. Too fast. The last ten days have been filled with such incredible adventures. Jake, Hunter and I did so many fun things I could barely keep up. Of all our crazy adventures, I cherish my daily discovery trips with Jake in his truck and my horseback riding lessons with Hunter the most.

At about three-thirty every day, Jake would knock on Riley's office door to remind me it was the end of the workday and the beginning of our road trip. He would usually leave Hunter behind to watch over the ranch while we'd head to a new spot around Fort

Collins. I discovered so many hidden gems and so many beautiful landscapes.

I still remember our first ride. He refused to start his truck unless I ran back to my place to grab my camera. I hadn't planned on taking photos, but he'd claimed what I was about to see was so magical I had to capture it with my lens. I'll admit, at first I thought he was overplaying it, but Jake was absolutely right. I had never seen such breathtaking scenery in my life. We'd drive around until the sky started changing in those chatoyant shades of warm red, yellow and orange.

God, how can things be this good and this confusing? Gwyn is convinced I've fallen hard for Jake, but I still refuse to admit it to myself. Sometimes I'll allow myself to believe there's more to what we've shared so far, but I usually snap out of my delusional state when I remember how worked up Jake was when Lindsay ambushed him wanting to take things to the next level. Obviously, he's not looking for anything too serious. The last thing I need is to create this fantasy in my mind just to find out he's only interested in a casual fling, one in which he shares me with his best friend. It's best if I keep my feelings for him safely locked up because I don't need another heartbreak.

That said, it hasn't prevented me from secretly looking forward to our daily rides. I don't know how to explain it, but when we're together, Jake's gaze is almost sweltering, causing my temperature to rise to intolerable levels.

I smile at the thought of our short getaways. A small thrill runs through me as I flash back to yesterday's ride.

We ended the day like we have every day for the past week, leaning against the hood of his truck, holding hands and marveling at the landscape. There's something truly magical about the way the sun sets over the Rocky Mountains and every night for the past week I've been in awe.

The scenery wasn't the only thing that took me aback yesterday. There was something different about Jake. I don't know how to explain it, but I swear there was a softness to his touch I've yet to experience. Although still confident and very much the alpha male I gladly surrender to, he was so tender. The moment was intoxicating. It was so perfect I would've stayed out there with him all night long.

Once it got too dark, we headed back to the ranch to join Hunter for a late dinner. Jake and I drove in a comfortable silence as I looked out my window, losing myself in the nocturnal stillness. Last night the moon was out, full and bright, lighting up the warm summer night sky. Furtively, I looked over at Jake, the dash lights casting a glow on his gorgeous face. A strand of his thick hair had fallen over his forehead and I watched his eyes, framed by beautiful lashes, as he scanned the road ahead of us. He was so focused. I'm not sure I've ever taken this much time to admire him before while he's awake. The combination of dark hair, translucent blue eyes, and bronzed skin mixed with the potency of his desire to take my pleasure to new heights—a talent that makes me want more of him—should be illegal in every state of this great country of ours. At that moment, he really did take my breath away.

I was staring at him so shamelessly he caught me a few times, but instead of turning away like I usually would, I held his suggestive gaze until his eyes flickered back to the road. A sly smile formed on his lips, his only acknowledgement that I was quietly devouring him.

By the time we got back to the ranch, I was as turned on as a light switch and I seriously considered running to my place to relieve the tension mounting between my legs before dinner. There was no way of explaining to Hunter that an innocent ride could be laced with so much raw sexuality.

When the three of us got together, the conversation was animated, like always, until I couldn't handle it anymore, at which point Hunter slung me over his shoulder and walked me up to my blue-eyed hunk's bedroom where both men ravished me and gave me orgasm after orgasm.

My horseback riding lessons with Hunter never ended with us getting naked or by me being so wet I could slide out of my panties because we were too busy laughing our heads off to ever turn it into anything sexy. Hunter was more than patient with me, but my awkwardness constantly derailed my horse until Hunter put an end to it by grabbing the reins so we could follow him back to the ranch. I lamented numerous times that I wasn't cut out to be a cowgirl and by the end of the week he agreed with me.

I'm sad my ten days of freedom with my guys is nearly drawing to an end... well, until we figure things out. I'm unsure how Jake, Hunter and I will be able to continue enjoying each other with so many people on the ranch. There's a part of me dying to know, but I'm so afraid of breaking this magical spell, I tell myself it's best to wait for one of them to come up with a plan.

Now I'm diligently working when my phone rings. When my best friend's name flashes across my screen, I can't help but smile. *I'm sure she's calling for more smut.*

"Are you calling for an update on my dirty love life and to find out if I've had my afternoon quickie yet?" I chuckle.

Gwyn and I have had numerous chats and she knows about every single toe-curling climax. She also reveled in my saucy adventures of the past week. I think she's been using me to live out one of her own fantasies and secretly, I've been enjoying every minute of it.

"No. I'm calling about something else."

"Oh. Why do you sound so serious?"

Her voice is unusually subdued. Gwyn is always so bubbly when we talk because she's always looking forward to my latest naughty tale, but today she seems very preoccupied.

"Allison—"

"Wait a minute," I interrupt. "Gwyn, you only call me by my full name when you have bad news. Is everything okay with you and Gaven?"

"We're fine. I've been debating calling you for the last thirty minutes, but Gaven pushed me to dial your number."

"Why in the world would you hesitate to call me? You're my best friend. What's going on?"

"Clark left my house half an hour ago. Right after he left, I was so distraught, I called Gaven in a state of panic."

Huh? "Panic? I don't understand any of this. Why in the world would he drop by your place again and, more importantly, why would you even open the door?"

"Trust me, I nearly slammed the door in his face, but the way he was begging for me to listen… it made me think maybe I should hear him out. After all, you're my best friend and when he said it concerns you, I was all ears."

"Puh-lease," I say, rolling my eyes. "What could Clark have to say that was so urgent? And why would you believe it has anything to do with me? We haven't been together in over three months. He's part of my past now. I'm sure his relationship with Paula, the woman I caught him cheating on me with, is blossoming beyond belief and his über-successful investment company with his business partner Jasper is raking in millions of dollars every month." I snort with disdain.

"Clark says he's been trying to get a hold of you for the past few weeks, but you've been ignoring his calls and his text messages."

"Gwyn, this conversation is getting weirder by the second. Since when do you care about Clark? I thought you made it clear I needed to move on and put him behind me, which is exactly what I've done. Why are you all of a sudden interested in his futile calls and his fake-urgent text messages?"

"Your ex was trying to get a hold of you because of a very serious matter. Frankly, I'm surprised you never told me about this in the past and I'm a little hurt I had to hear it from a person I have very little respect for."

"What are you talking about?" She's driving me mad with this cryptic conversation.

"You've always claimed you had no other involvement in Clark's company other than co-signing the lease to his extremely expensive Manhattan office space."

"I don't. I've been honest with you from the beginning. Why would I lie?" I'm so confused right now.

"According to Clark, you're the treasurer of his company."

"The what?"

Gwyn is the most straightforward person I know and I'm puzzled as to why she's skirting around the real reason why she's calling. "You know, a treasurer. The watchdog who oversees all aspects of financial management in a company. It's like being a company's money-keeper."

Instead of answering her preposterous accusation, I start laughing hysterically, slapping my free hand against my thigh and stomping my foot against the floor until her words put an end to my amusement.

"I don't think you'll find it so funny when I tell you Clark stood in my kitchen and looked me square in the eye before divulging that twelve of your investors were suing the hell out of you in a monster class-action suit against Venture App and its principals. And since you're the treasurer at your ex's company, they're suing your ass as well."

****

Get Your FREE SECRET Chapters!

Thank you for purchasing this romance book!

I'd love for you to lose yourself in more
sultriness, sexiness and steamy passion!

When you sign-up today, I'll send you the following
Secret Chapter for Part 4 of this serial:

*Jake's thoughts after dropping off Lindsay while driv-
ing back to the ranch to be with Allison and Hunter*

*** <u>PASSWORD FOR</u> Secret Chapter Part 4:
First-Rodeo

Note: the password is case sensitive!

Sign-up TODAY!

www.RomanceBooksRock.com

***If you've already signed-up to my list from
previous books, you can visit the same page to
download the Secret Chapters for this romance***

****

PART 5—BILLIONAIRES' INDULGENCE

Burning Desire

Chapter One

Holy Mother Mary.

My jaw is open and I'm gasping for air as I replay my best friend's words. My iPhone is still stuck to my ear, but it's as if I've gone blind, deaf and mute in a matter of seconds. My brain is hurting so much right now, it's not even funny. My best friend just dropped a bomb so devastating it would make the worst nuclear attack look like a playground. *Did she say a lawsuit?*

There's no way this is possible. I mean I do understand her words because after all, I speak English, but at the same time it's incomprehensible to me Gwyn would ever link my name to fraud. I knew something was up when she called me by my full name, but it never occurred to me Clark lied about my involvement in his company and it certainly never would have even popped into my head that my whole life was about to burst into flames for wrongful actions I never committed.

I've never managed the finances of my ex's company. The whole idea of me poring over complicated financial charts is laughable. Venture App is Clark and Jasper's pride and joy, not mine. Either Gwyn is delirious or Clark is out to get me.

I'm still lost in my thoughts when Gwyn brings me back to reality.

"Ali, are you still there?"

"Yes," I say in a meek voice. "Gwyn, I'm not a principal or a treasurer in Clark's company—I never have been. And I surely wouldn't know anything about disgruntled investors."

This whole discussion has my stomach tied in a knot and it's threatening to give me an ulcer. I'm trying to make sense of what Gwyn is sharing, but none of it is logical. I can barely keep track of my own finances, why in the world would anyone appoint me to manage a company's finances, let alone my ex who I caught cheating on me?

"You wouldn't lie to me, right?"

"Gwyn, I have nothing to hide. You're frustrating the hell out of me because it's as if you're speaking Chinese and I'm speaking Swahili. I'm sure this must be a big fat mistake. Clark is making this stuff up."

"You're sure?"

"Of course. We've been friends for a very long time and we've had our differences, but we've never had this type of tension between us, Gwyn. How can you even doubt me?" I say, ticked off.

"Clark was convincing at painting a pretty grim picture and I'm really worried about you."

"He's bullshitting. My only part in my ex's company was being a stupid woman who only had desperation as her last card to play. When he secured that office last year, Clark begged me to co-sign the lease every single day for two months straight until I caved in. His explanation at the time was Jasper's heavy student loan debt and bad credit were anchors preventing them from propelling the company forward. He was pressuring me and manipulating me by telling me that by signing the lease, I was showing him I believed in him, and hence I believed in us. I know now he was playing me for a fool, but at the time I really thought those papers could bring us closer. As you know, I've refused to co-sign the lease this year, so as far as I'm concerned, I have no involvement in this story anymore."

"Yeah, well, as I told you, that's not the song Clark is singing."

"Come on, Gwyn. We both know how much of a snake he can be. I'm not even sure why you're taking his claims seriously. For all we know, he's trying to weasel his way back into my life by going through you so I'd have no other option but to pay attention to his desperate pleas."

"Yeah, I was thinking the same, but when he revealed he's secured legal counsel and his business partner Jasper Reed has done the same, I became a little nervous. People don't hire an attorney unless it's important. When I questioned him why investors would go after you guys in such a vicious way, he cleverly avoided my question by telling me I needed to get in touch with you as soon as possible and urge you to secure your own legal representation. When he explained he and Jasper had a three-week lead time on you and they were getting ready for the impending civil trial, that's when I realized he wasn't bullshitting."

"But this makes no sense," I yell out as panic sets in. "I have absolutely no involvement in his company and I don't understand why I would need legal counsel to protect myself against investors I don't even know who could sue the hell out of me when I've done nothing wrong."

"Honey, I'm telling you everything I know. But I recommend you get yourself back here as soon as possible. You need to find a good attorney to fight this. If you're not the treasurer in Clark's company, you need to prove it so these investors don't go after you."

"Even though I'm no longer with him, the asshole manages to find a way to make my life miserable."

"I know you hate his guts, and I can't blame you, but I'd call Clark immediately after you hang up with me. Maybe he'll be more forthcoming with you than he was with me."

"That's a good idea and I need to get back to New York urgently."

"I'll be honest, the sooner you're back in the city, the sooner you'll be able to get to the bottom of things. If Clark is lying about your involvement in his company, you need to move heaven and earth to discover the truth."

"I'm scared, Gwyn," I confess, biting my nails. "I don't have the means to hire an attorney. You know what I've been dealing with over the past few months. Sure, I get paid at this job, but it's never going to cover the astronomical legal fees. I don't know how much these investors are suing Clark and Jasper for, but all this sounds like it's going to be a financial tsunami for me." I rub my temples with my free hand. The pressure building between my temples is unbearable.

"Since all of this was well over my head, I called Gaven and he confirmed my worst fears. Class-action suits usually mean some pretty angry people are looking for a colossal payday. These types of suits usually end up in a guilty verdict that represents millions if not hundreds of millions of dollars for the guilty party and a case like yours could also mean a prison sentence."

Fuck, now I really have a splitting headache. "Jesus."

"Sweetie, there are firms in the city that take on clients pro bono. If you've been wronged, I'm sure someone will want to help you. Why don't I ask Gaven if he knows of anybody in his circle who could represent you? I'm sure by the time you get back, we'll have figured something out."

"I pray to God you're right or else I'm really screwed."

CHAPTER TWO

JAKE

It's amazing how much I've come to look forward to my afternoon rides with Ali. It was an innocent suggestion at first to allow her to discover the area and take some breathtaking photos, but it's quickly turned into my favorite part of the day.

Riley's trip to California has allowed us to give into our hedonistic desires with unbridled gluttony. Sharing Ali with my best friend has been an extraordinary and unforgettable experience, but I'll be honest, in the past few days I've found myself more and more reluctant to allow Hunter to savor the sassy blonde. My best friend and I have always been very open when it comes to women, especially those we've had the pleasure of sampling together, but I never imagined myself falling for Ali. I was content gorging on her sinful body and I was extremely turned on by watching my best friend make her come, but lately, that pleasure has turned into dread.

There's something magical about the time Ali and I spend on the road until nightfall that's really brought us closer together and it's allowed me to appreciate every facet of her personality. Neither of us has said a word so far, but something has changed between us—I just know it. It's like an unspoken communion. There's no doubt I was instantly attracted to her, but in the last nine days I've also been able to discover her quirkier side, which I find irresistible. She comes across as shy and reserved at first, but in time she's allowed me in and I'm totally smitten. I usually start my countdown right after lunch knowing that I only have a few hours before she's all mine.

Yesterday afternoon was truly magical. I didn't want it to end and if I could've convinced her to spend the night sleeping cuddled next to my body at the back of my truck under the moonlight to avoid going back to the ranch, I would have.

Today, I'm particularly excited because we're traveling through time. I want to take her to the Holiday Twin Drive-In Theatre. This drive-in theatre is a throwback to the fifties and it's a great place to get nice and close. There's something kitschy and fun about eating snacks in my SUV while we watch a movie on a big screen outdoors. I hope she'll enjoy the experience as much as she's been thrilled by all of our past adventures.

After the movies, I plan on taking her to the lake again for a romantic picnic under the stars. I can't think of a more perfect backdrop for an intimate evening. I'll put some blankets at the back of my vehicle, I'll pack some wine and beer in a cooler and we'll stop by the Colorado Room for some dinner.

This is one of my favorite barbecue joints in town because I can't get enough of their infamous Sammys. Those sandwiches are out-of-this-world delicious. Since I can never choose, I'll order a few of their slow-roasted pork shoulder sandwiches topped with sweet tangy barbecue sauce served with apple and jicama slaw and I'll also get a couple of their braised short ribs topped with caramelized onions, sautéed peppers and gruyere cheese sauce. You really can't go wrong. I absolutely have to get her to try the Colorado Room's taters. The best way to describe them is deep-fried mashed potato balls. I've offered to pay good money to get my hands on the recipe so Isadora can make them for us, but the owner keeps turning me down.

When Ali is fully relaxed, I'll confess my feelings for her. There's only one way to know if this intense energy I've felt surge between us during these afternoon rides is mutual. My timing couldn't be more perfect. Hunter will be in Denver partying it up with two of his cousins from LA, so we'll have all night to enjoy each other, since he usually plays it safe and books a hotel room to sober up.

"Riley's impending return must have kept Ali really busy today," I say to myself as I approach my sister's office. I tried calling Ali to let her know I was running a little late for our date this afternoon, but it kept going straight to voicemail. I texted her a few times in the past hour, but she hasn't responded. I'm sure the fact that my sister is coming back tomorrow is most likely adding a lot of pressure. Knowing Riley, she must've sent Ali a mile-long to-do list. *Damn, the honeymoon is nearly over. I'm going to have to man up or things will get awkward real fast.* I still remember Ali desperately trying to understand how our relationship would unfold once my sister and her kids were back at the ranch, and even though I really didn't have an answer at the time, I'm very glad I didn't make any predictions because my feelings for her have dramatically changed. When Hunter's back tomorrow, I need to have a face-to-face with my best friend to let him know I've fallen hard for Ali and I want her all to myself.

Looks like she's having a grueling day.

As I reach my sister's office, I notice through the large window Allison hunched over with her elbows pinned against the desk. She's cradling her head in her hands. Although I'm not as carefree as Hunter, I'm sure I can find a way to bring back her dazzling smile regardless of the day she's had so far.

"Knock, knock, knock," I say jovially as I push the door open. "I hope you're ready for an amazing afternoon because I have some big plans for us. It's an adventure you'll never find in a million years in a city like New York." I stride towards her desk hoping I'll have piqued her curiosity. "I can't promise you'll be able to take loads of great photos, but I can promise a whole lot of fun."

I'm standing over her grinning ear to ear, but since she's made no effort to look up at me it hits me something must be wrong.

"Ali, what's going on?"

"I... I don't think I can make it today," she replies between sobs. Her head is still nestled between her hands and she shakes her head to emphasize her words.

I take a few steps forwards and kneel at her feet. "Why are you crying?"

"My life is an absolute disaster," she wails.

"Come on now, Ali, it can't be that bad. Is it about the workload my sister left you?"

"I'd never get bent out of shape just because of workload, Jake. This is far more serious. Actually it's devastating."

I don't know what might have changed so drastically in the last few hours, but she's really worked up and the sadness I read on her face breaks my heart.

"Why don't you share what's going on? Maybe I can help." I brush her hair back tenderly, trying to comfort her.

"I don't want to bother you with my drama. This has nothing to do with you. It has everything to do with the fact I consistently fall for the wrong men and I always end up picking up the broken pieces of my life. In this case, I'm royally screwed."

"Sounds like it has to do with your ex. I think you know by now I'm not immune to unexpected drama caused by an ex-lover. Why don't you tell me what the bastard did? Whatever it is you're dealing with, I'm here for you." I wipe away her tears, hating to see her so broken.

She blinks a few times, trying to assess if she can trust me. I smile at her and hold her gaze, hoping she's willing to trust me. After a few long minutes, she brings her shoulders down as if already defeated and sighs before speaking.

"I'm being sued by a bunch of people I've never met in my life and didn't know existed until an hour ago."

"Okay. I'll admit, it's not what I was expecting. I think you're going to have to start from the beginning because this is heavy shit." Why would anyone want to go after Ali?

For the next hour she spills her guts between sobs about her ex-boyfriend, the nasty breakup, the devastating conversation she had not long ago with her best friend Gwyn, the lawsuit, and her failed attempt at getting a straight answer from this idiot Clark who gave her the runaround until she hung up on him in frustration just before I walked into the office. By the time she's done, she's crying and shaking like a leaf.

I embrace her in my arms while consoling her. "Your best friend is right. You can't go at this alone. You need to hire the best attorneys out there if you're going to go against a class-action suit."

"But I've done nothing wrong," she wails.

"Sweetie, that's why you need to fight this." I rub her back, bringing her body closer to mine, hoping my warmth will calm her down.

"I don't even know where to start to find a New York lawyer willing to take on my case free of charge. I mean, do attorneys really help people like me out of the goodness of their heart?"

"Yes, some do. Not all attorneys are bad people, baby. Gwyn is right in recommending finding a lawyer who would take on your case pro bono, but you have to understand that top lawyers wouldn't spend a lot of their time working on a case they're never going to get paid for. In a city like New York where most sharp attorneys bill a thousand dollars an hour, you can be certain anyone who takes your case would be passing it along to a junior attorney. Now I'm not saying you can't get assigned a competent junior attorney, what I'm saying is why take chances?"

"What other options do I have, Jake? Even if I were to ask my parents for support, they'd never be able to come up with the kind of money I need to fight this. There's no way I can ever ask them to mortgage their house. It would just be inconceivable. I feel so alone in this."

I run my thumb along her trembling lip before leaning in and kissing her.

"Ali, first off, you don't know what you're fighting yet since your ex-boyfriend is tight-lipped about the situation other than to tell you to hire legal counsel. Second off, I agree. You shouldn't put your family's livelihood at stake for mistakes Clark is potentially responsible for. Third off, you're not alone. You have me now. Why don't you allow me to help?"

"I could never ask you to do anything like that. I'd rather die," she says, panicked by my suggestion.

"Sweetheart, you're not asking, I'm offering. We've shared so much already in the past few weeks and I'd hope that by now you'd see us as friends as much as lovers. I couldn't bear seeing you deal with this situation without stepping up."

"Oh," she lets out, surprised, before curling her lips into a faint smile. The dark cloud over her hazel eyes has lifted and she's gazing at me with a glimmer of hope. "Are you serious?"

"Ali, by the sound of it, your ex-scumbag-of-a-boyfriend has screwed you over and I want to make things right for you and straighten his mess out. Allow me to do that much for you."

Her mouth falls open in shock and I instinctively want to tear Clark limb from limb for having put her in harm's way with his callous actions. I don't know the full story yet, but I do know a class-action suit is serious shit and it means an unscrupulous dirtbag was willing to take advantage of innocent people by robbing them blind.

"Are you sure? I don't have the money to repay you."

I can't believe she's so stunned someone would want to lighten her burden and be there for her. What kind of lowlives has she dated in the past?

"Who said anything about you having to repay me?" I flash her a sly smile before dropping soft kisses against the neck I want to suck on for hours.

"I don't know how I can ever thank you for coming to my rescue like this."

"Seeing you smile again is all the thanks I need. I have more money than I'll ever need from the sale of my former dotcom company and Hunter and I have been extremely lucky because the ranch has been turning a solid profit year after year since we bought it. Why have all this money if I can't put it to good use? Not to mention I have the right connections—sharp people who can help us make sense of all of this. You're in trouble and you need me."

In all of my years in business, no one has ever sued me, but I have gone after a number of dishonest individuals and so far I've always won. The tech business is cutthroat and many less formidable competitors won't hesitate to use dishonest practices to gain an edge. I'd like to say I've always ended on top because I'm smarter than the crooks who were trying to wrong me, but it's really because our fortune has allowed us to hire top-gun attorneys. If you're going to fight fire with fire you need to be armed with a stellar legal team.

"So you know of a good attorney in New York?"

Her innocence is endearing and I have to fight off a smile so she doesn't think I'm making light of the situation.

"I know some of the best attorneys from coast to coast. I also know of a cleaner who'll help us find information your ex is unwilling to share."

"A cleaner? What are you talking about?"

"Your Clark must be hiding a lot. If you claim you're not a treasurer in his company and he's claiming you are, there's foul play somewhere and we need to dig deep in order to have solid data before our attorney stands in front of a judge. In the tech world, we have cleaners who can break into any computer, tap into wireless communication systems, dismantle any complex code and track anything that can be traced electronically. In my case, his name is Winston Hughes." Winston takes care of cleaning rich people's laundry and in the past few years his roster of clients has been heavily skewed towards tech moguls who all of a sudden find themselves with a lot to lose in the face of frivolous lawsuits. Winston's team consists of a bunch of nerds and former Army intelligence who put their incredible talent to good use clearing the names of their elite clients.

"Clark can be very sneaky and Jasper has always given me the creeps. Are you sure this Winston guy is going to be able to come up with anything?"

"Trust me, idiots like your ex and his business partner are no match for Winston and his team."

"Without you, I would've given into desperation." She looks so vulnerable now and the only thing I want to do is protect her.

"Don't you ever doubt I'm here for you. You hear me?"

She nods vehemently and fights off tears. "Okay, I won't."

"I'm going to stay by your side throughout this whole ordeal. If I have to hire more men to take over for my responsibilities on the ranch so it doesn't all fall on Hunter's shoulders, I will without a shred of hesitation."

"Oh, no," she says, widening her eyes and bringing her hand up to her mouth. "You can't do that on my account. I mean I don't want to add to your load," she protests.

"I don't think you heard me. There's no negotiation here, Ali. I'm in this with you. Period."

"Gosh. You don't know what it means to me to hear you say that."

"At some point you're going to have to fly back to New York to meet with the attorney and possibly stand trial. I'm coming with you because there's no way I'm letting you go alone. I'll be on that plane sitting right next to you and I'll stay in the Big Apple for as long as it takes for us to get resolution. Do you hear me?"

Her face brightens so much I know I've been able to cast away her worries.

"Thank you, thank you, thank you," she chants, jumping into my arms, covering my face with kisses.

God, I love feeling her curves against my body like this. I could stay wrapped around her all day long.

As much as I hate having to postpone my plans to confess how I've fallen for Ali and my desire to have her all to myself, it's clear she needs me now more than ever. Once we put this nightmare behind us, we can start making plans for a future together.

CHAPTER THREE

ALLISON

Three weeks later

I'm incredibly excited and nervous about to-morrow. In a little over twenty-four hours, I'll be back in New York City.

Two days ago, Jake's legal eagle, Aaron Schatzberg, asked us to jump on a flight and rush to the Big Apple. Although Jake kept begging me to have faith, I nearly lost all hope until Hilary McMillin, one of Winston's investigators, caught a lucky break when she got her hands on damaging evidence we needed in our fight against Clark and his business partner. The minute it became clear we had some solid proof, Aaron summoned us for a meeting at his office to prepare me to stand in front of a judge who will hopefully rule in my favor and clear me of any wrongdoing.

Between the endless conference calls with Aaron and the long hours I've spent every day on the phone with Winston's team, I've been mentally and emotionally drained. I usually would confide in my best friend, but she's been away on a buying trip for work, which made it nearly impossible for us to find a decent time to talk. She's been shopping her head off in Indonesia, Thailand and Bali. I've done my best to keep her up to date with the latest developments via text messages, but I didn't want to overwhelm her so we decided to talk when she got back.

She's been trying to get a hold of me all day, but I've been so busy, I couldn't even find one minute to dial her. I've had to let all her calls go to voicemail because between Riley, the lawyer and the cleaner, it's been absolutely insane. I figured it would be best for us to catch up at the end of the day when I'd be able to kick off my cowgirl boots and unwind with a glass of wine.

It's true I'm seeing her in two days for breakfast before she heads to the office, but since she left the country three weeks ago, there's so much to catch up on. Not to mention there's plenty I don't want to discuss in a public place. I'm happy I'm all packed and ready for my trip. Since I don't have to worry anymore, Gwyn and I can talk as long as we want.

When I dial her, she picks up immediately and I'm already giddy. "Oh my God, Gwyn. I've missed you so much." I'm so overjoyed right now, it's not even funny. I swear if we were on a Skype video chat, she'd see me jump up and down.

"Ali, sweetie. It seems like a lifetime. I feel like I've been gone so long I've had time to celebrate two birthdays." She laughs.

"I'm so happy to finally hear your voice again."

"I feel the same. I can't believe I was on the other side of the planet while you were dealing with all this shit. How's everything?"

"I won't lie. The last few weeks have been a rollercoaster filled with scary lows and heartwarming highs. I can't remember the last time I was this stressed out."

"Of course. This is your name and reputation we're talking about. I'd be losing my mind with worry as well."

"It's true the burden of having to prove my innocence has been weighing on me like an eight-hundred-pound gorilla, but it's lightweight compared to discovering Clark has been involved in malicious activities."

"What has the scumbag done now?"

"While we were together he always claimed he had big plans for Venture App—"

"Wait. Don't tell me he lied." She snorts.

"Yeah," I respond, matching her disdain. "He did have some lofty financial forecasts, he only omitted to share he was willing to reach his goals by any means possible—even if it involved duping a bunch of innocent investors."

"So it's true? He and Jasper stole all this money from these investors?"

"Gwyn, it's been disgusting to witness. He was never the person I thought he was and he didn't hesitate to throw me under the bus to save his own skin."

"Do you know how you ended up being an unsuspecting treasurer in his fraudulent company?"

"Not at all, but it all comes out in a couple of days. Jake's attorney, Aaron Schatzberg, is finally able to divulge more details. So I'm both looking forward to and dreading getting back to NYC. As much as I've tried, it's been nearly impossible for me to focus on work because my days have been so chaotic."

"How's your boss taking all this? I mean you'll be away for a while."

"To my great relief, Riley has been incredibly understanding about what I'm going through and she's given me the time I needed to sort this mess out as long as I made up for the hours—which I always did. While I'm back home, I'll continue working electronically. I won't be at the lawyer's office or in court all day."

"Good. So it's all out in the open with Riley?"

"Yeah. Jake insisted I let Hunter, Riley and Isadora know early on about what I was dealing with because he knew I would be distracted and he also knew I would be spending lots of time on the phone during my work hours. Isadora has taken it upon herself to cook the most delicious Southern comfort meals I've ever tasted in my life. It's her way of showing she cares and I love that woman so much for what she's done for me. Riley's four-year-old daughter, Erika, will come up to me and give me a big hug whenever she notices I'm sad or anxious and she's already quick at reminding me everything will be okay. She's so adorable, I'd totally adopt her if I could." I laugh.

"I'm so happy you have good people surrounding you."

"Gaven's been amazing. He's checked up on me daily—sometimes twice a day—to find out how I was holding up. He's such a sweetheart and a keeper."

"I love him to pieces. I asked him to reach out to you while I was gone and I'm so proud of him for going beyond and above."

"He certainly did."

"What about your parents? Did you finally confess?"

I sigh, still remembering the difficult conversation I had with my mom and dad. "It took a lot of courage, but I did manage to speak to my family about what was going on. Needless to say, the news was a shocker for my parents and my brothers."

"I have no doubt this must've scared the living daylights out of them when you told them."

"They were incredibly worried, but when I explained I wasn't alone, they were grateful I had someone like Jake in my corner fighting for justice."

"It takes a certain type of man to be willing to step up to the plate like he has."

Jake has unselfishly set aside so many of his own priorities in order to be at my beck and call. The turmoil in the pit of my stomach since I found out I was looking at a multimillion-dollar lawsuit has been eating at me little by little. I think Jake must've sensed that, because he's been particularly caring and protective of me. His business has been growing in leaps and bounds and he's also had the burden of hiring more staff to work on the ranch in order to respond to the insatiable demands of a roster of new clients, but he dropped anything he was doing if I needed him. No matter how many times I've told him how much I appreciate what he's doing for me, I still feel it's never enough. I haven't got a clue how I would've navigated this treacherous road without him.

"I couldn't be luckier to have so many amazing people in my corner rooting for me."

"On a different note, what about Jake and Hunter? What's going on with your two guys?"

"Hunter's also been supportive and as you know, Jake's been a real pillar of strength during these trying times."

"Okay, that's a great answer if you were speaking to your mom, but you know exactly what I mean." She chuckles.

"It's been complicated."

"I bet. Have the three of you…"

"Not really. Unfortunately, a few days after Riley got back from California, Hunter got an urgent call from his family. His grandmother had a serious heart attack and he had to rush back to Los Angeles to be by her side. He's been gone for nearly three weeks. Even though I've been going through my own personal hell, his own ordeal has saddened me because it's been really hard on him."

"Oh, I'm so sorry to hear that. How is his grandmother now?"

"It was touch and go for a long time, but he texted Jake a few days ago to let us know the doctors were allowing them to take her home."

"Man, you've been dealing with a lot."

"Yeah, it seems like this tsunami of bad news just swept over the ranch all at once."

"What about Jake? Has anything happened between the two of you since he's still living with you on the ranch?"

"Legal drama and the return of my boss don't bode well for our former debauchery. Hunter, Jake and I had to cool things off the minute Riley got back. It was a shock to my body at first to go without the warmth of these two men who made me climax over and over again, but this pending trial, Hunter's grandmother's condition and Jake's busy schedule covering for his business partner has put a damper on things. Not to mention the cooking reality TV show shot Riley's fame into the stratosphere and she now has more new business opportunities than she can handle, which means a lot more work for me."

"That's it? It's over?" I can hear the disapproval in her voice.

"I really don't know, Gwyn. Since I'm still hiding my feelings for Jake, I figured all these distractions were for the best."

"So you're going to keep your feelings for him bottled up forever?"

"I'm not like you. I'd never take the lead with a man. It's not my style."

"He's a great guy and you like him a lot, Ali. I don't understand why you don't just come out and tell him. You might be pleasantly surprised."

"I know where you're coming from, but in the last three weeks, Jake's been all business. Don't get me wrong, he's been watching over my case like a hawk, but he's also been unusually distant."

"Could it be because Riley's back? I'm sure he doesn't want to put you in a compromising position since she's the one who hired you."

"Maybe you're right, but I'm not going to rock the boat."

"That's not a good enough answer."

Damn, she's relentless.

I sigh heavily before speaking again. "I'll admit I've found it challenging to figure out the best way of approaching Jake. Every time I tried, he turned the conversation around so we're focusing on the trial. It really screwed me up for a while because I was afraid I was confusing gratitude for genuine feelings towards him, but when we're in the same room together, my heart skips a beat."

"You'll have five days alone with him, sweetie."

"We'll be so busy in New York—"

"It's the perfect time," she interrupts. "Think about it—no boss to watch over your shoulder, no nanny who could potentially catch the two of you, no nephews and nieces running around, no workers to manage and no business partner to handle. It's just the two of you."

"I... I don't know."

"Listen, I'm not going to pressure you on this one, Ali. You've been sharing your feelings about him for weeks now. I know this trial has derailed things for you, but from what you've described, I think you're making a huge mistake by remaining silent. I'd hate for you to regret letting him go without a fight."

I take in her words as I ponder on a possible way for me to let Jake how I feel.

"Let me think about it."

"You should, because life is too damn short to let every bump in the road throw you for a loop. You want him?"

"I do," I whisper, heavy-hearted.

"Then you should go after him. Period. End of story."

There's a long silence before she speaks again.

"Honey, I'm going to have to go. I'm still severely jet-lagged and my bed is calling me."

"Okay, I love you. I'll see you in a couple of days for an early-morning breakfast. I can't wait to hug you again."

"Same here, kiddo. Have a safe trip and I'll see you soon."

"I will." I sigh heavily, clutching the phone in my hands.

I know Gwyn is looking out for me and she wants me to be happy, but I'm not sure I have what it takes to be that forward with Jake.

CHAPTER FOUR

Hunter

"I haven't felt this rested since I left Fort Collins," I tell myself as I peel open my eyes. I let out a big yawn before stretching out my arm to grab my iPhone.

Wow. I slept twelve hours straight. I can't remember the last time I went to bed at eight o'clock at night. Damn, I was surely exhausted.

Even with my blinds still pulled down, it's obvious it's going to be another gloriously sunny day in LA, but that's not motivating enough to entice me out of bed. Just as I'm toying around with the idea of flipping to my side, pulling the covers over my head and falling asleep a little while longer, I hear a few of my stepsisters' kids fighting with each other. *Man, those boys are even more rambunctious than Riley's twins.* From the hustle and bustle going on in the kitchen downstairs, it's clear the household already has a headstart on me. *It's good to be home.*

The past three weeks have been the most stressful of my life. Although I had nightmares when my parents divorced when I was only ten years old, it pales in comparison to the idea of losing the woman I love the most on this planet. It's funny really, because in the last ten years I've been in and out of la-la land. When I'm back in town, it's usually either for business or to visit the woman who's captured my heart since she first took me into her arms.

I haven't spent this much time in Los Angeles since I left my dad's house to study at Stanford University. I would have much preferred to come back under better circumstances, but when my dad called to let me know that my grandmother Rose had had a heart attack and she had been admitted to the hospital, I dropped everything and I jumped on the next flight.

Luckily for me Jake knows exactly how important my grandmother is in my life and he took over my responsibilities at the ranch without asking any questions. Before I was packed and ready to go, he had already lined up workers to cover for me and he was looking for backup. He only said one thing before I left, but it meant the world to me. "You better call me if you need to talk. You don't have to go through this alone."

I considered renting a place while I was out here, but I decided to stay at my dad's house so that I can be as close as possible to my grandmother and the rest of the family. I don't think he'd ever say it aloud, but from the way we've been bonding, I think my dad is happy with my decision to stay in my old room. Although they're not affected directly, my three stepsisters have also been dropping by to make sure my dad is holding up.

It's been a long time since we've all been back home at the same time. It's funny how weddings, births or tragedy bring a family closer together. All of a sudden goals and deadlines fall by the wayside.

"Nana is still with us and that's all that matters," I say, pensively scratching the early-morning stubble on my chin.

I still remember how excruciatingly long the flight from Denver to LA was. It's only two and a half hours, but it felt like I was flying to Hong Kong and back. I'm usually a pretty easy-going guy, but I was a ball of nerves when I arrived at the hospital where my grandmother was staying. When I walked into Nana Rose's room and I saw her lying there pale as a ghost, it nearly brought me to my knees. In all of my life, I had never experienced such pain. My grandfather died ten years ago and I still remember crying over his loss, but it never felt like somebody was stabbing me in the heart.

Beatrix Rose Evans and I have the type of relationship few men will ever share with their grandmothers. I believe the love we share has shaped me into the man I am today. I do love my mother, I guess, but she's always given the impression she wasn't very interested in me or in anything that ever happened in my life. My maternal grandmother is still alive, but like all the other family members on my mother's side, I have a very distant relationship with her. For some reason I've never been able to warm up to my mom's mom. Of course, the fact that I left Arizona at sixteen to move in with my dad and my stepmother here in Los Angeles did little to bring us closer. She never made the effort and neither did I.

With my grandmother in hospital, we had practically lost all hope until one night I told my father to go back home for a decent night's rest. I promised I'd stand watch over my grandmother, allowing him the luxury of sleeping in his own bed for the first time in weeks.

Standing vigil in a hospital changes you. I've never seen my father look so broken or so helpless. That's telling considering he stands six feet six inches tall. He's always been larger than life to me. I've always seen him as unbreakable, but since I've come back home, I've seen a man nearly paralyzed by the fear of losing his beloved mother.

After straining to remain awake, I drifted into a deep sleep with my head resting on Nana Rose's lap while clutching her little hands like I had done so many times when I was a young boy. At some point in the middle of the night I felt soft fingers playing through my hair and I woke up abruptly. She had been in a coma for days and just like that she'd woken up and she was smiling down at me.

She was so frail it broke my heart, but at least she was alive and awake. It was clear that this feisty little woman was sending a message to God letting Him know she wasn't quite ready yet. Although the doctor's prognosis is extremely encouraging, I'm still keeping a very close eye on my nana.

Today, for the first time since I've arrived in Los Angeles, I woke up with another woman consuming my thoughts.

"I should call the ranch to find out how things are going," I mumble to myself as I flash back to the last night Jake and I shared the sexy blonde who's become an incredibly passionate and addicting lover in a very short period of time. I flip the covers from my naked body and run to the bathroom to cover up before any of my nephews barge into my bedroom. Back in Fort Collins, there's always a buffer. I can hear Riley's kids coming because little Erika is usually running to catch up after her brothers as they storm towards my house. Inevitably, her cries and her laughs are a warning sign and I always have time to get dressed, but it's not the case here.

After brushing my teeth, splashing my face with cold water and taking a quick shower, I jump into a pair of old track pants and I sit on my bed trying to decide if I should call Allison or Jake first. I'm just about to dial my best friend's number when a text comes in.

Remember me?

How the hell can I ever forget you?

Trying to charm my pants off?

I think I've done that a few times already.

Yes, you have. On a serious note, Jake said your grandmother's doing better, but I wanted to drop you a quick line to find out for myself.

It's good to hear from you. Thanks for your concern. She's doing better.

Thank God. I'm so relieved. How are you holding up?

I'm good. I have to remain strong for my dad. Is it okay if I call? We haven't talked in a while. Texting is great, but hearing your voice would be even better.

I didn't want to call just in case you were at the hospital, but sure, call. I can't wait to talk to you.

"Hey, you."

"Hunter, I miss you. Things aren't the same without you around."

"Of course not. Knowing my best friend, I bet you it's all work and no play." I chuckle.

She laughs. "See, that's exactly what I mean. Your sense of humor is contagious. Do you know when you'll come back to Fort Collins?"

"I won't leave just yet. My grandmother's doing much better, but I want to stick around. Is everything okay at the ranch other than the fact that Jake is working everyone like dogs?"

"Oh, everything is running like clockwork. Jake and I are getting ready to leave for New York tomorrow."

"Wow. It's approaching fast."

"Unfortunately it is."

I hear the nervousness in her voice. I don't blame her. She's dealing with a difficult situation.

"I'm sure I don't have to repeat myself. You have nothing to worry about with Aaron. He won't let you down. He'll fight tooth and nail to win. It's true most attorneys are known for their tenacity, but Schatzberg is as hardass as they come."

"Yeah. I already have that impression from the discussions I've had with him. He's pretty unimpressed with the shit Clark pulled."

"It never ceases to amaze me how low some people can go."

"I didn't see it coming, which makes me feel stupid considering how long Clark and I lived together."

"Please stop blaming yourself. Jake and I dealt with our fair share of scumbags when we still owned the dotcom company, but nothing like this. Your ex-boyfriend should win a freaking medal. Just when you think you've seen the worst in humans, some idiot comes out of the woodwork to prove you wrong."

"I'm just so grateful I don't have to go through this alone."

"Just like Aaron, Jake will never let you down. He takes things very seriously, too seriously sometimes, and he sees anything he takes on through until the very end. That's one of his biggest competitive advantages and that's also why I am so proud to call him my best friend. He'd rather die than not deliver on his promise."

"Although I'm extraordinarily grateful, I think maybe he's…"

She pauses. I expect her to continue, but after a few seconds I realize I might have to coax it out of her.

"You didn't finish your sentence."

"I don't know if I should."

I frown into the phone, surprised.

"Allison, what's up?"

"It's nothing. I'm sure I'm making a big deal out of nothing."

I'm sure she's genuinely concerned about my grandmother's health and that's why she called, but something else is troubling her. "If it were nothing you wouldn't bring it up, right?"

"I suppose."

"Come on. It's me you're talking to. You know you can tell me anything. Did you and Jake have a fight?"

"I wish. Maybe then he'd be willing to talk to me."

"You've totally lost me."

Even though I grew up surrounded by women, sometimes they can be so freaking confusing.

"Don't mind me. I'm sure I'm just being nervous about the upcoming trial."

"I'm not a mind-reader and I can't see your expression, but when you talk about the trial I don't hear the same trepidation in your voice as I do when you talk about Jake. Are you going to let me in?"

"He's been very distant, Hunter. I don't know if it's something I said or something I did, but he's not the same person he was before you left."

"Allison, there's a lot going on right now. Jake and I go way back and when he's overwhelmed he tends to shut down. I don't know how to explain it. It's almost as if he's saving his energy for the bigger fight."

"Has he said anything to you? About us?"

"When we talk we usually discuss matters related to the workers, new clients or existing ones. He's definitely mentioned how concerned he was about the trial and how confident he was in your legal team, but he hasn't shared much more. He hasn't delved into anything personal."

"It figures."

"How so?"

"It's just that…"

Why is it so hard for her to open up about what's clearly choking her?

She sighs. "It's almost as if he's treating me like a stranger. Unless we're talking about the trial, Riley's TV show or what's happening on the ranch, he's as silent as a monk."

I open my mouth to ask another question, but then it hits me. "Do you mean the two of you haven't been alone together since I left?"

"No."

"So you haven't been together intimately?"

I thought for sure Jake was going to take advantage of the fact that I'm away to keep our little blonde busy. I would've done the same thing.

"I could be running around the ranch or riding Romeo buck naked and he wouldn't even notice."

Oh, I'm sure he'd notice.

"And it bothers you?"

"It's not that it bothers me." She hesitates. "I really love what we shared together. I just thought that maybe… Never mind," she huffs. "I can't even form a coherent sentence. How do I expect you to be able to help me?" She laughs nervously.

"Just because you can't express it doesn't means it's not weighing on you."

"Exactly."

After a few minutes of contemplative silence I speak again. "Tell you what. I may not be ready to come back to Fort Collins yet, but my grandmother is doing better and I have so much family by her side twenty-four seven, I don't have to worry. Why don't I take a few days to be with you guys? I'll leave tomorrow for New York and it'll be just the three of us. If I'm there, I'm sure it won't take much for Jake to loosen up."

"I really appreciate it, but you don't have to do that. I don't want to cause any problems."

"Sharing you with my best friend is never a problem, sweetheart." I chuckle.

"Are you sure?"

"I don't make a habit of saying things I don't mean. I hope my presence will force the two of you to finally 'fess up about the way you feel about each other. Don't think I didn't notice how blissfully happy the two of you were when you came back to the ranch after those long evening rides."

These two are such idiots. If they just took a second to stop beating around the bush, they'd both realize how much they're into each other. Jake hasn't brought it up, and I'm surely not going to ask questions or he'll accuse me of meddling, but I've known this guy since we were sixteen. He's never looked at another woman the way he looks at Allison. The little blonde nearly melts every time my best friend is in the room. Seriously, they need to get their act together. Maybe a little push is all they need.

"Well… it's not what you think. It's just…"

"It's just what, Allison?"

"I mean I love being with both of you… you know that, don't you?"

I bite off a smile. It's so adorable the way she trips all over her words trying to hide what's blatantly obvious. "Sure. If you say so."

"Gosh," she exhales, defeated.

I ignore her hesitation. "It was really great talking to you, sweetheart. Let me get off the phone so I can book a flight. I'll see you and Jake in a couple of days in New York. I'll text him to let him know I'm coming. I'll arrive later in the day so I'm not a distraction. It's important for you to focus on the trial, but when nighttime comes we can all have a little fun."

"I'll see you in a few days, then. I can't wait for all of us to be together again."

Maybe this time around I should sit back and watch Jake fuck her silly. "I'm sure that'll get the conversation flowing really nicely between the two of them." I chuckle to myself as I cut off the call with Allison to speed-dial my travel agent.

CHAPTER FIVE

Allison

It's been nearly six weeks since I left New York and I never imagined coming back under these circumstances. Jake and I arrived late last night and I was so exhausted from a hectic week, it didn't take me long to crash. After a good night's sleep, I'm ready to take on this day.

As I put the finishing touches on my makeup, I can't help but be in awe of the place I'll call home while back in New York. *God, I still can't believe Jake has such deep pockets.* He booked us into the Surrey, one of Manhattan's most luxurious hotels. Even though I've been living in the city since attending the Fashion Institute of Technology, it was the first time I've heard of this swanky location. I gasped in shock when we walked into the lobby last night. This is undoubtedly out of my reach and beyond my comfort zone, but there I was standing next to my blue-eyed savior as a bona fide guest.

Everything about my surroundings spells money and class. From the warm reception we received when we arrived, it's obvious Jake is a regular at this intimate Upper East Side address. I thought the lobby was impressive, but nothing could have prepared me for our room... or should I say massive suite.

When we walked in, my jaw dropped. How can you describe such opulence? Our suite is furnished in a harmonious palette of grey and brown shades. It features several large bedrooms, a cozy fireplace, a private terrace and a deep soaking tub. I could seriously live here for the rest of my life. All the rooms are showstoppers, but the bathroom is the type of oasis you dream of having in your home one day, knowing unless you win the Powerball, it's unlikely to ever happen. The oversized glass-enclosed shower almost had me crying. I had never seen anything like it. When I spotted a couple plush robes hanging on the back of the bathroom door, I ran towards them like a kid running towards an ice cream truck. They looked so decadent and luxurious, I reached out and caressed them like you would a fluffy cat.

My reaction was so amusing to Jake, he declared he'd buy me my own robe before we went back to Fort Collins. When I peeked inside the robe, I read "by Pratesi" on the label. It's moments like these I wish I were more of a fashionista like Gwyn because I don't recognize the brand, but something tells me this robe cost more than my entire shoe collection.

This morning our suite is washed by a beautiful sun and I can appreciate the décor even more. I'm wearing the robe I was gushing over while getting myself ready before I slip into a brand-new suit I bought in Denver with Riley's help. I'm still so dazzled by our surroundings. Even though Jake is in the other room, I can't contain my excitement.

"Jake, I still can't believe you've booked this palace for us for a whole week," I shout through the crack of the door.

"What did you expect?" He chuckles. "This is a stomping ground for Hunter and I. We've been here so many times, we're practically on a first-name basis with most of the staff."

"Everything is so... you know... perfect. Even the latte I ordered this morning was decadent."

"I'm glad you like it." When I look up, there he is standing at the door, staring at me in the mirror. I'm suddenly very conscious of his gaze and I feel exposed although I'm fully covered. "Wait until we have dinner later." He smiles.

"I'm really excited about dinner because I'd never have the guts to walk into their world-renowned restaurant, Boulud, to even order a cup of tea, let alone a full meal," I say, freaked out by the idea of paying ten dollars for a cup of chichi hot beverage.

"You underestimate yourself." His deep boisterous laugh fills the room. I don't remember the last time I heard him laugh like this.

"I've never experienced anything remotely this high-end in my life."

Jake pushes the bathroom door open wider and takes a step inside. "And that's exactly why I keep coming back here."

"Well, it's good to be you."

"True, but right now, it's good to be you too." He winks and I can't help but smile.

"Maybe you're right, because I never thought this would be possible for me."

"I've been telling you, everything is possible, Ali. Even you winning this case and suing the hell out of your ex. Heck, that's exactly what we're going to do." He taps the tip of my nose with his index finger and we're both aware of the intimacy in his touch. He hasn't so much brushed his body next to mine in the last three weeks and in this moment I realize how much I've missed being so close to him. I look up at him, hoping things might get even more intimate, but the flicker in his glee bursts my bubble. I read the hesitation in his eyes before he speaks. "Speaking of which, I'd better get back to my laptop and finish answering Dirk's questions. My manager is an ace at what he does, but he's never had to be in charge on his own for so long. Not to mention Winston or Aaron might have some last-minute questions for us."

Before I can even answer, he's gone.

"Oh. Okay. Sure," I babble to myself. There he goes switching the conversation to business again. Although I'm elated to have a stellar legal team, I wish Jake could turn off the business talk for one minute.

For some strange reason, I was under the impression Jake had booked separate rooms since he's been so distant for weeks now, but to my surprise, when we got to the hotel he declared we'd be staying in the same suite. I was excited at first until we walked in and I discovered there were three bed-rooms. The three doors sent a clear message—there was a good chance I wouldn't be sharing his bed.

That night, after kicking off my shoes and slipping out of my clothes and into something more comfortable, I was hoping Jake and I would be able to reconnect and perhaps a bit more. Oh, boy, was I in for a rude awakening. After a few frustrating minutes with my eyes shifting back and forth from my e-reader to where he was working with his eyes glued to his laptop, I waved him good night hoping to catch his attention, but he was still busy ironing out a few details via email. I really appreciate everything he's done for me so far and I don't want to come across as a whining child, but I wish I knew why he went from scorching hot to cold with me.

When I woke up this morning, Jake had left me a note on the bathroom mirror letting me know he had gone for a two-hour workout at the hotel's gym. Since I had an early-morning breakfast with Gwyn I didn't mind, but I was hoping when I got back we might have spent some quiet time together before our long day at the attorney's office. But to my chagrin, he was all business.

When I realize things are going to be similar to the way they were last night, I head to the bath-room and take an obscenely long time to get ready in the hopes of avoiding worrying about how to catch

Jake's attention. The interaction we just shared is as intimate as it's been between us for a long time.

Focus your attention on your makeup instead of stressing out over how weird things are between us.

I'm about to apply a second coat of mascara when a naughty idea pops into my head. I throw the tube back into my makeup case and I lift my eyes toward the mirror. I put my hands on my hips and arch my left eyebrow while pinching my lips together as my mind churns. I'm definitely not as forward as Gwyn, but I know for certain she wouldn't back down so easily when she wants something—or someone.

In a bold attempt to channel my best friend, I slide out of the beautiful white robe that was hiding my secret weapon and hook it at the back of the bathroom door. I've tried my best to tempt Jake since I got back from breakfast, but it's now time to pull out the big guns—drop-dead-gorgeous lingerie. I bought this outrageous white slip with black lace detailing around the breast when I purchased my suit. Surprisingly, Riley was the one who pushed me to make the purchase. Her theory is the more buttoned-up the suit, the naughtier the underwear. I couldn't resist. *Okay, you so can do this.* I open the door and pretend to have forgotten something in my room.

"Oh, don't mind me. I forgot my stockings in the bedroom."

"Um, okay," he says without even a glance in my direction.

"Yeah, you guys have it easy."

"We do?"

Crap, still nothing.

"Yeah, you don't have to deal with half the shit we have to in order to look good," I laugh, walking on my tippy-toes to accentuate the undulation of my hips. *Come on, look at me.*

"Don't know how you ladies do it."

"It's such hard work, but the results are worth it, don't you think?"

Over here. I'm over here!

"I just need to jump into a suit and I'm ready for business." He chuckles, still focused on his damn laptop.

I purposely parade without a bra or panties underneath the soft fabric, praying the contour of my hardening nipples and my ass would be bait, but nothing, *nada, niet, niente, rien du tout.*

Oh, for the love of God. After a number of failed attempts walking from my bedroom to the bathroom and back, I give up. Defeated again, I cover my body under the robe. *Damn, he seems to see right through me.* What am I going to do? It's not as if I have the courage to plop my naked body on the desk in front of him and beg him to fuck me. I shake my head and squander the dream of touching his skin, tasting his mouth, and feeling his weight over me ever again. I have to accept things have changed between us.

Oh, well. I should finish getting ready.

In less than two hours, I'll be sitting in Aaron Schatzberg's office for our first face-to-face meeting. So far, Aaron and I have had numerous Skype video calls, but he didn't feel we needed to fly into the city until we had irrefutable proof under our belts.

I tie up my long mane into a low bun to look as polished as possible. I keep my makeup light because I've never been one to hide under powder and colors. I pop in a pair of pearl earrings my parents bought for me for my eighteen birthday and *voilà*! When I'm done, I catch a glimpse of myself in the mirror in front of me and I grin. The bright-eyed woman staring back at me is wearing an indecently pricey robe and a rosy glow from my early-morning brisk walk from the café where I met my best friend back to the hotel. I lean in closer to take in my jaw-dropping transformation and I squint, still unable to believe it's really me because I look unfamiliar to myself.

There's no denying it, I'm no longer the same person. There's some wisdom in my eyes that wasn't there before and I like the new me.

Look at you, Ali. You're all grown up.

I feel so confident about this day. I wish I could say the same about Jake and I. I hope Hunter's arrival later today will help us rekindle the magic we lost.

CHAPTER SIX

JAKE

Ali has been desperately trying to catch my attention all morning. I don't know what I was thinking when I booked one large suite for the both of us instead of getting her a separate room. I guess I wanted to be close by just in case she was stressing out over her case.

It was a sound idea at the time, but now it seems like the stupidest thing I've ever done considering how much I fucking want her. I woke up this morning with a monster hard-on wishing her warm little body was nestled into mine.

At least I had the good sense to let her go to bed first last night to avoid any temptations. I remember how puzzled she looked trying to figure out which room she should select. I knew she was waiting for my cue, but I let her make the decision on her own.

After she'd waved me good night, I waited until I was certain she was fast asleep before turning off my laptop and going to bed. I had to execute herculean strength to pick one of the empty rooms instead of sliding my body next to hers.

At one o'clock in the morning it was obvious my hard-on wasn't going to allow me to have a good night's rest. I flung back the covers and fisted my cock, hoping for some kind of salvation. I pumped hard up and down my shaft, wishing it was Ali's hands or her sweet lips. It didn't take me long to come like an animal. I had to bite my left hand to contain the sounds of my climactic explosion.

It's not that I don't want her badly, I just don't want things to get confused between us.

In order to curb my appetite for her curves, I extricated myself from bed at the crack of dawn and I hit the gym for two arduous hours. I was hoping the release of this pent-up energy would help, but my monster erection is still raging between my legs. Unable to withstand the pressure that serves as a reminder I haven't been inside Ali in a really long time, I retreated into my bedroom and jerked off again while she was getting ready in the bathroom. I swear if I keep this up, I won't be able to use my right hand for long.

She nearly broke my resolve a few minutes ago when I caught a glimpse of her hard nipples caressing the fabric of that naughty-as-hell thing she's been prancing around in. I had to bite my tongue to avoid jumping on her like a panther on an innocent gazelle. *God, my balls are aching for her.*

The last three weeks have been agonizing. I can't think of anything more tormenting than being so close to someone you crave with every fiber of your being while messy circumstances make things too complicated to give in to your desires. Riley's return made things uncomfortable and Hunter's grandmother's sudden hospitalization wasn't the time for me to have a heart-to-heart with my best friend. Not to mention it's been hell at the ranch adjusting to the new flow of lucrative business.

I want things to be completely clear between Ali and I before I take her again. She has to want me as much as I want her. Only her. But for now, if I can't have her in my bed and under me, then I'll sure as hell do right by her and protect her. Defend her. Stand up for her.

I'm still a little apprehensive about Hunter dropping by for a couple of days. I wimped out when he texted me. I told him it would be great to hang out with him in the Big Apple, but I haven't told him that the reality is I don't want to share Ali anymore. *I need to be upfront with him.* Since Aaron and his team will most likely need time to prep Ali for her first trial, I'll take this opportunity to slip out and meet Hunter to discuss things in the open. I hadn't planned on this taking place in New York City, but if I want to make things official with the woman I'm so determined to guard from harm, I might as well just get it over with. It's much better to have this conversation face to face than over the phone while Hunter's in LA taking care of his grandmother.

It's best to have one cross to bear at a time. Once the dust settles, everything is possible. *It's only a few more days, Jake.*

I've been playing around with the idea of taking her to the Hamptons after the trial and laying my cards on the table. I was thinking of making reservations at Pierre's. This French bistro is one of the Hamptons' most romantic locations and the perfect backdrop for what I have in mind. The atmosphere is warm and intimate, the food is spectacular and the view is breathtaking. I'll play it by ear since we still have a long week ahead of us, but one thing is certain, she'll be mine before we land in Denver again.

I'm in the middle of sending a few instructions to Dirk, my right-hand man at the ranch, when Ali steps out of the bathroom again, vying for my attention. This time instead of staying in the background, she approaches my desk wrapped in a terrycloth robe I'd rip off in a minute to fling her delicious body on top of this desk and fuck her senseless.

Peering over my laptop at her, I wink. "Everything okay?" My gaze cuts to hers. "Seems like you've been watching me from that bathroom over there all morning. Is there something you want to ask me?"

Ali blushes and widens her eyes, aware she's been busted. "Pfft. What makes you say that? I'm not watching you." Her hands go to her hips and she scrunches her nose to emphasize her point.

"Nice robe, but it won't do in public. We're due to leave soon so you should put some clothes on. We don't want to be late," I say, waggling my finger the length of her body.

Instead of answering, she tugs the front of her robe around her chest before huffing and turning on her heel. Her frustration is palpable, but it's best for both of us if I ignore my carnal urges.

With a sigh I return my focus to my screen, amused by her reaction. After I've answered all of Dirk's questions, I look at the time in the upper right-hand corner of my screen and realize we need to get out of here. This is New York and traffic can quickly become the kiss of death when you're already running late. I get up and walk to the chair near the small dining table and grab my silk tie. I put it on and tighten it around my neck before slipping into my Italian wool jacket. I look down at my Rolex watch. When Ali is still barricaded in the bathroom, I become concerned.

"Come on, Ali. We need to leave now or we'll be late. We don't want to hit any snags along the way." I walk back towards the desk to grab my MacBook Pro laptop and tuck it in its protective sleeve before shoving it inside my leather case.

A few minutes pass and she's still not out. I ready myself to call her again when the bathroom door opens behind me and I speak without turning around. "Are you ready?"

When I face her, I freeze. *Holy shit*. I take a step back and I nervously rake my fingers through my hair, very aware of how my cock is twitching inside my pants. *Jesus, she looks hot*. My gaze drags from her polished, coiffed updo all the way down to her outrageously sexy nude high heels. I open my mouth to speak, but it takes a few minutes for my brain to catch up. I'm so in awe right now, I must look like a man dying of thirst.

"Ali, you look dangerous in that suit."

"It's not too conservative?"

"Not at all. And look, we're both wearing navy," I say, grasping at an opportunity to keep the conversation from veering into something improper and bawdy.

"Oh, you're right," she says, smoothing the fabric of her skirt.

"Honestly, you're absolutely beautiful."

"My hair's okay?"

"Of course." I exhale. "I much prefer your hair when it's cascading over your shoulders"—*because fisting your mane while I ram you from behind gets me off like a rocket*—"but the way you have it off your face like this just brings more emphasis to your striking features." *It also exposes the neck I'd kiss for days. Would it be in poor taste to mark your flawless skin with a hickey right before a trial?*

"The blouse isn't too colorful, right?" She pulls open the lapel of her jacket and pushes her boobs towards me. *For God's sake, how the hell am I supposed to contain myself here?*

I heave a breath and force myself to focus on her eyes. With limited success since my eyes keep shifting downwards. "Not at all, it brightens your face." *If only you knew how much I'm dying to leap forward right now and rip it off you to have full access to your huge tits.*

"Would white have been a better option?"

We lock eyes and I feel as lost as a puppy. She's cute and sweet and so damn gorgeous it's hard to take a breath.

"Nah." I shake my head and close my eyes, desperately trying to ward off the hedonistic fantasies I'd love nothing more than to live out.

"Good. Riley helped me choose this outfit. It's not something I'd usually wear, but she said I needed to look the part in order to be taken seriously."

"She's right." *Damn, girl, if my dick is any indication, you're playing the role of seductress to a tee.*

"The shoes aren't too... you know..."

I drop my gaze to her feet and I instantly want to hit my knees on the floor and kiss her legs all the way up to her pussy. "No, I don't. What's wrong with the shoes?" *Other than the fact they're making my cock so hard right now, it's fucking killing me.*

"They're very high heels. I'm so short I wanted to give myself some height, but maybe something more sensible would have been better? What do you think?"

What would be sensible would be for your legs to be jacked up over my shoulders with those fuck-me pumps still glued to your feet as I drive in and out of your warm pussy. That's what I think. "Honestly, I'm no fashion guru, but I think everything you're wearing looks amazing on you."

"Thank you. I know we've gone over this many times, but I'm still a bit nervous," she confesses, patting her bun.

Goddammit, I could do a lot of dirty things to you right now. "You have the best legal team money can buy behind you." I close the gap between us and extend my arm without even noticing it. I brush my knuckles over her left cheek and she closes her eyes as she leans into my hand. "And you have me." My voice is deep and low. My dick twitches at the thought of taking her lips. So much for not confusing things. *Treacherous bastard.*

"You're right, I need to stop worrying or I'll go crazy." She nods while lifting the corner of her lips into a half smile.

I blink a few times, taking her beauty in as if this is the first time I've ever seen her. I'm torn between my need to be inside her and my commitment to protect her. Shaking my head to cast off the spell, I realize if we don't hop in a cab at this instant, I'll find myself in a compromising position with her underneath me.

"Let's hit the road," I say, reaching out to her. She takes a few steps forward and interlaces her fingers around mine.

Her touch instantly brings flashbacks of a whole lot of raunchy memories. *Jesus, this is going to be a very long five days.*

Doing my best to avoid giving in to my urgent need, I grab my laptop with my free hand and drag her out of our suite. If we don't head for the door, there's no telling what I'll do to her. "Are you ready to take on this day, Ali?"

She looks up at me with her sparkling hazel eyes and bats her long eyelashes a few times. "With you by my side, I am." *Damn.* I instantly feel a pang in my chest. Things were a whole lot easier when I was hiding behind my screen and immersing myself in work, but now there's nowhere for me to hide. It's just me and her.

I think I'm going to go out of my goddamn mind.

* * *

As we leave the hotel, the afternoon heat hits me like a wall, even in the suffocating shadows of the buildings overhead. I look up and down the street and I realize—I'm back in New York. There's nothing quite like summers in Manhattan and that's why I love living in Fort Collins so much. You don't have to deal with the oppressive heat, the heavy smog, the mobs of eager tourists or the stinking sewers.

The chauffeured car is already waiting for us when we emerge from the hotel. Lucky for us, lunch hour is a decent time to be travelling in Manhattan and within a few minutes we arrive in front of Aaron Schatzberg's office.

Ali and I ride the elevator up fifteen stories in silence. As much as I try, I can't take my eyes off of her—she's breathtaking. Since the elevator is packed with employees coming and going from lunch, we don't have to force ourselves to make small talk. When we get to Aaron's floor, I grab her by the hand again and I push my way out of the elevator. When I pull open the glass doors to Aaron's office a bubbly young receptionist greets us.

"Welcome to Schatzberg & Associates. Do you have a meeting?"

"Yes, we do. We're meeting Mr. Schatzberg. My name is Jake Carrington and this is Allison Randall. We have an appointment at twelve-thirty."

"Oh, yes, Mr. Schatzberg is expecting both of you. Let me call the attorney who'll take you to the boardroom where Mr. Schatzberg and your team of attorneys are waiting. If you'd like to have a seat, it shouldn't be more than a few minutes."

"Thank you very much," I respond before turning to Ali. "Do you want to sit?"

She shakes her head. "I'd rather stand," she answers, nervously biting her lower lip and crossing her arms around her chest. God knows I want to take her mouth into mine, but now is neither the time nor place.

"Jake, I'm getting anxious again," she confesses.

Goddammit, I just want to protect her. I grab hold of her shoulder and lower my head. "Look at me, Ali." She obeys without hesitation. "It's going to be all right. I know we're about to discover a lot more nasty things about your ex, but you can do this. Lean on me if you need to. I'm here for you. Okay?"

"Okay."

"Do you want me to get someone to fetch you a—"

A voice interrupts me and both Ali and I turn around at the same time to face the woman calling out my name.

"Mr. Carrington, how are you? My name is Rachel Coffman and I'm one of the attorneys assigned to your case," she says, extending her hand.

"It's a pleasure to meet you," I respond, taking her hand. "It's not my case. I'm here for moral support." I wink. "This is Allison Randall, the client."

"Of course. Ms. Randall, it's a pleasure to finally meet you." Rachel shakes Ali's hand with as much confidence as she did mine. "Rest assured, we have a power team assembled in the boardroom. If you'd like to follow me." Rachel marches ahead and we follow her through the maze of cubicles and offices until we hit a large room surrounded by glass windows.

Aaron's spared nothing. The boardroom is packed with attorneys and support staff who all have an important role in this case and I already have an eye on the mountain of snacks weighing down a table in the corner of the room.

Before we even open the door, Aaron greets me with a warm smile. We go way back and this man has saved my ass more times than I can count. No one goes after the bad guys like this legal eagle. Don't be fooled by his stature. Although he only stands five foot six, Aaron is a powerhouse capable of the impossible for his clients. It goes without saying such brilliance comes at a hefty price tag, but Ali is very much worth it.

As usual, Aaron is one step ahead of me and speaks before I even have time to open my mouth. "Jake, I never thought I'd see you again since you moved to spend your days tending to cattle."

"It had to be a darn good reason for me to come back to the Big Apple."

Aaron takes me in with a sly grin. *All right, we're about to get into a friendly war of words.*

"You're a disappointment, Carrington. You know that? If you're going to make a comeback, assume the role," he says, taking a step forward before flicking the lapel of my suit. "I expected to see you waltz in here in worn-out cowboy boots and a leather cowboy hat, chewing on a piece of hay or tobacco and wearing some tight jeans that make my female staff lose their heads, but instead you look like a goddamn tight-ass banker who spends his days crunching too many numbers in your bloody expensive imported suit."

I smile before I retort. "Just because I own a ranch and sometimes walk around in a cowboy hat to ward off the sun doesn't make me a bona fide cowboy. I'm much better at hiring them than pretending to be one... even if I can ride a horse."

"Fucking excuses. Was it too much to ask?"

I size Aaron up with a grin hanging from the corner of my mouth. "You kiss your mama with that mouth, Schatzberg?"

"You leave my mother out of this if you know what's good for you."

"Is that your way of saying you've missed me?"

"You wish," he says before embracing me in a man hug.

"Consider yourself lucky I still have you on speed dial," I joke.

"I'll keep that in mind the next time I send you my bill."

We both laugh.

"I missed you, Aaron."

"It's good to see you again, Jake." Aaron is still patting my back when I notice Ali looks like a deer in the headlights. She's obviously taken aback by our banter. I grin at her and mouth, "We're joking around." Reassured, she smiles back at me.

"I brought the client." Pulling myself away from my long-time friend, I bring the focus back to Ali.

"I finally get to meet the lovely Allison in person," he says, taking a step forward before cupping her hands in his. "My, my, my. If I weren't representing you, I wouldn't dream of leaving this meeting without your phone number."

Allison turns beet red so fast, Aaron bursts out laughing. "Oh," she manages to say with eyes as big as Frisbees.

"Aaron, don't you think you're laying it on a bit thick?" I mock.

"What can I say? It's impossible for me to remain unaffected by the charms of a beautiful woman."

I roll my eyes at Ali. Aaron is a master flirt able to charm his way out of any situation. His ability to seduce tough-as-nails judges has served his clients very well.

Since moving away from the dotcom industry and taking ownership of the ranch, I've hired a few corporate lawyers in Denver with whom I work closely. That said, I still have the lawyer who took care of the sale of our former tech company on my payroll and I've always kept Aaron close by. Since we're in the cattle business, there's still an opportunity for people to come after us with frivolous claims and I'm not willing to gamble when it comes to my defense team.

Jeff Bingaman, who owns a farm a few acres away from our ranch, got sued a few years back when false rumors came out he was doping his chicken and passing them off as organic and grain-fed. He fought tooth and nail and won. Unfortunately, it cost him an indecent amount of money and the negative press affected his business for months. It's amazing what kind of shit a vindictive former employee can stir up. Having a lawyer willing to draw blood makes good business sense in my opinion.

"It's a pleasure to finally meet you, Aaron."

"Are you ready to get started and find out how we're going to get you out of this royal mess?"

"I am."

"Good. The entire team is here and in the next forty-five minutes Gloria, my assistant, will wheel in lunch for all us. Let's get started. I hate to be the bearer of bad news, but I should warn you now…"

"Oh, no. What's wrong?" Ali asks nervously.

"Is there anything that happened since Allison and I left the hotel we should be concerned about?" I ask.

"On the contrary. Winston's team came through and our people here have been brilliant. We just got a few more juicy details about half an hour ago that will help Allison's case. This means we have a shitload to go over today. I doubt any of us will leave this office before seven tonight. It's going to be a long day and I promised the entire team drinks on me when we're done. Of course, you and Allison are my guests."

"That's the kind of warning I can live with."

"Glad to hear it, Allison. Come over here and take a seat. Jake, where do you want to sit?"

"Right next to Allison." I pull out the closest chair and sit next to the curvy blonde and she smiles at me with gratitude. When I take my place at the table, I lean in and whisper in her ear. "You didn't think I was going to leave you alone, did you?"

"It sounds like it's going to be a brutal day," she whispers back. "I'd understand if you needed to attend to things related to the ranch."

"The ranch can wait. We're in this together, remember?"

"Right." Her lips curl up and she rewards me with a huge smile.

"Okay, the two of you. Cut out the chitchat or else we'll never go for those drinks," Aaron says and both Ali and I sit up straight in our chairs like docile pupils.

"Allison, before we get started, let me introduce you to the team. You've already met Rachel. She's one of the junior attorneys assigned to your case. This is Steve Griffiths, he's another junior attorney. Both of these young people are sharks and promise to be top attorneys. This is Tanya Daley and Valerie Gooden. They're both paralegals and let me tell you, nothing slides by them. These people have been relentless in the past three weeks at uncovering the truth. We didn't want to let out too much information until today, but we're ready to open Pandora's box."

"Gosh, I'm not sure what to say. I can't thank you enough for helping me clear my name."

"We're here to protect and serve our clients. Call us old-fashioned, but we take our clients' needs to heart. But"—Aaron lets the words hang dramatically as if he's pleading in front of a jury—"your case had us all shaking our heads. Right, gang?"

All four heads nod in agreement.

"Why would you say that, Aaron? You must have seen worse cases in all your years in business."

"Jake, once we unpick the web of lies Clark and Jasper wove around Allison, you'll be amazed at the lengths people are willing to go to for greed."

"I can't wait to hear this."

"I'll pass the floor over to Steve, who will brief you on every detail we've discovered so far."

"Ms. Randall and Mr. Carrington, it's a pleasure to finally meet you."

"Please, Steve, no need to be so formal. I'm Jake and she's Allison," I mock.

"That sounds good to me." Steve turns his attention to Ali. "Allison, I believe Aaron has made it clear that the trial we have in three days is to establish your innocence and to get a judge to recognize you were never a principal of Venture App and therefore the class-action suit wouldn't be something you'd have to concern yourself with."

"Yes, Steve. I understand that."

"Good. The class-action suit will undoubtedly go on, but our job is to make sure those angry investors know you had nothing to do with stealing their money."

"I'm still not clear how my name got associated with Venture App as a treasurer."

"This is a simple case of two young traders willing to do anything to get what they wanted... even if that meant screwing you over."

"So you were able to establish I had nothing do to with this?" Ali asks nervously.

"Winston's team is genius, but in the last few days they've been on fire."

"How so, Steve?" I interrupt. Winston and I have been in contact numerous times, but I know how he works. He'll reveal the minimum until he's provided the attorney working the case with enough evidence to build a solid defense. Any leaks along the way could cost us dearly so I'll be hearing about the details of the case at the same time as the sexy woman sitting next to me.

"Allison kept saying she had no clue how she ended up a principal in her ex's company, but we needed to be sure she had no involvement."

"I didn't realize you didn't believe me. You thought I wasn't being upfront?" Ali asks, shocked.

"With all due respect, people lie to cover their ass all the time, but you seemed sincere. There's a reason why Rachel, Aaron and I kept drilling you with the same questions. We needed to determine your trustworthiness. Once we did, we moved on to the next step."

"Which is?"

"Jake, we needed proof from the horse's mouth to support Allison's claims. In other words, we needed a trail of communication between Jasper and Clark where they shared their master plan. Not an easy task when most communications now happen on cell phones."

"Didn't Winston find anything on their computers?"

"It's a new world we live in. Winston hacked their computers early on, but found very little. That's when we realized... it was all in the palm of their hands."

"That's so true. Clark lived with that phone glued to his hand. He even slept with it safely tucked under his pillow."

"Bingo, Allison. After trailing both of these idiots for a few days, it became clear we needed to tap into their phones to get a hold of the text messages they've exchanged over the past eight months."

"But how do you do that given the complexity of the telecommunications systems? It's not as if you could remotely access their deleted and archived messages. Any small-time coder can hack a computer these days in their sleep, but text messages are a whole other beast."

"God, I forgot you were a master coder, Jake." Aaron jumps into the conversation. "You're spot on. It was a nightmare, but Rachel here was brilliant."

"Aaron's right. Without Rachel's solution, we'd still be scrambling." Steven turns to his colleague. "Why don't you explain that part?"

"Thanks, Steve." The short redhead extricates herself from her chair and stands at the opposite end of the table from where Aaron is sitting. "We had a two-step plan. First, Winston installed monitoring software in proximity of their homes so we could track their conversations, which he did successfully. Once we knew there was something fishy going on, we needed irrefutable proof."

"Did you use spyware on their phones?"

"Jake, that's a good idea, since once installed, the software is practically invisible. In other words, there's no way neither of them could detect they're being spied upon. That said, there are laws against this kind of monitoring in this country, not to mention we'd still have to figure out a way to get our hands on their phones long enough to install the darn software."

"This sounds like a mind-numbing jigsaw puzzle."

"It was, but then I remembered—and I'm so sorry, Allison, for bringing this up—Clark had a roaming eye."

"Other parts of his body had a tendency to roam even more indecently than his eyes, if you know what I mean." Ali's sarcastic retort has us all in stitches.

"Point well taken, Allison. We needed to retrieve their old text messages legally in order to be able to use the evidence in court without risking them being thrown out by an overzealous judge."

"Don't keep us guessing. How did you do it?" I have to admit it, you can take the coder out of Silicon Valley, but you can never take the passion of breaking complex wireless systems apart out of my veins. I'm like a kid inside a candy shop.

"We used hot and sexy women."

"Huh? Come again?" *Okay, I didn't expect that.*

"What?" Ali gasps.

"It's summer in New York. Other than the oppressive heat, rich New Yorkers running away to the Hamptons and outdoor concerts, what else can you count on?"

Ali looks as puzzled as I do. "Rachel, I don't follow."

"I'll be honest, I'm with Allison on this one, neither do I."

"Street marketing," Aaron and his team all answer in unison, surprising the heck out of me.

"You could be speaking Russian right now, it would be the same thing."

"Allison, in the summer every company looking to boost their visibility and sales is giving away samples or trying to get some market data out of New Yorkers. We simply followed the trend by hiring a few attractive female models capable of stopping traffic with their good looks. We dressed them in slightly naughty schoolgirl outfits and then we placed them smack dab in front of Clark and Jasper's office. From that point on it was simply a matter of letting nature run its course. The plot was to lure both crooks in to believing they were entering a contest to win twenty-five thousand dollars if they answered one simple question..."

"Which is?" I press.

"What's the name of your cell phone carrier?"

"Why is that so important?"

"That information was going to make our lives a heck of a lot easier. Winston's team knew what the two con men looked like and where they worked, so it was a walk in the park for us to target them. Our models were well paid and willing to wait it out until the two clowns showed up... and they did. We had them fill out a short form with the date, their name and signature... and we were in business!"

"Oh, my God, I get it." I slap my palm against my forehead.

"You do?"

"Yes, Allison. This is truly brilliant. Rachel, let me see if I follow. Once you knew of their cell phone carriers you could go to those companies and ask them to hand over their records?"

Rachel opens her mouth to respond, but Aaron interrupts her. "Jake, if you ever get tired of tending to your cattle and living in the middle of nowhere, I'd take you on a partner at my firm in a heartbeat. Call me or text me when you're ready to come back to civilization." He winks.

"Careful what you wish for, buddy. And may I remind you there's life outside of New York City."

"Barely," he laughs. "But let Rachel continue explaining things."

"Jake, that's it. We got a judge to grant us a warrant. We hit a lucky streak since both Clark and

Jasper use the same company. V-Line Mobile Communications is worth several tens of billions of dollars and it took them about thirty seconds to hand over the records. They weren't going to risk their reputation for two petty criminals. Once Tanya and Valerie, our two paralegals extraordinaire, started reading old messages they'd exchanged, that's when everything started making sense."

"So how did I end up as a principal?" Ali asks.

"They forged your signature."

"What?"

"Clark and Jasper's business plan was to approach investors with deep pockets and convince them to invest in up-and-coming app companies for a whopping twenty-five percent profit share within six months. These were technically companies that were just about to hit the market, which made the offer even more tempting."

"Wow. I'd invest my own money with that kind of promise," I say.

"Yeah. It was too good to be true. They were clever, but sloppy, which played in our favor. The only way you can get a sophisticated investor to fork out money is to show them a profit, aka money in the bank."

"I don't think Clark ever made a profit. He kept complaining things were always slow when you get started and money would be tight for a while."

"Allison, regardless of his cockamamie story, there were no profits to be made—ever. They weren't working with any app companies. It was all smoke and mirrors. Jasper and Clark ran a modern Ponzi scheme and they were using the glitz of the app world to rob people blind."

"A what?"

"A Ponzi scheme. Jasper and Clark lured big money in by promising to pay an insanely high return to their investors. The only caveat is they weren't going to pay those poor people from profit earned, but rather by attracting new capital from new investors. Basically you rob Peter to pay Paul. The only thing they needed to line up those desperate investors was bait. They took out a loan for two hundred and fifty thousand dollars to look legit and have a beefed-up bank account to ease the minds of investors."

"There's no way I'd ever be so stupid. I've never signed loan papers for a quarter of a million dollars."

Rachel flashes Ali a sly smile before continuing. "We figured that much, but someone did on your behalf."

"Huh?"

"Clark and Jasper tricked the loan officer at the bank. God, they were clever," she responds, tapping her index finger against her chin in a pensive way.

"Clark, clever? Right," Ali mumbles under her breath.

"Rachel, you've got me intrigued. How did they get their hands on two hundred and fifty thousand dollars if Allison never co-signed the papers?"

"Jasper and Clark desperately needed that money, but Jasper's credit history is atrocious. The background check we did on him confirms there's no way in hell a bank in this country would ever loan him a dime. They needed to think fast in order to find an unsuspecting partner willing to give them the credentials they needed to look good in the eyes of the bank. They switched to plan B and that's where Allison came in."

"I'm sorry, Rachel, this makes no sense at all." Ali's annoyance is unmistakable.

"You gave them carte blanche when you co-signed the lease papers last year."

"How can signing a lease for an office equate to me signing my life away against two hundred and fifty thousand dollars?"

"We caught a string of text messages between Clark and Jasper where they masterminded copying the signature from the lease and transferring it onto the loan papers."

"You can't possibly get that kind of money without sitting face to face with someone. I mean, I know this is the land of opportunity, but come on," I say indignantly.

"You're right, Jake. That's why nine months ago, Dalton O'Donnell, the lending officer at Drake Bank of America, met in person with the three officers of Venture App—Clark Peterson, Jasper Reed and…" Rachel pauses mid-sentence and locks eyes with Ali. "Are you ready for this, Allison?"

"For the love of God, how bad can it be?"

"You. A woman by the name of Paula Bullock duped Mr. O'Donnell by posing as you."

"Paula? As in the woman my ex cheated on me with?"

"Your ex-boyfriend shrewdly wormed his way into convincing Paula to forge your signature. He promised her a small chunk of the profits and she willingly went along with his plans. We found several text messages where Clark was pushing Paula to learn how to reproduce your signature without needing to rely on the lease you had originally signed. It barely took her a week to master every nuance of your penmanship."

"Oh, that little bitch." Allison pinches her lips and folds her arms across her chest angrily. "She couldn't stop at stealing my boyfriend, she had to go after my reputation."

"I'm really sorry about this, Allison. What she did is reprehensible, but since we have solid proof she acted in a malicious way towards you, we can sue the hell out of her."

"You can, Rachel?"

"By forging your signature and by posing as you to secure a loan, she's committed several felonies and we'll go after her like a red-tailed hawk goes after its prey. She's guilty as sin and she's most definitely not going to get away with this. Had we not found those compromising text messages, you would have been the one taking the fall for all this."

"But I don't get it. How can she copy my signature so easily?"

"Unfortunately, you have an easy signature to reproduce."

"Crap."

"Once Paula mastered her criminal artistry, all three accomplices walked into Drake Bank of America to secure a big fat payday."

Allison shakes her head in disbelief. "I never thought Clark would stoop so low. I mean he was dishonest with me in our relationship, but it's a far cry from convincing someone to impersonate me to steal money."

Frankly, listening to all of this, I'm shocked anyone could be so devious. In the tech world when somebody tries to go after you it's all about money. What Clark did to Allison could have destroyed her reputation forever and landed her in jail for a very long time.

"There's still something puzzling me."

"What's that?"

"If Paula was so proficient at fooling people by forging my signature, why was Clark pressuring me into signing the lease for a second year in a row?"

"Ah, of course. Forgive me, I forgot to explain that one." Rachel flashes Allison a mocking smile while shaking her head. "I'm sure I don't have to tell you this by now, but your ex is a real gem and yes, I'm being sarcastic. When he first contacted you, he wasn't so much interested in you signing the lease as much as finding out how much you knew. Clark was simply trying to determine if the lawyers representing the investors they had conned had contacted you. From the text messages we retrieved, Paula had already signed the lease for the upcoming year by forging your signature."

"Of course she did," Ali says flatly.

"One more thing to keep in mind. Clark may have originally contacted you to snoop, but when he started texting those urgent messages, it's because he realized the shit had hit the fan and it became clear they weren't going to get out of the lawsuit. Since you weren't responding to his pleas, he went knocking at your best friend's door so she would have to dirty her hands and drop the bomb on you."

"What a coward."

"May I offer you a piece of advice, Allison?"

"Absolutely, please do."

"Paula is a loose cannon. She can forge your signature on any document. I highly recommend you get in touch with your financial institutions and the government to change your signature on every single piece of paper and identification document."

"Gosh, you think…"

"The best way to predict a criminal's next move is to go back in the archives and look at how they've behaved in the past. I can assure you this woman will strike again if you don't take the necessary steps to protect yourself."

"My God. Thank you so much for the warning," Ali answers in a shaky voice. "When we take a break I'll slip out to make some phone calls."

"This woman is a real menace. Why is she so determined to destroy Allison in this way?"

"It boils down to one word, Jake."

"Which one?" I frown.

"Love."

"Paula was in love with my ex?" Ali says.

Rachel nods. "From what we've been able to read, she would've done pretty much anything for Clark."

"I know I should be irritated right now, but for some reason none of this surprises me. I had my suspicions, but thanks for confirming them."

"I'm sure I don't have to tell you you're much better off without him."

"Nah. I came to that conclusion on my own a while ago."

I place my hand on Ali's forearm, wanting to make sure she's okay with everything she's heard so far. "Are you sure you're okay handling all of this?"

"Definitely."

"Rachel, did we ever find out how Allison's ex-boyfriend and his business partner got busted?"

"Jake, one of their first investors brought in a dozen other people with deep pockets looking for a fast return on their investments. From what the attorney representing the investors in the class-action suit shared, it seems Charles Edward Wineworth, a seventy-year-old former army colonel turned successful retailer, is the one who blew the whistle."

"How did he find out these two idiots were running a scam?"

"We won't find out until the trial takes place in two months, but these investors' attorneys are very prepared to tear Clark and Jasper apart. We're lucky we have enough to get Allison out of this shitty situation and you won't have to deal with a multimillion-dollar law suit looming over your head. Now that I've given you an overview, I believe we're going to take a few minutes for lunch and then Steve can explain how things will unfold when we stand in front of a judge in three days. We still have a lot to talk about and most importantly we need to make sure Allison is ready to stand trial."

"I'm sorry, Rachel, this all sounds like great news, but before we continue I have to ask another question."

"Go right ahead, Jake."

"Are you certain this is an airtight case and you have all the damaging proof against Paula, Clark and Jasper to guarantee a judge finds in Allison's favour?"

"We wouldn't be here if we didn't."

I open my mouth to ask another question, but Allison beats me to the punch. "You feel that confident? I mean, it's my life we're talking about here."

"Allison, we're all aware the stakes are extremely high in this case and I can assure you we're all very confident we have this one hands down." Rachel bounces her eyes from my gaze to Allison's, beaming at us with a triumphant smile.

I glance at my friend sitting at the head of the table and Aaron nods as if he's read my mind, silently confirming we have nothing to worry about.

"Thank you for putting my mind at ease." I turn to the gorgeous woman sitting next to me and I cup her hands in mine. "I told you this firm is the best legal powerhouse money can buy. God knows they aren't cheap, but damn, are they ever worth it."

The entire room roars. It's a mixture of relief and utter happiness at the fact we're one step closer to putting this nightmare behind us.

CHAPTER SEVEN

ALLISON

As Jake and I make our way back to the hotel after spending the last few hours unwinding with Aaron and his team at the world-renowned Rainbow Room, I can't help but thank my lucky stars.

When we arrived at the restaurant, Aaron took me aside and whispered in my ear a secret that had a huge impact on me. It seems everyone from Elizabeth Taylor to Cole Porter has danced at this restaurant. To say I was impressed is an understatement. I never imagined in my wildest dreams I'd have a chance to eat at such a prestigious spot.

Contrary to most places in the city, this is one eatery where you're sure to enjoy a spectacular meal even on the slowest day of the week. Overlooking the New York skyline, we were able to chill out sitting under the massive signature chandelier that characterizes this location so well while listening to a band play old-time hits. Once we all devoured our meals, Aaron suggested we linger at the stunning and sophisticated lounge featuring a wraparound outdoor terrace with a breathtaking panoramic views of the city for more tempting nibbles and overpriced drinks. It was such an eye-opener to discover how the other half lives.

As we whiz by Madison Avenue in the direction of the Surrey, I stare out the window, admiring the bright city lights. The streets are practically deserted. It may be the city that never sleeps, but the first day of the week has always been notoriously low-key in Manhattan.

Today was truly epic for me. I was able to experience first-hand the power of having a lot of money. Without Jake's generous offer, I would've winded up with an inexperienced junior attorney whose boss would've dumped my pro bono case in their lap to focus on high-paying clients. In other words, I would have gambled on my fate. *Jake came to my rescue big time.*

Since leaving the restaurant, we've been riding in silence. I suspect we're both lost in our thoughts reliving the main events of the day. In my case, I'm too apprehensive about the upcoming hours to attempt to make conversation. I'm not looking forward to going back to the hotel for another copycat evening of last night's stale and safe conversation. I'm sure Jake will be glued to his laptop and I'll be plotting out ways to let him know how I feel. *I wish I were more courageous and I could just blurt it out.*

Suddenly, I'm aware Jake is staring at me and I slowly turn my head to meet his beautiful blue eyes.

"You've been quiet all night," he says in a deep voice. "I'm sure everything Steve, Rachel and Aaron shared must make you really angry. No one can blame you, Ali. Your ex is a bona fide scumbag."

"Humph," I snarl. "I won't argue with you, but surprisingly, I'm okay. As long as I can clear my name and not have to deal with the financial blow of a class-action suit, I don't care anymore about how Clark's wronged me."

"So what is it then? Did you not like the restaurant Aaron selected?"

"Honestly, it was a surreal evening. There's no way I can ever complain about fine dining in New York. My friend Gwyn splurged and spoiled me rotten a few years back to celebrate my twenty-first birthday, but other than that, I stick to the more affordable local eateries. Tonight was a real treat for me."

"I agree. The food was outstanding and everything was cooked to perfection. It's not one of the cheapest restaurants in the Big Apple, but it's definitely one of the best."

"Are you kidding me? It's as if I've tapped into a secret society, between the swanky hotel where we're staying and the five-star meal."

Jake smiles and nods before putting a hand on my forearm. "Then why are you so quiet?"

The minute our skin touches, heat comes rushing to my face and my clit.

"It's been a really long day," I lie.

"Fortunately, we're not too far. You'll soon be able to enjoy a relaxing bath and then you can crash. Since we don't have to be back at Aaron's office until later in the afternoon, you'll have plenty of time to relax."

"Right." There's so much I want to tell him, but true to form, I wimp out. I simply force a smile and nod in agreement.

"Hunter tried texting you, but I think your phone was off."

"Oh," I say, surprised. "I've had it off all day. He must already be waiting for us at the hotel." I'm still conflicted about Hunter coming to New York to spend a few days with Jake and I, but hopefully his presence will put Jake in a different mindset. I replayed our conversation over in my head several times, but Hunter's words don't match my reality. If Jake has feelings for me, he had plenty of time during the flight and last night to express them. At least with Hunter in town, we'll all have a little fun and I might not be so on edge.

"Actually, Hunter can't make it."

"Did something happen to his grandmother?"

"She relapsed."

Shit. "I'm so sorry to hear that."

"Hunter doesn't want to leave her side."

"Of course. It makes total sense." Poor Hunter, he must be going through hell. "I'll call or text him when we get back to the hotel."

"I'm sure it'll mean a lot to him."

"I wish I could do more."

My heart sinks. Just when I had a glimmer of hope that tonight would be different, it turns out it won't. Jake will occupy one side of our gigantic suite and I'll lock myself in one of the bedrooms or I'll take a very long bath.

"It's just the two of us."

"Yeah. Seems like it."

As long as we keep the conversation to a nondescript topic, it seems Jake is happy to engage. God forbid we talk about what's really going on between us. *Great.* I turn my attention back to the streets so he doesn't read the disappointment in my gaze. My exasperation grows with each city light we cross until something detonates inside me. All day now, my heartache for Jake has been blossoming into the determination to simply confront him. I can't go on for the rest of this week acting like everything is okay when I've become invisible to the man who owns a big piece of my heart. *I need to know where I stand.*

The chauffeured black Lincoln Continental turns off of Madison Avenue onto 76th Street and before you know it we're parked in front of the hotel. I barely have time to grab the handle before my door swings open. The chauffeur gallantly helps me out of the car and I blush from the attention. *Another perk of having a lot of money.* I walk towards Jake's extended hand and I allow him to interlace his fingers into mine—as if he's done it a million times before.

We walk side by side into the hotel like long-time lovers almost oblivious to the bustling activity taking place in the lobby. Clearly, a group of guests has just arrived and they're all anxious to find a place to crash for the night. It's a struggle to reach the elevators and when we finally get there, Jake presses the button a few too many times, indicating he's as eager as I am to get back to our room.

When a car reaches the lobby, I exhale. The doors are just about to close when a pair of big strong hands clamp on them, forcing them to open again. A tall stranger smiles apologetically and before you know it, eight other tall burly men cram inside the car. It's so tight, Jake and I end up smashed against each other.

We play it cool, pretending this isn't the most awkward situation, but I feel his piercing eyes on me. I furtively look up and a mocking grin curls his lips. *Bastard.* I avoid brushing against his cock by taking a small step in front of me, afraid everyone on the elevator car might know how wet I am.

Jesus, this is the longest ride ever.

When the doors open, Jake pushes through the crowd and guides me towards our room by keeping his strong hand on the small of my back. We're walking so close to each other, but neither of us dares to speak. After letting me in, Jake waltzes in right behind me and struts around the suite turning a few lights on.

As soon as I enter, I drop my handbag on a small table near the couch and stride across the room. I kick off my insanely high heels and peel off my confining jacket before returning my focus to the tall man who's making me swoon. Overwhelmed by all of the emotions colliding inside me, I lean backwards against a wall to catch a glimpse of the man who's come to my rescue like a hero.

I drink him in shamelessly. Even after a very long day, he's still extraordinarily fuckable. *Damn, that's so annoying.* Despite a few unruly strands of hair flirting with his eyes, he still looks like a fierce businessman.

He drops his laptop case near the desk and he kicks off his expensive-looking shoes before peeling off his equally overpriced socks. As if I'm not in the room, he casually strips out of his tailored navy-blue jacket before removing his crisp white shirt. He places both on the back of the same chair they had been resting on earlier today and he's now standing in front of me in a form-fitting V-neck t-shirt.

My eyes drag over his lean muscles and I exhale, longing to touch him. Helpless, my gaze traces over the definition of his broad chest, his rock-hard abs, his strong shoulders and his buff biceps. The man is cut to such perfection it makes me want to delineate every dip and curve of his godlike physique with my tongue. *Jesus.*

I'm sure my lustful gaze must be burning his skin because he turns around and locks eyes with me. We stare at each other silently for a few long seconds like two people who have so much to say to each other but who don't know where to start until he breaks the ice.

"What? Why are you looking at me like this? There seems to be something on your mind you're not saying."

I open my mouth to deny his suspicions, but a force inside me takes over.

"Jake, I can't thank you enough for what you've done for me."

"Please. We've gone over this many times before. You know I would never have left you stranded alone."

I nod and I pinch my lips, determined not to allow this conversation to turn into another dreary exchange. "Yes, I know," I let out in a whisper. "But you've been so distant lately, it's killing me."

"Ali, there's been a lot going on with the trial and—"

"There you go again," I interrupt, lifting my chin defiantly. "You keep hiding behind this trial."

"I'm not."

He stares down at me. His jaw ticks. An uncomfortable silence stretches out between us until it becomes insufferable.

"What is it about me you don't like anymore, Jake?" It's more a plea than a question. We're both startled by my boldness. I didn't know I had it in me to speak my mind like this to a man.

"What are you talking about, Ali?"

"It's as if you don't see me anymore."

"Of course I see you."

"Well, you could've fooled me." I push myself off the wall and I take a decisive step forward, placing my hands on my hips.

"Ali, you've got it all wrong—"

"Are you kidding me? Although I was prancing around this place nearly naked this morning you couldn't even spare me one second. Whatever was happening on your laptop was so fascinating you couldn't look away."

"I don't want things to get weird between us."

"How in the world could things possibly get any weirder between us?"

"We live on the same property and you work for my sister. Let's not forget—"

"Yeah, I'm very aware of our living conditions. I thought being here together we might have been able to reconnect."

"It's not that simple. You're forgetting something very important."

"Why don't you enlighten me? Because right now I don't understand what the hell is going on between us."

"I've been wrestling to find the proper way of handling this," he says, waving his finger between us.

"Are you brushing off everything we've shared so far?" *Great. I was just a fun pastime.*

"No. Not at all."

"You don't have to lie," I say, throwing my hands up in the air. My frustration is consuming me.

"Ali, that's not—"

"Why don't you come out and say it so we can get this over with."

Put me out of my misery, please.

"What?"

"I know I never asked for anything from you and maybe I should've, but did you have to dismiss me so callously?"

"But I haven't." He looks almost hurt.

"Everything about your body language suggests you have." For once in my life I'm going to stand up for myself. I'm not going to allow a man to dispose of me like a dirty Kleenex.

"Ali—"

"Don't you 'Ali' me—"

"Allison!" he yells, demanding my attention. He narrows his eyes. The last time I saw this menacing look, he was staring at Lindsay. "You're not listening to me." He shakes his head and he chuffs out a laugh.

"This isn't funny, you know." I cross my arms over my chest.

"No, it's not. I'm not laughing because it's funny. I'm laughing at the irony of it all."

I huff. "No need to explain further. I get it," I say, opening my arms in a theatrical gesture.

He takes a long step towards me and fists both hands. "No, you fucking don't, because you won't stop talking long enough for me to explain myself."

All the blood drains from my face and my throat is so dry it's as if I've been roaming across the desert for the past week. "What more is there to explain?"

"Plenty. Everything about us started so suddenly."

"You don't have to go down memory lane, Jake. Just give me the quick summary," I hiss.

He's on me in a flash. One hand over my mouth, the other cradling the back of my head as he shoves me against a wall behind me. He holds me there with the weight of his own body, his legs on the outsides of mine, boxing me in. "It's not your turn to talk. Understood? For God's sake, woman, let me finish."

Holy shit. What just happened? My eyes widen and my nostrils flare at his command. I search his gaze and finally nod.

"If I wasn't so upset at you, I'd confess that your defiance is a real turn-on."

"Huh?" Did he say he was turned on?

My heart is beating so hard and so fast I'm dizzy and breathless. Or maybe it's from Jake covering my mouth with his strong hand as he slams me up against the wall. *Christ, I've never gotten so wet so fast in my entire life.*

"Do you think I'm not aware it's just the two of us? Trust me, it's been a struggle for me to restrain myself and not pounce on you," he says, arching a brow. "Do you remember the day of our last ride before Riley came back to the ranch?"

I nod.

"I had big plans for us that night. I had intended on letting you know how I truly feel about you, but the drama unfolding in your life took over and my need to be with you took a backseat." He frowns. "I was afraid you were dealing with so much already and I figured if I was patient it would pay off. You needed a protector, not another situation to handle. To make up for the past three weeks, I had planned on taking you away to the Hamptons before we went back to Denver later this week to see if there was a sliver of hope you might feel the same way I feel about you." He heaves a breath and leans his forehead against mine, bringing us eye to eye. *Jesus. Is that a declaration?* "I've been looking at you all day long, baby. You're so fucking beautiful," he murmurs, bending to kiss my neck, my collarbone, and the top swell of my boobs. "The only thing I wanted to do last night was to slide my body against your curves and fuck you until you passed out, but I didn't know if you wanted me in the same way." I furrow my brow, completely confused. "I desperately want you, Ali, but I don't think I can share you any-more... not even with my best friend. And I'm unsure if I'm entitled to demand such things of you."

If I were a betting woman, I'd lose a boatload of money right now because not even in my wildest dreams could I have ever imagined such a heart-wrenching confession from a man I want more than life itself.

I pull at the hand covering my mouth in a gentle plea. Jake removes his hand immediately. "Can I say something, please?" I ask now that the torrent of my anger has subsided.

His dark gaze turns electric blue again. "Go ahead." He smiles.

"I want to be with you too, Jake," I let out in a heated breath.

His eyes narrows and his lips press into a line. "What about Hunter?"

It takes me a split second, but finally every-thing makes sense. I understand why the man my heart aches for has been so aloof and distant for the past few weeks.

"What about him? He's not here, is he?" I retort, curling up my lips.

He searches my eyes for a long minute, perplexed, until the weight of my words hit him. In that instant I know he's read my heart. "Really?"

"Jake, he knows."

"He does?"

"Uh-huh." I duck my head, aware I've revealed too much.

Jake catches my chin in his fingers and forces me to meet his gaze. He's staring at me so intensely. One more minute and I'll ignite like a torch. "You're kidding. Did you open up to him?"

I shake my head and I drop my gaze.

"Ali," he says in a stern voice. "Look at me."

My eyes rise to meet his. "I didn't have to. He's known for a while and he's confronted me a few times about my feelings for you."

Jake frowns. "He's never brought it up with me. When did this happen?"

"At the cabin and then the morning after all three of us were together at his house... right before you came down for... right before I left Fort Collins when I texted him to ask after his grandmother. He suggested he call me back instead of us texting and during our conversation he brought it up again. And..." I hesitate, still unsure if I'm revealing too much. I mean, maybe this is something these two friends should hash out.

"And what?" he presses. "Ali, please, don't hold back on me now," he says in a whisper.

"Hunter said he'd willingly back off if I want to take things further with you."

"And do you want to take things further with me?"

"I've wanted this for many weeks now. I was just waiting for you to catch up." I flash him a cocky smile.

"You can't be fucking serious." I worry I've upset him, but soon I realize he's grinning from ear to ear and it's obvious my answer has taken him by surprise. "You're sure? Because once we start I'm going to be all over you and there'll be no stopping me."

Yes, please! "I've never been more sure about anything in my life."

He smiles and combs his fingers through his hair before locking eyes with me again. "I need to be with you, Ali. Fuck, what am I talking about? I want you so much it hurts. There was too much going on, forcing me to put a lid on my emotions, but I've got to tell you, every part of me is saying to never let you go. I want to wake up curled next to your sensual curvy body and I want to fall asleep with my head resting against your ample breasts. I don't want us to hide what we share anymore. Not from Hunter, not from my sister, not from anyone." *Oh, my Lord. I can't believe this is happening to me.* My mouth drops open and my chest heaves uncontrollably at his sweet declaration. "How does that sound?"

Nearly woozy from his proximity, his dazzling grin, and his piercing eyes, I struggle to reply. "I want it all," I finally manage.

We both laugh and Jake cradles my face in his hands. "I'm glad to hear you say that because I realize I forgot to ask you something very important."

"This is already as surreal as it gets. I don't know if I can handle much more."

"I have a feeling you'll be able to manage fine," he teases.

My heart is a bass drum pounding in my chest. *What else does he have on his mind?*

"Okay. Go ahead. I'm ready." I smile broadly, unable to contain my excitement.

"Will you be my girlfriend?"

"Ah," I gasp, bringing my hands up to cover his. I fight off tears swelling in my eyes, losing myself in this moment of pure bliss. "Me? Us? Together?" I'm babbling like a toddler, unable to think straight long enough to come up with a more coherent question.

"Was that a yes, a no or a maybe? I couldn't tell," he mocks.

"Did you actually ask me what I think you did?"

"Yup, and I hope with all my heart you'll say yes."

"Hearing you say all this is shaking the ground beneath my feet, Jake."

"In a good way, I hope, baby?"

"In the best possible way. I can't think of anything I'd want more," I whisper.

Is this really happening to me?

I'm shaking so hard I suspect the weight of Jake's body against mine is more responsible for holding me up than my own wobbly legs. My hand fists his t-shirt, pulling him in or pulling myself up—I'm not sure which. *I want him. No. I need him.*

He stares at me a long moment, his blue eyes blazing and his breathing hard. "I have this bone-deep urge to possess you, Ali."

Oh, my God.

"I'm all yours, Jake," I pant, head spinning and adrenaline rushing through my body like torrential rain in a tropical storm.

Slowly, he leans in, his tongue flicking my bottom lip, and we both laugh. Finally he crushes my lips and ravages me with a heated kiss that ignites my soul like a bonfire. In this moment, I realize how much I've missed his lips against mine. How much I miss tasting him.

Jake fists my hair that's still tied up in a bun and tilts my head backwards before grasping my jaw with his free hand and he absolutely devours the hell out of me in a breath-stealing, heart-melting, soul-stirring kiss. I whimper, I groan and I claw at his hair to try to pull him closer. He pushes his hips into my belly, grinding his hard cock against me until I'm panting and dripping. My panties are uncomfortably wet between my legs. I swear, I'm as close to an orgasm as I've ever been without him even touching my clit.

When he breaks away from me, I whine.

"Jake," I whisper.

He pushes me away and takes me in from head to toe. "Your hair."

"What about it? I thought you liked it this morning."

"That was hours ago when I could still withstand the aching between my legs, we're well past that now."

"Oh."

"I need to fist it freely while I fuck you."

Oh, God, he's talking dirty.

"Please untie it."

I obey, aware he's watching my every move.

"Good girl. I want to see your mane cascading over your big heavy tits once I undress you."

"Jake, please…"

"What? Does it shock you how much I desperately want you?"

"You're going to have to slow down," I beg, my heart beating against my chest as I try to halt my racing pulse. "It's been a few weeks already and I don't think I can keep up with you."

"You should know me by now. I don't slow down. I'm going to take you like I always do—deep and hard. I'm not here to comfort you, baby. I'm here to make sure you come screaming out my name when you climax so hard your eyes roll into the back of your head while you beg for mercy."

"Jesus." My jaw drops and I blink in an effort to regain my composure, but to no avail. His dirty mouth has always been my undoing.

"The dirty talk is to make sure you're nice and wet for my raging cock."

"Honestly, I think I'm far beyond that."

The sensual drizzle of my juices dripping down between my thighs is a definite sign my body is ready for him. He flashes me a devilish grin and I know I won't be able to walk tomorrow. But if it means he'll make me come over and over and over again, then frankly I don't care.

"Your suit was sexy early today, but now it's in the way of me ravishing you," he chuckles. With a precision flick of his fingers, he unbuttons my blouse and pushes it down my arms. "Much better," he mocks. Without asking for permission he unzips my navy-blue skirt and let its pool at my feet. He hooks his fingers into both sides of my panties and he squats down in front of me as he drags them all the way down to the floor. I was expecting him to get back up and tower over me, but starting at my feet, Jake drops little kisses while traveling up my body in a worshipful, purposeful line from my painted toes to my tummy, to my jaw, all the way up to my earlobe. "This is going to be fucking amazing," he breathes.

"Ohhhh," I say, a soft, plaintive exhalation. *How can he keep turning me on like a firecracker?*

"What happened to that salacious silky black and white piece of underwear you were taunting me with this morning when you were vying for my attention?" He's back on his feet with his face inches from mine.

"My boobs are too big to walk around without a bra. So I had to choose. I didn't want to be inappropriate the first time I met with my attorney." I grin, holding his gaze.

"As naughty as this bra and panties combination is, it's bothering me. After three weeks of jerking off like a horny teenager, I want to be buried inside your pussy as urgently as possible." Impatiently he unhooks the navy-blue bra with white embroidered detailing and slips it down my arms before tossing it to the side.

"Ah," I pant when the cool ambient air caresses my erected peaks.

"Fuck, I've missed these so badly," he growls as he leans down and fondles my boobs. He kisses the left one and then the right. And when he sucks a nipple into his mouth and flicks it with his tongue, I lose it and unleash a needful cry. "You like that, don't you?"

I'm so far gone, I struggle to find my words. "Yes," I manage. He knows full well how I come undone under his touch. It's been a very long time since he's assaulted my boobs like this and goddammit, have I ever missed it.

For long pleasurable minutes, he worships and tortures my breasts until I'm certain I'm going to melt like a pot of chocolate fondue. "I've missed your mouth and your tongue so much, Jake," I gasp.

"Really? Is that all you've missed?"

Instead of answering his question, I daringly cup his cock and I squeeze hard. He grits his teeth with delight while closing his eyes halfway.

"On your knees for being such a temptress," he says, pressing on my shoulders and urging me down.

Excited, I sink all the way down until my knees hit the floor. My body is wedged between his muscular thighs and the wall. I'm trapped. A sharp thrill makes my stomach feel like I'm descending at vertiginous speed from the highest hill on a daredevil rollercoaster. I can barely breathe past the anticipation of finally being able to take him into my mouth and suck him until he comes gushing at the back of my throat.

"Take me out and taste me. Now," he growls, unzipping his pants halfway. *Fuck.*

My body clenches with excitement. His commands are like little shots of aphrodisiac pangs, each one turning me on more and more. I unfasten his pants before yanking them along with his boxer briefs down far enough to free him. Nearly panting, I take him in my hand. Jake's groan is the sweetest victory. He's so in control all the time, but here he is coming undone in the palm of my hand. His cock is magnificent—hot, thick and long. Mine. I revel in the lubrication that his own moisture provides as I wrap my eager fingers around him and stroke him. Leaning forward, I wet my lips before wrapping them around his cock. *Finally.* I swirl my tongue around his head before sucking him in.

"Hmmm," I moan into his shaft. *Jesus, he tastes so good.*

"Fuck, Ali."

I wiggle my legs inwards, bringing them closer together to allow me to put an end to my suffering by squeezing my thighs together until I climax. Alas, it's nearly impossible for me to position myself while I still have his very big cock inside my mouth and still reach my clit. Desperate, I spread my legs wider before sliding my free hand between my legs seeking relief, but he stops me with a sharp tug at my hair.

"I don't remember telling you to touch yourself," he reprimands.

I look up and lock eyes with him. "I can't take it anymore," I beg.

"Don't worry. It won't be long before my fingers are all over your clit teasing, flicking and rubbing you until you come hard. Don't you dare rob me of this pleasure."

"Um," I whimper, unsure I possess the resolve to wait one more second to give in to my pending orgasm.

"Move your hand away from your clit, Ali," he commands. I hesitate, caught between the need to obey him and the inexorable need for relief. "Didn't you hear what I said? If you don't move your hand, you can forget about coming all over my mouth as my fingers pump your ass and the others pinch your clit."

Fuck.

I close my eyes, nearly drowning in his words. The threat of forfeiting such a delirious climax is all I needed to hear to change my mind.

"Good. Put your hand back on my dick where it belongs. Now open wide because my cock feels extremely neglected."

I barely have time to part my lips before he plunges his dick into my mouth in one stroke, hitting so deep at the back of my throat, I almost gag. *I guess no more nice and slow.* Jake doesn't stop, not for a second—he grips my hair in his fist and thrusts over and over again. He's savage, hungry, depraved, filling me up and raising my body temperature to perverted levels.

"You've got such a sweet little mouth, Ali." His fingers fist my hair and hold the back of my head in place dictating the cadence. He doesn't force me, but the threat of it is there. The thought alone is so intoxicating. Jake gives me time to explore all of him and to find a rhythm where my hands and my mouth work in a fluid motion. "Damn," he hisses. "I can't believe I was able to survive these past few weeks without you taking me in your mouth." Little gritty curses spill out of him, igniting my clit into a ball of fire. *I can suck him all day just to hear the hedonistic sounds he makes.* "Take me deeper. Make me come."

Gripping his thighs with my hands, I inhale a deep breath and I push my face forward onto his cock as far as I can take him. This isn't like any other blowjobs I've ever given before. Nah, those were tame compared to this. Jake is relentlessly fucking my mouth, yanking my head closer, fisting my hair tighter.

Holy Jesus. It's fast and it's furious and I want it all.

I suck in deeper, flicking my tongue against the underside of his cock as he pulls out of my mouth and pumps into me again.

"Are you naughty enough to take me all the way in, baby?" He brushes away the hair obstructing my view and I lift my eyes towards him. It's not a question. It's more of a challenge.

I defiantly hold his gaze to let him know I'm so up for it. He flashes me a half-grin and slides his hips backwards before thrusting inside my mouth with force. He pushes his huge head against the ridges of my throat. *Jesus.* I'm near the edge, gorging on him audaciously. Everything about this moment is overwhelming every sense in my body until there's nothing but my consuming need to suck him harder to elicit more of the savage grunts he's rewarding me with. My body heats up like the engine of a racecar as a flood of overpowering desire pools between my thighs. I'm so turned on, I can barely breathe. Everything about him is dominating me and forcing me to succumb. There is no way out. If I were to die right now choking on his cock, it would be the sweetest death I could ever imagine.

"Yeah, that's it. Suck me hard, baby," he grunts, pumping in and out of my mouth. *Holy shit.* Jake grabs me by the back of the head and the jaw, taking control of my movement and filling my throat with his dick. "Oh, Christ. Hold it, hold it, hold it. Fuck, yeah." He releases me and I gasp for air.

"No. I'm not done. I want more," I protest.

"Don't worry. I've got more to give," he mocks when he reads the desperation on my face. "I want to make sure you're okay."

"I was when you were inside my mouth." I'm startled by my own admission. The old Allison would never have had the guts to express herself this way, but then again I'm a whole new woman.

"Look at you, you little dirty girl. If you want me so badly, open up again."

He doesn't have time to ask twice. I impale my mouth on his hard dick, my lips closing around him. I take him all the way to the base of his shaft and I fight the instinct to pull back. *Damn, he's so huge.*

"That's a fucking hungry little mouth you have, isn't it?"

Oh, Lord. He can't keep talking dirty and prevent me from playing with my throbbing clit and still expect me to hold on to my sanity.

"Look at me, Ali."

Tilting my head as much I can with my mouth full of him, I meet his gaze. His dark blue eyes are glazed over by lust, mouth open with anticipation, chest heaving with desire. He's absolutely freaking gorgeous.

"Hmmm. You're so hungry for me. Aren't you?" His grunts are driving me insane and robbing me of my ability to speak. Without warning, Jake withdraws. "Answer me."

Why'd you do that?

"I am," I say, peering up at him, yearning to take him back in my mouth.

He flashes me a side smile filled with satisfaction. "Tell me my cock is the only one you want."

Is this really happening? Is this really my Jake? Is this man finally all mine? I'm so loving it. "I want only you."

"That's not the question I asked."

I narrow my eyes at him before smiling. "Your dick is the only one I want in my mouth, my pussy and my ass."

"I know you do. Open up, you little vixen." Jake grasps my hair with one hand and the other hand pulls down my jaw. And then his cock slides across my tongue. *Oh shit, shit, shit.* He's thrusting in and out of me, guided by my libidinous grunts. "God, I've thought of fucking your mouth for weeks. It's been so consuming I thought I was going to lose my goddamn mind."

I whimper in response. I was so certain I had lost him forever, but his words stir something addicting in me. *He wants me as much as I want him.*

"Baby, hold on." Jake's hips move with more determination and I barely have time to brace my hands against his thighs. He hits the back of my throat again and again. I steady myself to take in all of him, aware he's testing my tolerance. "This is fucking mind-blowing," he growls. Pressing my head backward into the wall, I surrender to the demands of his frantic thrusts, loving the way he's dominating my mouth and relishing the way he tastes. *Sweet mother of God.* Jake's warm cum fills my mouth before drizzling down the back of my throat. *Hot damn.*

He pulls out abruptly, then slides his hands under my arms and lifts me to my feet. His tongue slips inside my mouth and he boxes me against the wall with his chiseled body. "I love how you taste like me now." His hands run from my boobs to my stomach and down to my hips. It's impatient, impassioned and impetuous. I'm enraptured by the moment. My fingers dig into his shoulders and my thighs tremble from the core-shaking need enthralling me.

"Jake, please, don't tease me any longer," I rasp.

"I want to hear you beg for it. What do you want, Ali?" His fingers rake my thighs. He owns me.

"I... I need your cock inside me," I plead. I have no shame begging for an orgasm.

"Yeah. Good girl. I'm going to take you from behind and bury myself so deep inside you my balls will slap hard against your clit and you'll come from the contact."

"Good Lord," I moan as his tongue assaults mine again, making it nearly impossible to think. I shift my hips, desperate for his touch against my eager pussy.

His hard hands clamp down on my ass, causing me to gasp. "Ali, I'm warning you. The choice is up to you. You either remain still or I won't let you come."

"You can't do that," I protest.

"I love hearing the need in your voice. It's such a turn-on. But yes, I can, and I'll take your climax away from you if you keep this up."

"Please," I sob. I can't remember the last time I wanted someone so badly.

Jake kicks my feet apart and slides his fingers down my stomach until he reaches my slick pussy. He plunges two long fingers deep inside my wetness and I lose it. My body has been craving his touch for so long, the friction against my clit makes me come on contact. *I can't believe he does this to me.*

"Argh," I scream and my vision blurs. I'm inebriated by my release. I sag against Jake so helplessly that he has to hold me up. "Oh, oh, oh," I moan as he curls his demanding fingers against the front wall of my core and fucks me in rapid and precise bursts that keep his thick fingertips in constant contact with an excruciatingly sensitive area inside me—the same one he hit the first night he fucked me.

"You aren't getting my dick until you come again. I want you to come so hard you have to hold on to my arms to avoid collapsing to your knees. Do you hear me?"

The power emanating from him is so strong, it's as if a fire raging within is shooting through him and straight into me.

"No. I can't. I just can't." I'm almost weeping from the blissful intensity that nearly turns into passionate agony.

Jake braces his hand on the wall above my shoulder and nails me with a searing stare. "Oh, you sure as hell fucking can." He works his hand harder, shifting from an in-out to a front-to-back rhythm, zeroing in on my eager and needy clit. The movement of his hand makes me wetter and wetter, until I can only hear slippery sounds of my arousal.

"Jake..." My pulse is a frantic, pounding drumbeat. I wonder if he can see it.

"Don't fight it. Let go, baby."

An immeasurable amount of sensual pressure builds up around his fingers until I know without a shadow of a doubt not only will I come, but my explosive climax might cause me to lose consciousness—just as he demanded of me. I hold on tight to his arm like it's a lifejacket, needing something to hold, something to anchor me against the lustful tornado mounting inside me.

"That's right, sweetness," he rasps.

"Jake," I wail.

"Come for me," he grits out, his hand still moving, drawing my orgasm out until I can't decide if it's pleasure or pain.

"Oh… I'm… I'm coming." I tumble into the abyss of pure ecstasy.

Holy shit. I start to quake, my orgasm building, and I close my eyes. *Fuck.* I come undone with a scream I've never heard leave my body before. The spasms ripple through me with such intensity, it's as if I'm freefalling from a cliff into heaven.

"Good girl. Look at you. You're completely undone and I can't tell you how much I love seeing you like this. You came all over me, baby. Taste." He pushes his dripping fingers into my mouth.

Without hesitating, I grasp his wrist and I suck his fingers to the knuckle. He's made me come so hard in the last few minutes, not once but twice, and honestly my body so desperately needed him I'm willing to do anything he asks of me. As much as I've tried to give myself pleasure during these last few weeks of abstinence, nothing compares to this.

Jake's left hand cups my face as he pulls his fingers free of my mouth. He bends his knees to align his eyes with mine. "Did I push you too far?" he asks, brushing my damp hair away from my face and dropping a kiss on my nose. His gaze is serious, but his cocky smile betrays him.

"You keep doing this to me. It's as if you know my body better than I do."

"I didn't do anything to you. I'm simply giving you what your body craves. The truth is I've been dreaming of this since the last time we were together. I've been so steadfastly focused on protecting you…" He exhales, letting the sentence hang in the air. "Being so close to you and not being able to take you when I want and how I want nearly killed me. "

"Oh," I let out, surprised by his confession.

And just like that the cockiness is replaced by tenderness. "You're sure everything's okay?" The sweetness in his voice brings the sting of tears in my eyes. *My God, I think I've fallen head over heels for him.* No other man has ever been willing or able to take care of me like Jake.

My heart swells. "Everything is absolutely perfect."

A small, tender smile plays around his lips for a moment, and then it drops and I read the fire in his eyes. "Good. Shimmy your ass over there," he says, pointing his thumb over his shoulder. "and bend over the damn couch. I'm not nearly done with you yet."

CHAPTER EIGHT

JAKE

I lock eyes with Ali, waiting to see what she'll do, how she'll react to my command. *Fuck, I've missed gorging on her sinful body.* No matter how many times I take her, I'm never satiated. It's as if my body craves her constantly.

The sweet, submissive way she gives herself to me is intoxicating. She blows every one of my fantasies out of the water. She's everything I've ever wanted—brave, daring and willing to satisfy my every desire. I love how she's open to pursuing absolute abandonment, always trusting me and never resisting. Knowing she's willing to take our relationship to the next level is fueling something inexplicable inside me. I realize now how damned much I want—no, need—this woman. My Ali.

My eyes are still fixed on her as the seconds tick away, but she's still leaning against the wall catching her breath, and I smile inwardly.

"Keep me waiting and you'll be sorry. I'll make you pay so dearly you'll think the two orgasms I just gave you a few minutes ago were a warm-up."

When she still doesn't move, I grab her arm and drag her stumbling toward the couch.

"You can't keep pushing me around like this," she protests, curling her lips up in a delicious smile.

"The hell I can't. Not to mention the glee in your eyes is a telltale sign you're turned on and this rough play is getting you off."

When Ali lands on her back on the couch, her devilish eyes dart to the side as if she's thinking of escaping.

"I dare you to do it. I'd love nothing more than for you to give me a good reason to fuck your ass."

"You know I like it when take me to the wild side. So don't worry, you won't hear me protest." She throws me a challenging glance before wiggling her sexy body away from me and running across the room.

"I see. You want to play, huh? Then let's play."

She laughs as she dashes into the bathroom she's been obsessing over since she first laid eyes on it.

"Seriously?" I huff, amused by her friskiness. "You can't complain I haven't given you a fair warning." I run after her. There she is, standing in front of me naked with her hands on her hips as if to say, *Come and get it.* I grip the doorframe, blocking her exit, aware that if my rock-hard cock doesn't get relief soon, I'll explode. I drink her in from head to toe, mesmerized by every single curve of her delectable body.

"Oh, you're going to get it now," I warn, shaking my head.

"Uh-huh." She rolls her eyes at me. "Instead of making promises, why don't you come over here and fuck me."

"Is that a challenge?" I stop dead in my tracks and pin her with a dark stare. "What's gotten into you, Ali? You're so much bolder than usual. New York City is bringing out this minx I barely recognize and you're forcing me to punish you for demanding too much of me."

"Am I putting too much pressure on you? I guess you don't want me as badly as you profess to. Either that or older men can't keep up. After all, you're pushing thirty. Is that it?" She daringly smacks her own ass as if to prove her point.

"You little—"

Horny as hell, I close the gap between us until her sweet ass comes up against the countertop.

"Shit," she says on impact. "Okay, maybe I shouldn't have pushed your buttons like this. Is it too late to say I'm sorry?"

"Damn right it is." I grin before claiming her mouth in a hard kiss. Ali melts into me and she purrs.

Her hands wrap around the back of my neck and she slides her fingers into my hair, tugging, pulling and scratching. *Fuck. She's driving me mad.* "Jake, please."

"You don't have to ask twice, baby." Unable to hold back any longer, I turn her around, tear off my t-shirt and push her upper body forward until she hovers over the counter. I catch her by the arms and lower myself against her back until my lips touch her ear. "Since you're so intent on me fucking you, why don't you watch how you come undone in the mirror while my cock pounds you?"

"Hah," she exhales with eyes half closed. My blood is scalding hot with the need to bury myself as deep as possible inside her wetness. Ali bites down on her lip and nods. "I'd love that."

"I'm glad we're both in agreement." Our eyes lock for a long second before we both smile.

Without lowering my eyes, I unzip my pants and I take my cock in hand, aligning my head with her opening, ready to charge. *Fuck. I forgot.*

Unwillingly, I wrench back. "Wait. Let me get a condom."

Ali blinks as if pulling herself from a hazy fog. "I'm on the pill. I've been for a while," she says, staring at me. "And... I'm healthy... I mean I've always used a condom with other boyfriends."

Is she serious? Taking her bareback is a fucking dream. Nothing compares to that mind-blowing skin-on-skin sensation. "I'm clean as well, Ali. But I need to be one hundred percent sure you want this."

She nods. "I trust you. I want to feel you inside me and I don't want any barriers between us."

Satisfaction roars through me. *Goddammit, this is going to be unforgettable.* I pull down my pants and boxer briefs with one hand until they hit the floor.

I step out to free myself, ready to fuck her senseless. I tug her upward so I can whisper into her ear and meet her hazel eyes in the mirror. "Ali, tell me you want me inside you. Tell me you want me buried so fucking deep, I'll never want to find my way back out ever again."

She leans her cheek against mine. I could get drunk just admiring her exquisite face. "I want you to fill me up so completely you make it impossible for me to ever contemplate being with another." Something about the way she responds tells me her answer is bigger than this moment.

"Oh, my baby." That's all I need to hear.

Still holding her arms behind her back, I bend my knees, tilting her hips, and I slide my dick into her heady pussy. "Fuck, it's been too long," I growl.

"It has." She moans and bears her ass down on me, taking me in deeper.

Shit. She's so damn enticing, slippery and irresistible.

"Being inside of you like this without any barriers between us is overwhelming, unbelievable and electrifying all wrapped into one," I grunt, doing my best to steady myself to avoid shooting my load too early. "It's as if I'm plugged directly into your overpowering energy."

"Faster, Jake." Her eyes are glazed over with sheer lust and just looking at her this way sets me off.

I bottom out inside her, my balls settling against her clit. "That's it, swallow all of my dick." I slow down my cadence and bring it to a halt before leaning towards her to bite down on the soft tendon that runs between her neck and her shoulder. She screams out in ecstasy. She wiggles her body against my stomach, her hands fist and unfist, her nails scratching my skin.

"Christ, you can't be serious," she barks. "I'm going to go mental if you remain still like this. Please, don't do this. You have to move. I need you to move." Molten hazel eyes plead with me in the mirror, her hips gyrating, determined to tempt me back into motion.

I groan. "Jesus, Ali. Are you trying to fuck me?" I loosen my grip to allow her to move. The way I've got her arms restrained, there's only so much she can do. In her growing frustration she reaches between my legs and squeezes my balls hard.

"Oh, shit." She catches me by surprise and it takes me a fraction of a second to react. I let her struggle for a moment to allow her to work out her pent-up energy and then I tug her back against me. "What do you want?"

"I want more of you."

It takes an excruciating feat of discipline to hold still. I want to drive my throbbing cock so deep inside her until I explode gushing between her thighs, but I need to hear her beg once more. "Say it. Tell me exactly what you want from me or I'll leave you like this."

"You… You wouldn't…"

I curl up the side of my mouth and raise an eyebrow in lieu of an answer. She flushes from her cheeks down her neck to her chest, where her heavy tits hang, waiting for me to grope and tease them. She licks her lips before answering. "Please fuck me."

Oh, yeah. My dick jerks inside her, ready to give her exactly what she craves. "How do you want it?"

"You can fuck me here in the bathroom or you can drag my body onto the balcony or if you prefer to throw me on the king-size bed in the bedroom and fuck me until my legs tremble, I don't care. I just need you," she rushes out.

I reward her with a satisfied chuckle. "Ali, get ready for the ride of your life."

Obedient, she places her hands on each side of the counter and holds on tight as if her life depends on it. Her wicked smile and her urgent need escalate my desire for her. I lean on top of her body, my weight pressing her belly against the cold marble countertop, as I gently pull her long hair back to kiss her cheek. I grab on to her waist with my free hand and I enter her with eagerness. She gasps.

I hold her firmly as I direct the cadence of each thrust. My hips slap against her delicious ass and the faster and deeper I fuck her the more she begs for it.

"You've been dying to get my attention all day, well, now you have it."

I pull her closer to me so I can enter her even deeper. I release one hand from her hips to pull back her head as I stick my tongue in her ear while holding her gaze in the mirror. My heart is pounding like a drum and I'm sweating from being so turned on.

"Are you going to come for me again?"

"Huh," she whimpers. I catch a glimpse of her glazed eyes and I know she's so far gone she most likely no longer remembers her own name. I can't help but smile.

I reach down to caress her clit, alternating between soft and urgent touches. Each time I tease her node, I enter her deeper and deeper. She screams with pleasure as her pussy pulsates from my sensual touch. Her body convulses and her breath comes out in sharp pants.

"I asked you a question," I press.

"Ah," she pants, unable to answer.

"If you don't answer, I'll force it out of you, Ali," I warn.

"Shit," she grunts low.

I part her cheeks with my free hand and I slide a finger in her ass, delving, teasing and toying greedily. She's so caught up in her own ascent to heaven, she's unable to protest.

"I know you're close, baby. Answer me or I'll torture you longer."

"Yes, yes, yes. I'm going to explode again."

I'm so fucking aroused from watching her lose control at my mercy I know my pending release will be long and likely to cause me to pass out. The next stroke is merciless. I curse, then slowly withdraw and I swing my hips back before ramming back into her, shoving her whole body forward. I thrust over and over again, knocking a moan out of her every single time.

Her body trembles under the assault. "Oh, baby, I'm just getting started," I grunt.

"Oh, Jake," she cries out.

I stroke her clit with a lingering, almost punishing circular motion.

"God," she gasps, quivering.

"Let go, baby. Let go."

"Ahhhh. I'm close."

I grab her head in both hands before licking the inside of her ear as I pound faster into her. "Come hard for me, Ali," I order, pounding deep inside her again.

If the counter wasn't made of solid marble and wood, it would wobble beneath us with each one of my unrelenting thrusts. My fingers reach for her clit again and I caress her nub with urgency as I pound into her.

"Oh, Jesus. Jake, I can't take this. Please, please slow down," she pants.

"I'll only stop when you come undone screaming out my name and when I gush my warm cum inside your pussy." I sear her with a lustful gaze.

As if to teach her a lesson, I pound her with more determination. I grab her hips and I fuck her hard and fast, angling myself to hit her G-spot.

"Oh, yeah, oh, yeah, oh, yeah," she chants.

"Oh, baby, you're making me lose all my senses." *Damn, I can't remember the last time I fucked a woman bareback.*

Without warning, I wrench her up into an almost-standing position, one hand across her breasts, the other sliding towards her clit. I skate across her node with my middle finger and she bites her lower lip.

"Oh, oh, oh," she hushes in a low, broken voice.

"Ali, you're mine," I hiss, driving into to her voraciously. "Your sensual body. Your sweet pussy. Your hips. Your huge tits. And every other intoxicating and beautiful part of you. All mine," I grunt through gritted teeth. "I want you to come all over my dick," I order.

"Ah… Jake… I'm—" *She's gone.*

She closes her eyes, allowing the exhilarating warmth of her orgasm to spread through her, and it's so strong tears roll down her cheeks. Her climax clenches against my dick and her slick wetness coats me. "Jesus fucking Christ," I roar, fighting back my own inevitable release. It's all I can take before the fiery volcano heating up my insides demands total abandon.

"Holy hell." I mumble a string of inaudible words before letting out a muffled grunt.

As a new surge of excitement overtakes me, I'm entirely consumed by the ecstasy of my climax. I can't think straight. My orgasm plows through me and I jerk before pouring my climax inside her.

"Fuck, Ali," I cry out, thrusting one last time, moving helplessly through my release.

I collapse on top of her and I stay there for a few long minutes as my heavy breath brushes against her flushed face. I wrap my arms around her body and I hold on to her as if I never want to let her go. I kiss her once, twice, three times gently and reverently. Panting, Ali looks up at me in the mirror and the smile of satisfaction she wears pulls at the strings of my heart.

Easing up off of her with shaky legs, I carefully withdraw from her. *Damn, that was surreal.* Rubbing her hips, I say, "Stay right there for a minute." I walk across the bathroom in search of a small washcloth hanging from the rod. I turn on the water under the shower and wet the cloth before returning by her side. "Spread them wide." I grin at her as I place the warm cloth between her legs. Ali gasps on contact. She turns shy again, as if she's made self-conscious by the intimate act.

"I can do it… You don't have to—"

"I'm sure you can, love. But you're mine now and I want to take care of you," I say, wiping her clean. I throw the cloth to the floor and lock eyes with her again. "This was worth waiting for." I turn her around to face me before wrapping her in my arms.

"That was amazing. I can't believe I survived this long without having you inside me."

"I feel the same. That'll never happen again. I want to fuck you every morning and every night from now on, Ali."

"Oh," she says in a soft, timid exhalation.

"Is that okay with you?" I tease, brushing my nose against hers.

"It's more than okay. I'm all yours, Jake."

"I wouldn't want it any other way, Ali." I engulf her in my arms protectively.

I'm so wrapped up in her there's no way out for me and in this moment I know she'd be so easy to love.

CHAPTER NINE

ALLISON

One month later

I reach the main floor of Jake's ranch home to find Jake in the kitchen wearing only a pair of beat-up jeans that hang low on his hips, revealing the upper part of his muscular ass. There's no way he's wearing underwear and that's perfectly fine with me. His arms are braced on the granite counter and he's staring at his expensive Swiss-made espresso maker like he might be able to will the machine to brew faster.

My God, he's gorgeous with his hair all messed up like this. For a long moment, I drink him in, raking my gaze all over his long athletic body. His back is a sculpted canvas of muscles and even though he fucked me real good last night and again this morning, I still long to trace him with my fingers and my tongue. *He's so freaking hot and he's all mine.* I fell for Jake a long time ago, but in the last month since we've been living together in his house, I have to be honest with myself. I love this man with all my heart.

I take a step forward and he turns around. I can read his mind before he even speaks.

"Honey, are you going to live in this robe for the rest of your natural life?" he mocks.

"Good morning to you too, lover boy."

"Good morning, precious, but you still haven't answered my question."

I'm wearing the white terrycloth Pratesi robe Jake bought for me before we left the Surrey hotel. Since we got back, it's always the same song and dance in the morning. He forces me to put on clothes and I fight back like a three-year-old. I'd live in this robe if I could.

"What can I say? I love it and it's a present from you."

"I get it, but you do realize it's the first thing you slip into in the morning and the last thing you take off at night since we got back to Denver and you moved in with me?" He closes the gap between us and sweeps a strand of hair behind my ear.

Since I moved in with him. I still can't get used to these words. After he fucked me so many times I couldn't remember which city I was in after his declaration, Jake asked me to move in with him as I was snuggled in his arms. His sweet proposition rendered me silent. I couldn't speak for a long while because I was so utterly happy. It was impossible to find words to express the depth of emotions stirring in me and I was only able to nod while fighting back the tears.

Since I hadn't brought much with me when I left New York to accept the position as Riley's assistant, it took me about twenty minutes to move all of my belongings from the guesthouse to Jake's house. I've been blissfully living with him for the past glorious, unbelievable month.

"Stop teasing me."

"Fair enough." He flashes me a side grin. "I'll make sure to buy you another one when we return to New York next week."

"You don't have to, but having a backup robe is a brilliant idea." I smile. "I can't believe Paula's trial is fast approaching."

"I'm happy Aaron was able to get a trial fairly quickly. I don't want this hanging over your head any longer. Next week will be a double victory for you," he says, kissing the top of my head.

"You're right. I finally get the settlement money from Clark and Jasper's case and Aaron goes after Paula for all she's worth to punish her for what she's done to me."

Last month's trial was far more emotional than I ever could've imagined. I kept convincing myself I was fine, but walking in that courtroom and looking into Clark's eyes was the hardest thing I've ever had to do. The level of betrayal is beyond words.

I had only met Clark's business partner once at a company function and I didn't remember him much. Turns out Jasper is your typical untrustworthy bad guy. He's a shady-looking, short young man with a potbelly and a sly smirk that makes you wonder what other crimes he's gotten away with in the past.

Everything about him made my skin crawl. *Ew.* Even though this dark episode in my life is almost behind me, I still kick myself for having trusted Clark and for not seeing he was a smooth-talking scumbag.

"Exactly. Your ex will have to pay up. Not even his slimy attempt at hiding profits from his trades in an overseas bank account saved his sorry ass."

Two days before the trial, Winston's team was able to pinpoint a stash of money Clark and Jasper had transferred out of the country. Although they were running their Ponzi scheme operation at night, they were still working for one of the top trading houses in Manhattan by day. In other words, they had insight on a lot of lucrative opportunities. They scored big time with a stock and made an insane amount of money in a very short period of time. Once Aaron got wind of this, he made sure to get me the heftiest settlement possible. A judge awarded me seven hundred and fifty-eight thousand dollars in damages for the fact Clark and Jasper had attempted to damage my reputation in an irreparable way. Had Winston and Aaron not been able to uncover all of this incriminating proof against the man I once thought I loved, I would've ended up in prison for crimes I never committed.

Although I was immensely grateful to Jake for being willing to foot the eye-popping legal bill, I was elated when the judge requested the two idiots pay Aaron's fees. I still remember the look of disbelief on Clark, Jasper and Paula's faces. I had to bite the inside of my lip to avoid smiling in front of the judge. Since my ex and his business partner had money stashed away, the judge granted me my fair share because it wasn't money stolen from investors to fuel their Ponzi operation.

"I really can't believe it's almost over."

"You better believe it. You're innocent of all wrongdoing and you've been able to clear your name."

I nod, silently thanking the man who came to my rescue. "On a different topic—" The bell on the state-of-the-art Swiss-made machine interrupts me.

"Coffee?" He arches his eyebrows, perked up by the idea of finally being able to savor some dark goodness.

"Please."

Jake steps away from me to fix my cup, having learned in the last few weeks of living together how I like mine, and hands me a cup filled to the rim with piping hot liquid—an Americano.

"Thanks." I blow into it and take my first sip, watching him over the porcelain cup.

"How is it?"

"Perfect, like always."

"You were saying?" He hugs his own cup and leans against the counter.

"Did you have to spend a lot of time with Brett this morning?" I ask, meeting his gaze. He swallows and sets his cup on the counter.

"Nah. I texted him, but he said he was good and he had the weekend crew working and on schedule. I didn't bother going out. I figured I'd spend this

Saturday with my sexy girlfriend since we have the ranch all to ourselves…"

Darn. I grin into my next sip.

Since landing a number of very lucrative contracts with top restaurants from across the country, Jake and Hunter's business has been bursting at the seams. In order to keep things running smoothly at the ranch and to avoid getting too involved in the day-to-day operations, they had no other choice but to hire a weekend crew and a top-notch manager. Brett Peeters comes from a long line of ranchers and he's impressed the heck out of everybody since day one.

"You mean all to ourselves other than the ten men working on the property right now?"

"I mean without Riley, the kids and Hunter."

My boss is back in California shooting more episodes of her outrageously popular food reality show and she took her kids and her nanny with her. Hunter's grandmother is doing so well, his entire family organized a little party to celebrate the fact she's walking again. It's just my super-hunky boyfriend and me for the next few days.

"Exactly. We get to run around naked without a nosy little person barging in announced," he says, taking a step closer to me again.

"First off, Riley isn't little. She's five-eleven. And second off, that's no way to talk about your sister." I chuckle.

"Just because she's my younger sibling and she's your boss, she thinks she can waltz in here anytime she wants to catch up. She doesn't get it. Riley has always been completely oblivious to other people's need for privacy."

God, things have changed so dramatically in such a short period of time. Someone needs to come up with a better word than 'happy' to describe my current life.

When I called Gwyn to announce that Jake and I had opened up to each other, she nearly passed out. The phone went dead on her end for what seemed like an eternity. I could hear her breathing, but I figured it was such big news she needed time to absorb it all. Once she got over the initial shock, she insisted on having us over for dinner to meet the man who stole my heart.

Jake and Gaven got along famously while Gwyn spent the better part of that evening bouncing her eyes from mine to Jake's in disbelief. Before we left that night, she hugged me so hard I thought she was going to squeeze every last breath out of my lungs. Her happiness for me overflowed and I enjoyed every second of it.

Jake had a heart-to-heart with his best friend the second Hunter got back from Los Angeles. Although it was clear from the hints he kept dropping Hunter knew well before we were willing to admit anything and it's really no surprise he nearly killed himself laughing when Jake and I finally 'fessed up to our feelings for each other.

I was extraordinarily nervous the day my boyfriend and I sat down with Riley to let her know things had changed between us. I wasn't sure if I was still going to have a job or not. You can imagine my shock when my boss jumped to her feet, clapped her hands and started screaming joyously. Both Jake and I looked at her as if she had lost her marbles until she revealed she'd had a strong gut feeling during my first Skype interview with her that I would be the perfect woman for her big brother. She had hired me not only because of my talent and skills, but because she was hoping to play matchmaker. She was doubly elated to find out I was staying in Fort Collins since Cynthia had decided a few days ago that serving others in poorer countries was her true vocation. Turns out Cynthia loves living in Africa far more than she ever expected and she has no plan to come back soon.

"You're too hard on her." I gently punch his arm with my free hand. "Riley misses you because she's away half the time. Between the TV show, her blog, her own cooking show and the new eatery she's about to open in Denver in the fall, she rarely sees you. I'm sure when she's on the ranch she wants to spend every waking hour with you."

"Yeah, well, it's her fault for taking on so much. She doesn't have to open a restaurant in Denver. She already has too much on the go," he says, curling up his lips like an unimpressed boy.

Riley's popularity seems to explode every week to another level. She's become a mini-celebrity in Colorado and a few months ago a wealthy restaurateur approached her with an opportunity of a lifetime—her own restaurant with the backing of someone who had deep pockets and years of experience in the business.

"Admit it, you have a soft spot for my sister."

"I have no other choice but to root for Team Riley because she's my boss and also because I love her to pieces."

"Enough about my matchmaker-slash-celebrity chef sister. What do you want to do today?"

"Well, when you put it like that... It's the beginning of another glorious day in Fort Collins. We can go to the farmers' market, or we can take a long drive, or I can ride behind you and we can go all the way up to the river. I'm pretty easy-going."

"All great ideas, but I was thinking of something a little bit more low-key."

"Oh, I see where this is going." I roll my eyes. "If this involves us staying in bed all day, I might be convinced into giving you what you want."

"Good, because I need a lot of your affection." He lowers his eyes and I follow his gaze. I'm greeted by a massive erection I'm aching to jump on. "Do you see what you do to me? I can't even contain myself around you. I must have made you come at least four times last night, but I want more of you and I won't take no for an answer."

"Shouldn't we have breakfast?"

The smile pulling at his mouth speaks volumes. "I want to devour you before breakfast, after breakfast and every hour on the hour after that."

"You don't say," I purr. "So what do you have in mind?"

I curl my lips into a knowing smile when his attention moves over my face, to my chin, and down to the swell of my breasts. Since I'm completely naked under my robe, I'm sure he's able to catch a glimpse of my boobs. I stare up at him—at the familiar dark lashes and electric blue eyes, his five o'clock shadow at seven in the morning, and the sly smile he's been wearing since I woke him up—for the second time last night—three hours ago with my mouth on his cock. You'd think living together would slow things down for us, but it hasn't.

"Let's hear it. What type of debauchery do you have in mind, Mr. Carrington?"

"Oh, baby." He smiles warmly at me.

"How do you want me? Are you going to pull me by the hair all the way to the barn and tie me up again like you did a few weeks ago when we had the ranch all to ourselves? Have you bought new sex toys that will threaten to make me lose my mind? Or will you fuck my ass by pressing my body against the granite counter over there?" I say, pointing my finger over his shoulder. "Honestly, I don't care. You know you already own me and I'd never dream of refusing you." I step into him and nuzzle my body into his.

"Ali, you're my beautiful, wonderful and sweet little indulgence."

"Are you buttering me up for something even raunchier?" I side-eye him, waiting for his witty repartee.

I expect him to make a dirty comment, but his gaze softens. He looks away, almost shy, before returning his attention to me. *What's going on in his head?*

"I love you, Ali," he blurts out.

"What?" I gasp, pulling away from him, my eyes wide and jaw dropped open. "Are you kidding me right now?" I squeeze my eyes closed for a milli-second, heart pounding.

He takes a small step back to look at me for several long, heavy beats. His smile straightens, his eyes moving over my face in that way that feels like a lingering caress. He leans in and kisses me once, twice, and a third time.

"I said, I love you." He knows perfectly well his words are rocking my world.

I need a moment to collect my thoughts, inebriated by this enchanting interlude, before I speak again. "Jake, I love you too," I say between breaths.

"My feelings for you deepen every single day I wake up with your body nestled against mine."

"I love waking up every morning in your bed."

"Our bed," he corrects me.

"Our bed," I say in a whisper.

"I want you so intensely, Ali, all the time. Every day since you've moved in you've seduced me more and more. Everything about you is so attractive to me—your sultry looks, your arresting curves, your dazzling smile, your endless generosity and the way you so willingly submit yourself to my desires—no matter how naughty they are." He laughs. "Everything about you lures me in, makes me want you more, makes me want it all with you."

My mouth drops open. *Oh. My. God.* How many times have I dreamed of this moment? I tilt my head and hold his gaze, my whole body tingling with expectation.

"Jake, I'm wholeheartedly yours," I confess, standing on my tippy-toes and kissing up from his chest to his neck to his chin all the way up to his lips.

"I know we've only been together for a month, but I can't imagine not having you in my life anymore."

Oh, Lord. Is this really happening to me? His words are so dizzying my legs give in and he has to hold me to prevent me from falling from the shock of his love declaration. My heart's beating at such an insane rate, I'm certain he can see my pulse thrum.

"Jake, I think I fell for you the day you took me in the barn. I've never felt like this for anyone else in my life. My heart aches when we're apart and it swells with contentment when I seek refuge in your home at the end of the day."

"Our home."

"Our home." I grin from ear to ear, unable to contain this torrent running through my veins.

His lips crush mine, hard and demanding. His tongue penetrates my mouth and my body detonates. I moan into our kiss as thrilling excitement rips through me in waves of pure, smoldering bliss. I can't stop moving against him, greedy for the feeling to go on and on—forever.

God, I love him so much.

THE END

Dear Sexy Reader,

Thanks for giving *Billionaires' Indulgence* a read. What a wild ride, right?

Now that Allison and Jake have found their Happy Ever After, what happens to Hunter?

Find out how a business trip to expand the ranch's growth turns bad boy Hunter's world upside down.

You'll love this binge-read, because everyone loves a dirty-talking hero who's also dangerously loving.

Billionaire's Infatuation is a suspenseful and steamy romance novel.

Get it now.

Much love,

Scarlett Avery

P.S. Reviews are a beautiful thing!

P.P.S. I keep writing because of your hunger for my stories. Thank you for your fervor, love, and loyalty.

P.P.P.S. For access to an EXCLUSIVE Secret Chapter, go to the next page!

****

Get Your FREE SECRET Chapters!

Thank you for purchasing this romance!

I'd love for you to lose yourself in more
sultriness, sexiness and steamy passion!

When you sign-up today, I'll send you the following
Secret Chapter for Part 5 of this serial:

*Jake and Allison reveal their desire
to be together to Riley*

*** <u>PASSWORD FOR</u>
Secret Chapter Part 5:
Back-To-NYC

Note: the password is case sensitive!

Sign-up TODAY!

www.RomanceBooksRock.com

***If you've already signed-up to my list from previ-
ous books, you can visit the same page to download
the Secret Chapters for this romance ***

****

ABOUT THE AUTHOR

USA TODAY BESTSELLING AUTHOR Scarlett Avery dreams up captivating stories that allow you to escape for a few hours or a self-indulgent-binge-reading-weekend.

Her steamy novels feature delicious dirty-talking and swoon-worthy bad boys, smart and sassy women, edge-of-your-seat twists, plenty of steam, a sizzling roller coaster of a ride and always a happy ending.

You could say Scarlett is pretty unapologetic about how much she loves writing sexy romance.

Her steamy romance novels come in a range of saucy shades.

Fair warning…

Once you start reading Scarlett's novels, there's no going back!

www.ingramcontent.com/pod-product-compliance
Lightning Source LLC
Chambersburg PA
CBHW052343020726
47503CB00001B/80